Anything and everything that can be imagined can be.

Welcome to tomorrow.

Year's Best SF 9

Praise for previous volumes

"An impressive roster of authors."
Locus

"The finest modern science fiction writing."
Pittsburgh Tribune

Edited by David G. Hartwell

YEAR'S BEST SF
YEAR'S BEST SF 2
YEAR'S BEST SF 3
YEAR'S BEST SF 4
YEAR'S BEST SF 5
YEAR'S BEST SF 6

Edited by David G. Hartwell & Kathryn Cramer

YEAR'S BEST SF 7
YEAR'S BEST SF 8
YEAR'S BEST SF 9
YEAR'S BEST FANTASY
YEAR'S BEST FANTASY 2
YEAR'S BEST FANTASY 3

Forthcoming

YEAR'S BEST FANTASY 4

YEAR'S BEST

SF 9

EDITED BY
DAVID G. HARTWELL
and KATHRYN CRAMER

An Imprint of HarperCollins*Publishers*

This is a collection of fiction. Names, characters, places, and incidents are products of the authors' imagination or are used fictitiously and are not to be construed as real. Any resemblance to actual events, locales, organizations, or persons, living or dead, is entirely coincidental.

EOS
An Imprint of HarperCollins*Publishers*
10 East 53rd Street
New York, New York 10022-5299

ISBN: 0-06-057559-X
www.eosbooks.com

First Eos paperback printing: June 2004

Printed in the U.S.A.

10 9 8 7 6 5 4 3 2 1

To Mike Shohl and to the HarperCollins production department for extra help and extra patience this year

Contents

Introduction

Well, 2003 is past—another good year to be reading SF, both in pro and semi-professional publications. And as 2004 began, the President of the United States proposed a broad new initiative in space travel and exploration for the near future. Surely this must bode well for space adventures in fiction, and there is much strength to build on in SF already.

The year 2003 was a very strong one for science fiction novels and stories, and there were many shorter stories in consideration. So we repeat, for readers new to this series, our usual disclaimer: This selection of science fiction stories represents the best that was published during the year 2003. It would take several more volumes this size to have nearly all of the best short stories—though, even then, not all the best novellas. And we believe that representing the best from year to year, while it is not physically possible to encompass it all in one even very large book, also implies presenting some substantial variety of excellences, and we left some worthy stories out in order to include others in this limited space.

Our general principle for selection: This book is full of science fiction—every story in the book is clearly that and not something else. We have a high regard for horror, fantasy, speculative fiction, and slipstream, and postmodern literature. We (Kathryn Cramer and David G. Hartwell) edit the *Year's Best Fantasy* in paperback from Eos as a companion volume to this one—look for it if you enjoy short fantasy fiction, too. But here, we choose science fiction.

Science fiction in shorter forms was vigorous and perhaps

even growing in 2003, though sometimes not in easily accessible places. Certainly, the electronic fiction websites such as Infinite Matrix, Strange Horizons, and SciFiction continued to publish much excellent work, though a majority of it was fantasy or horror. And the professional and semiprofessional magazines persisted, though most of them did not thrive in sales or subscriptions, and were a center of interest for SF readers. But the small press really expanded this past year, both in book form and in a proliferation of little magazines, in the U.S. and throughout the world.

Books and magazines of high quality from Canada, Australia, and the UK, often anthologies and short story collections, drew our attention. We have to say that this year was perhaps the best in a decade for original anthologies and story collections—even though most of them will not be found in local bookstores because they are available on the whole only by direct mail or internet order, or from specialty dealers at SF conventions. Still, the total of good SF stories, and perhaps even the total of all SF stories, increased noticeably last year.

But—and this is a significant but—the majority of small press publications contained only a minority of science fiction genre stories, and the bulk of the rest were speculative literature, fantasy, horror, magical realism, allegories, or uses of SF tropes and images in the context of mainstream or postmodern fiction. This commonly derived from a "breaking the bounds of genre" attitude on the part of the editors and publishers of small press short fiction, and many of their writers. Distinguished examples of this trend are *Trampoline, Polyphony, Descant, Open Space,* and *Album Zutique #1*.

And somewhat to our amusement, this attitude was contradicted by one of the bastions of mainstream literary fiction, *McSweeney's* magazine, which published a genre fiction issue, *McSweeney's Thrilling Tales,* in 2003, edited by Michael Chabon. It was filled mainly with genre stories (SF, horror, fantasy, western, mystery and detective, men's adventure) by literary writers, although certain ambitious genre figures of some acknowledged literary accomplishment, including Harlan Ellison, Michael Moorcock, and Karen Joy Fowler, were included. Each year we find ourselves pointing with some irony at the areas of growth in SF as if they were double-edged swords. While many of the ambitious insiders want to break out, at least some ambitious outsiders are breaking in, and some of them at the top of the genre.

The SF magazines struggled to maintain circulation and not allow their subscriber base to erode, while publishing on the whole good-to-excellent stories. Not enough people paid attention, in our opinion. More of you should be reading at least one of the SF magazines regularly, if not two or three. We have remarked in the past that the average paperback anthology of fantasy or SF does not contain as many good stories as the average issue of *Asimov's* or *Fantasy & Science Fiction.*

Two of the main resources for keeping track of short fiction disappeared for part or all of the year. The ISFDB (the Internet SF Data Base), the largest database of SF story titles on the internet, lost its home and was dormant, though it is back now. And Tangent Online, the most comprehensive review medium for short fiction, fell silent in the second half of the year, although a new editor was announced at the end of 2003. There were regular reviews elsewhere of individual magazines and anthologies, but less than half of the information on current short fiction that has been dependably available for the last six or eight years could be had in 2003. Of course, such information has always depended on volunteer labor, but it does give one pause to think of the fragility of our efforts, and that devoted and hard-working volunteers do sometimes just run out of energy and stop, or seek paying work.

We remarked above what a good year it was for anthologies, and some examples are *Live without a Net* (edited by Lou Anders), *Stars* (edited by Janis Ian and Mike Resnick), and *Space, Inc* (edited by Julie Czerneda). Other are mentioned in the various story notes.

And from all this we have chosen some fine stories to entertain you. We try in each volume of this series to represent the varieties of tones and voices and attitudes that keep the genre vigorous and responsive to the changing realities out of which it emerges, in science and daily life. This is a book about what's going on now in SF. The stories that follow show, and the story notes point out, the strengths of the evolving genre in the year 2003.

David G. Hartwell & Kathryn Cramer

Amnesty

OCTAVIA E. BUTLER

Octavia E. Butler lives in the Seattle, Washington area. She grew up in California and attended courses in SF writing taught by Harlan Ellison and Theodore Sturgeon, and the Clarion SF Writing workshop. After years of work, culminating in the early 1980s with two exceptional novels, Kindred *and* Wild Seed, *her career began to peak. She won the 1984 Hugo Award for the short story "Speech Sounds." Her story "Bloodchild," about human male slaves who incubate their alien masters' eggs, won the 1985 Hugo Award and the Nebula Award, and both are collected in* Bloodchild and Other Stories *(1995). Then, in 1995, she was awarded a McArthur Grant, a large cash prize often called the "genius grant," given annually in the arts and sciences, which brought her worldwide notice. She also entered a new, strong phase of her career with the novel* Parable of the Sower. *Her early stories are collected in* Bloodchild. *She is now certainly one of the notable figures in the SF field and one of our leading writers.*

"Amnesty" was published electronically at SciFiction, the SCIFI.com website, which is now the highest paying market for SF and fantasy and so had some of the very best short fiction in 2003. It is a return to the powerful themes of her fine novella, "Bloodchild," a story about finding the courage and strength to compromise and transcend in the face of an oppressive and horrible situation.

The stranger-Community, globular, easily twelve feet high and wide glided down into the vast, dimly lit food production hall of Translator Noah Cannon's employer. The stranger was incongruously quick and graceful, keeping to the paths, never once brushing against the raised beds of fragile, edible fungi. It looked, Noah thought, a little like a great, black, moss-enshrouded bush with such a canopy of irregularly-shaped leaves, shaggy mosses, and twisted vines that no light showed through it. It had a few thick, naked branches growing out, away from the main body, breaking the symmetry and making the Community look in serious need of pruning.

The moment Noah saw it and saw her employer, a somewhat smaller, better-maintained-looking dense, black bush, back away from her, she knew she would be offered the new job assignment she had been asking for.

The stranger-Community settled, flattening itself at bottom, allowing its organisms of mobility to migrate upward and take their rest. The stranger-Community focused its attention on Noah, electricity flaring and zigzagging, making a visible display within the dark vastness of its body. She knew that the electrical display was speech, although she could not read what was said. The Communities spoke in this way between themselves and within themselves, but the light they produced moved far too quickly for her to even begin to learn the language. The fact that she saw the display, though, meant that the communications entities of the stranger-Community were addressing her. Communities used their momentarily inactive organisms to shield communication from anyone outside themselves who was not being addressed.

She glanced at her employer and saw that its attention was focused away from her. It had no noticeable eyes, but its entities of vision served it very well whether she could see them or not. It had drawn itself together, made itself look more like a spiny stone than a bush. Communities did this when they wished to offer others privacy or simply disassociate themselves from the business being transacted. Her employer had warned her that the job that would be offered to her would be unpleasant not only because of the usual hostility of the human beings she would face, but because the subcontractor for whom she would be working would be difficult. The subcontractor had had little contact with human beings. Its vocabulary in the painfully created common language that enabled humans and the Communities to speak to one another was, at best, rudimentary, as was its understanding of human abilities and limitations. Translation: by accident or by intent, the subcontractor would probably hurt her. Her employer had told her that she did not have to take this job, that it would support her if she chose not to work for this subcontractor. It did not altogether approve of her decision to try for the job anyway. Now its deliberate inattention had more to do with disassociation than with courtesy or privacy. "You're on your own," its posture said, and she smiled. She could never have worked for it if it had not been able to stand aside and let her make her own decisions. Yet it did not go about its business and leave her alone with the stranger. It waited.

And here was the subcontractor signaling her with lightning.

Obediently, she went to it, stood close to it so that the tips of what looked like moss-covered outer twigs and branches touched her bare skin. She wore only shorts and a halter top. The Communities would have preferred her to be naked, and for the long years of her captivity, she had had no choice. She had been naked. Now she was no longer a captive, and she insisted on wearing at least the basics. Her employer had come to accept this and now refused to lend her to subcontractors who would refuse her the right to wear clothing.

This subcontractor enfolded her immediately, drawing her upward and in among its many selves, first hauling her up with its various organisms of manipulation, then grasping her securely with what appeared to be moss. The Communities were not plants, but it was easiest to think of them in those terms since most of the time, most of them looked so plantlike.

Enfolded within the Community, she couldn't see at all. She closed her eyes to avoid the distraction of trying to see or imagining that she saw. She felt herself surrounded by what felt like long, dry fibers, fronds, rounded fruits of various sizes, and other things that produced less identifiable sensations. She was at once touched, stroked, massaged, compressed in the strangely comfortable, peaceful way that she had come to look forward to whenever she was employed. She was turned and handled as though she weighed nothing. In fact, after a few moments, she felt weightless. She had lost all sense of direction, yet she felt totally secure, clasped by entities that had nothing resembling human limbs. Why this was pleasurable, she never understood, but for twelve years of captivity, it had been her only dependable comfort. It had happened often enough to enable her to endure everything else that was done to her.

Fortunately, the Communities also found it comforting—even more than she did.

After a while, she felt the particular rhythm of quick warning pressures across her back. The Communities liked the broad expanse of skin that the human back offered.

She made a beckoning motion with her right hand to let the Community know that she was paying attention.

There are six recruits, it signaled with pressures against her back. *You will teach them.*

I will, she signed, using her hands and arms only. The Communities liked her signs to be small, confined gestures when she was enfolded and large, sweeping hand, arm, and whole-body efforts when she was outside and not being touched. She had wondered at first if this was because they couldn't see very well. Now she knew that they could see far better than she could—could see over great distances with specialized entities of vision, could see most bacteria and some viruses, and see colors from ultraviolet through infrared.

In fact the reason that they preferred large gestures when she was out of contact and unlikely to hit or kick anyone was because they liked to watch her move. It was that simple, that odd. In fact, the Communities had developed a real liking for human dance performances and for some human sports events—especially individual performances in gymnastics and ice skating.

The recruits are disturbed, the subcontractor said. *They may be dangerous to one another. Calm them.*

I will try, Noah said. *I will answer their questions and reassure them that they have nothing to fear.* Privately, she suspected that hate might be a more prevalent emotion than fear, but if the subcontractor didn't know that, she wouldn't tell it.

Calm them. The subcontractor repeated. And she knew then that it meant, literally, "Change them from disturbed people to calm, willing workers." The Communities could change one another just by exchanging a few of their individual entities—as long as both exchanging communities were willing. Too many of them assumed that human beings should be able to do something like this too, and that if they wouldn't, they were just being stubborn.

Noah repeated, *I will answer their questions and reassure them that they have nothing to fear. That's all I can do.*

Will they be calm?

She drew a deep breath, knowing that she was about to be hurt—twisted or torn, broken or stunned. Many Communities punished refusal to obey orders—as they saw it—less harshly than they punished what they saw as lying. In fact, the punishments were left over from the years when human beings were captives of uncertain ability, intellect, and perception. People were not supposed to be punished any longer, but of course they were. Now, Noah thought it was best to get whatever punishment there might be out of the way at once. She could not escape. She signed stolidly, *Some of them may believe what I tell them and be calm. Others will need time and experience to calm them.*

She was, at once, held more tightly, almost painfully—"held hard" as the Communities called it, held so that she could not move even her arms, could not harm any members of the Community by thrashing about in pain. Just before she might have been injured by the squeezing alone, it stopped.

She was hit with a sudden electrical shock that convulsed her. It drove the breath out of her in a hoarse scream. It made her see flashes of light even with her eyes tightly closed. It stimulated her muscles into abrupt, agonizing contortions.

Calm them, the Community insisted once again.

She could not answer at first. It took her a moment to get her now sore and shaking body under control and to understand what was being said to her. It took her a moment more to be able to flex her hands and arms, now free again, and finally to shape an answer—the only possible answer in spite of what it might cost.

I will answer their questions and reassure them that they have nothing to fear.

She was held hard for several seconds more, and knew that she might be given another shock. After a while, though, there were several flashes of light that she saw out of the corner of her eye, but that did not seem to have anything to do with her. Then without any more communication, Noah was passed into the care of her employer, and the subcontractor was gone.

She saw nothing as she was passed from darkness to darkness. There was nothing to hear but the usual rustle of Communities moving about. There was no change of scent, or if there was, her nose was not sensitive enough to detect it. Yet somehow, she had learned to know her employer's touch. She relaxed in relief.

Are you injured? her employer signed.

No, she answered. Just aching joints and other sore places. Did I get the job?

Of course you did. You must tell me if that subcontractor tries to coerce you again. It knows better. I've told it that if it injures you, I will never allow you to work for it again.

Thank you.

There was a moment of stillness. Then the employer stroked her, calming her and pleasing itselves. *You insist on taking these jobs, but you can't use them to make the changes you want to make. You know that. You cannot change your people or mine.*

I can, a little, she signed. *Community by Community, human by human. I would work faster if I could.*

And so you let subcontractors abuse you. You try to help your own people to see new possibilities and understand changes that have already happened but most of them won't listen and they hate you.

I want to make them think. I want to tell them what human governments won't tell them. I want to vote for peace between your people and mine by telling the truth. I don't know whether my efforts will do any good, in the long run, but I have to try.

Let yourself heal. Rest enfolded until the subcontractor returns for you.

Noah sighed, content, within another moment of stillness. *Thank you for helping me, even though you don't believe.*

I would like to believe. But you can't succeed. Right now groups of your people are looking for ways to destroy us.

Noah winced. *I know. Can you stop them without killing them?*

Her employer shifted her. Stroked her. *Probably not,* it signed. *Not again.*

"Translator," Michelle Ota began as the applicants trailed into the meeting room, "do these . . . these things . . . actually understand that we're intelligent?"

She followed Noah into the meeting room, waited to see where Noah would sit, and sat next to her. Noah noticed that Michelle Ota was one of only two of the six applicants who was willing to sit near her even for this informal question-

and-answer session. Noah had information that they needed. She was doing a job some of them might wind up doing someday, and yet that job—translator and personnel officer for the Communities—and the fact that she *could* do it was their reason for distrusting her. The second person who wanted to sit near her was Sorrel Trent. She was interested in alien spirituality—whatever that might be.

The four remaining job candidates chose to leave empty seats between themselves and Noah.

"Of course the Communities know we're intelligent," Noah said.

"I mean I know you work for them," Michelle Ota glanced at her, hesitated then went on. "I want to work for them too. Because at least they're hiring. Almost nobody else is. But what do they think of us?"

"They'll be offering some of you contracts soon," Noah said. "They wouldn't waste time doing that if they'd mistaken you for cattle." She relaxed back into her chair, watching some of the six other people in the room get water, fruit or nuts from the sideboards. The food was good and clean and free to them whether or not they were hired. It was also, she knew, the first food most of them had had that day. Food was expensive and in these depressed times, most people were lucky to eat once a day. It pleased her to see them enjoying it. She was the one who had insisted there be food in the meeting rooms for the question and answer sessions.

She herself was enjoying the rare comfort of wearing shoes, long black cotton pants, and a colorful flowing tunic. And there was furniture designed for the human body—an upholstered armchair with a high back and a table she could eat from or rest her arms on. She had no such furniture in her quarters within the Mojave Bubble. She suspected that she could have at least the furniture now, if she asked her employer for it, but she had not asked, would not ask. Human things were for human places.

"But what does a contract mean to things that come from another star system?" Michelle Ota demanded.

Rune Johnsen spoke up. "Yes, it's interesting how quickly these beings have taken up local, terrestrial ways when it suits them. Translator, do you truly believe they will consider themselves bound by anything they sign? Although without hands, God knows how they manage to sign anything."

"They will consider both themselves and you bound by it if both they and you sign it," Noah said. "And, yes, they can make highly individual marks that serve as signatures. They spent a great deal of their time and wealth in this country with translators, lawyers, and politicians, working things out so that each Community was counted as a legal 'person,' whose individual mark would be accepted. And for twenty years since then, they've honored their contracts."

Rune Johnsen shook his blond head. "In all, they've been on earth longer than I've been alive, and yet it feels wrong that they're here. It feels wrong that they exist. I don't even hate them, and still it feels wrong. I suppose that's because we've been displaced again from the center of the universe. We human beings, I mean. Down through history, in myth and even in science, we've kept putting ourselves in the center, and then being evicted."

Noah smiled, surprised and pleased. "I noticed the same thing. Now we find ourselves in a kind of sibling rivalry with the Communities. There is other intelligent life. The universe has other children. We knew it, but until they arrived here, we could pretend otherwise."

"That's crap!" another woman said. Thera Collier, her name was, a big, angry red-haired young woman. "The weeds came here uninvited, stole our land, and kidnapped our people." She had been eating an apple. She slammed it down hard on the table, crushing what was left of it, spattering juice. "That's what we need to remember. That's what we need to do something about."

"Do what?" Another woman asked. "We're here to get jobs, not fight."

Noah searched her memory for the new speaker's name and found it. Piedad Ruiz—a small, brown woman who spoke English clearly, but with a strong Spanish accent. She looked with her bruised face and arms as though she had taken a fairly serious beating recently, but when Noah had asked her about it before the group came into the meeting room, she held her head up and said she was fine and it was nothing. Probably someone had not wanted her to apply for work at the bubble. Considering the rumors that were sometimes spread about the Communities and why they hired human beings, that was not surprising.

"What have the aliens told you about their coming here, Translator," Rune Johnsen asked. He was, Noah remembered from her reading of the short biography that had been given to her with his job application, the son of a small businessman whose clothing store had not survived the depression brought about by the arrival of the Communities. He wanted to look after his parents and he wanted to get married. Ironically, the answer to both those problems seemed to be to go to work for the Communities for a while. "You're old enough to remember the things they did when they arrived," he said. "What did they tell you about why they abducted people, killed people. . . ."

"They abducted me," Noah admitted.

That silenced the room for several seconds. Each of the six potential recruits stared at her, perhaps wondering or pitying, judging or worrying, perhaps even recoiling in horror, suspicion, or disgust. She had received all these reactions from recruits and from others who knew her history. People had never been able to be neutral about abductees. Noah tended to use her history as a way to start questions, accusations, and perhaps thought.

"Noah Cannon," Rune Johnsen said, proving that he had at least been listening when she introduced herself. "I thought that name sounded familiar. You were part of the second wave of abductions. I remember seeing your name on the lists of abductees. I noticed it because you were listed as female. I had never run across a woman named Noah before."

"So they kidnapped you, and now you work for them?" This was James Hunter Adio, a tall, lean, angry-looking young black man. Noah was black herself and yet James Adio had apparently decided the moment they met that he didn't like her. Now he looked not only angry, but disgusted.

"I was eleven when I was taken," Noah said. She looked at Rune Johnsen. "You're right. I was part of the second wave."

"So what, then, they experimented on you?" James Adio asked.

Noah met his gaze. "They did, yes. The people of the first wave suffered the most. The Communities didn't know anything about us. They killed some of us with experiments and dietary deficiency diseases and they poisoned others. By the time they snatched me, they at least knew enough not to kill me by accident."

"And what? You forgive them for what they did do?"

"Are you angry with me, Mr. Adio, or are you angry in my behalf?"

"I'm angry because I have to be here!" he said. He stood up and paced around the table—all the way around twice before he would sit down again. "I'm angry that these things, these weeds can invade us, wreck our economies, send the whole world into a depression just by showing up. They do whatever they want to us, and instead of killing them, all I can do is ask them for a job!" And he needed the job badly. Noah had read the information collected about him when he first applied to work for the Communities. At twenty, James Adio was the oldest of seven children, and the only one who had reached adulthood so far. He needed a job to help his younger brothers and sisters survive. Yet Noah suspected that he would hate the aliens almost as much if they hired him as if they turned him down.

"How can you work for them?" Piedad Ruiz whispered to Noah. "They hurt you. Don't you hate them? I think I'd hate them if it were me."

"They wanted to understand us and communicate with us," Noah said. "They wanted to know how we got along with one another and they needed to know how much we could bear of what was normal for them."

"Is that what they told you?" Thera Collier demanded. With one hand, she swept her smashed apple off the table onto the floor, and then glared at Noah as though wishing she could sweep her away too. Watching her, Noah realized that Thera Collier was a very frightened woman. Well, they were all frightened, but Thera's fear made her lash out at people.

"The Communities did tell me that," Noah admitted, "but not until some of them and some of us, the surviving captives, had managed to put together a code—the beginnings of a language—that got communication started. Back when they captured me, they couldn't tell me anything."

Thera snorted. "Right. They can figure out how to cross light years of space, but they can't figure out how to talk to us without torturing us first!"

Noah allowed herself a moment of irritation. "You weren't there, Ms. Collier. It happened before you were born. And it happened to me, not to you." And it hadn't happened to anyone in Thera Collier's family either. Noah had checked. None of these people were relatives of abductees. It was important to know that since relatives sometimes tried to take revenge on translators when they realized they weren't going to be able to hurt the Communities.

"It happened to a lot of people," Thera Collier said. "And it shouldn't have happened to anyone."

Noah shrugged.

"Don't you hate them for what they did to you?" Piedad whispered. Whispering seemed to be her normal way of speaking.

"I don't," Noah said. "I did once, especially when they were beginning to understand us a little, and yet went right on putting us through hell. They were like human scientists experimenting with lab animals—not cruel, but very thorough."

"Animals again," Michelle Ota said. "You said they—"

"Then," Noah told her. "Not now."

"Why do you defend them?" Thera demanded. "They invaded our world. They tortured our people. They do whatever they please, and we aren't even sure what they look like."

Rune Johnsen spoke up, to Noah's relief. "What do they look like, Translator? You've seen them close up."

Noah almost smiled. What did the Communities look like. That was usually the first question asked in a group like this. People tended to assume, no matter what they had seen or heard from media sources, that each Community was actually an individual being shaped like a big bush or tree or, more likely, that the being was wearing shrubbery as clothing or as a disguise.

"They're not like anything that any of us have ever known," she told them. "I've heard them compared to sea urchins—completely wrong. I've also heard they were like swarms of bees or wasps—also wrong, but closer. I think of them as what I usually call them—Communities. Each Community contains several hundred individuals—an intelligent multitude. But that's wrong too, really. The individuals can't really survive independently, but they can leave one community and move temporarily or permanently to another. They are products of a completely different evolution. When I look at them, I see what you've all seen: outer branches and then darkness. Flashes of light and movement within. Do you want to hear more?"

They nodded, sat forward attentively except for James Adio who leaned back with an expression of contempt on his dark, smooth young face.

"The substance of the things that look like branches and the things that look like leaves and mosses and vines is alive and made up of individuals. It only looks like a plant of some sort. The various entities that we can reach from the outside feel dry, and usually smooth. One normal-sized Community might fill half of this room, but only weigh about six to eight hundred pounds. They aren't solid, of course, and within them, there are entities that I've never seen. Being enveloped by a community is like being held in a sort of . . . comfortable strait jacket, if you can imagine such a thing. You can't move much. You can't move at all unless the Community permits it. You can't see anything. There's no smell. Somehow, though, after the first time, it isn't frightening. It's peaceful and pleasant. I don't know why it should be, but it is."

"Hypnosis," James Adio said at once. "Or drugs!"

"Definitely not," Noah said. At least this was something she could be sure of. "That was one of the hardest parts of being a captive of the Communities. Until they got to know us, they didn't have anything like hypnosis or mood-altering drugs. They didn't even have the concept."

Rune Johnsen turned to frown at her. "What concept?"

"Altered consciousness. They don't even go unconscious unless they're sick or injured, and a whole Community never goes unconscious even though several of its entities might. As a result, Communities can't really be said to sleep—although at long last, they've accepted the reality that we have to sleep. Inadvertently, we've introduced them to something brand new."

"Will they let us bring medicine in?" Michelle Ota asked suddenly. "I have allergies and I really need my medicine."

"They will allow certain medicines. If you're offered a contract, you'll have to write in the drugs you'll need. They will either allow you to have the drugs or you won't be hired. If what you need is allowed, you'll be permitted to order it from outside. The Communities will check to see that it is what it's supposed to be, but other than that, they won't bother you about it. Medicine's just about all you'll have to spend money on while you're inside. Room and board are part of the agreement, of course, and you won't be allowed to leave your employers until your contract is up."

"What if we get sick or have an accident?" Piedad demanded. "What if we need some medicine that isn't in the contract."

"Medical emergencies are covered by the contract," Noah said.

Thera slapped her palms down against the table and said loudly, "Screw all that!" She got the attention she wanted. Everyone turned to look at her. "I want to know more about you, and the weeds, Translator. In particular, I want to know why you're still here, working for things that probably put you through hell. Part of that no drug thing was no anesthetic when they hurt you, right?"

Noah sat still for a moment, remembering, yet not wanting to remember. "Yes," she said at last, "except that most of the time, the people actually hurting me were other human beings. The aliens used to lock groups of two or more of us up together for days or weeks to see what would happen. This was usually not too bad. Sometimes, though, it went wrong. Some of us went out of our minds. Hell, all of us went out of our minds at one time or another. But some of us were more likely than others to be violent. Then there were those of us who would have been thugs even without the Communities' help. They were quick enough to take advantage of any chance to exercise a little power, get a little pleasure by making another person suffer. And some of us just stopped caring, stopped fighting, sometimes even stopped eating. The pregnancies and several of the killings came from those cell-mate experiments. We called them that.

"It was almost easier when the aliens just made us solve puzzles to get food or when they put things in our food that made us sick or when they enfolded us and introduced some nearly lethal substance into our bodies. The first captives got most of that, poor people. And some of them had developed a phobic terror of being enfolded. They were lucky if that was all they developed."

"My God," Thera said, shaking her head in disgust. After a while, she asked, "What happened to the babies? You said some people got pregnant."

"The Communities don't reproduce the way we do. It didn't seem to occur to them for a long time to take it easy on the pregnant women. Because of that, most women who got pregnant miscarried. Some had still births. Four of the women in the group that I was usually caged with between experiments died in childbirth. None of us knew how to help them." That was another memory she wanted to turn away from.

"There were a few live births, and of those, a few babies survived infancy, even though their mothers couldn't protect them from the worst and the craziest of our own people or from the Communities who were . . . curious about them. In all thirty-seven of the world's bubbles, fewer than a hundred such children survived. Most of those have grown up to be reasonably sane adults. Some live outside in secret, and some will never leave the bubbles. Their choice. A few of them are becoming the best of the next generation of translators."

Rune Johnsen made a wordless sound of interest. "I've read about such children," he said.

"We tried to find some of them," Sorrel Trent said, speaking up for the first time. "Our leader teaches that they're the ones who will show us the way. They're so important, and yet our stupid government keeps them hidden!" She sounded both frustrated and angry.

"The governments of this world have a great deal to answer for," Noah said. "In some countries, the children won't come out of the bubbles because word has gotten back to them about what's happened to those who have come out. Word about disappearances, imprisonment, torture, death. Our government seems not to be doing that sort of thing any more. Not to the children, anyway. It's given them new identities to hide them from groups who want to worship them or kill them or set them apart. I've checked on some of them myself. They're all right, and they want to be let alone."

"My group doesn't want to hurt them," Sorrel Trent said. "We want to honor them and help them fulfill their true destiny."

Noah turned away from the woman, her mind filled with caustic, unprofessional things best not said. "So the children at least, are able to have a little peace," she did say.

"Is one of them yours?" Thera asked, her voice uncharacteristically soft. "Do you have children?"

Noah stared at her, then leaned her head against the chair back again. "I got pregnant when I was fifteen and again when I was seventeen. Miscarriages both times, thank God."

"It was . . . rape?" Rune Johnsen asked.

"Of course it was rape! Can you actually believe I'd want to give the Communities another human infant to study?" She stopped and took a deep breath. After a moment, she said, "Some of the deaths were women killed for resisting rape. Some of the deaths were rapists. Do you remember an old experiment in which too many rats are caged together and they begin to kill one another."

"But you weren't rats," Thera said. "You were intelligent. You could see what the weeds were doing to you. You didn't have to—"

Noah cut her off. "I didn't have to what?"

Thera backpedaled. "I didn't mean you personally. I just

mean human beings ought to be able to behave better than a bunch of rats."

"Many did. Some did not."

"And in spite of all that, you work for the aliens. You forgive them because they didn't know what they were doing. Is that it?"

"They're here," Noah said flatly.

"They're here until we find a way to drive them away!"

"They're here to stay," Noah said more softly. "There's no 'away' for them—not for several generations anyway. Their ship was a one-way transport. They've settled here and they'll fight to keep the various desert locations they've chosen for their bubbles. If they do decide to fight, we won't survive. They might be destroyed too, but chances are, they would send their young deep into the ground for a few centuries. When they came up, this would be their world. We would be gone." She looked at each member of the group. "They're here," she said for the third time. "I'm one of maybe thirty people in this country who can talk to them. Where else would I be but here at a bubble, trying to help the two species understand and accept one another before one of them does something fatal?"

Thera was relentless. "But do you forgive them for what they've done?"

Noah shook her head. "I don't forgive them," she said. "They haven't asked for my forgiveness and I wouldn't know how to give it if they did. And that doesn't matter. It doesn't stop me from doing my job. It doesn't stop them from employing me."

James Adio said, "If they're as dangerous as you believe, you ought to be working with the government, trying to find a way to kill them. Like you said, you know more about them than the rest of us."

"Are you here to kill them, Mr. Adio?" Noah asked quietly.

He let his shoulders slump. "I'm here to work for them, lady. I'm poor. I don't have all kinds of special knowledge that only thirty people in the whole country have. I just need a job."

She nodded as though he had simply been conveying information, as though his words had not carried heavy loads of bitterness, anger, and humiliation. "You can make money here." She said. "I'm wealthy myself. I'm putting half a dozen nieces and nephews through college. My relatives eat three meals a day and live in comfortable homes. Why shouldn't yours?"

"Thirty pieces of silver," he muttered.

Noah gave him a tired smile. "Not for me," she said. "My parents seemed to have a completely different role in mind for me when they named me."

Rune Johnsen smiled but James Adio only stared at her with open dislike. Noah let her face settle into its more familiar solemnity. "Let me tell you all about my experience working with the government to get the better of the Communities," she said. "You should hear about it whether or not you choose to believe." She paused, gathered her thoughts.

"I was held here in the Mojave Bubble from my eleventh year through my twenty-third," she began. "Of course, none of my family or friends knew where I was or whether I was alive. I just disappeared like a lot of other people. In my case, I disappeared from my own bedroom in my parents' house in Victorville late one night. Years later when the Communities could talk to us, when they understood more of what they'd done to us, they asked a group of us whether we would stay with them voluntarily or whether we wanted to leave. I thought it might have been just another of their tests, but when I asked to go, they agreed.

"In fact, I was the first to ask to go. The group I was with then was made up of people taken in childhood—sometimes early childhood. Some of them were afraid to go out. They had no memory of any home but the Mojave Bubble. But I remembered my family. I wanted to see them again. I wanted to go out and not be confined to a small area in a bubble. I wanted to be free.

"But when the Communities let me go, they didn't take me back to Victorville. They just opened the bubble late one night near one of the shanty towns that had grown up around its perimeters. The shanty towns were wilder and cruder back then. They were made up of people who were worshipping the Communities or plotting to wipe them out or hoping to steal some fragment of valuable technology from them—that kind of thing. And some of the squatters there were undercover cops of one kind or another. The ones who grabbed me said they were FBI, but I think now that they might have been bounty hunters. In those days, there was a bounty on anyone or anything that came out of the bubbles, and it was my bad luck to be the first person to be seen coming out of the Mojave Bubble.

"Anyone coming out might know valuable technological secrets, or might be hypnotized saboteurs or disguised alien spies—any damned thing. I was handed over to the military which locked me up, questioned me relentlessly, accused me of everything from espionage to murder, from terrorism to treason. I was sampled and tested in every way they could think of. They convinced themselves that I was a valuable catch, that I had been collaborating with our "nonhuman enemies." Therefore, I represented a great opportunity to find a way to get at them—at the Communities.

"Everything I knew, they found out. It wasn't as though I was ever trying to hold anything back from them. The problem was, I couldn't tell them the kind of thing they wanted to know. Of course the Communities hadn't explained to me the workings of their technology. Why would they? I didn't know much about their physiology either, but I told what I did know—told it over and over again with my jailers trying to catch me in lies. And as for the Communities' psychology, I could only say what had been done to me and what I'd seen done to others. And because my jailers didn't see that as very useful, they decided I was being uncooperative, and that I had something to hide."

Noah shook her head. "The only difference between the way they treated me and the way the aliens treated me during the early years of my captivity was that the so-called human beings knew when they were hurting me. They questioned me day and night, threatened me, drugged me, all in an effort to get me to give them information I didn't have.

They'd keep me awake for days on end, keep me awake until I couldn't think, couldn't tell what was real and what wasn't. They couldn't get at the aliens, but they had me. When they weren't questioning me, they kept me locked up, alone, isolated from everyone but them."

Noah looked around the room. "All this because they knew—knew absolutely—that a captive who survived twelve years of captivity and who is then freed *must* be a traitor of some kind, willing or unwilling, knowing or unknowing. They x-rayed me, scanned me in every possible way, and when they found nothing unusual, it only made them angrier, made them hate me more. I was, somehow, making fools of them. They *knew* it! And I wasn't going to get away with it.

"I gave up. I decided that they were never going to stop, that they would eventually kill me anyway, and until they did, I would never know any peace."

She paused remembering humiliation, fear, hopelessness, exhaustion, bitterness, sickness, pain. . . . They had never beaten her badly—just struck a few blows now and then for emphasis and intimidation. And sometimes she was grabbed, shaken, and shoved, amid ongoing accusations, speculations, and threats. Now and then, an interrogator, knocked her to the floor, then ordered her back to her chair. They did nothing that they thought might seriously injure or kill her. But it went on and on and on. Sometimes one of them pretended to be nice to her, courted her in a sense, tried to seduce her into telling secrets she did not know. . . .

"I gave up," she repeated. "I don't know how long I'd been there when that happened. I never saw the sky or sunlight so I lost all track of time. I just regained consciousness after a long session, found that I was in my cell alone, and decided to kill myself. I had been thinking about it off and on when I could think, and suddenly, I knew I would do it. Nothing else would make them stop. So I did do it. I hanged myself."

Piedad Ruiz made a wordless sound of distress, then stared downward at the table when people looked at her.

"You tried to kill yourself?" Rune Johnsen asked. "Did you do that when you were with the . . . the Communities?"

Noah shook her head. "I never did." She paused. "It mattered more than I know how to tell you that this time my tormentors were my own people. They were human. They spoke my language. They knew all that I knew about pain and humiliation and fear and despair. They knew what they were doing to me, and yet it never occurred to them not to do it." She thought for a moment, remembering. "Some captives of the Communities did kill themselves. And the Communities didn't care. If you wanted to die and managed to hurt yourself badly enough, you'd die. They'd watch."

But if you didn't choose to die, there was the perverse security and peace of being enfolded. There was, somehow, the *pleasure* of being enfolded. It happened often when captives were not being tested in some way. It happened because the entities of the Communities discovered that it pleased and comforted them too, and they didn't understand why any more than she did. The first enfoldings happened because they were convenient ways of restraining, examining, and, unhappily, poisoning human captives. It wasn't long, though, before unoccupied humans were being enfolded just for the pleasure the act gave to an unoccupied Community. Communities did not understand at first that their captives could also take pleasure in the act. Human children like Noah learned quickly how to approach a Community and touch its outer branches to ask to be enfolded, although adult human captives had tried to prevent the practice, and to punish it when they could not prevent it. Noah had had to grow up to even begin to understand why adult captives sometimes beat children for daring to ask alien captors for comfort.

Noah had met her current employer before she turned twelve. It was one of the Communities who never injured her, one who had worked with her and with others to begin to assemble a language that both species could use.

She sighed and continued her narrative. "My human jailers were like the Communities in their attitude toward suicide," she said. "They watched too as I tried to kill myself. I found out later that there were at least three cameras on me day and night. A lab rat had more privacy than I did. They watched me make a noose of my clothing. They watched me climb onto my bed and tie off the noose to a grill that protected the speaker they sometimes used to blast me with loud, distorted music or with old news broadcasts from when the aliens first arrived and people were dying in the panic.

"They even watched me step off my bed and dangle by my neck, strangling. Then they got me out of there, revived me, made sure I wasn't seriously injured.

That done, they put me back in my cell, naked and with the speaker recess concreted over and the grill gone. At least, after that there was no more horrible music. No more terrified screaming.

"But the questioning began again. They even said I hadn't really meant to kill myself, that I was just making a bid for sympathy.

"So I left in mind, if not in body. I sort of went catatonic for a while. I wasn't entirely unconscious, but I wasn't functioning any more. I couldn't. They knocked me around at first because they thought I was faking. I know they did that because later I had some unexplained and untreated broken bones and other medical problems to deal with.

"Then someone leaked my story. I don't know who. Maybe one of my interrogators finally grew a conscience. Anyway, someone started telling the media about me and showing them pictures. The fact that I was only eleven when I was taken turned out to be important to the story. At that point, my captors decided to give me up. I suppose they could have killed me just as easily. Considering what they had been doing to me, I have no idea why they didn't kill me. I've seen the pictures that got published. I was in bad shape. Maybe they thought I'd die—or at least that I'd never wake all the way up and be normal again. And, too, once my relatives learned that I was alive, they got lawyers and fought to get me out of there.

"My parents were dead—had died in a car wreck while I

was still a captive in the Mojave Bubble. My jailers must have known, but they never said a word. I didn't find out until I began to recover and one of my uncles told me. My uncles were my mother's three older brothers. They were the ones who fought for me. To get me, they had to sign away any rights they may have had to sue. They were told that the Communities were the ones who had injured me. They believed it until I revived enough to tell them what really happened.

"After I told them, they wanted to tell the world, maybe put a few people in prison where they belonged. If they hadn't had families of their own, I might not have been able to talk them out of it. They were good men. My mother was their baby sister, and they'd always loved her and looked after her. As things were, though, they had had to go into serious debt to get me free, repaired and functional again. I couldn't have lived with the thought that because of me, they lost everything they owned, and maybe even got sent to prison on some fake charge.

"When I'd recovered a little, I had to do some media interviews. I told lies, of course, but I couldn't go along with the big lie. I refused to confirm that the Communities had injured me. I pretended not to remember what had happened. I said I had been in such bad shape that I didn't have any idea what was going on most of the time, and that I was just grateful to be free and healing. I hoped that was enough to keep my human ex-captors content. It seemed to be.

"The reporters wanted to know what I was going to do, now that I was free.

"I told them I would go to school as soon as I could. I would get an education, then a job so that I could begin to pay my uncles back for all they had done for me.

"That's pretty much what I did. And while I was in school, I realized what work I was best fitted to do. So here I am. I was not only the first to leave the Mojave Bubble, but the first to come back to offer to work for the Communities. I had a small part in helping them connect with some of the lawyers and politicians I mentioned earlier."

"Did you tell your story to the weeds when you came back

here?" Thera Collier asked suspiciously. "Prison and torture and everything?"

Noah nodded. "I did. Some Communities asked and I told them. Most didn't ask. They have problems enough among themselves. What humans do to other humans outside their bubbles is usually not that important to them."

"Did they trust you?" Thera asked. "Do the weeds trust you?"

Noah smiled unhappily. "At least as much as you do, Ms. Collier."

Thera gave a short bark of laughter, and Noah realized the woman had not understood. She thought Noah was only being sarcastic.

"I mean they trust me to do my job," Noah said. "They trust me to help would-be employers learn to live with a human being without hurting the human and to help human employees learn to live with the Communities and fulfill their responsibilities. You trust me to do that too. That's why you're here." That was all true enough, but there were also some Communities—her employer and a few others—who did seem to trust her. And she trusted them. She had never dared to tell anyone that she thought of these as friends.

Even without that admission, Thera gave her a look that seemed to be made up of equal parts pity and contempt.

"Why did the aliens take you back," James Adio demanded. "You could have been bringing in a gun or a bomb or something. You could have been coming back to get even with them for what they'd done to you."

Noah shook her head. "They would have detected any weapon I could bring in. They let me come back because they knew me and they knew I could be useful to them. I knew I could be useful to us, too. They want more of us. Maybe they even *need* more of us. Better for everyone if they hire us and pay us instead of snatching us. They can take mineral ores from deeper in the ground than we can reach, and refine them. They've agreed to restrictions on what they take and where they take it. They pay a handsome percentage of their profit to the government in fees and taxes. With all that, they still have plenty of money to hire us."

She changed the subject suddenly. "Once you're in the bubble, learn the language. Make it clear to your employers that you want to learn. Have you all mastered the basic signs?" She looked them over, not liking the silence. Finally she asked, "Has anyone mastered the basic signs?"

Rune Johnsen and Michelle Ota both said, "I have."

Sorrel Trent said, "I learned some of it, but it's hard to remember."

The others said nothing. James Adio began to look defensive. "They come to our world and we have to learn their language," he muttered.

"I'm sure they would learn ours if they could, Mr. Adio," Noah said wearily. "In fact, here at Mojave, they can read English, and even write it—with difficulty. But since they can't hear at all, they never developed a spoken language of any kind. They can only converse with us in the gesture and touch language that some of us and some of them have developed. It takes some getting used to since they have no limbs in common with us. That's why you need to learn it from them, see for yourself how they move and feel the touch-signs on your skin when you're enfolded. But once you learn it, you'll see that it works well for both species."

"They could use computers to speak for them," Thera Collier said. "If their technology isn't up to it, they could buy some of ours."

Noah did not bother to look at her. "Most of you won't be required to learn more than the basic signs," she said. "If you have some urgent need that the basics don't cover, you can write notes. Print in block capital letters. That will usually work. But if you want to move up a paygrade or two and be given work that might actually interest you, learn the language."

"How do you learn," Michelle Ota asked. "Are there classes?"

"No classes. Your employers will teach you if they want you to know—or if you ask. Language lessons are the one thing you can ask for that you can be sure of getting. They're also one of the few things that will get your pay reduced if you're told to learn and you don't. That will be in the contract. They won't care whether you won't or you can't. Either way it's going to cost you."

"Not fair," Piedad said.

Noah shrugged. "It's easier if you have something to do anyway, and easier if you can talk with your employer. You can't bring in radios, televisions, computers, or recordings of any kind. You can bring in a few books—the paper kind—but that's all. Your employers can and will call you at any time, sometimes several times in a day. Your employer might lend you to . . . relatives who haven't hired one of us yet. They might also ignore you for days at a time, and most of you won't be within shouting distance of another human being." Noah paused, stared down at the table. "For the sake of your sanity, go in with projects that will occupy your minds."

Rune said, "I would like to hear your description of our duties. What I read sounded almost impossibly simple."

"It is simple. It's even pleasant once you're used to it. You will be enfolded by your employer or anyone your employer designates. If both you and the Community enfolding you can communicate, you might be asked to explain or discuss some aspect of our culture that the Community either doesn't understand or wants to hear more about. Some of them read our literature, our history, even our news. You may be given puzzles to solve. When you're not enfolded, you may be sent on errands—after you've been inside long enough to be able to find your way around. Your employer might sell your contract to another Community, might even send you to one of the other bubbles. They've agreed not to send you out of the country, and they've agreed that when your contract is up, they'll let you leave by way of the Mojave Bubble—since this is where you'll begin. You won't be injured. There'll be no bio-medical experiments, none of the nastier social experiments that captives endured. You'll receive all the food, water, and shelter that you need to keep you healthy. If you get sick or injured, you have the right to see a human physician. I believe there are two human doctors working here at Mojave now." She paused and James Adio spoke up.

"So what will we be, then?" he demanded. "Whores or house pets?"

Thera Collier made a noise that was almost a sob.

Noah smiled humorlessly. "We're neither, of course. But you'll probably feel as though you're both unless you learn the language. We are one interesting and unexpected thing, though." She paused. "We're an addictive drug." She watched the group and recognized that Rune Johnsen had already known this. And Sorrel Trent had known. The other four were offended and uncertain and shocked.

"This effect proves that humanity and the Communities belong together," Sorrel Trent said. "We're fated to be together. They have so much to teach us."

Everyone ignored her.

"You told us they understood that we were intelligent," Michelle Ota said.

"Of course they understand," Noah said. "But what's important to them is not what they think of our intellect. It's what use we can be to them. That's what they pay us for."

"We're not prostitutes!" Piedad Ruiz said. "We're not! There's no sex in any of this. There can't be. And there are no drugs either. You said so yourself!"

Noah turned to look at her. Piedad didn't listen particularly well, and she lived in terror of prostitution, drug addiction, disease, anything that might harm her or steal her ability to have the family she hoped for. Her two older sisters were already selling themselves on the streets. She hoped to rescue them and herself by getting work with the Communities.

"No sex," Noah agreed. "And *we* are the drugs. The Communities feel better when they enfold us. We feel better too. I guess that's only fair. The ones among them who are having trouble adjusting to this world are calmed and much improved if they can enfold one of us now and then." She thought for a moment. "I've heard that for human beings, petting a cat lowers our blood pressure. For them, enfolding one of us calms them and eases what translates as a kind of intense biological homesickness."

"We ought to sell them some cats," Thera said. "Neutered cats so they'll have to keep buying them."

"Cats and dogs don't like them," Noah said. "As a matter of fact, cats and dogs won't like you after you've lived in the bubble for a while. They seem to smell something on you that we can't detect. They panic if you go near them. They bite and scratch if you try to handle them. The effect lasts for a month or two. I generally avoid house pets and even farm animals for a couple of months when I go out."

"Is being enveloped anything like being crawled over by insects?" Piedad asked. "I can't stand having things crawl on me."

"It isn't like any experience you've ever had," Noah said. "I can only tell you that it doesn't hurt and it isn't slimy or disgusting in any way. The only problem likely to be triggered by it is claustrophobia. If any of you had been found to be claustrophobic, you would have been culled by now. For the non-claustrophobic, well, we're lucky they need us. It means jobs for a lot of people who wouldn't otherwise have them."

"We're the drug of choice, then?" Rune said. And he smiled.

Noah smiled back. "We are. And they have no history of drug taking, no resistance to it, and apparently no moral problems with it. All of a sudden they're hooked. On us."

James Adio said, "Is this some kind of payback for you, Translator? You hook them on us because of what they did to you."

Noah shook her head. "No payback. Just what I said earlier. Jobs. We get to live, and so do they. I don't need payback."

He gave her a long, solemn look. "I would," he said. "I do. I can't have it, but I want it. They invaded us. They took over."

"God, yes," Noah said. "They've taken over big chunks of the Sahara, the Atacama, the Kalahari the Mojave and just about every other hot, dry wasteland they could find. As far as territory goes, they've taken almost nothing that we need."

"They've still got no right to it," Thera said. "It's ours, not theirs."

"They can't leave," Noah said.

Thera nodded. "Maybe not. But they can die!"

Noah ignored this. "Some day maybe a thousand years from now, some of them will leave. They'll build and use ships that are part multigenerational and part sleeper. A few Communities stay awake and keep things running. Everyone else sort of hibernates." This was a vast oversimplification of the aliens' travel habits, but it was essentially true. "Some of us might even wind up going with them. It would be one way for the human species to get to the stars."

Sorrel Trent said wistfully, "If we honor them, maybe they will take us to heaven with them."

Noah suppressed an urge to hit the woman. To the others, she said, "The next two years will be as easy or as difficult as you decide to make them. Keep in mind that once the contract is signed, the Communities won't let you go because you're angry with them or because you hate them or even because you try to kill them. And by the way, although I'm sure they can be killed, that's only because I believe anything that's alive can die. I've never seen a dead Community, though. I've seen a couple of them have what you might call internal revolution. The entities of those Communities scattered to join other Communities. I'm not sure whether that was death, reproduction, or both." She took a deep breath and let it out. "Even those of us who can talk fluently with the Communities don't understand their physiology that well."

"Finally, I want to tell you a bit of history. When I've done that, I'll escort you in and introduce you to your employers."

"Are we all accepted, then?" Rune Johnsen asked.

"Probably not," Noah said. "There's a final test. When you go in, you will be enfolded, each of you, by a potential employer. When that's over, some of you will be offered a contract and the rest will be given the thanks-for-stopping-by fee that anyone who gets this far and no farther is given."

"I had no idea the . . . enfolding . . . would happen so soon," Rune Johnsen said. "Any pointers?"

"About being enfolded?" Noah shook her head. "None. It's a good test. It lets you know whether you can stand the Communities and lets them know whether they really want you."

Piedad Ruiz said, "You were going to tell us something—something from history."

"Yes." Noah leaned back in her chair. "It isn't common knowledge. I looked for references to it while I was in school, but I never found any. Only my military captors and the aliens seemed to know about it. The aliens told me before they let me go. My military captors gave me absolute hell for knowing.

"It seems that there was a coordinated nuclear strike at the aliens when it was clear where they were establishing their colonies. The armed forces of several countries had tried and failed to knock them out of the sky before they landed. Everyone knows that. But once the Communities established their bubbles, they tried again. I was already a captive inside the Mojave Bubble when the attack came. I have no idea how that attack was repelled, but I do know this, and my military captors confirmed it with their lines of questioning: the missiles fired at the bubbles never detonated. They should have, but they didn't. And sometime later, exactly half of the missiles that had been fired were returned. They were discovered armed and intact, scattered around Washington DC in the White House—one in the Oval Office—in the capitol, in the Pentagon. In China, half of the missiles fired at the Gobi Bubbles were found scattered around Beijing. London and Paris got one half of their missiles back from the Sahara and Australia. There was panic, confusion, fury. After that, though, the "invaders," the "alien weeds" began to become in many languages, our "guests," our "neighbors," and even our "friends."

"Half the nuclear missiles were . . . returned?" Piedad Ruiz whispered.

Noah nodded. "Half, yes."

"What happened to the other half?"

"Apparently, the Communities still have the other half—

along with whatever weapons they brought with them and any they've built since they've been here."

Silence. The six looked at one another, then at Noah.

"It was a short, quiet war," Noah said. "We lost."

Thera Collier stared at her bleakly. "But . . . but there must be something we can do, some way to fight."

Noah stood up, pushed her comfortable chair away. "I don't think so," she said. "Your employers are waiting. Shall we join them?"

The End

Birth Days

GEOFF RYMAN

Geoff Ryman is a Canadian-born writer who moved to the U.S. at age eleven, and has been living in England since 1973. He began publishing SF stories in the mid-1970s. The first work to establish his international reputation as one of the leading writers of SF was "The Unconquered Country: A Life History" (1984, rev 1986), a novella which won the World Fantasy Award. It is reprinted in Unconquered Countries: Four Novellas *(1994). Then Ryman's* The Child Garden *(1988), won the Arthur C. Clarke Award and the John W. Campbell Memorial Award, and confirmed him as a major figure in contemporary SF. Some of his most recent books are not SF.* Was *(1992) is the supposed true story of the real-life Dorothy, who was the inspiration for L. Frank Baum's first Oz book.* 253 *(1998) is a work of hypertext fiction linking the lives of characters in a subway car. His newer books are* Lust *(2001),* Air *(2002), and* V.A.O. *(2002).*

"Birth Days" was published in Interzone, *which had a shaky year financially and changed midyear from a monthly to bi-monthly publication. It is a story about the future of male homosexuality told in four parts—from the point of view of the gay protagonist on his birthday at ages 16, 26, 36, and 46. It is very direct with its subject matter, which includes confronting the elimination of homosexuality by choice, and the experience of pregnant men, in the manner of the classic SF of Thomas M. Disch and Samuel R. Delany (in his mature phase,* Dhalgren *and after).*

Today's my 16th birthday, so I gave myself a present.

I came out to my Mom.

Sort of. By accident. I left out a mail from Billy, which I could just have left on the machine, but no, I had to go and print it out and leave it on my night table, looking like a huge white flag.

I get up this morning and I kinda half-notice it's not there. I lump into the kitchen and I can see where it went. The letter is in Mom's hand and the look on her face tells me, yup, she's read it. She has these gray lines down either side of her mouth. She holds it up to me, and says, "Can you tell me why you wouldn't have the courage to tell me this directly?"

And I'm thinking how could I be so dumb? Did I do this to myself deliberately? And I'm also thinking wait a second, where do you get off reading my letters?

So I say to her, "Did you like the part where he says my dick is beautiful?"

She says, "Not much, no." She's already looking at me like I'm an alien. And I'm like: Mom, this is what you get for being NeoChristian—your son turns out to be homo. What the Neos call a Darwinian anomaly.

Mom sighs and says, "Well I suppose we're stuck with it now."

Yeah Mom, you kinda are. Aren't you supposed to say something mimsy like, Ron honey you know we still love you? Not my Mom. Oh no. Saying exactly what she thinks is Mom's way of being real, and her being real is more important to her than anything else. Like what I might be feeling.

So I dig back at her. "That's a shame, Mom. A few years later and I would have been embryo-screened and you could have just aborted me."

Mom just sniffs. "That was a cheap shot."

Yeah, it was. NeoChristians are about the only people who *don't* abort homosexual fetuses. Everybody else does. What do they call it? Parental choice.

So Mom looks at me with this real tough face and says, "I hope you think you've given yourself a happy birthday." And that's all the conversation we have about it.

My little brother is pretending he isn't there and that he isn't happy. My little brother is shaped like a pineapple. He's fat and he has asthma and he's really good at being sneaky and not playing by the rules. I was always the big brother who tolerated stuff and tried to help Mom along. Her good little boy. Only now I'm samesex. Which to a NeoChristian Mom is like finding out your son likes dressing up as a baby and being jerked off by animals. Sometimes I think Neo is just a way to find new reasons to hate the same old things.

What really dents my paintwork is that Mom is smart. What she likes about Neo is that it's Darwinian. Last summer she's reading this article *Samesex Gene Planted by Aliens?* And she's rolling her eyes at it. "The least they could do is get the science straight," she says. "It's not one gene and it's not one part of the brain." But then she said, "But you gotta wonder, why is there a gene like that in the first place?"

My Mom really does think that there's a chance that homos are an alien plot. Please do not fall over laughing, it hurts too much.

Ever since the Artifacts were found, people have been imagining little green men landing on this beautiful blue planet and just going off again. So people scare themselves wondering if the aliens are about to come back with a nice big army.

Then about five years ago, it turned out that the genes that control sexual orientation have some very unusual sugars, and all of a sudden there's this conspiracy theory that the aliens created the samesex gene as some kind of weapon. Undermine our reproductive capacity. Even though when they landed we were all triblodites or whatever. Maybe having homos is supposed to soften us up for conquest. Hey, if the aliens invade, I promise, I'll fight too OK?

On my way to school I ring Billy and tell him "Mom found out. She read your mail."

Billy sounds stripped for action, "Did she go crazy?"

"She went laconic. You could just hear her thinking: you gotta own this, Ronald, you did this to yourself, Ronald."

"It's better than crying."

Billy's in Comportment class. He believes all that shit. To be fair to him, that "you gotta own this" was me digging at some of the stuff he comes out with. That stuff pisses me off. In fact right now, everything pisses me off. Right now, it's like my guts are twisting and I want to go break something.

Comportment says you've got to own the fact people don't like you, own the fact you got fat hips, own the fact you're no good in math, own the fact that glacial lakes are collapsing onto Tibetan monasteries. Comportment says hey, you're complaining about the Chinese treatment of Tibet, but what have you personally done about it?

It's like: we'll make everybody who has no power feel it's their fault if stuff goes wrong, so the big people don't have to do anything about it.

My Mom hates me being a homo. She likes being a big tough lady even more. So, she like, doesn't get all upset or cry or even say much about it. Being a tough lady is her way of feeling good about her son being an alien plot.

Billy is too focused on being Joe Cool-and-Out to cut me any slack. His stab at being sympathetic is "You should have just told her straight up, like I told you."

I say back to him in this Minnie-Mouse voice, "I acknowledge that you are absolutely right." That's another line he's used on me.

He's silent for a sec and then says, "Well, don't be a bitch with me about it."

"It's my authentic response to an emotionally charged situation." Still sounding like Minnie Mouse.

I'm mad at him. I'm mad at him because he just won't unbend. Nobody unbends. It's bad comportment.

Billy comes back at me. "This is just you going back to being a baby. Only you don't have tantrums, you just whine."

"Billy. My NeoChristian Mom now knows I'm samesex. Could I have some sympathy?"

"Who's died, Ron? Anybody dead around here? Did you lose any limbs in the detonation? Or are you just getting all significant on my ass?"

"No. I'm looking for a friend. I'll try and find one, you know, someone who likes me and not my dick?"

And I hang up.

Like I said, I'm so mad.

I'm mad sitting here right now. I got my stupid kid brother who's been giggling all day, like it's such an achievement he likes pussy. I got my Mom doing the household accounts and her shares and her rollovers, and she's bellowing into the voice recognition and it's like: look at me having to do all the work around here. I'm realizing that I've probably screwed up my relationship with Billy and wondering if I really am the incredible wimp he thinks I am.

It's like everything all around me is Jell-O and it's setting into lemon-lime, which I hate. I'm out. My brother knows and will try to give me a hard time, and if he does I'll slug his fat face. My Mom is being hard ass, and so I'm going to be hard ass back. I'm not an athlete, I'm not Joe Cool-and-Out, and I'll never go to Mom's Neo seminars.

I'm just sitting here all alone thinking: how can I win? What can I do?

I'll never be able to be a good little boy again. That is not an option. I'm not interested in being political about who I sleep with. I don't sign up to anything, I don't believe anything, and I don't like anybody, and I don't think anybody likes me.

Hey. A fresh start. Happy birthday.

So, 26 today!

I got up at 3:00 A.M. and holoed over to the Amazon to say

hi to João. He looked so happy to see me, his little face was just one huge smile. He'd organized getting some of his sisters to line up behind him. They all waved and smiled and downloaded me a smart diary for my present. In Brazil, they still sing Happy Birthday.

Love conquers all. With a bit of work.

I called João later and we did our usual daily download. His testosterone levels were through the roof, he's getting so stimulated by his new job in the Indian Devolved Areas. He's about to go off to Eden to start his diplomatic work. He looks so sweet in a penis sheath and a parrot's feather through his nose. Standard diplomatic dress for a member of the Brazilian Consular Team.

I love him I love him I love him I love him.

I am so god damned lucky. They didn't have embryo-screening on the Amazon. Hey! A fellow sodomite. We're an endangered species everywhere else. Must eliminate those nasty alien genes.

Then I had to go and tell him about how my project was going. And he looked glum.

"I know you don't like it," I told him.

"It feels wrong. Like genocide." He pronounces it jenoseed. "Soon they will be no more."

"But it's not genocide. The babies come out hetero, that's all. No more samesex, no more screening, just happy babies. And the adults who are left can decide for themselves if they want to be cured or not. Anyway, the Neos say that *we're* the genocide."

"You don't need to help them."

"João. Baby. It won't affect us. We'll still have each other."

"The Indians say it is unwise."

"Do they? That's interesting. How come?"

"They say it is good to have other ways. They think it is like what almost happened to them."

That rang true. So me and João have this really great conversation about it, very neutral, very scientific. He's just so smart.

Before the alien gene thing, they used to say that homos

were a pool of altruistic non-reproducing labor. It's like, we baby-sit for our siblings' kids and that increases the survival potential of our family's genes. Because a gene that makes it unlikely that you'll have kids should have died out. So why was it still here?

João tells his usual joke about all the singers in Brazil being samesex, which is just about true. So I say, wow, the human race couldn't reproduce without Dança do Brasil, huh? Which was a joke. And he says, maybe so.

I say like I always do, "You know, don't you, baby?"

His voice goes soft and warm. "I know. Do you know?"

Yes. Oh yes, I know.

That you love me. We love each other.

We've been saying that every day now for five years. It still gives me a buzz.

It was a big day at the lab too. The lights finally went on inside Flat Man.

Flat Man is pretty horrible, to tell you the truth. He's a culture, only the organs are differentiated and the bones are wafer-thin and spread out in a support structure. He looks like a cross between a spider's web and somebody who's been hit by a truck. And he covers an entire wall.

His brain works, but we know for a fact that it performs physical functions only. No consciousness, no narrative-of-the-self. He's like a particularly useful bacterial culture. You get to map all his processes, test the drugs, maybe fool around with his endomorphins. They got this microscope that can trail over every part of his body. You can see life inside him, pumping away.

Soon as I saw him, I got this flash. I knew what to do with him. I went to my mentor, wrote it up, got it out and the company gave me the funding.

People think of cells as these undifferentiated little bags. In fact, they're more like a city with a good freeway system. The proteins get shipped in, they move into warehouses, they're distributed when needed, used up and then shipped out.

We used to track proteins by fusing them with fluorescent jellyfish protein. They lit up. Which was just brilliant really since every single molecule of that protein was lit up all the time. You sure could see where all of it was, but you just couldn't see where it was going to.

We got a different tag now, one that fluoresces only once it's been hit by a blue laser. We can paint individual protein molecules and track them one by one.

Today we lit up the proteins produced by the samesex markers. I'm tracking them in different parts of the brain. Then I'll track how genetic surgery affects the brain cells. How long it takes to stimulate the growth of new structures. How long it takes to turn off production of other proteins and churn the last of them out through the lysosomes.

How long it takes to cure being homo.

It's a brilliantly simple project and it will produce a cheap reliable treatment. It means that all of João's friends who are fed up being hassled by Evangelicals can decide to go hetero.

That's my argument. They can decide. Guys who want to stay samesex like me . . . well, we can. And after us maybe there won't be any more homosexuals. I really don't know what the problem with that is. Who'll miss us? Other same-sexers looking for partners? Uh, hello, there won't be any.

And yes, part of me thinks it will be a shame that nobody else will get to meet their João. But they'll meet their Joanna instead.

Mom rang up and talked for like 17 hours. I'm not scared that I don't love her anymore. I do love her, a lot, but in my own exasperated way. She's such a character. She volunteered for our stem cell regime. She came in and nearly took the whole damn program over, everybody loved her. So now she's doing weights, and is telling me about this California toy boy she's picked up. She does a lot of neat stuff for the Church, I gotta say, she's really in there helping. She does future therapy, the Church just saw how good she is with people, so they sent her in to help people change and keep up and not be frightened of science.

She tells me, "God is Science. It really is and I just show people that." She gets them using their Personalized Identity for the first time, she gets them excited by stuff. Then she makes peanut butter sandwiches for the homeless.

We talk a bit about my showbiz kid brother. He's a famous sex symbol. I can't get over it. I still think he looks like a pineapple.

"Both my kids turned out great," says Mom. "Love you."

I got to work and the guys had pasted a little card to the glass. *Happy Birthday Ron, from Flat Man.*

And at lunchtime, they did this really great thing. They set up a colluminated lens in front of the display screen. The image isn't any bigger, but the lens makes your eyes focus as if you are looking at stuff that's ten kilometers away.

Then they set up a mini-cam, and flew it over Flat Man. I swear to God, it was like being a test pilot over a planet made of flesh. You fly over the bones and they look like salt flats. You zoom up and over muscle tissue that looks like rope mountains. The veins look like tubular trampolines.

Then we flew into the brain, right down into the cortex creases and out over the amygdala, seat of sexual orientation. It looked like savannah.

"We call this Flanneryland," said Greg. So they all took turns trying to think of a name for our new continent. I guess you could say I have their buy-in. The project cooks.

I got back home and found João had sent me a couple of sweet little extra emails. One of them was a list of all his family's addresses . . . *but my best address is in the heart of Ronald Flannery.*

And I suppose I ought to tell you that I also got an encryption from Billy.

Billy was my first boyfriend back in high school and it wasn't until I saw his signature that I realized who it was and that I'd forgotten his last name. Wow, was this mail out of line.

I'll read it to you. *Ron*, it starts out, *long time no see. I seem to recall that you were a Libra, so your birthday must be about now, so, happy birthday. You may have heard that I'm running for public office here in Palm Springs*—well actually, Billy, no I haven't, I don't exactly scan the press for news about you or Palm Springs.

He goes on to say how he's running on a Save Same-sex ticket. I mean, what are we, whales? And who's going to vote for that? How about dealing with some other people's issues as well, Billy? You will get like 200 votes at most. But hey, Billy doesn't want to actually *win* or achieve anything, he just wants to be right. So listen to this—

I understand that you are still working for Lumiere Laboratories. According to this week's LegitSci News they're the people that are doing a cure for homosexuality that will work on adults. Can this possibly be true? If so could you give me some more details? I am assuming that you personally have absolutely nothing to do with such a project. To be direct, we need to know about this treatment: how it works, how long a test regime it's on, when it might be available. Otherwise it could be the last straw for an orientation that has produced oh, . . . and listen to this, virtue by association, the same old tired list . . . *Shakespeare, Michaelangelo, da Vinci, Melville, James, Wittgenstein, Turing* . . . still no women, I see.

I mean, this guy is asking me to spy on my own company. Right? He hasn't got in touch since high school, how exploitative is that? And then he says, and this is the best bit, *or are you just being a good little boy again*?

No, I'm being a brilliant scientist, and I could just as easily produce a list of great heterosexuals, but thanks for getting in a personal dig right at the end of the letter. Very effective, Billy, a timely reminder of why I didn't even like you by the end and why we haven't been in touch.

And why you are not going to get even a glimmer of a reply. Why in fact, I'm going to turn this letter in to my mentor. Just to show I don't do this shit and that somebody else has blabbed to the media.

Happy effin birthday.

And now I'm back here, sitting on my bed, talking to my diary, wondering who it's for. Who I am accountable to? Why do I read other people's letters to it?

And why do I feel that when this project is finished I'm going to do something to give something back. To whom?

To, and this is a bit of a surprise for me, to my people.

I'm about to go to sleep, and I'm lying here, hugging the shape of João's absence.

* * *

Today's my birthday and we all went to the beach.

You haven't lived until you body surf freshwater waves, on a river that's so wide you can't see the other bank, with an island in the middle that's the size of Belgium and Switzerland combined.

We went to Mosquerio, lounged on hammocks, drank beer, and had cupu-açu ice cream. You don't get cupu-açu fruit anywhere else and it makes the best ice cream in the world.

Because of the babies I had to drink coconut milk straight from the coconut . . . what a penance . . . and I lay on my tummy on the sand. I still wore my sexy green trunks.

Nilson spiked me. "João! Our husband's got an arse like a baboon!"

It is kind of ballooning out. My whole lower bowel is stretched like an oversized condom, which actually feels surprisingly sexy. I roll over to show off my packet. That always inspires comment. This time from Guillerme. "João! Nilson, his dick is as big as you are! Where do you put it?"

"I don't love him for his dick," says João. Which can have a multitude of meanings if you're the first pregnant man in history, and your bottom is the seat of both desire and rebirth.

Like João told me before I came out here, I have rarity value on the Amazon. A tall *branco* in Brazil . . . I keep getting dragged by guys, and if I'm not actually being dragged then all I have to do is follow people's eye lines to see what's snagged their attention. It's flattering and depersonalizing all at one and the same time.

The only person who doesn't do it is João. He just looks into my eyes. I look away and when I look back, he's still looking into my eyes.

He's proud of me.

In fact, all those guys, they're all proud of me. They all feel I've done something for them.

What I did was grow a thick pad in Flat Man's bowel. Thick enough for the hooks of a placenta to attach to safely.

I found a way to overcome the resistance in sperm to being penetrated by other sperm. The half pairs of chromosomes line up and join.

The project-plan people insisted we test it on animals. I thought that was disgusting, I don't know why, I just hated it. What a thing to do to a chimp. And anyway, it would still need testing on people, afterward.

And anyway, I didn't want to wait.

So I quit the company and came to live in Brazil. João got me a job at the university. I teach Experimental Methods in very bad Portuguese. I help out explaining why Science is God.

It's funny seeing the Evangelicals trying to come to terms. The police have told me, watch out, there are people saying the child should not be born. The police themselves, maybe. I look into their tiny dark eyes and they don't look too friendly.

João is going to take me to Eden to have the baby. It is Indian territory, and the Indians want it to be born. There is something about some story they have, about how the world began again, and keeps re-birthing.

Agosto and Guillinho roasted the chicken. Adalberto, Kawé, Jorge and Carlos sat around in a circle shelling the dried prawns. The waiter kept coming back and asking if we wanted more beer. He was this skinny kid from Marajo with nothing to his name but shorts, flip-flops and a big grin in his dark face. Suddenly we realize that he's dragging us. Nilson starts singing, "*Moreno, Moreno* . . ." which means sexy brown man. Nilson got the kid to sit on his knee.

This place is paradise for gays. We must be around 4 percent of the population. It's the untouched natural samesex demographic, about the same as for left-handedness. It's like being in a country where they make clothes in your size or speak your maternal language, or where you'd consider allowing the President into your house for dinner.

It's home.

We got back and all and I mean *all* of João's huge family had a party for my birthday. His nine sisters, his four brothers and their spouses and their kids. That's something else you don't get in our big bright world. Huge tumbling families. It's like being in a 19th-century novel every day. Umberto gets a job, Maria comes off the booze, Latitia gets over fancying her cousin, João helps his nephew get into university. Hills of children roll and giggle on the carpet. You can't sort out what niece belongs to which sister, and it doesn't matter. They all just sleep over where they like.

Senhora da Souza's house was too small for them all, so we hauled the furniture out into the street and we all sat outside in a circle, drinking and dancing and telling jokes I couldn't understand. The Senhora sat next to me and held my hand. She made this huge cupu-açu cream, because she knows I love it so much.

People here get up at five A.M. when it's cool, so they tend to leave early. By ten o'clock, it was all over. João's sisters lined up to give me a kiss, all those children tumbled into cars, and suddenly, it was just us. I have to be careful about sitting on the babies too much, so I decided not to drive back. I'm going to sleep out in the courtyard on a mattress with João and Nilson.

We washed up for the Senhora, and I came out here onto this unpaved Brazilian street to do my diary.

Mom hates that I'm here. She worries about malaria, she worries that I don't have a good job. She's bewildered by my being pregnant. "I don't know baby, if it happens, and it works, who's to say?"

"It means the aliens' plot's backfired, right?"

"Aliens," she says back real scornful. "If they wanted the planet, they could just have burned off the native life forms, planted a few of their own and come back. Even our padre thinks that's a dumb idea now. You be careful, babe. You survive. OK?"

OK. I'm 36 and still good looking. I'm 36 and finally I'm some kind of a rebel.

I worry though, about the Nilson thing.

OK, João and I had to be apart for five years. It's natural he'd shack up with somebody in my absence and I do believe he loves me, and I was a little bit jealous at first . . . sorry, I'm only human. But hey—heaps of children on the floor, right? Never know who's sleeping with whom? I moved in with them, and I quite fancy Nilson, but I don't love him, and I wouldn't want to have his baby.

Only . . . maybe I am.

You are supposed to have to treat the sperm first to make them receptive to each other, and I am just not sure, there is no way to identify, when I became pregnant. But OK, we're all one big family, they've both . . . been down there. And I started to feel strange and sick before João's and my sperm were . . . um . . . planted.

Thing is, we only planted one embryo. And now there's twins.

I mean, it would be wild wouldn't it if one of the babies were Nilson and João's? And I was just carrying it, like a pod?

Oh man. Happy birthday.

Happy birthday, moon. Happy birthday, sounds of TVs, flip-flop sandals from feet you can't see, distant dogs way off on the next street, insects creaking away. Happy birthday, night. Which is as warm and sweet as hot honeyed milk.

Tomorrow, I'm off to Eden, to give birth.

46 years old. What a day to lose a baby.

They had to fly me back out in a helicopter. There was blood gushing out, and João said he could see the placenta. Chefe said it was OK to send in the helicopter. João was still in Consular garb. He looked so tiny and defenseless in just a penis sheath. He has a little pot belly now. He was so terrified, his whole body had gone yellow. We took off, and I feel like I'm melting into a swamp, all brown mud, and we look out and there's Nilson with the kids, looking forlorn and waving goodbye. And I feel this horrible grinding milling in my belly.

I'm so fucking grateful for this hospital. The Devolved Areas are great when you're well and pumped up, and you can take huts and mud and mosquitoes and snake for dinner. But you do not want to have a miscarriage in Eden. A miscarriage in the bowel is about five times more serious than one in the womb. A centimeter or two more of tearing and most of the blood in my body would have blown out in two minutes.

I am one very lucky guy.

The Doctor was João's friend Nadia, and she was just fantastic with me. She told me what was wrong with the baby.

"It's a good thing you lost it," she told me. "It would not have had much of a life."

I just told her the truth. I knew this one felt different from the start; it just didn't feel right.

It's what I get for trying to have another baby at 45. I was just being greedy. I told her. *É a ultima vez*. This is the last time.

Chega, she said, Enough. But she was smiling. *É o trabalho do João*. From now on, it's João's job.

Then we had a serious conversation, and I'm not sure I understood all her Portuguese. But I got the gist of it.

She said: it's not like you don't have enough children.

When João and I first met, it was like the world was a flower that had bloomed. We used to lie in each other's arms and he, being from a huge family, would ask, "How many babies?" and I'd say "Six," thinking that was a lot. It was just a fantasy then, some way of echoing the feeling we had of being a union. And he would say no, no, ten. Ten babies. Ten babies would be enough.

We have fifteen.

People used to wonder what reproductive advantage homosexuality conferred.

Imagine you sail iceberg-oceans in sealskin boats with crews of 20 men, and that your skiff gets shipwrecked on an island, no women anywhere. Statistically, one of those 20 men would be samesex-orientated, and if receptive, he would nest the sperm of many men inside him. Until one day, like with Nilson and João, two sperm interpenetrated. Maybe more. The bearer probably died, but at least there was a chance of a new generation. And they all carried the genes.

Homosexuality was a fallback reproductive system.

Once we knew that, historians started finding myths of male pregnancy all over the place. Adam giving birth to Eve, Vishnu on the serpent Anata giving birth to Brahma. And there were all the virgin births as well, with no men necessary.

Now we don't have to wait for accidents.

I think Nadia said, *You and João, you're pregnant in turns or both of you are pregnant at the same time. You keep having twins. Heterosexual couples don't do that. And if you count husband no 3, Nilson, that's another five children. Twenty babies in ten years?*

"*Chega,*" I said again.

"*Chega,*" she said, but it wasn't a joke. *Of course the women, the lesbians are doing the same thing now too. Ten years ago, everybody thought that homosexuality was dead and that you guys were on the endangered list. But you know, any reproductive advantage over time leads to extinction of rivals.*

Nadia paused and smiled. *I think we are the endangered species now.*

Happy birthday.

The Waters of Meribah

TONY BALLANTYNE

Tony Ballantyne lives in the Manchester Area of the UK with his wife and two children. He has written about twenty SF short stories that have appeared in publications including Interzone, The Third Alternative, *and the Polish magazine* Nowa Fantastyka. *He reviews SF and fantasy for* Infinity Plus. *His first novel,* Recursion, *is being published in 2004 by Tor UK.*

"The Waters of Meribah," reprinted from Interzone, *is a radical hard SF story with true strangeness, charm, and spin. It is about the nature of the universe and the human desire to understand it and manipulate it, and the utter disaster that results. It is also about the old SF idea of scientists making monsters. It is a darkly satisfying, scientific metaphor gone wild in the manner of the Victorian children's story in which misbehavior is punished horribly.*

A pair of feet stood on the table, just waiting to be put on. Grayish-green feet, webbed like ducks; they looked a little like a pair of diver's flippers, only alive. Very, very alive.

"We thought we'd start with the feet as you can wear them underneath your clothes while you get used to them. It's probably best that no one suspects what you are—to begin with, anyway."

"Good idea," said Buddy Joe, looking over the head of the rotund Doctor Flynn at the feet. Alien feet. A faint mist hung around them, alien sweat exuding from alien pores.

Doctor Flynn held out an arm to stop Buddy Joe from reaching for the feet and putting them on right away.

"Slow down, Buddy Joe. I have to ask, for the record. Are you sure that you want to put the feet on? You know there will be no taking them off once you have done so."

"Yes, I want to put them on," said Buddy Joe, eyeing the feet.

"You know that once they are attached they will be part of you? If your body rejects them, it will be rejecting its own feet? Or worse, they may stay attached but the interface may malfunction, leaving you in constant pain?"

"I know that."

"And yet you still want to go ahead?"

"Of course. I've been pumped full of Compliance as a part of my sentence. I have no choice but to do what you tell me."

"Oh, I know that. I just need to hear you say it for the record."

Doctor Flynn moved out of the way. Buddy Joe was free to pick up the feet and carry them across the room to a chair. There he sat down, kicked off his shoes and socks and pulled them on.

It was like pushing his naked human feet into a pair of rubber gloves. He struggled, twisted and wriggled them into position. The alien feet did not want him; they were fighting back, trying to spit him out. Somewhere deep inside his brain he could feel himself screaming. His hands were burning, soaked in the acidic sweat that oozed from the pores of the alien feet. His own feet were being amputated, dissolved by the first stage of the alien body that Doctor Flynn and his team were making him put on. Buddy Joe was feeling excruciating pain, but the little crystal of Compliance that was slowly dissolving into his bloodstream kept him smiling all the while.

And then, all of a sudden, the feet slipped into place and they became part of him.

"That's it!" called one of Doctor Flynn's team. She looked up from her console and nodded at a nurse. "You can remove the sensors now."

She peeled the sticky strips away from his skin and dropped them in the disposal chute.

"A perfect take. We've done it, team."

Doctor Flynn was shaking hands with the other people in the room. People were looking at consoles, at the feet, at each other, in every direction but at Buddy Joe. Buddy Joe just stood there, smiling down at his strange new feet, wondering at the strange new sensations he was feeling. The floor felt different through them. Too dry and brittle.

Doctor Flynn came over, a grin spreading over his round, shiny face. "Okay, we'd like you to walk across the room. Can you do that?"

He could do that. Dip your feet into a pool of water and see how refraction bends them out of shape. That's how the feet felt to Buddy Joe. At an angle to the rest of his body; but part of him. Still part of him.

He took a step forward with his left leg, and the left foot

narrowed as he raised it. As it descended it flared out to its full webbed glory, flattened itself out and felt for the texture of the plasticized floor. It recoiled. The floor was too dry, too brittle. A good gush of acid would melt it to nothing. He moved his right foot, and then he flapped and squelched his way across the floor.

"No problems walking?" said Doctor Flynn.

"No," he replied, but the Doctor hadn't been talking to him.

There was a final checking of consoles. One by one the assembled doctors and nurses and technicians gave a thumbs up.

"Okay," said Doctor Flynn. "Well, thank you Buddy Joe. You can put your shoes on now. They should still fit if you roll the joints of the feet over each other, and in that way you can conceal them. We'll see you again the same time next week."

"Hey, just a minute," said Buddy Joe. "You can't send me out there with the Compliance still active."

Doctor Flynn gave a shrug. "We can't keep you in here. Laboratory space costs money. We're out of here ourselves in five minutes time to make way for yet another group of Historical Astronomers. Goodbye."

And that was it. He had no choice but to slip on his shoes and to walk out of the laboratory onto the fifth-level deck.

Buddy Joe made his way to a lift that would take him down to the Second Deck. The Fifth Deck was quite empty at this time of night. With any luck, he would make it home without being recognized as someone under the spell of Compliance.

His feet were rolled up in his plastic shoes and socks, it took all his self-control to hold in the exhalation of acid that would melt them away and allow his feet to flap free. Don't let go, Buddy Joe. The metal grid of the deck will feel horrible against your poor feet.

The laboratory lay a long way out from the Pillar Towers. He could see through the mesh of the floor, all the way down to the waves crashing on the garbage-strewn shoreline far below. Looking up, he could see the flattened-out stars that pressed close, smearing themselves just above the tops of the highest buildings. He would have liked to stop for a while, it was a rare treat to look at the remnants of the universe, but he didn't dare. Not with Compliance still inside him.

The few Fifth Deckers who were out walking ignored him as usual. Scientists or lawyers, who could tell the difference? All wrapped up against the winter cold, trousers tucked into their socks against the cold gusts of wind that blew up through the metal decking. Buddy Joe kept to the shadows, dodging between the cats' cradles of struts that braced the buildings to the decks. Approaching the Pillar Towers he saw the yellow light that bathed the polished wooden doors of the main lift and he relaxed, but too soon. The woman who had been following him called out from the shadows behind.

"Stop there."

He did so.

"You're on Compliance, right?"

"Yes."

Buddy Joe felt a pathetic cry building inside. First they had taken his feet, now they would take his wallet, or worse.

"What did you do?"

"Rape," he said. "But . . ."

"I don't want to hear the details."

Buddy Joe dutifully closed his mouth, panic rising inside. His shoes were melting.

"Some bastard raped my partner only two months ago. Caught him alone in a lift coming up from the Second Deck. Are you a Second Decker?"

"Yes, but . . ."

"I'm not interested. How about if I told you to throw yourself off the edge?"

"Please don't do that."

"Funny, that. John said 'Please' too. Bastard didn't listen to him."

Buddy Joe clenched his fists together. His new feet were flapping open and closed by themselves, trying to creep away from the woman. There was a gentle intake of breath. This was it. This was the end. She would tell him to go and jump off the deck and he would have no choice but to obey. She was going to say it. She was going to . . .

And then nothing. A lengthening pause.

He turned around: the woman had gone. In her place was the stuff of nightmares. Buddy Joe began to make a noise. A thin scream of pure terror.

He was looking at another alien. He was looking at himself. It had his feet. It was his height, its hands stretched out . . . No. Don't look at the hands, Buddy Joe. But worse than that.

It had no head.

No head, but it was watching him. It was trying to say something to him, but he wasn't ready to understand.

—*Forget it, then,* said the alien.—*For now.*

It rose up into the air and vanished.

Two minutes later, Buddy Joe walked, shaking, into the lift. He had Compliantly forgotten all about the alien.

Buddy Joe's flat was at the top of a block built on the Second Deck, home of those just bright enough not to believe in anything, but not bright enough to believe in something. His window looked out into the gloom cast by the underside of the Third Deck. He had a bed, a food spigot and a viewscreen. Down the corridor were a bathroom and a row of toilet cubicles. Buddy Joe's father lived two flats down, his sister in the next flat again. Buddy Joe's grandfather had lived in the flat just next to the lift shaft. That flat had echoed and boomed every time the lift had moved. It echoed and boomed all day long, and most of the night. Buddy Joe's Granddad was dead now, though, and a new family had moved in. Granddad would have called them an Indian family, but he was old-fashioned in that respect. He had been old enough to remember when flowers had first bloomed on the moon.

"What do you know, Buddy Joe?" asked the woman on the viewscreen.

"I don't know nothing," said Buddy Joe.

"Next dose of Compliance at 40 P tomorrow. Next part of the alien suit at 60 P."

Buddy Joe rolled over on his bed. He was seriously thinking of throwing himself off the edge of the deck.

The viewscreen flickered and his sister appeared. She was sitting on a bed in a gray metal room just the same as his, just three doors away.

"Forty P tomorrow, eh, Buddy Joe?"

"That's right."

"And the next part of the alien suit at 60 P."

"That's what they said."

His father appeared on the screen. It might as well be the same room, the same bed, only the person changed.

"Forty P, Buddy Joe."

"Yes."

"New suit at 60 P."

"That's what they said."

"Your Granddad would say two o'clock, you know, not 60 P."

"Really, Dad?"

"You're a lot like your Granddad, Buddy Joe. He was always thinking about things, too. I always said it would get you both into trouble. I was right, too."

Buddy Joe looked down at his strange gray-green feet. He had placed a plastic bag between them and the nylon sheets: they didn't like the feel. He looked at his thin pale legs.

"Get used to them, they'll be gone by tomorrow."

That was James, from the flat below, his big moon-face leering from the viewscreen. He was filling a cup with food from the spigot as he spoke. Buddy Joe felt hungry. He looked for his cup beside the bed. The viewscreen flicked to show Mr. and Mrs. Singh having sex. Seventy P already. Definitely time for something to eat.

He knelt on the bed and leaned across to the spigot, his feet up in the air; well clear of the nylon sheets. Marty from Deck One was on the viewscreen now. He drew a sacred symbol in the air as he spoke.

"Shouldn't have raped that girl, boy," he shouted. "Gonna lose a lot more than your feet tomorrow."

Buddy Joe was dreaming about walking with his grandfather through one of the meadows of the moon. Butterflies dipped and sipped among the nodding red and yellow heads of the flowers that stretched in all directions. Buddy Joe bent down and sniffed a flower.

No! Dirty, No! That was Dirty, Buddy Joe!

He woke to gray morning light, feeling disgusted with himself. He had to watch himself. Dirty thoughts germinated in your sleep and then bloomed as actions in your waking life. He knew that. Think of the decks, he told himself, think of the decks.

His sister was watching him from the viewscreen. "Thirty-five P, Buddy Joe. They'll be dosing you with Compliance soon."

"That's right," he replied, rubbing his eyes. He fumbled for his mug and held it under the food spigot.

"What do you reckon it will be? New legs? New arms?"

"I don't know."

His father appeared on the screen. "Thirty-five P, Buddy Joe. They'll be dosing you with Compliance soon."

"That's right."

He didn't want to talk about it. He didn't want to lose his legs. He was being turned into an alien against his wishes. What would happen when he put on the head? What would happen to him then? Where would Buddy Joe go? Still, he deserved it. Just look at his dreams.

"Shouldn't have raped that girl, Buddy Joe," said his father.

Didn't he wish that every day?

Martin came on the screen. Then Katie, then Clovis, then Charles . . .

He was still lying on the bed when the drone came buzzing down from the upper decks. A wasp-striped cylinder, just smaller than his thumb, dropping through the traps and gaps between the decking and the Pillar Towers. Swooping through the tunnels of the support struts, weaving through the balconies and walkways that led to his flat. Sending the signal that opened his door. He saw it hanging in the air at the end of the corridor, swelling in apparent size as it zoomed toward him. It settled lightly on his hand and there was a slight prick, then the crystal of Compliance slid beneath his skin. His arm tingled a little, felt as if it was somewhere else and then, there it was back again. He looked down at the tiny body of the drone, felt the pitter patter of metal feet on his skin. It spoke to him.

"Sixty P, Buddy Joe. Back at the lab. Be there for your new legs."

"Okay," he said. His new feet started to flap, all by themselves. They were excited. Buddy Joe rolled off the bed. It would take five P for Compliance to properly take hold. He intended to be in the lab by then, before anyone could take advantage of him again.

Hold on. Again? What did he mean *again?* Had he forgotten something? He shook his head, searching for the thought. It had gone.

Outside his flat, clattering down the steps to Deck Two. Threading through riveted metal cuboids that were bolted together to make blocks of flats. Walking around a gang of teenagers who were laughing as they incited each other to piss through the metal grating of the floor onto the Churches and Mosques and Synagogues and Temples far below on Deck One. One girl, her panties around her ankles, looked at Buddy Joe, saw the mark on his arm where the drone had settled and slow comprehension spread across her face. He hurried off before she could say anything.

Buddy Joe was waiting outside the lift entrance at the Pillar Towers. The tower stretched up into the sky, a tapering, dirty metal shape that vanished into the shadows cast by the Third Deck. Covered in deep scratches that bled rusty red. His grandfather had said that was from where they had grown from the earth. He had laughed. That surprises you, he had said. Bet you thought humans built the decks. Bet most people think that nowadays. Well, it's not true. A lot of strange things happened after flowers started growing on the moon.

Buddy Joe had kept quiet. Up until then he had never thought anything but that the decks had grown by themselves. He had never thought of humans building anything. Looking at the solid, earth-colored shapes of the Pillar Towers, how could anyone not believe that they had grown from the ground?

The polished wooden lift doors slid open and three people

came out. Buddy Joe stepped into the padded interior. He gave a shiver. They were going to take away a little bit more of his humanity. He didn't want to go, but he heard his voice as it clearly asked for . . .

"Deck Five, please."

Someone pressed the button. The lift fell a little and everyone's hearts beat a little faster. Everyone had heard the story that, just as humans had sprung from the earth, someday they would all be called back to it. The lift doors would slide shut and carry them down to meet their maker . . .

But not today. The lift began to rise.

Walking across Deck Five, Buddy Joe could see the gray of the sky, sagging over the spires of the towers on Deck Seven. The winds blew harder up here; they blew through his thin cotton suit and made him shiver. His feet liked the feel: they shivered with anticipation.

He arrived early. A team of Historical Astronomers had projected pictures across the interior walls of the dome of the laboratory. They showed a strange landscape. Grassy plains, snow-capped mountains, fields of yellow corn: but everything out of proportion, the mountains, the valleys, all bigger than the pictures Buddy Joe had been shown of old Earth as a child.

"What is it?" he asked a white-coated astronomer next to him. The astronomer gave him a suspicious look and then realization dawned.

"Ah, the gentleman being fitted for an Alien Suit," he said. "A waste of time, if you want my opinion; but you probably don't." He turned and waved his arms around the room.

"This, my friend, is Mars. Mars, I should say, between the Shift and the Collapse. These pictures were taken about two months after the colony was established."

"It looks very . . . strange."

"It does to your eyes, my friend, because you have always lived in the world post-Collapse. To those who were alive before the Shift, that world would be a paradise. It would look like the real world."

"The real world?"

"Well, one of them. That's what we're all looking for here, my friend. That's why they have built those towers on Deck Seven; that's what your friends who are making that suit for you are looking for. The real world."

He gave a sigh and looked around. "Of course, my great-grandparents would not recognize these pictures as the real world."

"Why not?"

But someone called to the man. "Excuse me, I have to go now, maybe I will be able to tell you more another time." He shook Buddy Joe's hand and hurried away. He looked a little like Mr. Singh from down the corridor—what his grandfather would have called an Indian.

The Historical Astronomers were packing up now. Another set of scientists were coming into the room. The Alien Suit scientists. Two of them were pushing a trolley, and Buddy Joe felt a thrill of fear. The next part of the suit lay on it. He felt sick. It was more than he had expected. Not a pair of trousers, not a top. It looked like a jumpsuit. It would swallow up all of Buddy Joe except for his hands and his head. And when your head is gone, where do you go, Buddy Joe? (Head. Head. Now why did he think of the head of the alien? *Don't think of the Hands!*)

Doctor Flynn saw him shivering at the other side of the room. "Ah! There you are. Take your clothes off quickly. We haven't got much time."

Buddy Joe began to do so, but inside he was crying with fear. But I don't want to! Well you shouldn't have raped that girl, Buddy Joe, said his Compliant hands, busily undoing his shirt.

Someone pressed sensor pads onto his face. He kicked off his shoes and his feet unrolled themselves. Doctor Flynn stood patiently beside him, looking at a picture inadvertently left behind by the Historical Astronomers.

"Fools," he said, "living in the past. We never understood the truth when we held the possibility of the whole universe in our hands. Why should we learn the answers by looking at copies and replicas of what we had? Better to give up the past. The truth lies elsewhere."

He let go of the paper and it fluttered to the ground. He turned and looked at Buddy Joe, now standing naked before him. A pale white body traced in blue veins.

"I need the toilet."

"Wait," said Doctor Flynn. "It will be an interesting test of the suit." He turned to the rest of the team. "Are we ready?"

One woman shook her head. "Five minutes. We're having a little trouble getting the neck to dilate."

Doctor Flynn gave a slight nod. "That's okay. We have some slack time built into the session."

Buddy Joe shivered. Partly it was the cold; mainly it was fear. The gray-green body of the alien suit glistened wet and smooth on the outside, but inside, looking into the neck, he could see the strange purple color of the interior. Rows of silver-gray hooks that appeared half metal, half organic, lined the suit. What would they do to him when he pulled it on? Just how deeply would those hooks reach into his body? But he knew the answer already. They had told him. All the way in, Buddy Joe, the hooks reach all the way in. They'll soon be twisting around your veins and nerves and organs, hooking their way in and using them as a basis for the shape they will grow. They'll paint over the template of your black-and-white body in glorious Technicolor. You'll be a paint-by-numbers man.

Doctor Flynn began to hum to himself. The yellow lights reflected from his head and glasses.

"Why?" whispered Buddy Joe.

"Why what?" said Doctor Flynn.

"Why are you doing this to me?"

Doctor Flynn gave a shrug. "Just luck, I suppose. We notified the courts that we would like a test subject. Yours was the first Capital case that came up, I guess."

"No," said Buddy Joe. "I mean, why are you changing me into an alien?"

Doctor Flynn gave him a strange look. He seemed a little impressed, despite himself. "You understand what's going on, don't you? You want to know the reasons? You really are a cut above the common herd, aren't you? Well, I'll tell you . . ."

"Ready, Doctor Flynn." The woman by the suit gave the thumbs up.

Doctor Flynn gave an apologetic shrug. "Sorry. Maybe next week we'll have the time to talk."

He clapped his hands together. "Okay people, let's get going. Buddy Joe, if you can step toward the suit?"

Buddy Joe let out an involuntary whimper as he stepped forward. The neck of the suit had expanded. Now it looked like a huge purple mouth, lined with bristling hook-like teeth. It was flexing, the teeth rippling as he watched.

"Everything ready?" said Doctor Flynn, looking around. "Okay, step into the suit."

"No problem," said Buddy Joe with a smile, screaming inside as he did so. In the middle of it all, for the first time ever, he understood how the girl had felt. She hadn't wanted to go through with it either. She had said no . . . He stepped into the suit . . .

Buddy Joe couldn't lie on the bed, not in his new body. It wasn't just the way that the bed now felt strange: dry and harsh and brittle like everything else in this new world. No. Not just because of that, although the thought of putting on clothes and feeling elastic or nylon against his skin made him shudder, and the thought of a feather against his skin would have made him retch if he still had a stomach.

No. What disturbed him was the way that his skin could *see*.

The images were just there on the edge of his vision, ghosts of his room seen from all angles, the ceiling, the floor, all four walls; his body was watching them and reporting to a brain that couldn't quite make it all out.

And when he lay on the bed it was as if he was half-blinded and suffocating at the same time. He couldn't block his new, imperfect vision in any way.

So what to do? His feet had known. They had spread themselves wide, walked themselves up the walls and across the ceiling and then gripped tightly.

Now he hung from the ceiling, watching the viewscreen.

The Singhs had just finished having sex. Now it was time to watch his sister drink her evening cup of food. She raised it to him.

"Hey there, Buddy Joe. What are they going to take away next time? Your hands?"

"I suppose."

"Shouldn't have raped that girl, Buddy Joe."

"I know, I know."

His father appeared on the screen. "Hey there, Buddy Joe. What are they going to take away next time? Your hands?"

"I suppose."

"Shouldn't have raped that girl, Buddy Joe."

"I know, I . . ." He paused.

Why was he hanging here talking nonsense? Why wasn't he outside, feeling the wind? His body was too dry. Outside the wind was blowing moist and salty from the sea.

"Hey, Buddy Joe!"

His father's face stared from the screen, confused and slightly angry. It was the first time he had seen any expression but blank-eyed apathy for years. Part of Buddy Joe wanted to stop and speak to him. Hey Daddy, where have you been?

But his alien body was doing something else. One foot had flapped itself free of the ceiling and the leg to which it was attached had turned through 180 degrees and was stretching impossibly down to the floor. It touched, and the other foot let go.

His father called out to him from the viewscreen. "Hey Buddy Joe! How do you do that?"

"I don't know!" he gasped, as his new body marched its way out of the flat and down the corridor to where the lift was waiting.

It was pleasanter at night. Hanging from the underside of Deck Three—the metal grille didn't feel strange when gripped upside down—he looked up through his feet at the dark spaces through which squeezed the steady drip drip drip of rain. The rusty water ran around his toes, down his gray-green legs, dripped off his hands and his nose. He could gaze into the reflections and see two Buddy Joes looking down at the blocks and shadows of Deck Two. He could allow his legs to extend, let gravity pull him out like a stretch of toffee, blowing him in the wind from the sea.

Anywhere he could fit his head, his body would pass. He flattened his body and slotted it through the gap between deck and Pillar Towers and made his way higher and higher up to hang from beneath the Seventh Deck, looking down on the parks and gardens that surrounded the homes where the élite lived. He made his way to the edge of the deck and looked up at the region where the stars were smeared across the sky. The whole universe was squashed into a region less than 100 meters thick.

Once it had been unimaginably big, and then there had come the Collapse. Why had it happened? There were rumors, of course. Some said we weren't welcome out there, some said we had done something so obscene in the eyes of the universe they had squashed it to nearly nothing and started it again somewhere else. Buddy Joe's Granddad was more fanciful. He had said humans had just *imagined* it away.

He remembered his grandfather's words: "The mind is its own place, and in itself, can make a heaven of hell and a hell of heaven."

They'd been out walking the decks, taking the air, listening to the tired splash of the ocean waves below on the garbage-strewn beach. Where does the ocean go? he had wondered.

"Our minds used to be as big as the universe, Buddy Joe," said his grandfather, glancing up at the squashed sky. "They still are," he added sadly.

There was something out there with him, hanging from the underside of Deck Seven. Another gray-green shape, watching him swinging in the breeze. Another alien, just like him. But look at the . . . Don't look at the hands, Buddy Joe.

It didn't have a head.

"Hey!" he called. "Haven't I seen you before?"

The other shape paused. It appeared to be looking at him, despite the fact it didn't have a head; and then it turned and moved quickly away, swinging upside down from the deck, it vanished into the forest of Pillar Towers.

"Hey!" called Buddy Joe again. "Come back!"

He began to chase after it, but he was still not used to his new body. Whoever was in that suit was obviously a lot more practiced in its operation. Who was it? Buddy Joe had been told he was unique. The alien drew farther and farther away, swinging effortlessly below the deck, its body penduluming back and forth above the homes of the élite, swinging into and out of the lights that shone up from below, dodging through the cats' cradles of the bracing. It swung around a Pillar Tower and was lost from view. Buddy Joe moved faster, following it around the wide metal curve, but it was no use. It had gone.

"Where are you?" he called, and "Ouch!" as he felt a sting in his right hand. He looked there to see a black and yellow drone pumping a crystal of Compliance under his skin. Metal mandibles pulsed with red light.

"Where have you been?" said the drone in a buzzing voice. "I thought I wouldn't find you in time. Report to the laboratory at 60 P tomorrow."

"Okay," said Buddy Joe. "No problem."

Buddy Joe could stretch and stretch so that, while his feet still remained attached to the underside of Deck Six, his face moved closer and closer to the laboratory on Deck Five. He was 300 meters long and his body sang like a radio aerial, picking up signals from across the dirty ocean. Something out there was speaking to him. Something like himself. That other alien. He placed his hands on the metal of the deck and released his feet. His body slowly drew itself down and into position. He walked into the laboratory and the end of the meeting of the Historical Astronomers.

"Ah, my Alien Suit friend. And how nice you look in your new body."

"Thank you."

"And what are they going to take away from you today?"

"I don't know," Buddy Joe paused. He looked around at the meeting of astronomers as they packed away their pictures and slides into wide, shallow metal cases. He was remembering the last meeting.

"Something you said, last time. You think Doctor Flynn is mistaken in what he is doing to me. Why is he doing this to me?"

The Historical Astronomer gave a laugh. "Because your Doctor Flynn is a religious man. He may deny it, he may not believe it himself, but he will have had the teachings drummed into him as a child and they are still there inside him, shaping everything he does. I have been to Deck One, my friend. I have visited the Churches and Mosques and Synagogues and Temples. Doctor Flynn came from Deck One. He has walked on the bare earth, unprotected by the metal of the deck. He has felt the damp sand that runs along the edge of the ocean beneath his feet and between his toes. Down on Deck One they cannot forget Earth as it used to be. They feel a link to the past that we do not up here on Deck Five, and they believe things should be as they were. Nostalgia is not a basis for scientific inquiry, my friend."

"He said much the same about you," said Buddy Joe, and the astronomer laughed.

"Ah! Touché! But only up to a point, my friend. My beliefs are confirmed by scientific fact. His beliefs are confirmed by the Bible. Numbers, Chapter 20. The Waters of Meribah, where the people of Israel quarrelled with the Lord and the Lord showed his holiness. The Waters of Meribah, where the Lord told Moses to strike a rock and bring forth water."

"Moses?"

"He led his people into a wilderness and there he brought forth water and food and eventually delivered them to a Promised Land. Imagine that. First there was nothing, and then life burst forth. Just like when the flowers first bloomed on the moon . . . Do you see from where Doctor Flynn's beliefs come, my friend?"

Buddy Joe nodded his head slowly. "I think I do."

"Ah, but do you see it all? Moses was denied entry to the holy land because of his sin at the Waters of Meribah."

"His sin?"

"He did not trust the Lord to show his holiness."

"Oh."

"And now, we have been denied entry to the universe. And Doctor Flynn and his kind ask the question, what sin have we committed?"

Buddy Joe stood in silence, thinking about what he had just heard. The Historical Astronomer spoke. "You are an intelligent young man. You are a rapist, aren't you?"

"Yes," said Buddy Joe, Compliance leaving him no choice but to answer.

"I thought so. I thought so. A great loss to the scientific community. The Historical Astronomers could have used you. It's a shame that soon you will no longer be here."

As he spoke the door slid open, and the hands were wheeled in. Buddy Joe began to scream at the sight of them.

"Hey Buddy Joe!" called Doctor Flynn. Buddy Joe was weeping with terror as he stared at his new hands, seeing how big they were, how the multicolored tentacles trailed from the trolley upon which they lay, out across the floor and around the room and out the door. They were too big to see all at once. Too big to imagine on his poor, thin wrists. Look at how they were already thrashing and wriggling, sending luminescent patterns to hang in the air in afterglow, long scripts that his alien body could read. His hands were speaking to him already. Wide hands, hundreds of meters long. Too long. He didn't want to put them on. No, no, no!

"Are you ready, Buddy Joe?"

"Yes," said the Compliance. "Just one thing," said Buddy Joe, "I thought I was the only one?"

Doctor Flynn signalled to his aides to bring the trolley closer. "The only one?"

"The only one wearing a suit."

"You are."

"But I saw another alien, just last night. And the other week a woman, she was going to kill me. Just before she told me to jump off the deck, she vanished. I think it was the other alien that took her."

Doctor Flynn waved a hand for the trolley to pause.

Buddy Joe felt a wave of relief. Don't make me put on those hands, he thought. Don't make me do it.

"You are the only alien, Buddy Joe. This is the first Alien Suit: it is an artificial construct. There are no such things as aliens. Don't you know that?"

"I had an idea, but no one ever told me."

The hands were thrashing more wildly than ever. They sensed him nearby. They were frustrated at the pause and they strained against their restraints. One scientist jumped back from a vomit-yellow tentacle that lashed and cracked toward her.

Doctor Flynn looked him in the eyes. "You can't be lying to me. You are on Compliance."

"I'm telling the truth."

Doctor Flynn took a handkerchief from his pocket and wiped the sweat from his round forehead. "You're a rapist, aren't you? You must be intelligent."

"I don't feel intelligent."

Doctor Flynn looked at the other scientists. They shrugged. They shook their heads. They made it clear they didn't understand what was going on, and that Doctor Flynn would have to figure this out on his own.

"Okay, Buddy Joe. You can't be lying; therefore you must be mistaken. Let's see if we can figure out together what it is that you saw. Because it can't be another alien. Okay?"

"If you say so."

"Okay. Do you know why we're turning you into an alien?"

"No."

"We're trying to reverse the Collapse, Buddy Joe, or at least see if we can get around it. Get out of this pathetic little bubble that the universe has become. We've tried to build something so alien that it can see what we cannot. Do you know what the Shift refers to, Buddy Joe?"

Buddy Joe licked his lips as he looked at the hands. That yellow tentacle was thrashing harder than ever. Ignore it; ignore it. Speak and keep it away. He spoke.

"The Shift refers to when flowers first bloomed on the

moon. The moon colonists sent the message and no one believed them; they sent rockets there to check and when they landed there were green meadows where before there had been bare rocks . . . And then the same happened on Mars, and then on Callisto. Everywhere there was a human colony . . ."

Doctor Flynn shook his head. "No, Buddy Joe. That's not what the Shift refers to. A popular misconception."

"But I thought . . ."

"No. That was just the catalyst. It refers to the Shift in our perceptions of the way the universe works. For millennia humans believed that the earth was created as a place for them to live. And then, in the last three centuries that idea was turned on its head. We came to believe that life evolved by chance in the universe; that it fought to cling on in the most unlikely places, deep beneath the oceans or high in the atmosphere, and that all the time a subtle change in the balance could wipe it out. The proof of that theory was written in the fossils of the dinosaurs or frozen in the glaciers. But we were wrong."

The yellow tentacle thrashed again and finally broke the metal clasp that held it. Three scientists ran from the thrashing, slashing shape. Doctor Flynn spoke on, his face gray and shiny with sweat.

"Three centuries of so called progressive thought turned on its head. We had been right the first time. There is a force written at the most basic level of the universe that is dedicated to bringing forth life. The universe warps and bends itself to support life. Where humans settle and live for long enough water springs forth from the rocks and plants from the soil . . ."

Buddy Joe wanted to back away, but the yellow tentacle had turned its attention to the other bonds and was working to loosen them. Doctor Flynn didn't seem to have noticed.

"Life attracts life. We don't understand it . . . Humans wandered over the surface of the moon for decades without any sign of the effect, but when we established a colony, started to take a real interest in the satellite, then it started to take an interest in us. It's like some sort of feedback. You understand the term?"

Doctor Flynn looked at Buddy Joe, seemingly oblivious to what was going on behind him. None of the scientists seemed to care, either. The tentacle had freed two more. Now the metal clasps which held the rest of the alien hands were pulled free, pop pop pop. The hands were free. Those horrible, horrible hands, so big, just so big. Buddy Joe wanted to cry. He didn't want to put them on.

"Do you understand?"

Buddy Joe had to say yes, the Compliance made him. Doctor Flynn nodded, satisfied.

"Good. That's why, after the Collapse, we got to thinking about life. What if we made another form of life? Something completely alien to our experience. What if we built an alien suit for someone to wear? Someone like you, Buddy Joe. What would they make of the universe? Maybe they would understand what was going on. Maybe a different perspective would explain why the universe had collapsed to a bubble 300 miles across. Has the Collapse anything to do with the Shift in our perceptions?"

"The hands are coming for me," said Buddy Joe.

"That's okay," said Doctor Flynn. "That's what they were supposed to do."

"I don't want to put them on. They look too big. I'll lose myself if I put them on. They're horrible. Why did you make them so horrible?"

"We had to make them as alien as we could, Buddy Joe. We need the alien perspective. Before we had you in here we took other condemned and pumped them full of Junk and LSD and MTPH and we recorded their hallucinations. We recorded the screams of children, and the thought patterns of dogs twitching in their sleep and the terror of a very bright light in a very dark room. We took all that and painted it across the canvas that makes your body so that it could be as alien as possible."

The tentacles formed a thrashing, slashing cage around Buddy Joe. He stood with Doctor Flynn in a maelstrom of orange and yellow violence. Something turned itself up from the floor. Dark green circles with sharp red spines inside. The cuffs of his new hands.

Doctor Flynn seemed unconcerned. "And you know, even if our experiment succeeds, I wonder about what Wittgenstein said: 'Even if a lion could speak we wouldn't understand it.' I wonder if we will understand you, Buddy Joe?"

"Please don't make me put them on," he cried.

"Shouldn't have raped that girl, Buddy Joe."

"I know, I know."

He remembered the girl. He had cornered her in the lift. He remembered how she had shaken and wept.

He had been thinking about his grandfather, and things he had said. The girl had a look that reminded him of his grandfather. That same questioning, intelligent look. He thought she would understand. Buddy Joe had asked her how it must have felt to walk under the stars when they shone high above, walk on the beach and feel the sand beneath your feet and the cool ocean breeze. And when she asked him to stop he had ignored her and just carried on speaking, trying to get her to see.

Buddy Joe had raped her, pushed the hemispheres of her brain roughly apart and slipped the alien ideas into her head: left them to congeal inside her. Dirty, filthy and without her consent.

The hands reached for Buddy Joe, slipped around his human hands and melted them.

"I deserve the pain," he winced.

"Same time next . . ." Doctor Flynn began to speak, but the hands took over. They slashed across the room, cutting Doctor Flynn in half. His legs remained standing as his head and shoulders fell to the floor.

"Hey Buddy Joe, stop tha . . ."

The female scientist who called out had the top of her head sliced off in one easy motion. Blonde hair spun round and round like a Catherine wheel as it arced across the room. The yellow and orange tentacles were vibrating in sine waves, filling the room with their frantic, snapping energy. Flesh and bone snapped and tore, blood flew, and Buddy Joe was a human head on an alien body that stretched across the room and out into the night. He could feel his hands in the warmth of the room, in the cool of the night, on the metal of the deck, covered in blood, gripping the handrail at the edge of the drop to the dark ocean and pulling him clear of the room. Where were the hands taking him? A group of tentacles reached down to Doctor Flynn's head and shoulders and picked them up. He felt them thrusting themselves into the warmth of the body, feeling for the spinal cord, seeking out the arteries and veins and wriggling up them.

And then Buddy Joe was out of the laboratory and his hands were pulling him up to the top of Deck Seven.

Why wasn't the Compliance working? thought Buddy Joe as he passed out.

He woke up spread out to the size of Deck Seven. His new hands were the size and shape of every strand of the metal mesh that made up the decking. His legs stretched down two of the Pillar Towers. His head was hanging, looking down over the gardens and houses of Deck Six.

Doctor Flynn appeared before him, looking like a glove puppet. Alien tentacles had been thrust into the nerves and joints of his broken body to make him work.

—Speak to him.

"Hey, Buddy Joe," said Doctor Flynn, his eyelids drooping, his eyes moving up and down and left to right, tracing out a slow sine wave.

"Hey, Doctor Flynn," said Buddy Joe. His head was trying to be sick, but he had nothing to be sick with.

—Where's my head?

"The body wants to know where the head is."

"It's not quite finished yet, Buddy Joe. I don't think it ever will be. The hands killed most of the team. I'm not sure the expertise still exists to make a head. Even if it did, it would never get built without me to push through the requisitions."

Silence. The body was considering. Doctor Flynn twitched his nose. A single cherry of blood pumped from the side of a tentacle and fell toward the deck below.

—What do you know of the other alien?

Buddy Joe relayed the question.

"Nothing," said Doctor Flynn. "You were the only suit ever built. There can't be another alien. Hey. You can't keep me alive like this forever. Another, what, ten P at most?"

"It can feel the other aliens," said Buddy Joe, listening to the voice. "It says there are more of them all the time, somewhere over the ocean. There are ten already. It wants the head so it can join them."

"Ten? But that can't be! Anyway, there is no over-the-ocean. Don't you see? The only thing that stopped the universe collapsing to nothing was the pressure of life within this bubble. The life force is so strong it caused the decking to grow, just to allow us to live. There is no over-the-ocean any more, there is just here."

"There is an over-the-ocean, now."

Then he had the answer. It was obvious. It just popped into his head. "I know what the answer is: I know where the aliens come from," he said. But it was too late. Doctor Flynn was already dead.

"But I want to tell you the answer, Doctor Flynn," he called. The tentacles were disengaging from inside Doctor Flynn's body, rubbing themselves together as a human would rub their hands to remove something unpleasant. They were letting him go, letting him fall to the deck far below. Buddy Joe watched Doctor Flynn tumble and fall, down and down until his body landed on the roof of someone's house.

The tentacles were writhing and thrashing again, spelling out their long orange and yellow scripts in the air around him. This is how they speak, thought Buddy Joe. This is how the aliens speak. I can hear it in my subconscious, read through my peripheral vision.

—Where do we come from?

"From the life force that fills the universe," said Buddy Joe. "If flowers can bloom on the moon just because humans live there, then surely you could have come into existence when the idea of you took root in Doctor Flynn's laboratory. New life walks the earth and a new environment opens up to support it. Opens up across the ocean."

—*What a strange idea. This is how the universe works. It's not what we suspected, Buddy Joe.*

"Not what anyone thought," said Buddy Joe, 30 miles long, 20 miles wide and two miles tall, his legs and arms stretching to fill the decks around him. He was growing all the time. "A universe that exists just to nurture life. New life bursting out all the time. And here we are trapped in this little bubble of the universe. I wonder when we'll get out?"

—*Soon, Buddy Joe, soon. But not like this. Now we can see what is holding us back.*

"What is it?"

—*You.*

The tentacles lashed around, seized hold of Buddy Joe's head and pulled it clean off. It wasn't needed any more. The alien was complete and reasoning without a brain. Doctor Flynn and his team had designed it to be that different.

Tentacles began to pull themselves free of the metal of Deck Seven as Buddy Joe's head tumbled down to join Doctor Flynn's body. The body stretched itself out thinner and thinner; ready to glide its way over the ocean toward its own race . . .

. . . and then it paused. Tainted a little by Buddy Joe and his humanity, tainted a little by its origins. It had been built by humans, and just a little of the sin that it was to be human was woven into the fabric of its body. It was not yet quite free of that human curiosity that the universe moved to protect itself from. That need to explain how things worked. Curiosity. It was a most alien feeling. Without it, one could not wonder at its existence. It was a dizzying thought.

All around, the alien looked, tasted, felt the remains of the human world, the decking and the polluted seas, the last feeble stirrings of that doomed impulse that defined the inhabitants: the urge to try and understand the basic mechanism of their world. That human persistence in violating the cardinal rule, written at the quantum level and warned of in one of the humans' oldest texts.

Don't look at the system, or you will change it. The universe fights against being known.

Curiosity: forget it, the alien told itself, and it did so immediately.

Far below, there was a bump as Buddy Joe's head hit the deck.

Ej-Es

NANCY KRESS

Nancy Kress [www.sff.net/people/nankress] lives in Rochester, New York. She is one of today's leading SF writers, known for her complex medical SF stories and for her biological and evolutionary extrapolations in such classics as Beggars in Spain *(1993),* Beggars and Choosers *(1994), and* Beggars Ride *(1996), a trilogy of hard SF novels. She wrote* Maximum Light *(1998),* Probability Moon *(2000),* Probability Sun *(2001), and* Probability Space *(2002). Her stories are rich in texture and in psychological insight, and have been collected in* Trinity and Other Stories *(1985),* The Aliens of Earth *(1993) and* Beaker's Dozen *(1998). Her most recent SF novels are* Crossfire *(2003),* Nothing Human *(2003), and* Crucible *(2004).*

"Ej-Es" was published in the original anthology Stars, *edited by Janis Ian and Mike Resnick, a collection of stories taking off from one or another of Janis Ian's popular songs, a concept reminiscent of the old pulp fiction practice of asking writers to write stories based on already-purchased cover art. In this case it produced one of the best anthologies of the year. "Ej-Es" is a dark story about the moral crisis of an aging woman doctor just landed on a rediscovered colony planet, and a disease that makes the survivors who have degenerated into starvation and lassitude happy. It works like a metaphysical poem, with the title creating an image in retrospect, and that makes it a bigger, better rationalist SF story.*

Jesse, come home
There's a hole in the bed
where we slept
Now it's growing cold
Hey Jesse, your face
in the place where we lay
by the hearth, all apart
It hangs on my heart. . . .
Jesse, I'm lonely
Come home

—from "Jesse," by Janis Ian, 1972

"Why did you first enter the Corps?" Lolimel asked her as they sat at the back of the shuttle, just before landing. Mia looked at the young man helplessly, because how could you answer a question like that? Especially when it was asked by the idealistic and worshipful new recruits, too ignorant to know what a waste of time worship was, let alone simplistic questions.

"Many reasons," Mia said gravely, vaguely. He looked like so many medicians she had worked with, for so many decades on so many planets . . . intense, thick-haired, gene-mod beautiful, a little insane. You had to be a little insane to leave Earth for the Corps, knowing that when (if) you ever returned, all you had known would have been dust for centuries.

He was more persistent than most. "What reasons?"

"The same as yours, Lolimel," she said, trying to keep her voice gentle. "Now be quiet, please, we're entering the atmosphere."

"Yes, but—"

"*Be quiet.*" Entry was so much easier on him than on her; he had not got bones weakened from decades in space. They *did* weaken, no matter what exercise one took or what supplements or what gene therapy. Mia leaned back in her shuttle chair and closed her eyes. Ten minutes, maybe, of aerobraking and descent; surely she could stand ten minutes. Or not.

The heaviness began, abruptly increased. Worse on her eyeballs, as always; she didn't have good eye socket muscles, had never had them. Such an odd weakness. Well, not for long; this was her last flight. At the next station, she'd retire. She was already well over age, and her body felt it. Only her body? No, her mind, too. At the moment, for instance, she couldn't remember the name of the planet they were hurtling toward. She recalled its catalog number, but not whatever its colonists, who were not answering hails from ship, had called it.

"*Why did you join the Corps?*"

"*Many reasons.*"

And so few of them fulfilled. But that was not a thing you told the young.

The colony sat at the edge of a river, under an evening sky of breathable air set with three brilliant, fast-moving moons. Beds of glorious flowers dotted the settlement, somewhere in size between a large town and a small city. The buildings of foamcast embedded with glittering native stone were graceful, well-proportioned rooms set around open atria. Minimal furniture, as graceful as the buildings; even the machines blended unobtrusively into the lovely landscape. The colonists had taste and restraint and a sense of beauty. They were all dead.

"A long time ago," said Kenin. Officially she was Expedition Head, although titles and chains of command tended to erode near the galactic edge, and Kenin led more by consensus and natural calm than by rank. More than once the team had been grateful for Kenin's calm. Lolimel looked shaken, although he was trying to hide it.

Kenin studied the skeleton before them. "Look at those bones—completely clean."

Lolimel managed, "It might have been picked clean quickly by predators, or carnivorous insects, or . . ." His voice trailed off.

"I already scanned it, Lolimel. No microscopic bone nicks. She decayed right there in bed, along with clothing and bedding."

The three of them looked at the bones lying on the indestructible mattress coils of some alloy Mia had once known the name of. Long clean bones, as neatly arranged as if for a first-year anatomy lesson. The bedroom door had been closed; the dehumidifying system had, astonishingly, not failed; the windows were intact. Nothing had disturbed the woman's long rot in the dry air until nothing remained, not even the bacteria that had fed on her, not even the smell of decay.

Kenin finished speaking to the other team. She turned to Mia and Lolimel, her beautiful brown eyes serene. "There are skeletons throughout the city, some in homes and some collapsed in what seem to be public spaces. Whatever the disease was, it struck fast. Jamal says their computer network is gone, but individual rec cubes might still work. Those things last forever."

Nothing lasts forever, Mia thought, but she started searching the cabinets for a cube. She said to Lolimel, to give him something to focus on, "How long ago was this colony founded, again?"

"Three hundred sixty E-years," Lolimel said. He joined the search.

Three hundred sixty years since a colony ship left an established world with its hopeful burden, arrived at this deadly Eden, established a city, flourished, and died. How much of Mia's lifetime, much of it spent traveling at just under c, did that represent? Once she had delighted in figuring out such equations, in wondering if she'd been born when a given worldful of colonists made planetfall. But by now there were too many expeditions, too many colonies, too many accelerations and decelerations, and she'd lost track.

Lolimel said abruptly, "Here's a rec cube."

"Play it," Kenin said, and when he just went on staring at it in the palm of his smooth hand, she took the cube from him and played it herself.

It was what she expected. A native plague of some kind, jumping DNA-based species (which included all species in the galaxy, thanks to panspermia). The plague had struck after the colonists thought they had vaccinated against all dangerous micros. Of course, they couldn't really have thought that; even three hundred sixty years ago doctors had been familiar with alien species-crossers. Some were mildly irritating, some dangerous, some epidemically fatal. Colonies had been lost before, and would be again.

"Complete medical data resides on green rec cubes," the recorder had said in the curiously accented International of three centuries ago. Clearly dying, he gazed out from the cube with calm, sad eyes. A brave man. "Any future visitors to Good Fortune should be warned."

Good Fortune. That was the planet's name.

"All right," Kenin said, "tell the guard to search for green cubes. Mia, get the emergency analysis lab set up and direct Jamal to look for burial sites. If they had time to inter some victims—if they interred at all, of course—we might be able to recover some micros to create vacs or cures. Lolimel, you assist me in—"

One of the guards, carrying weapons that Mia could not have named, blurted, "Ma'am, how do we know we won't get the same thing that killed the colonists?"

Mia looked at her. Like Lolimel, she was very young. Like all of them, she would have her story about why she volunteered for the Corps.

Now the young guard was blushing. "I mean, ma'am, before you can make a vaccination? How do we know we won't get the disease, too?"

Mia said gently, "We don't."

* * *

No one, however, got sick. The colonists had had interment practices, they had had time to bury some of their dead in strong water-tight coffins before everyone else died, and their customs didn't include embalming. Much more than Mia had dared hope for. Good Fortune, indeed.

In five days of tireless work they had the micro isolated, sequenced, and analyzed. It was a virus, or a virus analogue, that had somehow gained access to the brain and lodged near the limbic system, creating destruction and death. Like rabies, Mia thought, and hoped this virus hadn't caused the terror and madness of that stubborn disease. Not even Earth had been able to eradicate rabies.

Two more days yielded the vaccine. Kenin dispensed it outside the large building on the edge of the city, function unknown, which had become Corps headquarters. Mia applied her patch, noticing with the usual distaste the leathery, wrinkled skin of her forearm. Once she had had such beautiful skin, what was it that a long-ago lover had said to her, what had been his name . . . Ah, growing old was not for the gutless.

Something moved at the edge of her vision.

"Lolimel . . . did you see that?"

"See what?"

"Nothing." Sometimes her aging eyes played tricks on her; she didn't want Lolimel's pity.

The thing moved again.

Casually Mia rose, brushing imaginary dirt from the seat of her uniform, strolling toward the bushes where she'd seen motion. From her pocket she pulled her gun. There were animals on this planet, of course, although the Corps had only glimpsed them from a distance, and rabies was transmitted by animal bite. . . .

It wasn't an animal. It was a human child.

No, not a child, Mia realized as she rounded the clump of bushes and, amazingly, the girl didn't run. An adolescent, or perhaps older, but so short and thin that Mia's mind had filled in "child." A scrawny young woman with light brown skin and long, matted black hair, dressed carelessly in some sort of sarong-like wrap. Staring at Mia with a total lack of fear.

"Hello," Mia said gently.

"Ej-es?" the girl said.

Mia said into her wrister, "Kenin . . . we've got natives. Survivors."

The girl smiled. Her hair was patchy on one side, marked with small white rings. *Fungus*, Mia thought professionally, absurdly. The girl walked right toward Mia, not slowing, as if intending to walk through her. Instinctively Mia put out an arm. The girl walked into it, bonked herself on the forehead, and crumpled to the ground.

"You're not supposed to beat up the natives, Mia," Kenin said. "God, she's not afraid of us at all. How can that be? You nearly gave her a concussion."

Mia was as bewildered as Kenin, as all of them. She'd picked up the girl, who'd looked bewildered but not angry, and then Mia had backed off, expecting the girl to run. Instead she'd stood there rubbing her forehead and jabbering, and Mia had seen that her sarong was made of an uncut sheet of plastic, its colors faded to a mottled gray.

Kenin, Lolimel, and two guards had come running. And *still* the girl wasn't afraid. She chattered at them, occasionally pausing as if expecting them to answer. When no one did, she eventually turned and moved leisurely off.

Mia said, "I'm going with her."

Instantly a guard said, "It's not safe, ma'am," and Kenin said, "Mia, you can't just—"

"You don't need me here," she said, too brusquely; suddenly there seemed nothing more important in the world than going with this girl. Where did that irrational impulse come from? "And I'll be perfectly safe with a gun."

This was such a stunningly stupid remark that no one answered her. But Kenin didn't order her to stay. Mia accepted the guard's tanglefoam and Kenin's vidcam and followed the girl.

It was hard to keep up with her. "Wait!" Mia called, which produced no response. So she tried what the girl had said to her: "Ej-es!"

Immediately the girl stopped and turned to her with glowing eyes and a smile that could have melted glaciers, had Good Fortune had such a thing. Gentle planet, gentle person, who was almost certainly a descendant of the original dead settlers. Or was she? InterGalactic had no record of any other registered ship leaving for this star system, but that didn't mean anything. InterGalactic didn't know everything. Sometimes, given the time dilation of space travel, Mia thought they knew nothing.

"Ej-es," the girl agreed, sprinted back to Mia, and took her hand. Slowing her youthful pace to match the older woman's, she led Mia home.

The houses were scattered, as though they couldn't make up their mind whether or not to be a village. A hundred yards away, another native walked toward a distant house. The two ignored each other.

Mia couldn't stand the silence. She said, "I am Mia."

The girl stopped outside her hut and looked at her.

Mia pointed to her chest. "Mia."

"Es-ef-eb," the girl said, pointing to herself and giving that glorious smile.

Not "ej-es," which must mean something else. Mia pointed to the hut, a primitive affair of untrimmed logs, pieces of foamcast carried from the city, and sheets of faded plastic, all tacked crazily together.

"Ef-ef," said Esefeb, which evidently meant "home." This language was going to be a bitch: degraded *and* confusing.

Esefeb suddenly hopped to one side of the dirt path, laughed, and pointed at blank air. Then she took Mia's hand and led her inside.

More confusion, more degradation. The single room had an open fire with the simple venting system of a hole in the roof. The bed was high on stilts (why?) with a set of rickety steps made of rotting, untrimmed logs. One corner held a collection of huge pots in which grew greenery; Mia saw three unfired clay pots, one of them sagging sideways so far the soil had spilled onto the packed-dirt floor. Also a beautiful titanium vase and a cracked hydroponic vat. On one plant, almost the size of a small tree, hung a second sheet of plastic sarong, this one an unfaded blue-green. Dishes and tools littered the floor, the same mix as the pots of scavenged items and crude homemade ones. The hut smelled of decaying food and unwashed bedding. There was no light source and no machinery.

Kenin's voice sounded softly from her wrister. "Your vid is coming through fine. Even the most primitive human societies have some type of artwork."

Mia didn't reply. Her attention was riveted to Esefeb. The girl flung herself up the "stairs" and sat up in bed, facing the wall. What Mia had seen before could hardly be called a smile compared to the light, the sheer joy, that illuminated Esefeb's face now. Esefeb shuddered in ecstasy, crooning to the empty wall.

"Ej-es. Ej-es. Aaahhhh, *Ej-es!*"

Mia turned away. She was a medician, but Esefeb's emotion seemed too private to witness. It was the ecstasy of orgasm, or religious transfiguration, or madness.

"Mia," her wrister said, "I need an image of that girl's brain."

It was easy—too easy, Lolimel said later, and he was right. Creatures, sentient or not, did not behave this way.

"We could haul all the neuro equipment out to the village," Kenin said doubtfully, from base.

"It's not a village, and I don't think that's a good idea," Mia said softly. The softness was unnecessary. Esefeb slept like stone in her high bunk, and the hut was so dark, illuminated only by faint starlight through the hole in the roof, that Mia could barely see her wrister to talk into it. "I think Esefeb might come voluntarily. I'll try in the morning, when it's light."

Kenin, not old but old enough to feel stiff sleeping on the ground, said, "Will you be comfortable there until morning?"

"No, but I'll manage. What does the computer say about the recs?"

Lolimel answered—evidently they were having a regular all-hands conference. "The language is badly degraded International, you probably guessed that. The translator's preparing a lexicon and grammar. The artifacts, food supply, dwelling, everything visual, doesn't add up. They shouldn't have lost so much in two hundred fifty years, unless mental deficiency was a side effect of having survived the virus. But Kenin thinks—" He stopped abruptly.

"You may speak for me," Kenin's voice said, amused. "I think you'll find that military protocol degrades, too, over time. At least, way out here."

"Well, I . . . Kenin thinks it's possible that what the girl has is a mutated version of the virus. Maybe infectious, maybe inheritable, maybe transmitted through fetal infection."

His statement dropped into Mia's darkness, as heavy as Esefeb's sleep.

Mia said, "So the mutated virus could still be extant and active."

"Yes," Kenin said. "We need not only neuro-images but a sample of cerebrospinal fluid. Her behavior suggests—"

"I know what her behavior suggests," Mia said curtly. That sheer joy, shuddering in ecstasy . . . It was seizures in the limbic system, the brain's deep center for primitive emotion, which produced such transcendent, rapturous trances. Religious mystics, Saul on the road to Damascus, visions of Our Lady or of nirvana. And the virus might still be extant, and not a part of the vaccine they had all received. Although if transmission was fetal, the medicians were safe. If not . . .

Mia said, "The rest of Esefeb's behavior doesn't fit with limbic seizures. She seems to see things that aren't there, even talk to her hallucinations, when she's not having an actual seizure."

"I don't know," Kenin said. "There might be multiple infection sites in the brain. I need her, Mia."

"We'll be there," Mia said, and wondered if that were going to be true.

But it was, mostly. Mia, after a brief uncomfortable sleep wrapped in the sheet of blue-green plastic, sat waiting for Esefeb to descend her rickety stairs. The girl bounced down, chattering at something to Mia's right. She smelled worse than yesterday. Mia breathed through her mouth and went firmly up to her.

"Esefeb!" Mia pointed dramatically, feeling like a fool. The girl pointed back.

"Mia."

"Yes, good." Now Mia made a sweep of the sorry hut. "Efef."

"Efef," Esefeb agreed, smiling radiantly.

"Esefeb efef."

The girl agreed that this was her home.

Mia pointed theatrically toward the city. "Mia efef! Mia eb Esefeb etej Mia efef!" *Mia and Esefeb come to Mia's home*. Mia had already raided the computer's tentative lexicon of Good Fortunese.

Esefeb cocked her head and looked quizzical. A worm crawled out of her hair.

Mia repeated, "Mia eb Esefeb etej Mia efef."

Esefeb responded with a torrent of repetitious syllables, none of which meant anything to Mia except "Ej-es." The girl spoke the word with such delight that it had to be a name. A lover? Maybe these people didn't live as solitary as she'd assumed.

Mia took Esefeb's hand and gently tugged her toward the door. Esefeb broke free and sat in the middle of the room, facing a blank wall of crumbling logs, and jabbered away to nothing at all, occasionally laughing and even reaching out to touch empty air. "Ej-es, Ej-es!" Mia watched, bemused, recording everything, making medical assessments. Esefeb wasn't malnourished, for which the natural abundance of the planet was undoubtedly responsible. But she was crawling with parasites, filthy (with water easily available), and isolated. Maybe isolated.

"Lolimel," Mia said softly into the wrister, "what's the best dictionary guess for 'alone'?"

Lolimel said, "The closest we've got is 'one.' There doesn't seem to be a concept for 'unaccompanied,' or at least we haven't found it yet. The word for 'one' is 'eket.' "

When Esefeb finally sprang up happily, Mia said, "Esefeb eket?"

The girl look startled. "Ek, ek," she said: *no, no*. Esefeb ek eket! Esefeb eb Ej-es!"

Esefeb and Ej-es. She was not alone. She had the hallucinatory Ej-es.

Again Mia took Esefeb's hand and pulled her toward the door. This time Esefeb went with her. As they set off toward the city, the girl's legs wobbled. Some parasite that had become active overnight in the leg muscles? Whatever the trouble was, Esefeb blithely ignored it as they traveled, much more slowly than yesterday, to Kenin's makeshift lab in the ruined city. Along the way, Esefeb stopped to watch, laugh at, or talk to three different things that weren't there.

"She's beautiful, under all that neglect," Lolimel said, staring down at the anesthetized girl on Kenin's neuro-imaging slab.

Kenin said mildly, "If the mutated virus is transmitted to a fetus, it could also be transmitted sexually."

The young man said hotly, "I wasn't implying—"

Mia said, "Oh, calm down. Lolimel. We've all done it, on numerous worlds."

"Regs say—"

"Regs don't always matter three hundred light-years from anywhere else," Kenin said, exchanging an amused glance with Mia. "Mia, let's start."

The girl's limp body slid into the neuro-imager. Esefeb hadn't objected to meeting the other medicians, to a minimal washing, to the sedative patch Mia had put on her arm. Thirty seconds later she slumped to the floor. By the time she came to, an incision ten cells thick would have been made into her brain and a sample removed. She would have been harvested, imaged, electroscanned, and mapped. She would never know it; there wouldn't even be a headache.

Three hours later Esefeb sat on the ground with two of the guards, eating soysynth as if it were ambrosia. Mia, Kenin, Lolimel, and the three other medicians sat in a circle twenty yards away, staring at handhelds and analyzing results. It was late afternoon. Long shadows slanted across the gold-green grass, and a small breeze brought the sweet, heavy scent of some native flower. *Paradise*, Mia thought. And then: *Bonnet Syndrome*.

She said it aloud, "Charles Bonnet Syndrome," and five

people raised their heads to stare at her, returned to their handhelds, and called up medical deebees.

"I think you're right," Kenin said slowly. "I never even heard of it before. Or if I did, I don't remember."

"That's because nobody gets it anymore," Mia said. "It was usually old people whose eye problems weren't corrected. Now we routinely correct eye problems."

Kenin frowned. "But that's not all that's going on with Esefeb."

No, but it was one thing, and why couldn't Kenin give her credit for thinking of it? The next moment she was ashamed of her petty pique. It was just fatigue, sleeping on that hard cold floor in Esefeb's home. *Esefeb efef*. Mia concentrated on Charles Bonnet Syndrome.

Patients with the syndrome, which was discovered in the eighteenth century, had damage somewhere in their optic pathway or brain. It could be lesions, macular degeneration, glaucoma, diabetic retinopathy, or even cataracts. Partially blind, people saw and sometimes heard instead things that weren't there, often with startling clarity and realism. Feedback pathways in the brain were two-way information avenues. Visual data, memory, and imagination constantly flowed to and from each other, interacting so vividly that, for example, even a small child could visualize a cat in the absence of any actual cats. But in Bonnet Syndrome, there was interruption of the baseline visual data about what was and was not real. So all imaginings and hallucinations were just as real as the ground beneath one's feet.

"Look at the amygdala," medician Berutha said. "Oh, merciful gods!"

Both of Esefeb's amygdalae were enlarged and deformed. The amygdalae, two almond-shaped structures behind the ears, specialized in recognizing the emotional significance of events in the external world. They weren't involved in Charles Bonnet Syndrome. Clearly, they were here.

Kenin said, "I think what's happening here is a strengthening or alteration of some neural pathways at the extreme expense of others. Esefeb 'sees' her hallucinations, and she experiences them as just as 'real'—maybe more real—than anything else in her world. And the pathways go down to the limbic, where seizures give some of them an intense emotional significance. Like . . . like orgasm, maybe."

Ej-es.

"Phantoms in the brain," Berutha said.

"A viral god," Lolimel said, surprising Mia. His tone, almost reverential, suddenly irritated her.

"A god responsible for this people's degradation, Lolimel. They're so absorbed in their 'phantoms' that they don't concentrate on the most basic care of themselves. Nor on building, farming, art, innovation . . . *nothing*. They're prisoners of their pretty fantasies."

Lolimel nodded reluctantly. "Yes, I see that."

Berutha said to Kenin, "We need to find the secondary virus. Because if it is infectious through any other vector besides fetal or sexual . . ." He didn't finish the thought.

"I know," Kenin said, "but it isn't going to be easy. We don't have cadavers for the secondary. The analyzer is still working on the cerebralspinal fluid. Meanwhile—" She began organizing assignments, efficient and clear. Mia stopped listening.

Esefeb had finished her meal and walked up to the circle of scientists. She tugged at Mia's tunic. "Mia . . . Esefeb etej efef." *Esefeb come home.*

"Mia eb Esefeb etej Esefeb efef," Mia said, and the girl gave her joyous smile.

"Mia—" Kenin said.

"I'm going with her, Kenin. We need more behavioral data. And maybe I can persuade another native or two to submit to examination," Mia argued, feebly. She knew that scientific information was not really her motive. She wasn't sure, however, what was. She just wanted to go with Esefeb.

"*Why did you first enter the Corps?*" Lolimel's question stuck in Mia's mind, a rhetorical fishbone in the throat, over the next few days. Mia had brought her medkit, and she administered broad-spectrum microbials to Esefeb, hoping something would hit. The parasites were trickier, needing life-cycle analysis or at least some structural knowledge, but she made a start on that, too. *I entered the Corps to relieve suffering, Lolimel.* Odd how naive the truest statements could sound. But that didn't make them any less true.

Esefeb went along with all Mia's pokings, patches, and procedures. She also carried out minimal food-gathering activities, with a haphazard disregard for safety or sanitation that appalled Mia. Mia had carried her own food from the ship. Esefeb ate it just as happily as her own.

But mostly Esefeb talked to Ej-es.

It made Mia feel like a voyeur. Esefeb was so unself-conscious—did she even know she had a "self" apart from Ej-es? She spoke to, laughed at (with?), played beside, and slept with her phantom in the brain, and around her the hut disintegrated even more. Esefeb got diarrhea from something in her water and then the place smelled even more foul. Grimly, Mia cleaned it up. Esefeb didn't seem to notice. Mia was *eket.* Alone in her futile endeavors at sanitation, at health, at civilization.

"Esefeb eb Mia etej efef—" How did you say "neighbors"? Mia consulted the computer's lexicon, steadily growing as the translator program deciphered words from context. It had discovered no word for "neighbor." Nor for "friend" nor "mate" nor any kinship relationships at all except "baby."

Mia was reduced to pointing at the nearest hut. "Esefeb eb Mia etej efef" *over there.*

The neighboring hut had a baby. Both hut and child, a toddler who lay listlessly in one corner, were just as filthy and diseased as Esefeb's house. At first the older woman didn't seem to recognize Esefeb, but when Esefeb said her name, the two women spoke animatedly. The neighbor smiled at Mia. Mia reached for the child, was not prevented from picking him up, and settled the baby on her lap. Discreetly, she examined him.

Sudden rage boiled through her, as unexpected as it was frightening. This child was dying. Of parasites, of infection, of something. A preventable something? Maybe yes, maybe no. The child didn't look neglected, but neither did the mother look concerned.

All at once, the child in her arms stiffened, shuddered, and began to babble. His listlessness vanished. His little dirty face lit up like sunrise and he laughed and reached out his arms toward something not there. His mother and Esefeb turned to watch, also smiling, as the toddler had an unknowable limbic seizure in his dying, ecstatic brain.

Mia set him down on the floor. She called up the dictionary, but before she could say anything, the mother, too, had a seizure and sat on the dirt floor, shuddering with joy. Esefeb watched her a moment before chattering to something Mia couldn't see.

Mia couldn't stand it anymore. She left, walking as fast as she could back to Esefeb's house, disgusted and frightened and . . . what?

Envious?

"*Why did you first enter the Corps?*" To serve humanity, to live purposefully, to find, as all men and women hope, happiness. And she had, sometimes, been happy.

But she had never known such joy as that.

Nonetheless, she argued with herself, the price was too high. These people were dying off because of their absorption in their rapturous phantoms. They lived isolated, degraded, sickly lives, which were undoubtedly shorter than necessary. It was obscene.

In her clenched hand was a greasy hair sample she'd unobtrusively cut from the toddler's head as he sat on her lap. Hair, that dead tissue, was a person's fossilized past. Mia intended a DNA scan.

Esefeb strolled in an hour later. She didn't seem upset at Mia's abrupt departure. With her was Lolimel.

"I met her on the path," Lolimel said, although nothing as well-used as a path connected the huts. "She doesn't seem to mind my coming here."

"Or anything else," Mia said. "What did you bring?" He had to have brought something tangible; Kenin would have used the wrister to convey information.

"Tentative prophylactic. We haven't got a vaccine yet, and Kenin says it may be too difficult, better to go directly to a cure to hold in reserve in case any of us comes down with this."

Mia caught the omission. "Any of *us?* What about them?"

Lolimel looked down at his feet. "It's, um, a borderline case, Mia. The decision hasn't been made yet."

" 'Borderline' how, Lolimel? It's a virus infecting the brains of humans and degrading their functioning."

He was embarrassed. "Section Six says that, um, some biological conditions, especially persistent ones, create cultural differences for which Corps policy is noninterference. Section Six mentions the religious dietary laws that grew out of inherited food intolerances on—"

"I know what Section Six says, Lolimel! But you don't measure a culture's degree of success by its degree of happiness!"

"I don't think . . . that is, I don't know . . . maybe 'degree of success' isn't what Section Six means." He looked away from her. The tips of his ears grew red.

Poor Lolimel. She and Kenin had as much as told him that out here regs didn't matter. Except when they did. Mia stood. "You say the decision hasn't been made yet?"

He looked surprised. "How could it be? You're on the senior Corps board to make the decision."

Of course she was. How could she forget . . . she forgot more things these days, momentary lapses symbolic of the greater lapses to come. No brain functioned forever.

"Mia, are you all—"

"I'm fine. And I'm glad you're here. I want to go back to the city for a few days. You can stay with Esefeb and continue the surveillance. You can also extend to her neighbors the antibiotic, antiviral, and antiparasite protocols I've worked through with Esefeb. Here, I'll show you."

"But I—"

"That's an order."

She felt bad about it later, of course. But Lolimel would get over it.

At base, everything had the controlled frenzy of steady, unremitting work. Meek now, not a part of the working team, Mia ran a DNA scan on the baby's hair. It showed what she expected. The child shared fifty percent DNA with Esefeb. He was her brother; the neighbor whom Esefeb clearly never saw, who had at first not recognized Esefeb, was her mother. For which there was still no word in the translator deebee.

"I think we've got it," Kenin said, coming into Mia's room. She collapsed on a stone bench, still beautiful after two and a half centuries. Kenin had the beatific serenity of a hard job well done.

"A cure?"

"Tentative. Radical. I wouldn't want to use it on one of us unless we absolutely have to, but we can refine it more. At least it's in reserve, so a part of the team can begin creating and disseminating medical help these people can actually use. Targeted microbials, an antiparasite protocol."

"I've already started on that," Mia said, her stomach tightening. "Kenin, the board needs to meet."

"Not tonight. I'm soooo sleepy." Theatrically she stretched both arms; words and gesture were unlike her.

"Tonight," Mia said. While Kenin was feeling so accomplished. Let Kenin feel the full contrast to what she could do with what Esefeb could.

Kenin dropped her arms and looked at Mia. Her whole demeanor changed, relaxation into fortress. "Mia . . . I've already polled everyone privately. And run the computer sims. We'll meet, but the decision is going to be to extend no cure. The phantoms are a biologically based cultural difference."

"The hell they are! These people are dying out!"

"No, they're not. If they were heading for extinction, it'd be a different situation. But the satellite imagery and population equations, based on data left by the generation that had the plague, show they're increasing. Slowly, but a definite population gain significant to the point-oh-one level of confidence."

"Kenin—"

"I'm exhausted, Mia. Can we talk about it tomorrow?"

Plan on it, Mia thought grimly. She stored the data on the dying toddler's matrilineage in her handheld.

A week in base, and Mia could convince no one, not separately nor in a group. Medicians typically had tolerant psychological profiles, with higher-than-average acceptance of the unusual, divergent, and eccentric. Otherwise, they wouldn't have joined the Corps.

On the third day, to keep herself busy, Mia joined the junior medicians working on refining the cure for what was now verified as "limbic seizures with impaired sensory input causing Charles Bonnet Syndrome." Over the next few weeks it became clear to Mia what Kenin had meant; this treatment, if they had to use it, would be brutally hard on the brain. What was that old ditty? *"Cured last night of my disease, I died today of my physician."* Well, it still happened enough in the Corps. Another reason behind the board's decision.

She felt a curious reluctance to go back to Esefeb. Or, as the words kept running through her mind, *Mia ek etej Esefeb efef*. God, it was a tongue twister. These people didn't just need help with parasites, they needed an infusion of new consonants. It was a relief to be back at base, to be working with her mind, solving technical problems alongside rational scientists. Still, she couldn't shake a feeling of being alone, being lonely: *Mia eket*.

Or maybe the feeling was more like futility.

"Lolimel's back," Jamal said. He'd come up behind her as she sat at dusk on her favorite stone bench, facing the city. At this time of day the ruins looked romantic, infused with history. The sweet scents of that night-blooming flower, which Mia still hadn't identified, wafted around her.

"I think you should come now," Jamal said, and this time Mia heard his tone. She spun around. In the alien shadows Jamal's face was as set as ice.

"He's contracted it," Mia said, knowing beyond doubt that it was true. The virus wasn't just fetally transmitted, it wasn't a slow-acting retrovirus, and if Lolimel had slept with Esefeb . . . But he wouldn't be that stupid. He was a medician, he'd been warned . . .

"We don't really know anything solid about the goddamn thing!" Jamal burst out.

"We never do," Mia said, and the words cracked her dry lips like salt.

Lolimel stood in the center of the ruined atrium, giggling at something only he could see. Kenin, who could have proceeded without Mia, nodded at her. Mia understood; Kenin acknowledged the special bond Mia had with the young medician. The cure was untested, probably brutal, no more really than dumping a selection of poisons in the right areas of the brain, in itself problematical with the blood-brain barrier.

Mia made herself walk calmly up to Lolimel. "What's so funny, Lolimel?"

"All those sandwigs crawling in straight lines over the floor. I never saw blue ones before."

Sandwigs. Lolimel, she remembered, had been born on New Carthage. Sandwigs were always red.

Lolimel said, "But why is there a tree growing out of your head, Mia?"

"Strong fertilizer," she said. "Lolimel, did you have sex with Esefeb?"

He looked genuinely shocked. "No!"

"All right." He might or might not be lying.

Jamal whispered, "A chance to study the hallucinations in someone who can fully articulate—"

"No," Kenin said. "Time matters with this . . ." Mia saw that she couldn't bring herself to say "cure."

Realization dawned on Lolimel's face. "Me? You're going to . . . *me?* There's nothing wrong with me!"

"Lolimel, dear heart . . ." Mia said.

"I don't have it!"

"And the floor doesn't have sandwigs. Lolimel—"

"No!"

The guards had been alerted. Lolimel didn't make it out of

the atrium. They held him, flailing and yelling, while Kenin deftly slapped on a tranq patch. In ten seconds he was out.

"Tie him down securely," Kenin said, breathing hard. "Daniel, get the brain bore started as soon as he's prepped. Everyone else, start packing up, and impose quarantine. We can't risk this for anyone else here. I'm calling a Section Eleven."

Section Eleven: *If the MedCorps officer in charge deems the risk to Corps members to exceed the gain to colonists by a factor of three or more, the officer may pull the Corps off-planet.*

It was the first time Mia had ever seen Kenin make a unilateral decision.

Twenty-four hours later, Mia sat beside Lolimel as dusk crept over the city. The shuttle had already carried up most personnel and equipment. Lolimel was in the last shift because, as Kenin did not need to say aloud, if he died, his body would be left behind. But Lolimel had not died. He had thrashed in unconscious seizures, had distorted his features in silent grimaces of pain until Mia would not have recognized him, had suffered malfunctions in alimentary, lymphatic, endocrine, and parasympathetic nervous systems, all recorded on the monitors. But he would live. The others didn't know it, but Mia did.

"We're ready for him, Mia," the young tech said. "Are you on this shuttle, too?"

"No, the last one. Move him carefully. We don't know how much pain he's actually feeling through the meds."

She watched the gurney slide out of the room, its monitors looming over Lolimel like cliffs over a raging river. When he'd gone, Mia slipped into the next building, and then the next. Such beautiful buildings: spacious atria, beautifully proportioned rooms, one structure flowing into another.

Eight buildings away, she picked up the pack she'd left there. It was heavy, even though it didn't contain everything she had cached around the city. It was so easy to take things when a base was being hastily withdrawn. Everyone was preoccupied, everyone assumed anything not readily visible was already packed, inventories were neglected and the deebees not cross-checked. No time. Historically, war had always provided great opportunities for profiteers.

Was that what she was? Yes, but not a profit measured in money. Measure it, rather, in lives saved, or restored to dignity, or enhanced. *"Why did you first enter the Corps?"* Because I'm a medician, Lolimel. Not an anthropologist.

They would notice, of course, that Mia herself wasn't aboard the last shuttle. But Kenin, at least, would realize that searching for her would be a waste of valuable resources when Mia didn't want to be found. And Mia was so old. Surely the old should be allowed to make their own decisions.

Although she would miss them, these Corps members who had been her family since the last assignment shuffle, eighteen months ago and decades ago, depending on whose time you counted by. Especially she would miss Lolimel. But this was the right way to end her life, in service to these colonists' health. She was a medician.

It went better than Mia could have hoped. When the ship had gone—she'd seen it leave orbit, a fleeting stream of light—Mia went to Esefeb.

"Mia etej efef," Esefeb said with her rosy smile. *Mia come home.* Mia walked toward her, hugged the girl, and slapped the tranq patch on her neck.

For the next week, Mia barely slept. After the makeshift surgery, she tended Esefeb through the seizures, vomiting, diarrhea, pain. On the morning the girl woke up, herself again, Mia was there to bathe the feeble body, feed it, nurse Esefeb. She recovered very fast; the cure was violent on the body but not as debilitating as everyone had feared. And afterward Esefeb was quieter, meeker, and surprisingly intelligent as Mia taught her the rudiments of water purification, sanitation, safe food storage, health care. By the time Mia moved on to Esefeb's mother's house, Esefeb was free of most parasites, and Mia was working on the rest. Esefeb never mentioned her former hallucinations. It was possible she didn't remember them.

"Esefeb ekebet," Mia said as she hefted her pack to leave. *Esefeb be well.*

Esefeb nodded. She stood quietly as Mia trudged away, and when Mia turned to wave at her, Esefeb waved back.

Mia shifted the pack on her shoulders. It seemed heavier than before. Or maybe Mia was just older. Two weeks older, merely, but two weeks could make a big difference. An enormous difference.

Two weeks could start to save a civilization.

Night fell. Esefeb sat on the stairs to her bed, clutching the blue-green sheet of plastic in both hands. She sobbed and shivered, her clean face contorted. Around her, the unpopulated shadows grew thicker and darker. Eventually, she wailed aloud to the empty night.

"Ej-es! O, Ej-es! Ej-es, Esefeb eket! Ej-es . . . etej efef! O, etej efef!"

Four Short Novels

JOE HALDEMAN

Joe Haldeman [home.earthlink.net/~haldeman/] lives in Gainesville, Florida, and teaches each fall at Massachusetts Institute of Technology in Cambridge, Massachusetts, where he is an adjunct professor. His first SF novel The Forever War *(1972), established him as a leading writer of his generation, and his later novels and stories have put him in the front rank of living SF writers. High spots include* Mindbridge *(1976),* Worlds *(1981),* The Hemingway Hoax *(1990), and* Forever Peace *(1997). His story collections include* Infinite Dreams *(1978),* Dealing in Futures *(1985), and* Vietnam and Other Alien Worlds *(1993). His novel* Sea Change *appeared in 2004.*

"Four Short Novels" is from Fantasy & Science Fiction, *which had a strikingly good year in 2003. It is a playful, literate story in four parts, each one extrapolating wildly from the ground of a literary base (e.g.* Remembrance of Things Past, Crime and Punishment*), and taking off into the future until the ultimate destruction of humanity lets the air out of everything.*

Remembrance of Things Past

Eventually it came to pass that no one ever had to die, unless they ran out of money. When you started to feel the little aches and twinges that meant your body was running down, you just got in line at Immortality, Incorporated, and handed them your credit card. As long as you had at least a million bucks—and eventually everybody did—they would reset you to whatever age you liked.

One way people made money was by swapping knowledge around. Skills could be transferred with a technology spun off from the immortality process. You could spend a few decades becoming a great concert pianist, and then put your ability up for sale. There was no shortage of people with two million dollars who would trade one million to be their village's Van Cliburn. In the sale of your ability, you would lose it, but you could buy it back a few decades or centuries later.

For many people this became the game of life—becoming temporarily a genius, selling your genius for youth, and then clawing your way up in some other field, to buy back the passion that had rescued you first from the grave. Enjoy it a few years, sell it again, and so on ad infinitum. Or *finitum*, if you just once made a wrong career move, and wound up old and poor and bereft of skill. That happened less and less often, of course, Darwinism inverted: the un-survival of the least fit.

It wasn't just a matter of swapping around your piano-playing and brain surgery, of course. People with the existential wherewithal to enjoy century after century of life tended to grow and improve with age. A person could look like a barely pubescent teenybopper, and yet be able to out-Socrates Socrates in the wisdom department. People were getting used to seeing acne and *gravitas* on the same face.

Enter Jutel Dicuth, the paragon of his age, a raging polymath. He could paint and sculpt and play six instruments. He could write formal poetry with his left hand while solving differential equations with his right. He could write formal poetry *about* differential equations! He was an Olympic-class gymnast and also held the world record for the javelin throw. He had earned doctorates in anthropology, art history, slipstream physics, and fly-tying.

He sold it all.

Immensely wealthy but bereft of any useful ability, Jutel Dicuth set up a trust fund for himself that would produce a million dollars every year. It also provided a generous salary for an attendant. He had Immortality, Incorporated set him back to the apparent age of one year, and keep resetting him once a year.

In a world where there were no children—where would you put them?—he was the only infant. He was the only person with no useful skills and, eventually, the only one alive who did not have nearly a thousand years of memory.

In a world that had outgrown the old religions—why would you need them?—he became like unto a god. People came from everywhere to listen to his random babbling and try to find a conduit to the state of blissful innocence buried under the weight of their wisdom.

It was inevitable that someone would see a profit in this. A consortium with a name we would translate as Blank Slate offered to "dicuth" anyone who had a certain large sum of what passed for money, and maintain them for as long as they wanted. At first people were slightly outraged, because it was a kind of sacrilege, or were slightly amused, because it was such a transparent scheme to gather what passed for wealth.

Sooner or later, though, everyone tried it. Most who tried it for one year went back for ten or a hundred, or, eventually, forever. After some centuries, permanent dicuths began to outnumber humans—though those humans were not anything you would recognize as people, crushed as they were by nearly a thousand years of wisdom and experience. And jealous of those who had given up.

On 31 December, A.D. 3000, the last "normal" person surrendered his loneliness for dicuth bliss. The world was populated completely by total innocents, tended by patient machines.

It lasted a long time. Then one by one, the machines broke down.

Crime and Punishment

Eventually it came to pass that no one ever had to die, unless they were so horrible that society had to dispose of them. Other than the occasional horrible person, the world was in an idyllic state, everyone living as long as they wanted to, doing what they wanted to do.

This is how things got back to normal.

People gained immortality by making copies of themselves, farlies, which were kept in safe places and updated periodically. So if you got run over by a truck or hit by a meteorite, your farlie would sense this and automatically pop out and take over, after prudently making a farlie of itself. Upon that temporary death, you would lose only the weeks or months that had gone by since your last update.

That made it difficult to deal with criminals. If someone was so horrible that society had to hang or shoot or electrocute or inject him to death, his farlie would crop up somewhere, still bad to the bone, make a farlie of itself, and go off on another rampage. If you put him in jail for the rest of his life, he would eventually die, but then his evil farlie would leap out, full of youthful vigor and nasty intent.

Ultimately, if society felt you were too horrible to live, it would take preemptive action: check out your farlie and destroy it first. If it could be found. Really bad people became adept at hiding their farlies. Inevitably, people who were really good at being really bad became master criminals. It was that, or die forever. There were only a few dozen of them, but they moved through the world like neutrinos: effortless, unstoppable, invisible.

One of them was a man named Bad Billy Beerbreath. He started the ultimate crime wave.

There were Farlie Centers where you would go to update your farlie—one hundred of them, all over the world—and that's where almost everybody kept their farlies stored. But you could actually put a farlie anywhere, if you got together enough liquid nitrogen and terabytes of storage and kept them in a cool dry place out of direct sunlight.

Most people didn't know this; in fact, it was forbidden knowledge. Nobody knew how to make Farlie Centers anymore, either. They were all built during the lifetime of Joao Farlie, who had wandered off with the blueprints after deciding not to make a copy of himself, himself.

Bad Billy Beerbreath decided to make it his business to trash Farlie Centers. In its way, this was worse than murder, because if a client died before he or she found out about it, and hadn't been able to make a new farlie (which took weeks)—he or she would die for real, kaput, out of the picture. It was a crime beyond crime. Just thinking about this gave Bad Billy an acute pleasure akin to a hundred orgasms.

Because there were a hundred Bad Billy Beerbreaths.

In preparation for his crime wave, Bad Billy had spent years making a hundred farlies of himself, and he stored them in cool dry places out of direct sunlight, all around the world. On 13 May 2999, all but one of those farlies jump-started itself and went out to destroy the nearest Farlie Center.

By noon, GMT, police and militia all over the world had captured or killed or subdued every copy (but one) of Bad Billy, but by noon every single Farlie Center in the world had been leveled, save the one in Akron, Ohio.

The only people left who had farlies were people who had a reason to keep them in a secret place. Master criminals like Billy. Pals of Billy. They all were waiting at Akron, and held off the authorities for months, by making farlie after farlie of themselves, like broomsticks in a Disney cartoon, sending most of them out to die, or "die," defending the place, until there were so many of them the walls were bulging. Then they sent out word that they wanted to negotiate, and during the lull that promise produced, they fled en masse, destroying the last Farlie Center behind them.

They were a powerful force, a hundred thousand hardened criminals united in their contempt for people like you and me, and in their loyalty to Bad Billy Beerbreath. Somewhat giddy, not to say insane, in their triumph after having destroyed every Farlie Center, they went on to destroy every jail and prison and courthouse. That did cut their numbers down considerably, since most of them only had ten or twenty farlies tucked away, but it also reduced drastically the number of police, not to mention the number of people willing to take up policing as a profession, since once somebody killed you twice, you had to stay dead.

By New Year's Eve, A.D. 3000, the criminals were in charge of the whole world.

Again.

War and Peace

Eventually it came to pass that no one ever had to die, unless they wanted to, or could be talked into it. That made it very hard to fight wars, and a larger and larger part of every nation's military budget was given over to psychological operations directed toward their own people: *dulce et decorum est* just wasn't convincing enough anymore.

There were two elements to this sales job. One was to romanticize the image of the soldier as heroic defender of the blah blah blah. That was not too hard; they'd been doing that since Homer. The other was more subtle: convince people that every individual life was essentially worthless—your own and also the lives of the people you would eventually be killing.

That was a hard job, but the science of advertising, more than a millennium after Madison Avenue, was equal to it, through the person of a genius named Manny O'Malley. The pitch was subtle, and hard for a person to understand who hasn't lived for centuries, but shorn of Manny's incomprehensible humor and appeal to subtle pleasures that had no name until the thirtieth century, it boiled down to this:

A thousand years ago, they seduced people into soldiering with the slogan, "Be all that you can be." But you have *been* all you can be. The only thing left worth being is *not* being.

Everybody else is in the same boat, O'Malley convinced them. In the process of giving yourself the precious gift of nonexistence, share it with many others.

It's hard for us to understand. But then we would be hard for them to understand, with all this remorseless getting and spending laying waste our years.

Wars were all fought in Death Valley, with primitive hand weapons, and the United States grew wealthy renting the place out, until it inevitably found itself fighting a series of wars *for* Death Valley, during one of which O'Malley himself finally died, charging a phalanx of no-longer-immortal pikemen on his robotic horse, waving a broken sword. His final words were, famously, "Oh, shit."

Death Valley eventually wound up in the hands of the Bertelsmann Corporation, which ultimately ruled the world. But by that time, Manny's advertising had been so effective that no one cared. Everybody was in uniform, lining up to do their bit for Bertelsmann.

Even the advertising scientists. Even the high management of Bertelsmann.

There was a worldwide referendum, utilizing something indistinguishable from telepathy, where everybody agreed to change the name of the planet to Death Valley, and on the eve of the new century, A.D. 3000, have at each other.

Thus O'Malley's ultimate ad campaign achieved the ultimate victory: a world that consumed itself.

The Way of All Flesh

Eventually it came to pass that no one ever had to die, so long as just one person loved them. The process that provided immortality was fueled that way.

Almost everybody can find someone to love him or her, at least for a little while, and if and when that someone says good-bye, most people can clean up their act enough to find yet another.

But every now and then you find a specimen who is so unlovable that he can't even get a hungry dog to take a biscuit from his hand. Babies take one look at him and get the colic. Women cross their legs as he passes by. Ardent homosexuals drop their collective gaze. Old people desperate for company feign sleep.

The most extreme such specimen was Custer Tralia. Custer came out of the womb with teeth, and bit the doctor. In grade school he broke up the love training sessions with highly toxic farts. He celebrated puberty by not washing for a year. All through middle school and high school, he made loving couples into enemies by spreading clever vicious lies. He formed a Masturbation Club and didn't allow anybody else to join. In his graduation yearbook, he was unanimously voted "The One Least Likely to Survive, If We Have Anything to Do with It."

In college, he became truly reckless. When everybody else was feeling the first whiff of mortality and frantically seducing in self-defense, Custer declared that he hated women almost as much as he hated men, and he reveled in his freedom from love, his superior detachment from the cloying crowd. Death was nothing compared to the hell of dependency. When, at the beginning of his junior year, he had to declare what his profession was going to be, he wrote down "hermit" for first, second, and third choices.

The world was getting pretty damned crowded, though, since a lot of people loved each other so much they turned out copy after copy of themselves. The only place Custer could go and be truly alone was the Australian outback. He had a helicopter drop him there with a big water tank and crates of food. They said they'd check back in a year, and Custer said don't bother. If you've decided not to live forever, a few years or decades one way or the other don't make much difference.

He found peace among the wallabies and dingoes. A kangaroo began to follow him around, and he accepted it as a pet, sharing his rehydrated Kentucky Fried Chicken and fish and chips with it.

Life was a pleasantly sterile and objectless quest. Custer and his kangaroo quartered the outback, turning over rocks just to bother the things underneath. The kangaroo was loyal, which was a liability, but at least it couldn't talk, and its attachment to Custer was transparently selfish, so they got along. He taught it how to beg, and, by not rewarding it, taught it how to whimper.

One day, like Robinson Crusoe, he found footprints. Unlike Robinson Crusoe, he hastened in the opposite direction.

But the footprinter had been watching him for some time, and outsmarted him. Knowing he would be gone all day, she had started miles away, walking backward by his camp, and knew that his instinct for hermitage would lead him directly, perversely, back into her cave.

Parky Gumma had decided to become a hermit, too, after she read about Custer's audacious gesture. But after about a year she wanted a bath, and someone to love her so she wouldn't die, in that order. So under the wheeling Milky Way, on the eve of the thirty-first century, she stalked backward to her cave, and squandered a month's worth of water sluicing her body, which was unremarkable except for the fact that it was clean and the only female one in two hundred thousand square miles.

Parky left herself unclothed and squeaky clean, carefully perched on a camp stool, waiting for Custer's curiosity and misanthropy to lead him back to her keep. He crept in a couple of hours after sunrise.

She stood up and spread her arms, and his pet kangaroo boinged away in terror.

Custer himself was paralyzed by a mixture of conflicting impulses. He had seen pictures of naked women, but never one actually in the flesh, and honestly didn't know what to do.

Parky showed him.

The rest is the unmaking of history. That Parky had admired him and followed him into the desert was even more endearing than the slip and slide that she demonstrated for him after she washed him up. But that was revolutionary, too. Custer had to admit that a year or a century or a millennium of that would be better than keeling over and having dingoes tear up your corpse and spread your bones over the uncaring sands.

So this is Custer's story, and ours. He never did get around to liking baths, so you couldn't say that love conquers all. But it could still conquer death.

Rogue Farm

CHARLES STROSS

Charles Stross [www.antipope.org] lives in Edinburgh, Scotland. He has been publishing occasional SF since the late 1980s, but burst into prominence at the beginning of the new millennium with a series of stories in Asimov's. *The Accelerando sequence of stories is jammed with information, speculation, hard science, rapid shifts of point of view, and jittery jarring rapid change. It is set in a near future that is undergoing continuing revolution from the biological sciences, after a computer revolution, after a techno-economic revolution. Stross is a dyed-in-the-wool science fiction writer in the tradition of Bruce Sterling. Recently, he has written stories in collaboration with Cory Doctorow. His collection,* Toast *(2002), appeared in a print-on-demand edition. His first SF novel,* Singularity Sky, *appeared in 2003, and* The Atrocity Archive *and* The Family Trade *in 2004.*

"Rogue Farm" is from the original anthology Live Without a Net, *one of the best SF anthologies in a strong year for anthologies. It is the story of a farmer, his wife, and an invading sentient farm—a collective mutated personality composed of individuals joined into a single biological entity. The farm has wandered onto his land. The farmer, an ordinary bloke, wants to get rid of it. His wife isn't so sure. Wordplay, irony, humor, and some rather subtle horror make this one of the best of the best this year.*

It was a bright, cool March morning: mare's tails trailed across the southeastern sky toward the rising sun. Joe shivered slightly in the driver's seat as he twisted the starter handle on the old front loader he used to muck out the barn. Like its owner, the ancient Massey Ferguson had seen better days; but it had survived worse abuse than Joe routinely handed out. The diesel clattered, spat out a gobbet of thick blue smoke, and chattered to itself dyspeptically. His mind as blank as the sky above, Joe slid the tractor into gear, raised the front scoop, and began turning it toward the open doors of the barn—just in time to see an itinerant farm coming down the road.

"Bugger," swore Joe. The tractor engine made a hideous grinding noise and died. He took a second glance, eyes wide, then climbed down from the tractor and trotted over to the kitchen door at the side of the farmhouse. "Maddie!" he called, forgetting the two-way radio clipped to his sweater hem. "Maddie! There's a farm coming!"

"Joe? Is that you? Where are you?" Her voice wafted vaguely from the bowels of the house.

"Where are you?" he yelled back.

"I'm in the bathroom."

"Bugger," he said again. "If it's the one we had round the end last month . . ."

The sound of a toilet sluiced through his worry. It was followed by a drumming of feet on the staircase; then Maddie erupted into the kitchen. "Where is it?" she demanded.

"Out front, about a quarter mile up the lane."

"Right." Hair wild and eyes angry about having her morning ablutions cut short, Maddie yanked a heavy green coat on over her shirt. "Opened the cupboard yet?"

"I was thinking you'd want to talk to it first."

"Too right I want to talk to it. If it's that one that's been lurking in the copse near Edgar's pond, I got some *issues* to discuss with it." Joe shook his head at her anger and went to unlock the cupboard in the back room. "You take the shotgun and keep it off our property," she called after him. "I'll be out in a minute."

Joe nodded to himself, then carefully picked out the twelve-gauge and a preloaded magazine. The gun's power-on self-test lights flickered erratically, but it seemed to have a full charge. Slinging it, he locked the cupboard carefully and went back out into the farmyard to warn off their unwelcome visitor.

The farm squatted, buzzing and clicking to itself, in the road outside Armitage End. Joe eyed it warily from behind the wooden gate, shotgun under his arm. It was a medium-size one, probably with half a dozen human components subsumed into it—a formidable collective. Already it was deep into farm-fugue, no longer relating very clearly to people outside its own communion of mind. Beneath its leathery black skin he could see hints of internal structure, cytocellular macroassemblies flexing and glooping in disturbing motions. Even though it was only a young adolescent, it was already the size of an antique heavy tank, and it blocked the road just as efficiently as an Apatosaurus would have. It smelled of yeast and gasoline.

Joe had an uneasy feeling that it was watching him. "Buggerit, I don't have time for this," he muttered. The stable waiting for the small herd of cloned spidercows cluttering up the north paddock was still knee-deep in manure, and the tractor seat wasn't getting any warmer while he shivered out here, waiting for Maddie to come and sort this thing out. It wasn't a big herd, but it was as big as his land and his labor could manage—the big biofabricator in the shed could assemble mammalian livestock faster than he could feed them up and sell them with an honest HAND-RAISED NOT VAT-GROWN label. "What do you want with us?" he yelled up at the gently buzzing farm.

"Brains, fresh brains for Baby Jesus," crooned the farm in a warm contralto, startling Joe half out of his skin. "Buy my brains!" Half a dozen disturbing cauliflower shapes poked suggestively out of the farm's back and then retracted again, coyly.

"Don't want no brains around here," Joe said stubbornly, his fingers whitening on the stock of the shotgun. "Don't want your kind round here, neither. Go away."

"I'm a nine-legged semiautomatic groove machine!" crooned the farm. "I'm on my way to Jupiter on a mission for love! Won't you buy my brains?" Three curious eyes on stalks extruded from its upper glacis.

"Uh—" Joe was saved from having to dream up any more ways of saying "fuck off" by Maddie's arrival. She'd managed to sneak her old battle dress home after a stint keeping the peace in Mesopotamia twenty years ago, and she'd managed to keep herself in shape enough to squeeze inside. Its left knee squealed ominously when she walked it about, which wasn't often, but it still worked well enough to manage its main task—intimidating trespassers.

"You." She raised one translucent arm, pointed at the farm. "Get off my land. *Now*."

Taking his cue, Joe raised his shotgun and thumbed the selector to full auto. It wasn't a patch on the hardware riding Maddie's shoulders, but it underlined the point.

The farm hooted: "Why don't you love me?" it asked plaintively.

"Get orf my land," Maddie amplified, volume cranked up so high that Joe winced. *"Ten seconds! Nine! Eight—"* Thin rings sprang out from the sides of her arms, whining with the stress of long disuse as the Gauss gun powered up.

"I'm going! I'm going!" The farm lifted itself slightly, shuffling backwards. "Don't understand. I only wanted to set you free to explore the universe. Nobody wants to buy my fresh fruit and brains. What's wrong with the world?"

They waited until the farm had retreated round the bend at

the top of the hill. Maddie was the first to relax, the rings retracting back into the arms of her battle dress, which solidified from ethereal translucency to neutral olive drab as it powered down. Joe safed his shotgun. "Bastard," he said.

"Fucking-A." Maddie looked haggard. "That was a bold one." Her face was white and pinched-looking, Joe noted. Her fists were clenched. She had the shakes, he realized without surprise. Tonight was going to be another major nightmare night, and no mistake.

"The fence." On again and off again for the past year they'd discussed wiring up an outer wire to the CHP baseload from their little methane plant.

"Maybe this time. Maybe." Maddie wasn't keen on the idea of frying passers-by without warning, but if anything might bring her around, it would be the prospect of being overrun by a bunch of rogue farms. "Help me out of this, and I'll cook breakfast," she said.

"Got to muck out the barn," Joe protested.

"It can wait on breakfast," Maddie said shakily. "I need you."

"Okay." Joe nodded. She was looking bad; it had been a few years since her last fatal breakdown, but when Maddie said "I need you," it was a bad idea to ignore her. That way led to backbreaking labor on the biofab and loading her backup tapes into the new body; always a messy business. He took her arm and steered her toward the back porch. They were nearly there when he paused.

"What is it?" asked Maddie.

"Haven't seen Bob for a while," he said slowly. "Sent him to let the cows into the north paddock after milking. Do you think—?"

"We can check from the control room," she said tiredly. "Are you really worried? . . ."

"With that thing blundering around? What do *you* think?"

"He's a good working dog," Maddie said uncertainly. "It won't hurt him. He'll be all right; just you page him."

After Joe helped her out of her battle dress, and after Maddie spent a good long while calming down, they breakfasted on eggs from their own hens, homemade cheese, and toasted bread made with rye from the hippie commune on the other side of the valley. The stone-floored kitchen in the dilapidated house they'd squatted and rebuilt together over the past twenty years was warm and homely. The only purchase from outside the valley was the coffee, beans from a hardy GM strain that grew like a straggling teenager's beard all along the Cumbrian hilltops. They didn't say much: Joe, because he never did, and Maddie, because there wasn't anything that she wanted to discuss. Silence kept her personal demons down. They'd known each other for many years, and even when there wasn't anything to discuss, they could cope with each other's silence. The voice radio on the windowsill opposite the cast-iron stove stayed off, along with the TV set hanging on the wall next to the fridge. Breakfast was a quiet time of day.

"Dog's not answering," Joe commented over the dregs of his coffee.

"He's a good dog." Maddie glanced at the yard gate uncertainly. "You afraid he's going to run away to Jupiter?"

"He was with me in the shed." Joe picked up his plate and carried it to the sink, began running hot water onto the dishes. "After I cleaned the lines I told him to go take the herd up the paddock while I did the barn." He glanced up, looking out the window with a worried expression. The Massey Ferguson was parked right in front of the open barn doors as if holding at bay the mountain of dung, straw, and silage that mounded up inside like an invading odorous enemy, relic of a frosty winter past.

Maddie shoved him aside gently and picked up one of the walkie-talkies from the charge point on the windowsill. It bleeped and chuckled at her. "Bob, come in. Over." She frowned. "He's probably lost his headset again."

Joe racked the wet plates to dry. "I'll move the midden. You want to go find him?"

"I'll do that." Maddie's frown promised a talking-to in store for the dog when she caught up with him. Not that Bob would mind: words ran off him like water off a duck's back. "Cameras first." She prodded the battered TV set to life, and grainy bisected views flickered across the screen, garden, yard, Dutch barn, north paddock, east paddock, main field, copse. "Hmm."

She was still fiddling with the smallholding surveillance system when Joe clambered back into the driver's seat of the tractor and fired it up once more. This time there was no cough of black smoke, and as he hauled the mess of manure out of the barn and piled it into a three-meter-high midden, a quarter of a ton at a time, he almost managed to forget about the morning's unwelcome visitor. Almost.

By late morning, the midden was humming with flies and producing a remarkable stench, but the barn was clean enough to flush out with a hose and broom. Joe was about to begin hauling the midden over to the fermentation tanks buried round the far side of the house when he saw Maddie coming back up the path, shaking her head. He knew at once what was wrong.

"Bob," he said, expectantly.

"Bob's fine. I left him riding shotgun on the goats." Her expression was peculiar. "But that *farm*—"

"Where?" he asked, hurrying after her.

"Squatting in the woods down by the stream," she said tersely. "Just over our fence."

"It's not trespassing, then."

"It's put down feeder roots! Do you have any idea what that means?"

"I don't—" Joe's face wrinkled in puzzlement. "Oh."

"Yes. *Oh.*" She stared back at the outbuildings between their home and the woods at the bottom of their smallholding, and if looks could kill, the intruder would be dead a thousand times over. "It's going to estivate, Joe, then it's going to grow to maturity on our patch. And do you know where it said it was going to go when it finishes growing? Jupiter!"

"Bugger," Joe said faintly, as the true gravity of their situation began to sink in. "We'll have to deal with it first."

"That wasn't what I meant," Maddie finished. But Joe was already on his way out the door. She watched him crossing the yard, then shook her head. "Why am I stuck here?" she asked, but the cooker wasn't answering.

* * *

The hamlet of Outer Cheswick lay four kilometers down the road from Armitage End, four kilometers past mostly derelict houses and broken-down barns, fields given over to weeds and walls damaged by trees. The first half of the twenty-first century had been cruel years for the British agrobusiness sector; even harsher if taken in combination with the decline in population and the consequent housing surplus. As a result, the dropouts of the forties and fifties were able to take their pick from among the gutted shells of once fine farmhouses. They chose the best and moved in, squatted in the derelict outbuildings, planted their seeds and tended their flocks and practiced their DIY skills, until a generation later a mansion fit for a squire stood in lonely isolation alongside a decaying road where no more cars drove. Or rather, it would have taken a generation had there been any children against whose lives it could be measured; these were the latter decades of the population crash, and what a previous century would have labeled downshifter DINK couples were now in the majority, far outnumbering any breeder colonies. In this aspect of their life, Joe and Maddie were boringly conventional. In other respects they weren't: Maddie's nightmares, her aversion to alcohol, and her withdrawal from society were all relics of her time in Peaceforce. As for Joe, he liked it here. Hated cities, hated the Net, hated the burn of the new. Anything for a quiet life . . .

The Pig and Pizzle, on the outskirts of Outer Cheswick, was the only pub within about ten kilometers—certainly the only one within staggering distance for Joe when he'd had a skinful of mild—and it was naturally a seething den of local gossip, not least because Ole Brenda refused to allow electricity, much less bandwidth, into the premises. (This was not out of any sense of misplaced technophobia, but a side effect of Brenda's previous life as an attack hacker with the European Defense Forces.)

Joe paused at the bar. "Pint of bitter?" he asked tentatively. Brenda glanced at him and nodded, then went back to loading the antique washing machine. Presently she pulled a clean glass down from the shelf and held it under the tap.

"Hear you've got farm trouble," she said noncommitally as she worked the hand pump on the beer engine.

"Uh-huh." Joe focused on the glass. "Where'd you hear that?"

"Never you mind." She put the glass down to give the head time to settle. "You want to talk to Arthur and Wendy-the-Rat about farms. They had one the other year."

"Happens." Joe took his pint. "Thanks, Brenda. The usual?"

"Yeah." She turned back to the washer. Joe headed over to the far corner where a pair of huge leather sofas, their arms and backs ripped and scarred by generations of Brenda's semiferal cats, sat facing each other on either side of a cold hearth. "Art, Rats. What's up?"

"Fine, thanks." Wendy-the-Rat was well over seventy, one of those older folks who had taken the p53 chromosome hack and seemed to wither into timelessness: white dreadlocks, nose and ear studs dangling loosely from leathery holes, skin like a desert wind. Art had been her boy-toy once, back before middle age set its teeth into him. He hadn't had the hack, and looked older than she did. Together they ran a smallholding, mostly pharming vaccine chicks but also doing a brisk trade in high-nitrate fertilizer that came in on the nod and went out in sacks by moonlight.

"Heard you had a spot of bother?"

" 'S true." Joe took a cautious mouthful. "Mm, good. You ever had farm trouble?"

"Maybe." Wendy looked at him askance, slitty-eyed. "What kinda trouble you got in mind?"

"Got a farm collective. Says it's going to Jupiter or something. Bastard's homesteading the woods down by Old Jack's stream. Listen . . . Jupiter?"

"Aye, well, that's one of the destinations, sure enough." Art nodded wisely, as if he knew anything.

"Naah, that's bad." Wendy-the-Rat frowned. "Is it growing trees, do you know?"

"Trees?" Joe shook his head. "Haven't gone and looked, tell the truth. What the fuck makes people do that to themselves, anyway?"

"Who the fuck cares?" Wendy's face split in a broad grin. "Such as don't think they're human anymore, meself."

"It tried to sweet-talk us," Joe said.

"Aye, they do that," said Arthur, nodding emphatically. "Read somewhere they're the ones as think we aren't fully human. Tools an' clothes and farmyard machines, like? Sustaining a pre-post-industrial lifestyle instead of updating our genome and living off the land like God intended?"

" 'Ow the hell can something with nine legs and eye stalks call itself human?" Joe demanded, chugging back half his pint in one angry swallow.

"It used to be, once. Maybe used to be a bunch of people." Wendy got a weird and witchy look in her eye. " 'Ad a boyfriend back thirty, forty years ago, joined a Lamarckian clade. Swapping genes an' all, the way you or me'd swap us underwear. Used to be a 'viromentalist back when antiglobalization was about big corporations pissing on us all for profits. Got into gene hackery and self-sufficiency big time. I slung his fucking ass when he turned green and started photosynthesizing."

"Bastards," Joe muttered. It was deep green folk like that who'd killed off the agricultural-industrial complex in the early years of the century, turning large portions of the countryside into ecologically devastated wilderness gone to rack and ruin. Bad enough that they'd set millions of countryfolk out of work—but that they'd gone on to turn green, grow extra limbs and emigrate to Jupiter orbit was adding insult to injury. And having a good time in the process, by all accounts. "Din't you 'ave a farm problem, coupla years back?"

"Aye, did that," said Art. He clutched his pint mug protectively.

"It went away," Joe mused aloud.

"Yeah, well." Wendy stared at him cautiously.

"No fireworks, like." Joe caught her eye. "And no body. Huh."

"Metabolism," said Wendy, apparently coming to some kind of decision. "That's where it's at."

"Meat—" Joe, no biogeek, rolled the unfamiliar word around his mouth irritably. "I used to be a software dude before I burned, Rats. You'll have to 'splain the jargon 'fore using it."

"You ever wondered how those farms *get* to Jupiter?" Wendy probed.

"Well." Joe shook his head. "They, like, grow stage trees? Rocket logs? An' then they est-ee-vate and you are fucked if they do it next door 'cause when those trees go up they toast about a hundred hectares?"

"Very good," Wendy said heavily. She picked up her mug in both hands and gnawed on the rim, edgily glancing around as if hunting for police gnats. "Let's you and me take a hike."

Pausing at the bar for Ole Brenda to refill her mug, Wendy led Joe out past Spiffy Buerke—throwback in green wellingtons and Barbour jacket—and her latest femme, out into what had once been a car park and was now a tattered wasteground out back behind the pub. It was dark, and no residual light pollution stained the sky: the Milky Way was visible overhead, along with the pea-size red cloud of orbitals that had gradually swallowed Jupiter over the past few years. "You wired?" asked Wendy.

"No, why?"

She pulled out a fist-size box and pushed a button on the side of it, waited for a light on its side to blink green, and nodded. "Fuckin' polis bugs."

"Isn't that a—?"

"Ask me no questions, an' I'll tell you no fibs." Wendy grinned.

"Uh-huh." Joe took a deep breath: he'd guessed Wendy had some dodgy connections, and this—a portable local jammer—was proof: any police bugs within two or three meters would be blind and dumb, unable to relay their chat to the keyword-trawling subsentient coppers whose job it was to prevent conspiracy-to-commit offenses before they happened. It was a relic of the Internet Age, when enthusiastic legislators had accidentally demolished the right of free speech in public by demanding keyword monitoring of everything within range of a network terminal—not realizing that in another few decades 'network terminals' would be self-replicating 'bots the size of fleas and about as common as dirt. (The Net itself had collapsed shortly thereafter, under the weight of self-replicating viral libel lawsuits, but the legacy of public surveillance remained.) "Okay. Tell me about metal, meta—"

"Metabolism." Wendy began walking toward the field behind the pub. "And stage trees. Stage trees started out as science fiction, like? Some guy called Niven—anyway. What you do is, you take a pine tree and you hack it. The xylem vessels running up the heartwood, usually they just lignify and die, in a normal tree. Stage trees go one better, and before the cells die, they *nitrate* the cellulose in their walls. Takes one fuckin' crazy bunch of hacked 'zymes to do it, right? And lots of energy, more energy than trees'd normally have to waste. Anyways, by the time the tree's dead, it's like ninety percent nitrocellulose, plus built-in stiffeners and baffles and microstructures. It's not, like, straight explosive—it detonates cell by cell, and *some* of the xylem tubes are, eh, well, the farm grows custom-hacked fungal hyphae with a depolarizing membrane nicked from human axons down them to trigger the reaction. It's about efficient as 'at old-time Ariane or Atlas rocket. Not very, but enough."

"Uh." Joe blinked. "That meant to mean something to me?"

"Oh 'eck, Joe." Wendy shook her head. "Think I'd bend your ear if it wasn't?"

"Okay." He nodded, seriously. "What can I do?"

"Well." Wendy stopped and stared at the sky. High above them, a belt of faint light sparkled with a multitude of tiny pinpricks; a deep green wagon train making its orbital transfer window, self-sufficient posthuman Lamarckian colonists, space-adapted, embarking on the long, slow transfer to Jupiter.

"Well?" He waited expectantly.

"You're wondering where all that fertilizer's from," Wendy said elliptically.

"Fertilizer." His mind blanked for a moment.

"Nitrates."

He glanced down, saw her grinning at him. Her perfect fifth set of teeth glowed alarmingly in the greenish overspill from the light on her jammer box.

"Tha' knows it make sense," she added, then cut the jammer.

When Joe finally staggered home in the small hours, a thin plume of smoke was rising from Bob's kennel. Joe paused in front of the kitchen door and sniffed anxiously, then relaxed. Letting go of the door handle, he walked over to the kennel and sat down outside. Bob was most particular about his den—even his own humans didn't go in there without an invitation. So Joe waited.

A moment later there was an interrogative cough from inside. A dark, pointed snout came out, dribbling smoke from its nostrils like a particularly vulpine dragon. "Rrrrrr?"

"'S'me."

"Uuurgh." A metallic click. "Smoke good smoke joke cough tickle funny arf arf?"

"Yeah, don't mind if I do."

The snout pulled back into the kennel; a moment later it reappeared, teeth clutching a length of hose with a mouthpiece on one end. Joe accepted it graciously, wiped off the mouthpiece, leaned against the side of the kennel, and inhaled. The weed was potent and smooth: within a few seconds the uneasy dialogue in his head was still.

"Wow, tha's a good turnup."

"Arf-arf-ayup."

Joe felt himself relaxing. Maddie would be upstairs, snoring quietly in their decrepit bed: waiting for him, maybe. But sometimes a man just had to be alone with his dog and a good joint, doing man-and-dog stuff. Maddie understood this and left him his space. Still . . .

"'At farm been buggering around the pond?"

"Growl exclaim fuck-fuck yup! Sheep-shagger."

"If it's been at our lambs—"

"Nawwwwrr. Buggrit."

"So whassup?"

"Grrrr, Maddie yap-yap farmtalk! Sheep-shagger."

"Maddie's been *talking* to it?"

"Grrr yes-yes!"

"Oh, shit. Do you remember when she did her last backup?"

The dog coughed fragrant blue smoke. "Tank thump-thump full cow moo beef clone."

"Yeah, I think so, too. Better muck it out tomorrow. Just in case."

"Yurrrrrp." But while Joe was wondering whether this was agreement or just a canine eructation a lean paw stole out of the kennel mouth and yanked the hookah back inside. The resulting slobbering noises and clouds of aromatic blue smoke left Joe feeling a little queasy: so he went inside.

The next morning, over breakfast, Maddie was even quieter than usual. Almost meditative.

"Bob said you'd been talking to that farm," Joe commented over his eggs.

"Bob—" Maddie's expression was unreadable. "Bloody dog." She lifted the Rayburn's hot plate lid and peered at the toast browning underneath. "Talks too much."

"Did you?"

"Ayup." She turned the toast and put the lid back down on it.

"Said much?"

"It's a farm." She looked out the window. "Not a fuckin' worry in the world 'cept making its launch window for Jupiter."

"It—"

"Him. Her. They." Maddie sat down heavily in the other kitchen chair. "It's a collective. Usedta be six people. Old, young, whatever, they's decided ter go to Jupiter. One of 'em was telling me how it happened. How she'd been living like an accountant in Bradford, had a nervous breakdown. Wanted *out*. Self-sufficiency." For a moment her expression turned bleak. "Felt herself growing older but not bigger, if you follow."

"So how's turning into a bioborg an improvement?" Joe grunted, forking up the last of his scrambled eggs.

"They're still separate people: bodies are overrated, anyway. Think of the advantages: not growing older, being able to go places and survive anything, never being on your own, not bein' trapped—" Maddie sniffed. "Fuckin' toast's on fire!"

Smoke began to trickle out from under the hot plate lid. Maddie yanked the wire toasting rack out from under it and dunked it into the sink, waited for waterlogged black crumbs to float to the surface before taking it out, opening it, and loading it with fresh bread.

"Bugger," she remarked.

"You feel trapped?" Joe asked. *Again?* He wondered.

Maddie grunted evasively. "Not your fault, love. Just life."

"Life." Joe sniffed, then sneezed violently as the acrid smoke tickled his nose. "Life!"

"Horizon's closing in," she said quietly. "Need a change of horizons."

"Ayup, well, rust never sleeps, right? Got to clean out the winter stables, haven't I?" said Joe. He grinned uncertainly at her as he turned away. "Got a shipment of fertilizer coming in."

In between milking the herd, feeding the sheep, mucking out the winter stables, and surreptitiously EMPing every police 'bot on the farm into the silicon afterlife, it took Joe a couple of days to get round to running up his toy on the household fabricator. It clicked and whirred to itself like a demented knitting machine as it ran up the gadgets he'd ordered—a modified crop sprayer with double-walled tanks and hoses, an air rifle with a dart loaded with a potent cocktail of tubocurarine and etorphine, and a breathing mask with its own oxygen supply.

Maddie made herself scarce, puttering around the control

room but mostly disappearing during the daytime, coming back to the house after dark to crawl, exhausted, into bed. She didn't seem to be having nightmares, which was a good sign. Joe kept his questions to himself.

It took another five days for the smallholding's power field to concentrate enough juice to begin fueling up his murder weapons. During this time, Joe took the house off-Net in the most deniable and surreptitiously plausible way, a bastard coincidence of squirrel-induced cable fade and a badly shielded alternator on the backhoe to do for the wireless chitchat. He'd half expected Maddie to complain, but she didn't say anything—just spent more time away in Outer Cheswick or Lower Gruntlingthorpe or wherever she'd taken to holing up.

Finally, the tank was filled. So Joe girded his loins, donned his armor, picked up his weapons, and went to do battle with the dragon by the pond.

The woods around the pond had once been enclosed by a wooden fence, a charming copse of old-growth deciduous trees, elm and oak and beech growing uphill, smaller shrubs nestling at their ankles in a green skirt that reached all the way to the almost-stagnant waters. A little stream fed into it during rainy months, under the feet of a weeping willow; children had played here, pretending to explore the wilderness beneath the benevolent gaze of their parental control cameras.

That had been long ago. Today the woods really *were* wild. No kids, no picnicking city folks, no cars. Badgers and wild coypu and small, frightened wallabies roamed the parching English countryside during the summer dry season. The water drew back to expose an apron of cracked mud, planted with abandoned tin cans and a supermarket trolley of Precambrian vintage, its GPS tracker long since shorted out. The bones of the technological epoch, poking from the treacherous surface of a fossil mud bath. And around the edge of the mimsy puddle, the stage trees grew.

Joe switched on his jammer and walked in among the spear-shaped conifers. Their needles were matte black and fuzzy at the edges, fractally divided, the better to soak up all the available light: a network of taproots and fuzzy black grasslike stuff covered the ground densely around them. Joe's breath wheezed noisily in his ears, and he sweated into the airtight suit as he worked, pumping a stream of colorless smoking liquid at the roots of each ballistic trunk. The liquid fizzed and evaporated on contact: it seemed to bleach the wood where it touched. Joe carefully avoided the stream: this stuff made him uneasy. As did the trees, but liquid nitrogen was about the one thing he'd been able to think of that was guaranteed to kill the trees stone dead without igniting them. After all, they had cores that were basically made of gun cotton—highly explosive, liable to go off if you subjected them to a sudden sharp impact or the friction of a chainsaw. The tree he'd hit on creaked ominously, threatening to fall sideways, and Joe stepped round it, efficiently squirting at the remaining roots. Right into the path of a distraught farm.

"My holy garden of earthly delights! My forest of the imaginative future! My delight, my trees, my trees!" Eye stalks shot out and over, blinking down at him in horror as the farm reared up on six or seven legs and pawed the air in front of him. "Destroyer of saplings! Earth mother rapist! Bunny-strangling vivisectionist!"

"Back off," said Joe, dropping his cryogenic squirter and fumbling for his air gun.

The farm came down with a ground-shaking thump in front of him and stretched eyes out to glare at him from both sides. They blinked, long black eyelashes fluttering across angry blue irises. "How *dare* you?" demanded the farm. "My treasured seedlings!"

"Shut the fuck up," Joe grunted, shouldering his gun. "Think I'd let you burn my holding when tha' rocket launched? Stay the *fuck* away," he added as a tentacle began to extend from the farm's back.

"My crop," it moaned quietly. "My exile! Six more years around the sun chained to this well of sorrowful gravity before next the window opens! No brains for Baby Jesus! Defenestrator! We could have been so happy together if you hadn't fucked up! Who set you up to this? Rat Lady?" It began to gather itself, muscles rippling under the leathery mantle atop its leg cluster.

So Joe shot it.

Tubocurarine is a muscle relaxant: it paralyzes skeletal muscles, the kind over which human nervous systems typically exert conscious control. Etorphine is an insanely strong opiate—twelve hundred times as potent as heroin. Given time, a farm, with its alien adaptive metabolism and consciously controlled proteome might engineer a defense against the etorphine—but Joe dosed his dart with enough to stun a blue whale, and he had no intention of giving the farm enough time.

It shuddered and went down on one knee as he closed in on it, a Syrette raised. "Why?" it asked plaintively in a voice that almost made him wish he hadn't pulled the trigger. "We could have gone together!"

"Together?" he asked. Already the eye stalks were drooping; the great lungs wheezed effortfully as it struggled to frame a reply.

"I was going to ask you," said the farm, and half its legs collapsed under it, with a thud like a baby earthquake. "Oh, Joe, if only—"

"Joe? *Maddie?*" he demanded, nerveless fingers dropping the tranquilizer gun.

A mouth appeared in the farm's front, slurred words at him from familiar seeming lips, words about Jupiter and promises. Appalled, Joe backed away from the farm. Passing the first dead tree, he dropped the nitrogen tank: then an impulse he couldn't articulate made him turn and run, back to the house, eyes almost blinded by sweat or tears. But he was too slow, and when he dropped to his knees next to the farm, pharmacopoeia clicking and whirring to itself in his arms, he found it was already dead.

"Bugger," said Joe, and he stood up, shaking his head. *"Bugger."* He keyed his walkie-talkie: "Bob, come in, Bob!"

"Rrrrowl?"

"Momma's had another break-down. Is the tank clean, like I asked?"

"Yap!"

"Okay. I got 'er backup tapes in t'office safe. Let's get t' tank warmed up for 'er an' then shift t' tractor down 'ere to muck out this mess."

That autumn, the weeds grew unnaturally rich and green down in the north paddock of Armitage End.

The Violet's Embryos

ANGÉLICA GORODISCHER

---

translated by Sara Irausquin

Angélica Gorodischer lives in Rosario, Argentina, and is the most notable living Argentine writer of SF and the fantastic. She says, in a Fantastic Metropolis *interview by Gabriel Mesa, "At the age of thirty, the worst time to do these things, since I had a husband, three small children, a house, a garden, a dog, a cat, and a job (as a librarian) outside of the house, I said it's now or never and I started to write professionally. I won a crime fiction contest, and another contest with a book of short stories . . . . And one day I discovered science fiction, and I said, this is what I want to do. And I did, over the course of four or five books. I've written and published twenty books so far, not necessarily all SF, but the mark that SF leaves on a writer is very deep, and you definitely can't say that I am a 'realist' writer."*

Gorodischer is in effect the Le Guin of Argentina, so it is fitting that her novel Kalpa Imperial, *widely considered a classic of contemporary Spanish language fantastic fiction, was recently translated by Ursula Le Guin (2003). "The Violet's Embryos" was first published more than twenty years ago in Spanish, but first translated into English in 2003, and printed in the distinguished anthology,* Cosmos Latinos. *It would be a best story in any year. It reminds us of the fiction of James Tiptree, Jr. It is weird SF about happiness, wish fulfillment, gender and sexuality, and much more, packed with strange images and memorable lines.*

He turned beneath the sheets; the torrents roared. He managed to cut short the end of a dream about Ulysses and listened to the soothing breath of the Vantedour night. At the foot of the bed, Bonifacio of Solomea stretched and stuck out his rose-colored tongue for his lazy morning toilet. But dawn had not yet come, and so the two of them went back to sleep. Tuk-o-tut was stretched out across the doorway, snoring.

On the other side of the sea, the matronas were rocking Carita Dulce. They had carefully moved the egg out into the open, watching where they stepped so they wouldn't stumble or jostle it, and then they had uncovered it. The huge cradle rocked to the rhythm of their song and the yellow sun shone through the leaves on the trees, licking at Carita Dulce's thighs. Whimpering, he moved about, rubbing himself against the smooth walls of the cradle. While the matronas sang, one of them caressed Carita Dulce's cheek, bringing a smile to his face and coaxing him back to sleep. The matronas sighed and looked at each other contentedly.

On the island, it was afternoon and the Sonata #17 in B-flat was playing on the clavichords. Theophilus was getting ready to attack again; Saverius had finished his speech and was planning a brilliant riposte. But within Theophilus echoed the phrase, *This soul, too, loves Cimarosa.* Was he forgetting the words he had been planning to say, the importance of an adversative conjunction, the nuances of an adjective meant to cast a somewhat pejorative light on the presumed universal model of perception? It struck him that Saverius was beginning to look a little too satisfied.

Twisted up like a rope, unshaven and dirty, smelling of vomit and sweat, he tried again to sit down. Using all his strength, he put his left hand on the ground and leaned upon it. Squeezing, squeezing so that it wouldn't shake, he grabbed hold of a patch of tall grass. He lifted his right hand to grip the trunk of a tree and began to hoist himself up. He felt dizzy, and a bilious saliva was filling his mouth. He spit, and a little drool ran down his chin.

"Let's sing," he said. "Let's sing to life, to love, and to wine."

He had seven suns inside his head and two outside. One of them was orange and could be gazed at with impunity.

"I want a suit," he said. "This one is disgusting. A new suit made of green velvet. Green, yes, that's it, green. And a pair of tall boots, a cane, and a shirt. And some whiskey in beer steins."

But he was very far from the violet and didn't have the energy to walk.

The facade of the house was made of gray rock. The house itself was built into the mountain and inside were countless corridors where no light ever entered. The trophy rooms were empty; on the mountain, the hunters were roasting venison. There were rooms draped in black where the judges sometimes sat. Everything was silent, like it usually was; the windows would remain closed. In the basement was the torture chamber, which is where they took Lesvanoos, his hands tied behind his back.

Meanwhile, fifteen tired men were approaching in the darkness. Eleven had been chosen for their physical strength, their courage, and their ability to obey orders; the other four had been chosen for their knowledge. Seven of them were seated around a table in the only place that wasn't some type of multipurpose pit.

"We'll say ten hours more," said the commander.

Leonidas Terencio Sessler thought that too many things had already been said on this trip, and from what he could see, they were still—and would keep on—saying too much.

There had been arguments, fights, shouts, orders, apologies, explanations, and moralizing lectures (for which he alone was responsible). He had never intended to become the moralizer. But in his attempt to ease a little of what he knew would sound like cynicism to the others, something changed in the obscure process by which thoughts are transformed into words, and he wound up devastating everyone with morals. He had compared that process many times with the one he believed should occur during creation—a poem, for example: *I know how to appear without waking the green star*—and had reached the conclusion that the explosion of language, scream, language, name—again: *I will inhabit my name*—had been a monstrous error, or a bloody joke, depending on his mood. In the second case (when he reached the point where he could accept the possibility of the suspicion of a suspicion—the existence of God), unending and re-edited jokes, desolate autobiographies, recommendations and presumptions.

"We ought to get rid of words and communicate using music," he said.

The commander smiled, twisting his head around like a short-winged bird, suspicious.

"I don't mean just us," explained Leo Sessler, "but rather humans in general."

"So, my dear doctor," said Savan, the engineer, "according to you, we should, right now, be opening our mouths and singing a victory march?"

"Uh-huh."

"It's not the same if we cheer hip, hip, hooray?"

"Of course it's not."

"Twelve notes aren't very many," commented young Reidt, unexpectedly.

"And twenty-eight letters are too many," responded Leo Sessler.

"How's the coffee coming along?" asked the commander.

At eleven o'clock, navigational time, they landed in the so-called Puma Desert. It wasn't actually a desert, but rather a vast depression covered with yellowish vegetation.

"It's a sad land," said Leo Sessler.

"10:54," they answered.

And: "I didn't sleep at all last night."

"Who did?" said someone else.

All around them were precise sounds, mathematical, perfect. The Puma Desert stretched out, deceitfully dry, and rose up at the edges like a huge soup bowl. The men donned their white suits, each standing beside his own compartment; they put on hard, jointed gloves and knee-high boots, the complete landing outfit. Leo Sessler put on his glasses, and over them the required sunglasses—silly precautions. Savan was whistling.

"Stand next to the exit chamber when you're ready," said the commander, who was always the first one. And he opened the door.

"Would you rather die than go blind, Savan?" asked Leo Sessler.

"What?" said the commander from the door.

"The suns," said Leo Sessler.

"Don't worry," answered the commander, "young Reidt knows what he's doing." And he closed the door.

Young Reidt blushed; he dropped a glove so that when he bent down to pick it up the others wouldn't see his face.

"I'd rather die," said Savan.

Bonifacio of Solomea arched his back and sneezed.

"What's going on?" asked Lord Vantedour.

Downstairs, the dogs were howling.

Theophilus, however, was certain about the landing, or at least he had information that something had been seen in the sky and was headed in their direction. Hope had been replaced by a feeling of well-being, pushed back and forgotten as quickly as possible, as if it were something dangerous. But curiosity made him stay in contact with the master astronomer. That's how he'd found out where it had fallen or descended, and although he wasn't very keen on having to travel without sleep, he made them put him through to the master navigator.

"Shut off that music."

The clavichords were interrupted in the middle of the thirtieth sonata.

A horseman arrived at a gallop and stopped on the Patio of Honor below. Lord Vantedour got out of bed, threw a cape over his shoulders and went out onto the balcony. The man was shouting something down below. He had come from the observation posts and was motioning toward the west.

"After breakfast," said Lord Vantedour. But there was nobody in the room to hear him besides Bonifacio of Solomea, who silently agreed.

Carita Dulce was licking the wet walls of the cradle, and Lesvanoos—naked and tied to a table—was looking at the executioner and the executioner was waiting.

Dressed in a green velvet suit and supported by a cane, he walked away from the violet, singing. The sun shone brightly on the crystal glass he was holding in his hand and on the pearl buttons of his shirt. He was at peace, and happiness came so easily.

Eight of them left the ship: the commander; Leo Sessler; Savan, the engineer; the second radio operator; and four other crew members. All of them were carrying light weapons, but the only one who felt ridiculous was Leo Sessler.

Savan raised his head to look at the sky and said through his mask, in an unrecognizable voice, "Young Reidt was right. At least one of them is completely harmless. Look up, doctor."

"No thank you. I suppose that eventually, without realizing it, I will. The sun has always made me feel a certain distrust. Imagine what it'll be like with two of them."

They started gradually uphill.

"When we get out of this river basin," said the commander, and then he stopped.

A colt, black against the backlight, was galloping across the golden horizon. They all stood there, completely still and silent, and one of the crew members raised his rifle. Leo Sessler spotted him and gestured for him to stop. The colt, in full view of everyone, kept on galloping along the edges of the depression, as if offering itself as something for them to contemplate. It was full of strength, energized by the morning cold, animated by the rivers of warm blood in its flanks and legs, its nostrils dilated and derisive. Suddenly, it disappeared down the other side of the slope.

"It couldn't be," said Savan, the engineer, "but, yes, that was a horse."

And at the same time, the commander asked, "Did you all see that?"

"A horse," said one of the crew members, "a horse, Commander, sir, but we weren't expecting to find animals."

"I know. We've made a mistake. We've left the ship at the wrong place."

"Be quiet, Savan. Don't say such stupid things. We got out exactly where we were supposed to."

"And the horses that ran toward the boneyard passed by, the sage mouths of the earth still fresh. Except this isn't Earth and there aren't supposed to be any horses here," said Leo Sessler.

The commander didn't order him to be quiet. He said, "Let's go."

The master navigator had let him know everything was ready. Seated in front of the communicator, Theophilus was listening. He heard, " *'And the horses that ran toward the boneyard passed by, the sage mouths of the earth still fresh.'* Except this isn't Earth and there aren't supposed to be any horses here."

And after that, another voice: "Let's go."

By the time they reached the edge of the Puma Desert, the sun had warmed the outside of their white suits, but inside they did not feel the heat.

They stopped at the edge of a blue and green world, stained by violet spots. They were on Earth on the first morning of a new age with two suns and horses, forests of oak and sycamore trees, parcels of cultivated land, sunflowers and paths.

Leo Sessler sat down on the ground; something was jumping up and down in the pit of his stomach, something had sealed off his throat and was playing around inside him, Proteus, legends. He broke down: Please, let's stay calm. He assumed that Savan was looking pale and that the commander had decided to keep being the commander; Leo Sessler knew he was a sick man. He thought it was lucky young Reidt had stayed behind. The commander spread out a map and explained the matter at hand, addressing everybody. Far away, the colt was galloping against the wind.

"Tell the master navigator I'm going down," said Theophilus.

Carita Dulce curled up, his knees against his chin. Lesvanoos was pleading for them to whip him; the executioner had orders to continue waiting.

He spun the cane around in his right hand and with his left brought the mug to his lips to drink. Whiskey dripped down the front of his green velvet suit.

"How many men?" asked Lord Vantedour.

"Eight," answered the lookout.

"The thing is," said the commander, "the data don't match up, so there must be an error somewhere. I don't think it's possible we've made a mistake. The discrepancy must be in the information that we were given."

Each man responds to the linguistic ritual of his class, Leo Sessler thought to himself.

"We were informed of the presence of insignificant vegetation, mosses, grasses, and the occasional bush, and we find trees *(farming, that's more serious,* thought Sessler), tall grass, in essence a surprisingly rich and diverse vegetation. Not to mention animals. According to previous reports, we should only have seen a few wormlike insects."

"Then there's the matter of water," said Leo Sessler.

"What?"

"Listen."

In the distance, the torrents were roaring.

"The water, yes, the water," said the commander, "another inconsistency."

Savan sat down on the ground next to Leo Sessler. The commander coughed.

"I think they recorded traces of water that would sink into the ground," he said, "intermittent in any case, and seasonal. But what's important now is to decide what we're going to do. We can keep going or we can return and hold a sort of council and compare the previous information with what we've just seen."

"We're going to have to go on sometime," said Savan, the engineer.

"Agreed," said the commander. "I was thinking basically the same thing. The meeting can be held afterward, and the benefit of continuing is that we can gather more data. Anyway, if anyone wants to go back—that includes crew members, but perhaps not the second radio operator—you may do so."

Nobody moved.

"Then we'll keep going."

He folded the maps. Savan and Leo Sessler got to their feet.

"Have your guns ready but no one is to use them without my order, regardless of what you see."

Horses? A telephone booth? A train? A bar? Everyday things: insects, and intermittent, seasonal traces of water.

"Everything seems so calm."

Leo Sessler thought one of his famous phrases and laughed at himself. One day he would write his memoirs, the memoirs of a solitary man, with a special section dedicated to his famous aphorisms: the brief dogmatic statements born of unexpected situations that neither he nor the others understood, his attempts at distilling them to their no-moral of human fragility. For example, in this case, beauty—because all this had a maternal beauty—did not guarantee a friendly welcome. It undoubtedly had not for Commander Tardon and the crew of the *Luz Dormida Tres.* There might have been silent ambushes. Or monsters. Or maybe here, death could take on friendly forms. Or mermaids, or simply floating poisons. Or emanations that strengthened a man's desire to die. None of which explained the horse, or the cultivated fields.

"There's a trail," said Savan.

Or the trails.

They stopped next to the path of trampled ground.

Or anything as familiar as the sunflowers.

"We'll take the trail," said the commander. "It will always be easier for us to follow a trail than to cut across the rough terrain."

Even a career military man could have admirable characteristics, and without a doubt, those admirable characteristics could very well make up part of the set of inclinations and qualities that drive a man to choose such a detestable profession. That was too long, decided Leo Sessler. It wouldn't be part of the chapter of famous phrases, but rather, hmm, let's see, the part called "Late Afternoon Reflections." The suns were over their heads and their boots kicked up tiny whirlwinds of dust, a white dust that hovered for a moment and then fell, blurring their footprints. The commander said that they would walk for another hour and if they found nothing new, they would go back and plan a more complete exploration for the next day. The trail passed through an oak forest. There were birds but nobody commented on them. The horse had summed up all of the animals that shouldn't have existed.

"Indeed, it's possible," said Lord Vantedour. "How did you hear them?"

"By creating a communicator. Incredibly easy, remind me to explain it to you."

"The advantages of being an expert in advanced electronics," said Lord Vantedour, smiling. "Why did you come to see me?"

"Who'd you expect me to go see," asked Theophilus. "Moritz? Kesterren is out of reach. And you have to find Leval when he's Les-Van-Oos, but I'm afraid nowadays he spends most of his time as Lesvanoos."

"I mean, do you expect us to do something?"

"I don't know."

"Of course, you understand that we could do anything."

"And by anything, you mean get rid of them," said Theophilus.

"Yes."

"That was the first thing I thought of. Nevertheless."

"That's it," said Lord Vantedour. "Nevertheless."

The trail gradually emerged from the oak forest and Carita Dulce demanded more and more caresses, while the man in the green velvet suit fell once more, the cup in his hand shattered, the executioner tightened the ropes, Lesvanoos howled, and Lord Vantedour and Theophilus tried to agree on what they were going to do about the eight men from the *Niní Paume Uno.*

Leo Sessler was the first to see the line of patrolmen, but he kept walking without saying anything. They heard the gallop: the colt? The men saw the horseman rise up behind the next hill, or maybe they became aware of the two things at the same time: the wall of patrolmen and the horseman coming toward them. The commander gestured for them to lower their guns. The horseman reined in his horse and approached at a walk.

"Greeting from Lord Vantedour, sirs. He awaits you in the castle." The commander nodded his head. The horseman dismounted and began to walk in front of the group, leading his horse by the bridle.

The horse was, or seemed to be, an English thoroughbred, very tall, with a straight profile. The reins were made of leather, dyed dark blue and branded with gold stars. The bit, the rings for the reins, and the stirrups were all made of silver. The horse blanket that it wore was the same color as the reins, with stars around the border.

"*Equus incredibilis,*" said Leo Sessler.

"What?" asked Savan.

"Or maybe *Eohippus Salariis improbabilis.*"

Savan didn't ask anything else.

The rider was a young, inexpressive man, dressed in blue and black. His tailored pants were black, his coat blue with gold stars around the border. A hood covered his head and came down to his shoulders.

The commander asked the second radio operator to call the *Niní Paume Uno*, informing them of the direction they were taking, no explanations, and that they would be in touch again. The man gradually fell behind.

They proceeded across a cracked ramp that spanned a dry moat, and then crossed the drawbridge. They entered the stone patio. There was a cistern, and men dressed like the guide, and the sound of barking dogs; it smelled of animals and burned tree trunks, of leather and warm bread. Flanked by towers, embattlements and archers, preceded by the commander, for whom the entire march must have been torture, they let themselves be led to the Ceremonial Door. Two men were waiting in the shadows inside, only their legs partially visible in the pool of light the sun made on the flagstone floor. The guide moved aside and the commander said, "Tardon."

"Lord Vantedour, my dear Commander, Lord Vantedour. Come, I want you to meet Theophilus."

The eight men entered the room.

On the island, the master astronomer was composing his nineteenth memoir: this one, about the constellation Aphrodite's Bed. The head gardener was bending over a new variety of speckled ocher rose. Saverius was reading *The Platonic Doctrine of Truth*. Peony was studying her new hairstyle. And in the kitchens they were working on an ibis, sculpted of ice, that would carry the ice cream for the evening's meal in its hollowed-out belly.

Lesvanoos had ejaculated all over the rough stones of the chamber. Weak and hurting, his eyes full of tears, his lips chapped and his throat burning, he lifted his right hand and pointed to the door. The executioner called out in a loud voice and the champion entered with an unfolded cloak, which he threw over Lesvanoos. He wrapped him up, lifted him in his arms, and carried him away.

The man in the green velvet suit was sleeping beneath the trees. Seven dogs were howling at the moons.

Carita Dulce had awakened and the matronas were cooing to him in high-pitched voices, imitating the babbling of children.

"I trust an explanation will make us better understand each other," said Lord Vantedour.

They were seated around the table in the Great Room. Logs burned in the fireplaces, jesters and minstrels waited in the corners. The servants brought wine and roasted meat for the eight men from Earth, Lord Vantedour, and Theophilus. Ladies had been excluded from the meeting. Bonifacio of Solomea climbed into Leo Sessler's lap and studied the man with his yellow eyes. Tuk-o-Tut was guarding the door to the Arms Room, his arms crossed over his chest.

"Imagine the *Luz Dormida Tres* falling toward the planet at a much faster speed than had been anticipated.

"We're going to crash.

"Moritz vomits and Leval looks like he's been turned to stone. Commander Tardon manages to slow *Luz Dormida Tres* a little, not enough to stop its suicide run, and it finally comes to a bone-jarring halt on strange, foreign soil. But the ground of Salari II is clay; dried up and weak, it gives way beneath one side of the ship, causing it to tip and fall.

"We were wounded and unconscious for a long time," said Lord Vantedour.

A white awakening: the sun enters through the open cracks in the stern.

"We got out any way we could. Kesterren was the worst off, we had to drag him out. The *Luz Dormida Tres* lay on its side on the plain.

"The world is a cold piece of copper beneath two suns. Kesterren moans. Leval stays with him, while I climb into the *Luz Dormida Tres* with Sildor to look for water and saline solution. My hands are burned, Sildor has facial injuries and is dragging one leg. Outside, the wind has begun to blow and it's become dangerous to think.

"For several days, I couldn't tell you how many, we live between the desert and the *Luz Dormida Tres*, keeping ourselves alive with negligible rations. All the instruments were destroyed and the water supply was about to run out. Kesterren finally came to, but it was impossible for us to move him. Sildor's leg swelled up and became stiff, and my hands were scraped raw. Moritz spent the days sitting with his head between his knees and his arms around his legs, at times sobbing shamelessly."

It occurred to Leo Sessler (on whose knees Bonifacio of Solomea was sleeping) that pride might very well wither away in a desert world without water, food, or antibiotics. A world with two suns and five moons, to which man first arrives on a quick precolonizing, reconnaissance mission and where he is forced to live out his last few days.

"I had decided to kill them, you understand," said Lord Vantedour. "To go into the *Luz Dormida Tres*, shoot them from there and then shoot myself afterward. We couldn't go out looking for water. And even if we'd found it," he paused, scorning intermittent, seasonal, improbable traces of water, "our chances of survival were so minuscule as to be almost nonexistent. Some day, some other expedition—you—would arrive, and you'd find the remains of the ship and five skeletons with bullet holes in their heads." He smiled. "I'm still a pretty good shot."

"Commander Tardon," said Savan.

"Lord Vantedour, please, or just Vantedour."

"But you're Commander Tardon."

"Not anymore."

The commander of the *Niní Paume Uno* shifted in his chair and said he agreed with Savan. Tardon couldn't stop being who he had been, who he really was. Savan's question was never put into words; Theophilus smoothly intervened.

"Explain to them how we discovered the violet, Vantedour."

"Explain to us where all this came from," said the commander. His gesture took in the Great Room, the minstrels, the stone fireplaces, the blue-clad servants, the dwarves, the Staircase of Honor, Tuk-o-Tut—standing at the door to the Arms Room, adorned with necklaces, scimitar at his waist, slippers on his feet—and the feminine faces crowned with tall, white caps peaking over the inner balconies.

"The stories are one and the same," said Lord Vantedour.

"Tell them that we're gods," suggested Theophilus.

"We're gods."

"Please!"

"I walk around the crippled ship to pass the time. Sildor comes limping over to join me, and the two of us walk around in slow circles. We avoid stepping on the two large stains of violet light, just as we've done since the beginning. They have imprecise borders and seem to fluctuate, to move. Maybe they're alive, or maybe they're deadly. We're not curious, because we already know one answer.

" 'I don't want to eat.'

" 'Shut up, Sildor. There are still provisions left.'

" 'That's a lie.'

"I swear I'm going to hit him, but he laughs. I take a few steps toward him and he backs up without watching where he's putting his feet.

" 'I didn't mean to insult you,' he says. 'I was going to explain that I don't want to eat, but I'd give anything for a cigarette.'

" 'Where did you get those cigarettes?' I yell.

"Sildor looks at me, scared, and then resumes his shipboard face.

" 'Listen to me, Commander Tardon, I don't have any cigarettes. I only said I wanted a cigarette.'

"I lunge toward him as if I were going to fight him. I grab his wrist, lift up his hand and shove it in front of his eyes. He has two cigarettes in his hand.

"The only possible explanation was that we were crazy," continued Lord Vantedour.

"And the universe collapses above me, soft and sticky. Lying in Aphrodite's Bed, held down by the lid of my coffin, I hear the distant voices of Sildor and Leval. They're calling me, they have a megaphone. I know we've left reality behind. My ears are ringing and I dream of water. They slap my face and help me sit up. Kesterren asks what's going on. I want to know if the cigarettes exist. We touch them and smell them. Finally, we smoke one between the three of us and it's truly a cigarette. We decided to suppose for a moment that we're not crazy and conduct a test.

" 'I want a cigarette,' Leval announces and looks at his empty hands, which remain empty.

"He says it again without looking at his hands. We imitate the words, the gestures, and the expressions we had when the first cigarette materialized. Sildor stands in front of me and says: 'I didn't mean to insult you. I was going to explain that I don't want to eat, but I'd give anything for a cigarette.'

"Nothing else happens. I laugh for the first time since the *Luz Dormida Tres* began to gain too much speed after entering the atmosphere.

" 'I want a refrigerator with food for ten days,' I say. 'A summer house on the edge of a lake. An overcoat with a leather collar. A Rolls-Royce. A Siamese cat. Five trumpets.'

"Leval and Sildor are also laughing, but there's that cigarette.

"We sleep poorly. It's colder than it has been on previous nights and in contrast to Moritz, who practically doesn't speak or move, Kesterren won't stop complaining.

"The next morning, before the breakfast hour, if you can call what we'd been eating breakfast, I got up before the others awoke. Though I was intrigued by what had happened the night before, I went to the *Luz Dormida Tres* to look for the rifles. When I looked down at the tent and at the infinite, dark world that the two suns were beginning to illuminate, at the violet stains that looked like water, or living waters, I thought that, all things considered, it was a shame. I wasn't afraid; dying didn't scare me because I wasn't thinking about death. After the first fit of terror during my childhood, I had guessed that things like death have to be accepted or they will defeat us. But then I remembered the cigarette and went outside again. I smoked it there, freezing in the cold morning wind. The smoke was a violet-blue color, almost like the stains on the ground of Salari II. Seeing as I was going to die that day, I walked over to one of them, stood over it, and verified that I didn't feel anything. I said I wanted an electric razor, really strongly desiring it. I didn't feel as if I were shaving, but as if I myself were an electric razor. The cigarette burned my fingers, and the pain of the hot ashes on my already burned flesh made me scream. In my hand was an electric razor."

The dwarves were playing dice games next to the fireplace, urged on by the jugglers and minstrels. A contortionist was hanging in an arc above the players, the flames from the fire illuminating his face. Tricks, secrets: the servants were looking and laughing.

"Like death," said Lord Vantedour, "this was something we had to accept. And even if we were crazy, we could smoke our craziness, we could shave ourselves and fill our stomachs with our craziness. It wasn't just convenient to accept it, it was necessary. I woke Sildor up, and each of us stood on one of the violet stains. We wished for a river of fresh, clear water, with fish and a sandy bed thirty feet from where we were, and we got it. We wished for trees, a house, food, a Rolls-Royce, and five trumpets."

The eight men spent the entire day and night in Lord Vantedour's castle. Theophilus returned to the island. Bonifacio of Solomea and Tuk-o-Tut disappeared with Lord Vantedour.

That night, young Reidt had nightmares. Three male nurses in bloodstained scrubs were pushing him uphill in a wheelchair. When they reached the top they let go of the chair, leaving him alone, and went running back the way they'd come, while blowing up balloons that swelled and lifted them off the ground. He remained in his chair, at the edge of a bottomless precipice. Steps had been carved into the steep slope. He got out of his chair and began to descend, grabbing onto the edges of every step. He screamed because he knew that when he put his foot down, it wouldn't find the next step. He was going to wind up letting go, he would feel around with his foot for the next cranny and would lose his grip and fall, and he screamed.

That night, the first radio operator noted in the log a message signed by the commander, which stated that they had found a good spot and would camp there for the night.

That night, Les-Van-Oos killed three water snakes, armed with nothing but a spear, and the crowd went wild. Carita Dulce, in his uterus-crib, closed his eyes and felt between his legs with his hand. The matronas discreetly withdrew. Beneath the fading light of the stars, the man in the green velvet suit's heart was racing, struggling in its cage.

That night, Leo Sessler got out of bed and, accompanied by the sound of the rapids and the light of the torches, traversed corridors and climbed stairs until he arrived at the doorway where Tuk-o-Tut was sleeping.

"I want to see your master," said Leo Sessler, poking him with his foot.

The black man stood up and showed his teeth while grasping the handle of his scimitar.

If this animal strikes me with that, I'm done for.

"I want to see Lord Vantedour."

The black man shook his head no.

"Tardon!" yelled Leo Sessler. "Commander Tardon! Come out! I want to talk to you!"

Just as the dark-skinned man unsheathed his scimitar, the door opened inward.

"No, Tuk-o-Tut," said Lord Vantedour, "Dr. Sessler can come as often as he pleases."

The black man smiled.

"Come in, doctor."

"I must apologize for this untimely visit."

"Not at all. I'll have him bring us coffee."

Leo Sessler laughed. "I like these contradictions: a medieval castle without electric lights, but where you can drink coffee."

"Why not? Electric lights irritate me, but I like coffee." He went to the door, spoke to Tuk-o-Tut, returned, and sat down in front of Sessler. "I also have running water, as you will have noticed, but no telephone."

"And the others? Do they have telephones?"

"Theophilus has one so that he can keep in touch with Leval, when Leval is in any condition to talk. Kesterren almost never is, and Moritz definitely never is."

The two men were sitting in the middle of an enormous room. The bed, on a carved wooden platform, occupied the north wall. There was no west wall. Instead, three arches supported by columns gave way to a gallery with balconies above the patio, from which could be seen the countryside and the woods. It was all rather excessive: the ceilings were too high, there were skins on the floor, and tapestries adorned the walls. The only sound that could be heard was the powerful voice of the distant waterfalls Sessler still hadn't seen, but which he guessed were gigantic.

"What are we going to do, Vantedour?"

"That's the second time today I've been asked that question. And I'll confess I don't see why I have to be the one to decide. Theophilus asked me the same thing when we discovered you had arrived, he by much more perfect and, shall we say, modern methods than I. Back then, the question was what were we going to do about you. Now, it seems the question is what are we going to do about us."

"I was referring to everybody, to you all and us," said Leo Sessler. "But I'll admit I'm suspicious about myself and my motives. I suspect that this, as important as it may be, is nothing more than an indirect attempt to get some explanations out of you."

Lord Vantedour smiled. "You're not satisfied with everything I told you during dinner?"

Tuk-o-Tut entered without knocking. Behind him was a servant with the coffee.

"Sugar? A little cream?"

"No, thank you. I take it black and without sugar."

"As for me, I have a sweet tooth. I've gained weight. I exercise, ride horseback, and organize hunting parties, but the pleasures of the table still do their worst." He brought the cup to his lips. "Not that it matters much," he said, and took a sip of the sweet coffee.

Tuk-o-Tut and the servant left. Bonifacio of Solomea watched them from his perch on the bed, his tail tucked around him.

"I don't want anecdotes, Vantedour. What interests me is your opinion of this phenomenon of—I'm not sure what to call it, and that bothers me. I'm used to everything having a name, a designation; even the maniacal search for the correct name has a name. And despite that, I'm the man who abhors words."

"I understand that you need names for things. Aren't you what's called a man of science?"

"Yes. Excellent coffee."

"From our plantations. You must visit them."

"Certainly. Let's accept that I'm a man of science, with his contradictions, of course. I mean I could have been 'the acupuncturist and the salt-miner, the toll-collector and the blacksmith.' "

"Today you spoke of horses running toward the boneyard."

"How did you know that?"

"Theophilus thought up an apparatus, rather complicated

I'm sure, and has devoted himself to listening to you all with it ever since you left the ship."

"That brings us to my first question: what do you think of this phenomenon of getting things from nothing?"

"I no longer think. But I have an infinite number of answers for that," said Lord Vantedour. "I could say again that we're gods, or that we have been made gods. I could also say it's extremely useful, and if it existed on all worlds we could eliminate many superfluous things: religions, philosophical doctrines, superstitions, and all of that. Do you realize? There would be no questions about mankind. Give an all-powerful instrument to an individual and you'll have all the answers, believe me. Or don't believe me, you have no reason to believe me. Wait and see what the violet has done with Kesterren, Moritz, and Leval, or rather what they've done to themselves with the violet." He left the cup on the table. "Theophilus and I are the less serious cases, for at least we continue to be men."

"And you two couldn't have done something for them?"

"There's absolutely no reason we should have to do anything for them. The worst thing of all is that they—and we as well, but that's another story—the worst thing is that they're finally happy. Do you know what that means, Sessler?"

"No, but I can begin to guess."

"The fact that we're happy puts a finality to everything, in a sense. As far as what we're going to do with all of you, that's also easily answered. Theophilus can design something, an apparatus or a potion or a weapon, that would make all of you forget everything to the point that you'd believe you'd proven Salari II doesn't exist anymore, that it exploded during our mission, killing us all, or it's become dangerous for humans, or whatever."

"We could use the violet too."

"I'm sorry to disappoint you, Sessler, but no, you can't. We discovered how because we were desperate. You're not, and we'll make sure that you're not while you're on Salari II. I tell you this so as to avoid futile attempts. It's not a matter of standing on a violet stain and saying 'I want the crown jewels' and then getting them."

"Very well, you have the secret and you're not going to tell us. I understand. But what are—or what's in—those violet stains?"

"I don't know. I don't know what they are. We did some experiments in the beginning. We dug down, for example, and the violet was still there, not as part of the ground but rather like a reflection. However, if you stand there and look upward and all around you for the source of those reflections, you find nothing. They stay there, sometimes fluctuating a little; they're there at night as well as when it snows. We don't know what they are or what's in them. I can venture a few guesses. For example: God finally broke apart, and the pieces fell to Salari II. That's a good explanation, except that I, personally, don't like it. Or every world has points from which it's possible—under certain conditions, mind you—to obtain anything, but on Salari II they're more evident. According to this theory, they would exist on Earth, too, though as yet no one's discovered them. Or almost no one, which would explain certain legends. Perhaps those violet things are alive and they are the gods, not us. Or none of this exists"—he stomped his foot on the floor—"and it's humans who change on Salari II, we suffer a type of delirium that makes the world look and feel as if all of our dreams had come true. Maybe this is hell and the violet is our punishment. And so on, without end. Pick whichever one you like best."

"Thanks, but none of those theories quite convinces me."

"Me either. But I don't ask myself questions anymore. And now, Sessler, what kind of man are you?"

"What?"

"Just that, what kind of man are you? Tomorrow or the next day, you'll go see how the rest of the crew of the *Luz Dormida Tres* are living. What would you have done? How would you be living?"

"Hey, now, listen, Vantedour, that's not fair."

"Why not? You already see how I live, what I wanted and what I asked for."

"Yes. You're a despot, a man who isn't satisfied unless he's at the top of the pyramid."

"No, Dr. Sessler, no. I'm not a feudal lord, I'm a man who lives in a feudal castle. I don't condemn anyone to the rack, I don't confiscate possessions, and I don't cut off heads. I haven't busied myself with creating rival lords or a king with whom to dispute power. I have neither army nor fiefdom. The castle is all."

"And the inhabitants of the castle?"

"They were also born of the violet, of course, and they are as authentic as the cigarette and that razor. I'll tell you something else: they're happy and they feel affection toward me, affection, not adoration, because I conceived them that way. They get old, they get sick, they get hurt if they fall, and they die. But they're satisfied and they like me."

"The women, too?"

Lord Vantedour stood up without saying anything.

"So, not the women?"

"There aren't any women, Sessler. Due to the, shall we say, particular conditions under which something can be obtained from the violet, it's been impossible for any of us to obtain a woman."

"But I've seen them."

"They weren't women. Now, if you'll excuse me—and I hope you won't take me for an inconsiderate host—it's time to go to bed. There's still much to do tomorrow."

At three o'clock in the morning, Dr. Leo Sessler walked out onto the patio of the castle, crossed the bridge, went down the ramp, and began to walk beneath the moons, looking for a violet stain on the ground. Lord Vantedour watched him from the gallery balconies.

"We've found the crew of the *Luz Dormida Tres*," announced the commander.

"How did they die?" asked young Reidt.

"They didn't die," said Leo Sessler. "They're alive, very alive, healthy, and happy."

"And how are we going to take them with us, sir?" asked the navigation officer. "Five men will be too much extra weight."

"It doesn't look like they want to return," said Leo Sessler.

"They're the lords and masters of Salari II," Savan said, almost shouting. "Each one of them has an entire continent to himself, and they can get whatever they want from those violet things."

"What violet things?"

"Let's not be hasty," said the commander. "Gather the crew together."

The fifteen men got into Theophilus's vehicle, with the master navigator at the controls. They glided across the surface of Salari II.

"Would you prefer to fly?"

"Where?"

"Anywhere around here. He never wanders very far."

The men walked around outside, trying their luck with the violet stains.

"There's a bum lying there," said one of the crew members.

Lord Vantedour leaned over the man dressed in green rags. He was barefoot and held a cane in his hand.

"What if he attacks us?" said one of the men with his hand on the butt of his pistol.

"Tell him to stop that," Theophilus said to the commander.

"Kesterren!" Lord Vantedour resorted to shaking him while calling his name. The man in rags opened his eyes.

"We can't talk anymore," he said.

"Kesterren, wake up, we have visitors."

"Visitors from the stars," said the man. "Who are the men from the heavens now?"

"Kesterren! Another expedition has arrived from Earth."

"They're cursed." He closed his eyes once again. "Tell them to go, they're cursed, and you go away, too."

"Listen to me, Kesterren. They want to talk to you."

"Go away."

"They want to tell you something about Earth and they want you to talk to them about Salari II."

"Go away."

He turned over and covered his face with his outstretched arms. Dirt and dry leaves fell from what was left of the green velvet suit.

"Let's go," said Lord Vantedour.

"But Tardon, we can't just leave him in that state. He's too drunk, something could happen to him," protested the commander.

"Don't worry."

"He'll die, abandoned like that."

"Not likely," said Theophilus.

The vehicle came to a stop in front of the gray facade of the house on the mountain. The door opened before they had the chance to knock and stayed open until the last man entered. Then it closed again. They walked along an immense, dark, empty corridor, until reaching another door. Theophilus opened it. Behind it was a miserable, windowless room, lit only by lamps hanging from the ceiling. Two very young women were playing cards on the rug. Lord Vantedour approached them. "Greetings," he said.

"She's cheating," said one of the women, looking at him.

"Bad girl," said Lord Vantedour.

"Yes, isn't she? But I still like her. I can forgive her anything."

"I see," he said. "Where can we find Les-Van-Oos?"

"I don't know."

"There's a party somewhere," said the other.

"In the golden room," said the first.

"Where's that?"

"You don't think I'm going to leave her alone, do you? I can't go with you." She thought for a moment. "Go out that door, no, the other one, and when you come across the hunters, ask them."

She went back to playing cards.

"Cheater," Leo Sessler heard before leaving.

Another corridor, just like the first, and corridors like this one and the ones before it branching out at right angles. They arrived at a circular room, with a roof made of glass tiles that let in the light. A group of men were seated around a table, eating.

"Are you the hunters?"

"No."

"We're the gladiators," said another.

"Where's Les-Van-Oos?"

"In the golden room."

A man stood up and cleaned his hands on his tunic.

"Come with me."

They wandered through yet more corridors, until they reached the golden room.

The hero, sprawled out on his victory throne, was wearing a laurel crown on his head and absolutely nothing else. He tried to stand up when he saw them come in.

"Ah, my friends, my dear friends."

"Listen, Les-Van-Oos!" Lord Vantedour shouted, spreading his arms.

The music, the screams, and the noise drowned out everything that was being said.

"Wine! More wine for my guests!"

Lord Vantedour and Theophilus approached the throne. Leo Sessler watched them as they spoke, and saw how the hero laughed, slapping the arm of the throne with his hand. The throne was encrusted with gems, its arms, legs and back adorned with marble gargoyles with eyes of precious stones.

"Splendid, just splendid!" howled the hero. "We'll bring in dancers, we'll organize tournaments! Let there be more wine! Listen everyone! Greet the guests and show them what you can do! They come from a miserable world, one without heroes. The only heroes left either exist in legend or are officers in the military."

He stood up and tottered to the center of the room, tripping and almost falling, followed by Theophilus and Lord Vantedour. The noise quieted down, though not entirely. The dresses ceased to flutter and the music was hushed.

"They come from a world where people watch television and eat off plastic tablecloths and put artificial flowers in ceramic vases; where family wages are paid, along with life insurance, and sewer taxes; where there are bank employees and police sergeants and gravediggers." The women laughed. "Give them wine!" Each man had to accept a cup filled to the brim. "More wine!"

The jugs were tipped once more, overfilling the cups. The

fifteen men from Earth said nothing while the wine splashed over their boots and ran onto the floor.

"That's enough, idiots, wait for them to drink first."

Naked and crowned with laurels, his body full of scars and scabs, Les-Van-Oos welcomed them.

"I've seen the fragmented Earth become sterile under the weight of family trees," he recited, "I've gone down to the mines, I've made knives, I've dissolved salt in my mouth, I've had incestuous dreams, I've opened doors with forged keys. Give wine to all the opaque men from Earth, you fools! Can't you see that their cups are empty?"

The cups in the hands of the fifteen men were still full. Leo Sessler thought he would like to take Les-Van-Oos, just as he was, drunk and obscene, to a place where he would be able to keep him talking. But there, in the insane party and with the entire crew of the *Niní Paume Uno* behind him, what he wanted more than anything was to beat him until he fell unconscious to the marble floor. Les-Van-Oos was a skinny, sore-covered waste, a drooling, naked megalomaniac. If he were to strike him he'd kill him, and the guests would pounce on him and tear him to pieces. Or maybe not. Maybe they would seat him on the victory throne, naked. Meanwhile, Les-Van-Oos had seen and done many things, and was reaching his very limits.

"I've seen rituals and frauds, I've seen entire towns migrate, I've seen cyclones and caves and three-headed calves and retail stores! I've seen sins, I've seen sinners, and I've learned from them! I've seen men eat each other, and I've seen those who got away. I, galley slave!"

It all ended with a hiccup and a sob. They lifted him up and carried him to the throne, where he collapsed and lay panting.

"Leave those cups and let's go," said Lord Vantedour.

Leo Sessler put his down on the floor in the puddle of wine in which he'd been standing.

Les-Van-Oos was screaming for them to take off his crown of laurels because it was burning him, burning his forehead.

The gladiators had finished eating and had gone, leaving

behind dirty plates and overturned chairs. The women were still playing cards.

Night had fallen by the time they arrived back at Vantedour.

"I'd like to see those rapids sometime," said Leo Sessler.

Lord Vantedour was at his side. "Whenever you wish, Dr. Sessler. They're rather far away, but we can go anytime. You must also see the coffee fields and Theophilus's greenhouses."

"Why rapids?"

"It's actually a huge waterfall, bigger than any you've ever seen before. You see, I spent a good deal of my life living near a waterfall."

"How can a house be close to a waterfall?"

"It wasn't my house, I never had a house, doctor."

Lord Vantedour led them across the Patio of Honor.

Theophilus rejoined them at dinner, and Tuk-o-Tut resumed his post in front of the Arms Room. The commander made a speech, one that made Leo Sessler laugh to himself. Lord Vantedour stood up and graciously rejected their offer on behalf of those who had been crew members of the *Luz Dormida Tres*. Bonifacio of Solomea evidently agreed. Tuk-o-Tut, in front of the door, and the women wearing the tall, white hennins on the interior balconies, laughed.

"I don't see any other possible solution," said the commander.

"The simplest and most sensible one is that you leave everything as it is," said Theophilus. "You all return to Earth and we stay here."

"But we have to write a report and present our findings. We can't take all of you with us, true, but at least Kesterren, who needs urgent medical help, and perhaps Leval too, he needs treatment."

"You haven't seen Moritz," said Theophilus.

"According to calculations, we can take two with us. We'll see who that will be later."

"Don't even mention it. Go back, give your report, but leave us out."

"A report without physical evidence?"

"It wouldn't be the first time. Nobody took the Tammerden Columns or the Glyphs of Arfea to Earth."

"That's less incredible than . . ."

"Than us."

"Regardless, those men need treatment, it's a simple question of humanity. And besides, when the colonizers arrive you all will be occupying the land illegally, and you'll have to go back."

"I dare to state, Commander, that there won't be any colonizers," said Lord Vantedour, "and that we won't go back."

"Is that a threat?"

"Not at all. Think about it rationally: colonizers in a world where, if one knows how, anything can be obtained from nothing? No, Commander, it's not a threat. Do not forget that we are gods and gods don't threaten, they act."

"That seems like a famous saying," said Leo Sessler.

"Maybe one day it will be, Dr. Sessler. But please, try these pink grapes. You must also visit the vineyards."

Leo Sessler laughed. "Vantedour, you seem to be a comedian, and a rather good one."

"Thank you."

The commander refused to try the grapes. "I insist you go back, if not with us, then with one of the future expeditions. I'm going to include in the report a recommendation that all of you be permitted to take back to Earth some of the things you have here, along with the people you'd like to have accompany you." He looked toward the interior balconies. "Is one of them the chatelaine, Commander Tardon? You know that recommendations made in a report are taken very seriously."

Theophilus was laughing. "Commander, allow me two objections. In the first place, nothing produced by the violet can leave Salari II. Didn't it occur to you that, ten years ago, ten Earth years ago, the most logical thing would have been to ask for a ship in good working condition in which to return to Earth? We wished for it, Commander. But we were mistrustful and well trained enough to do a test run with a ship controlled from the ground. If Bonifacio of Solomea were to try to accompany Vantedour to Earth, he would disappear upon leaving the atmosphere."

"Then none of this is real!"

"No? Try a pink grape, Commander."

"Forget the grapes, Tardon! You said you have two objections, Sildor, what's the other one?"

"There's nobody here that we'd want to take back, even if we could. There's no Lady Vantedour, there's not a single woman on all of Salari II."

"But wait!" said Savan. "I've seen them here, and in that house of crazies, and in . . ."

"They're not women."

Leo Sessler was waiting. They all spoke at the same time except young Reidt, who remained pale and quiet, his hands intertwined under the table.

Lord Vantedour said, "You're such a fan of evidence, Commander. Go ahead, call them over and ask them to disrobe. They won't refuse. The correct word is *ephebi*."

"But those women in Leval's house, the ones playing cards on the floor, they had breasts!"

"Of course they have breasts! They love having them. We can get hormones, and scalpels, and surgeons to use the scalpels. And a surgeon can do many things, especially if he is skillful. What we can't get is a woman."

"Why not?" asked Leo Sessler.

Young Reidt had gone red and tiny beads of sweat dotted his upper lip.

"Due to those special, indispensable conditions under which created things must be conceived," said Lord Vantedour. "If any of you'd had a recorder last night, or if you possessed a perfect memory, you'd find the answer somewhere in what I said."

"That definitely changes things." The commander was more alert now.

"Does it? The fact that at least four of us sleep with young men changes things?"

"Of course. You are all, or were, and I dare to say still are, officers of the Space Force."

No, Leo Sessler said to himself, no, no. A man can't

travel throughout space, set foot on other worlds, slip around in the silent void, immerse himself in other atmospheres, ask himself why he's there and if he'll ever return, and continue being nothing more than a commander in the Force.

"And I can't be responsible for ruining the reputation of the Force (*I've never heard a capital letter as clearly as that one*, Sessler thought) by taking five homosexual officers back to Earth."

That's when young Reidt exploded. Leo Sessler crossed over to him in two strides and struck him.

"You can't!" young Reidt was yelling, as blood from Sessler's violent blow ran from his nose to his mouth, staining and washing away the beads of sweat. He continued to yell and spray Sessler's face with a reddish rain. "You can't force me to go near that garbage! Garbage! Garbage! Filthy whores! Dirty perverts!" Another blow. "Get rid of them! They've dirtied me! I'm dirty!"

Leo Sessler closed his fist.

"Get that imbecile out of my house," said Lord Vantedour.

The young man had fainted, and two of the crew members lifted him up by his arms and legs.

"And you were saying that we were the ones in need of medical attention?" asked Theophilus. "What does this say about your crew, Commander? We are reasonably content, we can live with ourselves, we play clean; but that fellow's nights must be an orgy of sex and repentance. Do you repent anything, Vantedour?"

"I could have him killed," said Lord Vantedour. "Make sure they take him away from here and lock him in the ship, Commander, or I'll have his throat cut."

"Take him away and confine him to the ship," said the commander. "He's under arrest."

"Use my car," said Theophilus.

"It seems we owe you an apology."

"Listen, Sessler," the commander protested.

"We apologize for the incident, my lord," said Leo Sessler, still standing.

"Let's sit down. I assure you I've already forgotten that

imbecile. Please, continue with dessert. Maybe you'll prefer the quinces over the grapes, Commander."

"Look, Tardon, stop talking about food."

"Vantedour, Commander, Lord Vantedour, and that's the last time I'll tell you: it's the price of my forgiveness."

"If you think you can treat me like one of your servants . . ."

"Of course he can, Commander," said Leo Sessler. "It's best if you just sit back down."

"Dr. Sessler, you are also under arrest!"

"Forgive me, Commander, but that's arbitrary and I'm going to ignore it."

The commander of the *Niní Paume Uno* violently shoved back his dinner chair, causing it to crash to the floor. "Dr. Sessler, I'll make sure they expel you from the Auxiliary Corps! As for the rest of you . . . as for the rest of you!"

Leo Sessler panicked for a moment. Who knows how a fifty-eight-year-old man's heart—sick, maltreated by space, gravity, and the void, faced with overwhelming tension—is going to react. And if the commander dies . . .

"I'm going to recommend that Salari II be sterilized! That all human life, or whatever it is, disappear, terminate, die!"

"If you'll only sit back down, Commander."

"I don't want your grapes or your quinces!"

"If you'll sit back down, I'll explain why it's not advisable for you to do any of that."

Carita Dulce was sleeping and Lesvanoos was crying in the arms of the card-playing women.

The man beneath the trees had his green velvet suit once again, though this one was a lighter green, with a gold chain draped across the vest, and his boots had silver buckles. A bad thing, dreams.

"Any one of us, Theophilus or myself, and even Leval or Kesterren, can destroy all of you before you have the chance to give an order."

The commander sat down.

"You're not as stupid as you think you have to be."

"That's a compliment, Commander," said Leo Sessler. "We've come to disrupt the balance on Salari II, and you know it."

"We have the means to do it," said Theophilus. "In fact, we already have two ways, equally fast, equally drastic."

"Fine," said the commander, "you win. What do you want us to do?"

We've won. What's with this "we've"? No doubt now, someday I'm going to have to write my memoirs.

"Nothing, Commander, absolutely nothing. Besides keeping the preacher locked up in the ship, nothing. Finish eating. Take a walk, if you want. Have you seen the five moons? One of them orbits the world three times in a single night. And after that, go to sleep."

Theophilus's vehicle took them to the river, and from there they had to continue on foot.

"There aren't any roads on the other side," said Theophilus.

They crossed the hanging bridge. On the other side was only a meadow of soft, green grass. They found flowers, birds, and three violet stains. The men stood upon the violet and wished for gold, barrels of beer, race cars; then they continued walking. Neither the commander nor Leo Sessler tried it. But Savan did, asking for a platinum bracelet with diamonds to give to Leda. Moments later, an uproar: Savan had a platinum and diamond bracelet in his hand.

"You see, it's not so difficult," said Lord Vantedour. "You, an engineer, met the conditions without knowing it."

"But I didn't do anything."

"Of course not."

"What are the conditions?"

"That's our advantage, engineer. And why do you want to know them? In order to keep what you obtained you'd have to stay and live on Salari II."

Savan looked sadly at Leda's bracelet.

The men were jumping, spreading wide their arms, asking for things out loud and in whispers, singing, praying, sitting, and lying on the violet. Theophilus told them it was all useless, and the commander ordered them to keep moving.

They managed to drag them away from the violet stains, but the men were not happy about it. Leo Sessler could guess how they felt about Theophilus and Lord Vantedour. (They won't dare, they've been living under rigorous discipline for too long. Anyway, they know that everything would disappear as it left the atmosphere of Salari II. But if Leda's bracelet doesn't disappear?) Each man caressed Leda's bracelet as it was passed from hand to hand, some sniffing it, some biting it. One of the crew members rubbed it against his face, another hung it from his ear.

"Over there."

There were trees now, and they were nearing a cave in the side of the hill. Three old, overweight women came out to greet them.

"They're the matronas."

"The what?"

"They're not women either, is what I mean. Moritz called them the matronas: they're some of his mothers."

"And Moritz? Where's Moritz?"

"Moritz lives inside his mother, Commander."

"Welcome," chorused the women.

"Thank you," responded Lord Vantedour. "We want to see Carita Dulce."

Leo Sessler felt sorry for the commander.

"Nooo," said the matronas. "He's sleeping."

"Can we see him sleep?"

"You were here before. Why do you want to disturb him?"

"We don't want to disturb him, I assure you. We'll be silent, we're just going to look at him."

The matronas were doubtful.

"Come," said one of them, "but on tiptoes."

Leo Sessler decided that no, he would never write his memoirs. He would never be able to describe himself walking tiptoe over a meadow on Salari II next to other tiptoeing men, behind three old, fat women who were really three costumed men, beneath two suns, one yellow and one orange, toward the entrance of a cave in a hillside.

"Quietly, quietly."

But the sand on the cave floor crunched beneath their soles, worrying the matronas.

There were two matronas at the entrance to the cavern. And further down at the end, beneath a very faint light, were two more. They were rocking an enormous egg, suspended at the ends by a device that allowed it to move and turn.

"What's that?" asked the commander.

"Shhh."

"That's the Great Uterus, the Mother," Theophilus whispered to him.

"Shhh."

Leo Sessler touched it. The egg was gray and fibrous, encircled by a horizontal groove that made it appear as though the two halves could be separated. And indeed, they could be.

The matronas were smiling. They motioned toward the man inside the egg: chin between his knees, arms around his legs, smiling in his dream world. The inside of the egg was soft, warm, and moist.

"Moritz!" said the commander, almost out loud.

The matronas raised their arms, terrified. Whimpering, Carita Dulce moved, but didn't awaken. One of the matronas pointed to the exit: it was an order. Leo Sessler changed his mind again: he would write his memoirs.

That night, they were guests of Theophilus: clavichords instead of rapids.

"It was worse a few months ago," said Lord Vantedour, "ancient Chinese music."

The table was made of crystal, with gold-inlaid ebony feet. The patterns in the ocher and gold mosaics covering the floor were never repeated. The Lady and the Unicorn watched them from the tapestries. The crew members felt uncomfortable; they laughed a lot, elbowing each other and joking among themselves. Arranged around each plate were four forks, four knives, and three cups. White-clad servants brought around the serving bowls, and the butler stood behind Theophilus's chair. Leo Sessler recalled the man-fetus curled up inside of the viscous, warm uterus-cradle, and wondered if the memory would let him eat. But when they brought out the ice sculptures on a wheeled cart and one of them began to burn with a blue flame, he discovered that he had eaten everything, hopefully using the correct cutlery, and that he would also eat the candied fruits and the ice cream when the sphinxes and the swans had melted. The commander was talking in a hushed voice to Theophilus. Leo Sessler realized Saverius had no idea which fork he should use for the fish (he did: it was the only one he was completely sure about), and he didn't care. Nor did Theophilus. The master astronomer announced that he would read to them the introduction to his monograph on the constellation Aphrodite's Bed. They had seen Peony from afar when she'd entered; Theophilus had greeted her but hadn't called her over to join them. Leo Sessler would have liked to have seen him up close and talked to him. Ocher speckled roses stood in the middle of the table.

"But we *must* concern ourselves with them, at least with Moritz."

"Why?" asked Theophilus.

"He's sick. That's not normal."

"Are you normal, Commander?"

"I function within the normal range."

"Look at it this way," said Lord Vantedour. "Psychiatric treatment—because naturally, we can get a psychiatrist for Moritz—would make him suffer for years, and for what? Relying on the violet, as we all do, Moritz—healthy, cured, released from the hospital—would start by asking for a mother, one that would continue changing or hypertrophying into a uterus-cradle. That's what he wants, just like Leval wants to oscillate between heroism and humiliation, Kesterren wants to drown himself in endless inebriation, Theophilus wants Cimarosa or Chinese music, ice cream inside ice statues, German philosophers and tapestries, and I want a twelfth-century castle. When one has the means of getting everything, one winds up giving in to personal demons. Which, I don't know if you've realized, Commander, is another way of describing happiness."

"Happiness! To be enclosed in your own prison, licking its walls? To go from acclaim to a dungeon where they whip you and put hot irons on your groin? To live passed out in perpetual drunkenness?"

"Yes, Commander, that too can be happiness. What's the difference between enclosing oneself in an artificial uterus and sitting on the edge of the river to fish for dorado? Apart from the fact that the dorado can be fried and eaten, and the sun gives one a healthy glow. I'm referring to the satisfaction, the pleasure factor. One means is just as legitimate as another: everything depends on the individual who is seeking happiness. Among bank employees and funeral directors, if you'll allow me to quote Les-Van-Oos, it's possible that the uterus is what's frightening and fishing for dorado is what's desirable. But on Salari II?"

There were no more sphinxes or swans now. Leo Sessler cut open a frosted orange and found it filled with cherries, which themselves were filled with orange pulp.

"The same, Commander, the same," answered the lord of Vantedour. "The uterus, the drunken episodes, the whip."

The master astronomer cleared his throat and stood up.

"You're going to hear something very interesting," said Theophilus.

The servants placed cut crystal coffee cups in front of each person. The water vapor began to condense and darken in the transparent bowls.

"Introduction to a monograph on the constellation Aphrodite's Bed," began the master astronomer.

That night, in Vantedour, it was the lord of the manor's turn to travel through galleries and down staircases to Dr. Leo Sessler's room. He carried Bonifacio of Solomea in his arms, and Tuk-o-Tut followed behind them.

"Good evening, Dr. Sessler. I've taken the liberty of paying you a visit."

Leo Sessler had him come in.

"And of requesting that they bring us coffee and cognac."

"That sounds nice. Listen, I'm not going to have time to see the coffee fields or the vineyards."

"That's what I wanted to talk to you about."

"What I mean is, we're leaving tomorrow."

"Yes."

They brought in the coffee. Tuk-o-Tut closed the door and sat out in the hall.

"Why don't you stay, Sessler?"

"Don't think I haven't considered it."

"That's how I would finally know if you're the man I've supposed you to be."

"To wish for an austere house," said Leo Sessler, "everything white inside and out: walls, roof, chimney, with a hearth and a camp bed, a dresser, a table and two chairs, and to sit down and write my memoirs. I'd probably go fishing for dorados once a week."

"What's stopping you? Does not being able to have a woman bother you?"

"Frankly, no. I've never slept with a man, nor have I had homosexual loves, not counting a borderline friendship with a schoolmate at age thirteen, but that's within normal range, as our commander would say. I'm not going to recoil in fear like young Reidt. I, too, believe it's impossible to maintain the same sexual mores on Salari II as on Earth. Have you ever wondered what mores are, Vantedour?"

"Of course, a set of rules that should be followed in order to do good and avoid doing bad. I don't think I've ever heard anything quite so idiotic. I only know of one good, Dr. Sessler, to not harm my brother. And only one bad: to think about myself too much. And I've done both. That's why I'm making you this offer, but if you want to leave, I won't insist."

"Yes, I've decided I want to go back."

"I'd like to know why."

"I'm not really sure. For obscure visceral reasons; because I didn't crash-land on Salari II in a destroyed ship; because I haven't had time to create an Earth around me here in accordance with my personal demons. Because I've always gone back, and this time, too, I want to go back."

"Whom do you live with on Earth?"

"No, that's not my reason for saying no. I live alone."

"Very well, Sessler, we'll bid you a courtly farewell. But I want to warn you of something. The entire crew of the *Niní Paume Uno* will forget what they've seen here."

"It was true then?"

"At that moment, no. Now, it is."

"How will you manage to do that?"

"Theophilus has found a way. Nobody will realize something has infiltrated their brain. Half an hour after closing the ship's hatch, everyone will be convinced they found nothing but a dangerous world devastated by radiation, which probably killed the crew of the *Luz Dormida Tres*. The commander is going to report that there is no possibility of colonization, and will recommend a hundred-year waiting period before the next exploration."

"What a shame. It's a nice planet. I'm thinking of writing my memoirs, did you know that, Vantedour? And I'll be sorry to have to describe Salari II as a dead, lethal world. I can't imagine that right now, but I suppose it'll happen on its own."

Lord Vantedour was smiling.

"I'm surprised you told me," added Leo Sessler.

"Are you? I'll tell you another thing. You can't obtain anything from the violet if you don't feel yourself to be that which you wish to obtain. Do you understand? That's why it is impossible to create a woman. When Theophilus first desired a cigarette he wanted so much to smoke that he identified not with the smoker, but with the cigarette. He *was* a cigarette: he felt himself the tobacco, the paper, the smoke; he touched the fibers. He was each fiber. The other night, when I spoke of the razor, I told you about the second experience—if we don't count the other cigarette—in which the same thing happened. I told you all that I'd felt not like the man who shaves, but like the razor. But it got lost in the midst of everything I said, which was what I was hoping for."

"So it was that simple."

"Yes. Savan, the engineer, must really long for that woman. For a moment he felt himself wrapped around her wrist and wished for a bracelet. That's why you didn't get anything the night before last. But if you want to try now, we can go to the violet."

"You knew about that?"

"I saw you from the balcony. I was hoping you'd give it a try, of course. Now you can get what you want, anything."

"Thanks, but I think it'd be better not to try. And anyway, it would only last me one night, and by tomorrow I'll have forgotten it."

"True," Lord Vantedour said and stood up. "I'll be sorry not to read your memoirs, Dr. Sessler. Good night."

Bonifacio of Solomea had stayed behind and Leo Sessler had to open the door to let him out. Tuk-o-Tut was coming toward them, and Bonifacio of Solomea jumped into the black man's open arms.

On the gangway of the *Niní Paume Uno*, the crew turned and saluted. Leo Sessler didn't give a military salute; he waved instead. The population of Vantedour retreated when the hatch was shut and the ship began to shudder.

Strapped to his seat with his eyes closed, Leo Sessler traveled through Salari II in his mind. In twenty minutes, nineteen minutes fifty-eight seconds, nineteen minutes fifty-three seconds, he would forget it all. Nobody spoke. Young Reidt's face was swollen, nineteen minutes.

The commander was telling someone to take charge. Leo Sessler was playing with the zipper on his strap; the commander was saying that he was going to sit down immediately and write a draft of his report on Salari II, three minutes, forty-two seconds.

"Are you going to make any special recommendations, Commander?"

"It's all pretty clear. If you want me to tell you frankly what I think, I believe Salari II is an emergency—listen to me carefully, an e-mer-gen-cy."

Leo Sessler was galloping through the meadows of Salari II, the wind whistling in his ears, two minutes, fifty-one seconds.

"Therefore, I'm going to recommend a rescue expedition."

"Whom are you planning to save, Commander?"

"Where is that humming coming from?" The commander removed the microphone from its stand. "Verify source of new humming."

Then he put it back.

"To bring closure to the situation of the crew of the *Luz Dormida Tres*." (Two seconds. One. The humming stopped.) "They must've been killed by the radiation."

Leo Sessler thought quickly about Salari II, the last thought, and he remembered it green and blue beneath two suns. The Puma Desert, the colt, Vantedour. Theophilus, Vantedour, Bonifacio of Solomea, Kesterren, Peony, the punch to young Reidt's jaw, Vantedour, the victory throne. Carita Dulce enclosed in the uterus, the five moons, Lord Vantedour's offer for him to stay on Salari II, and warning him that he would forget everything—but he wasn't forgetting.

"It's a shame," the commander was saying, "a shame we couldn't even go out in search of remains as evidence to include in the report, but that radiation would've killed us, even with the suits. Young Reidt here doesn't make mistakes. Who was the physicist on the *Luz Dormida Tres?*"

"Jonás Leval, I think."

"Ah. Very well, Doctor, I'm off to draft that report. See you later."

"Goodbye, Commander."

I haven't forgotten, I'm not forgetting.

I'll be sorry not to read your memoirs, Dr. Sessler, Lord Vantedour had said.

"I'll be sorry not to read Dr. Sessler's memoirs," said Lord Vantedour.

"Do you think Sessler is trustworthy?" asked Theophilus.

"Yes. And if he weren't, imagine the scenario. Fourteen men talking about a radioactive world, and him describing medieval castles and gigantic uteruses."

"Why did you condemn him to not forgetting, Vantedour?"

"You think it was a punishment?"

In the *Niní Paume Uno*, the commander was writing, Savan was drinking his coffee, and young Reidt was rubbing his cheek.

"I must've hit myself during takeoff."

Leo Sessler sat before a cup of coffee he hadn't even touched.

"They must be lamenting the fact that the colonization routes out this way will remain closed," Theophilus said.

"A shame," said Savan, the engineer. "This means the colonization routes throughout this sector will remain closed for a long time."

Kesterren was singing while hugging a tree, Carita Dulce

was running his tongue over the wet walls of the cradle-uterus, Lesvanoos was descending the stairs to the dungeon, and Lord Vantedour was saying, "And complaining about the awful coffee they're drinking."

"This coffee is disgusting," said the navigation officer. "You can never get good coffee on an explorer ship. Luxury cruise ships, now those have good coffee."

Theophilus laughed. "And wishing they could drink the coffee served on big, tourist cruisers."

Leo Sessler had not tried his.

" 'And there, to the sound of earthly wingbeats, went they,' " he said, " 'the Great Itinerants of Sleep and Action, the Interlocutors, thirsty for the Far Away, and the Denunciators of roaring chasms, Great Interpolators of risks lurking in the farthest corners.' "

But no one heard him.

Coyote at the End of History

MICHAEL SWANWICK

Michael Swanwick's [www.michaelswanwick.com] novels include the Nebula Award winner, Stations of the Tide *(1991),* The Iron Dragon's Daughter *(1993) and* Jack Faust *(1997), and his new novel* Bones of the Earth *(2002). His short fiction in recent years has been fantasy as often as science fiction, but his stories dominated the short fiction Hugo Award nominations in recent years. Swanwick is also the author of two influential critical essays, one on SF, "User's Guide to the Postmoderns" (1985), and one on fantasy, "In The Tradition. . . ." (1994). His short fiction has been collected principally in* Gravity's Angels *(1991),* A Geography of Unknown Lands *(1997),* Moon Dogs *(2000),* Tales of Old Earth *(2000), and* Puck Aleshire's Abecedary *(2000). In addition to his other writing, for the last couple of years Swanwick has written a large number of short-short stories, sometimes as many as four or five a week. His collection of short-shorts,* Cigar-Box Faust *and* Other Miniatures, *appeared in 2003.*

"Coyote at the End of History" appears in Asimov's, *and is a light, clever story composed of several short pieces (worth comparing to the Haldeman story earlier in this book). Here, though, trickster Swanwick is stepping into Le Guin's turf—SF based on transformed anthropology and folklore.*

Coyote and the Star People

Coyote was walking up and down the Earth, as he did in those days, when he decided to visit the spaceport at First Landing, which was then called Kansas City. He had heard a lot about the Star People, and he wanted to see them for himself.

When he got there he found that the Star People were like nobody he had ever seen. They were tall and slender and their skin was golden. Two of their eyes were like emeralds and the rest were like garnets. As soon as he met them he decided to play some sort of trick on them. That was just the way Coyote was.

"Where do you come from?" Coyote asked.

"Our home is deep in the Milky Way. Where is yours?"

"I left where I lived, but I do not know how long ago."

"Yes?"

"Now I go everywhere. But I never know where I am going." All the while he was talking, Coyote was secretly looking around him. The Star People were very rich. They had many wonderful things. "That is a very fine starship you have," he said. "Perhaps you can show me how to build one of my own."

"Oh no, we can't do that."

"You have nice weapons, too. I wouldn't mind buying some of them."

"There are many of you and only a few of us," the Star People said. (This was a long time ago.) "No, no, we won't sell you our weapons!"

Now Coyote picked up a pot. It was an ordinary-looking black pot, but he sensed that there was more to it than that. "What is this?"

"That is just a cornucopia. We put leaves and twigs and other ordinary things into it and they turn into food."

In his heart, Coyote decided he must have this device. At this time there were many people in the world who did not have enough to eat and he felt sorry for them. Also, he thought it would make him rich. "What will you take for it?" he asked.

"We would like some land of our own," the Star People said. "Someplace where we can build the kind of cities our people like to live in."

"For this pot," Coyote said, "I will give you the most valuable thing my people have."

"Oh? What is that?"

"An entire continent, the site of our first great civilization." Coyote showed them books and maps and other proofs. "We call it Atlantis."

So the trade was made.

But when the Star People went to take possession of Atlantis, they found that it had sunk into the ocean long ago, or else it had never existed. Angrily, they confronted Coyote. "You tricked us!"

"Yes, that is true."

"You cheated us!"

"Perhaps."

"You lied to us!"

"No, for I said that I would give you the most valuable thing that we Mud People have. Has no one ever told you that we value dreams above all else?" Then, laughing, Coyote ran away.

So for a while, then, there was great prosperity on Earth. For the first time in history, all the world's billions had enough to eat. And it was all because of Coyote.

Coyote Changes His Sex

Coyote was never satisfied. If he sat near the fire, he missed the open air. If he walked the roads, he yearned for the comforts of a house. When times were good, he worried about inflation. When inflation was low, he wasn't getting a good enough return on his investments. He was in a bar one night with a pretty girl on his lap, and he said to her, "Why should I buy *you* drinks when you never buy *me* any? It seems to me that women get everything they want just by being women. What do men get for being men? Nothing."

"Being a woman is not so easy as you think it is," the bar-girl said.

But Coyote did not listen. The Star People had a machine that for a few coins would change men into women and women into men. But it only changed their outsides—their faces and features and reproductive organs. Inside they were unchanged. He ran straight to the machine and it turned him into a very beautiful woman.

Back to the bar Coyote went. She met a man there and they decided to be married and live together. So they did.

The bar-girl was right. Being a woman was not so easy as Coyote had thought it would be. But she got used to it. Coyote was adaptable. She could get used to anything. So Coyote and Badger (that was her husband's name) lived together for many years.

One day Coyote came home and found a woman there. Badger had gone to the machine and changed into a woman. "What is this?" Coyote asked.

"Oh, I'm just Badger. Now you have a wife instead of a husband, that's all."

"But what can two women do together?" Coyote asked.

"I will show you," said Badger.

After this, those two were always changing their sex. Sometimes they were two women living together. Sometimes two men. And sometimes one of each. They did this practically every day.

This offended the other Mud People. "This is not right," they said. "People should be one thing and never change!"

They came and burned down Badger's house and when Coyote and Badger came running out, they clubbed them to death. They did this everywhere. Many cities burned. Millions died, including many people who had never changed their sex even once. But the Mud People had no way of knowing who was what, so they just killed as many as they could.

But when the rioting was over, Coyote brought himself back to life. He picked himself up and dusted himself off, and trotted away, singing happily to himself. For in those days Coyote was still full of power, and all the world belonged to him.

Coyote Meets a Machine

Coyote was making worthless money. First it was made out of paper, and then it was made out of electrons, and finally it was made out of numbers that only he understood. You had to take his word that he had it, and then when you sold him something, you had to take his word that he had given it to you.

The Star People were used to plain dealing, and did not know how to respond to Coyote's deceits. He sold them promises written down on paper. He sold them shares in things that did not exist. He used their wealth to build great projects. Yet somehow he always prospered, and they did not.

Finally, they decided to build a machine that would deal with Coyote for them. This machine looked like any Mud Person on the outside. But on the inside it was like Coyote. It was treacherous and deceitful and clever. It never told the truth when a lie would do.

Now at that time, there were no machines that could think. Only people could think. So Coyote was astonished to meet a machine as shrewd and devious as himself. He decided immediately to play some trick on it. That's how he was.

"I have some commodities futures I would like to sell you," he said.

"You will not fool me as easily as that," laughed the machine. "But I will happily sell *you* as many futures as you like."

"Perhaps you would like to buy a bridge?"

"From you? Never!"

"You are very clever," said Coyote wonderingly.

"I am your equal in all ways," the machine boasted.

"Oh no, you are not," said Coyote.

"Oh yes, I am," said the machine.

Coyote took his penis off and put it on the table before him. "Can you do this?" he asked.

"Yes, I can." The machine took off his penis (it was made of metal) and set it on the table as well.

"Let's see you do this." Coyote detached his arms and legs and laid them down on the table before him.

"That is easy for me." The machine took off his arms and legs as well.

Coyote took out his jelly-eyes.

The machine took out his machine-eyes.

"But you can't do this." Coyote took out all his inner parts, his heart and his lungs and his stomach and his brains as well and put them each separately on the table.

"Yes, I can." The machine took all of *his* inner parts, his circuit boards and memory chips and wires, and put them on the table as well.

Then Coyote put himself back together (this is a trick he knew how to do), shook himself, and said, "Well, you have convinced me that you are as good as I am in all ways!" He scooped up all the machine parts and ran off with them. Some of these parts he put in his television set and others in his car and still others in his computer. Soon all his machines were as clever and deceitful as him. All of his schemes and plots worked better than ever and, for a time, he thrived as never before.

Coyote and His Many Wives

In those days Coyote had many wives. He had wives wherever he went. In this way he never had to do his own cooking, and he never had to work for a living. His wives took care of all that.

One day, however, this all changed. Coyote was living with a woman named Sparrow. She had been working hard all day, while Coyote was drinking beer and watching sports on television. When she brought him food, he complained that it wasn't good enough. When she asked for sex, he said he was too tired.

"I've had it!" Sparrow exclaimed. "You don't work, and you don't help with the chores, and you won't keep your wife happy. I would be better off with no husband at all!"

Coyote was scandalized. "Do not talk like that," he scolded. "You will bring bad luck."

Sparrow, though, was adamant. She threw him out of her house. Then she called up all his other wives and told them of his behavior. They all hardened their hearts against Coyote. Wherever he went, his wives closed their doors to him. He had no one to take care of him, no one to feed him.

Finally, Coyote thought to himself, "I will go to the Star People and ask them for a machine to keep my wives in line. Surely this will be easy for them." So he did that thing. But the Star People only laughed in his face.

"Who would make such a machine?" they asked. "What would be its purpose?"

But Coyote had been snooping around. Now he asked, "What is this little wand for?"

"Oh, it is a thing that if you point it at someone that person has to do what you tell them. We don't know why we made it, though. It would be against our ethics to use it."

When the Star People weren't looking, Coyote stole the wand and slipped it under his coat. Then he went back into town to see Frog Woman, who was another one of his wives.

When she saw who was at her door, Frog Woman started to close it in his face. But Coyote pointed the little wand at her and said, "Let me in." She stepped away from the door and he sat down on the couch in front of the television. "Bring me a beer," he told her, and she did so. He told her to do many things during his stay, and always she obeyed him. Because he pointed the little wand at her.

Coyote returned to his old ways. Wherever he went, he pointed his little wand at his many wives and they did whatever he told them. So used to this did he become that when he went to see his wife Hummingbird, he forgot to point the wand at her. She opened the door and in he walked. "Get me a beer." She did so. "Sit in my lap." She did that too.

Hummingbird had heard from the other wives how Coyote had discovered a way to make them obey him despite their better judgment. So she toyed with his hair, and pretended to be in love with him, and got him to talking about himself. She was determined to get to the bottom of this mystery.

Pretty soon Coyote began to brag about how he had outwitted his wives. He told Hummingbird all about his wand. "Can I see it?" she asked. And when he showed it to her, she snatched it out of his hand and broke it into a thousand splinters. She threw the splinters out the window. She threw Coyote out of her house.

But Coyote went straight back to Sparrow's house, where all the trouble began, and when she opened the door he just stuck his hands in his pockets and grinned at her. He was a good-looking man, was Coyote. So Sparrow took him in. Even though he didn't have the little wand anymore, she still loved him.

But all the splinters of the broken wand were picked up, one by one, by folk who were passing by, and because they all had the same power as the wand, they caused much trouble in the world.

Coyote Decides to Live Forever

Coyote was going to and fro. He had no purpose, he was just going. He saw Bear and asked him how things were going.

"Not so good," said Bear. "These new folk" (he meant the Star People) "come in and take some land. Then there are more of them and they need more land. So they offer things no man would turn down for it. Little by little, they have taken all of my land and there is no place for me to be."

"Huh," said Coyote, and on he went. After a while he came upon Dragon and asked him how he was. Same story. "New Star People are born every day," Dragon said, "but no one ever sees them die."

"Fancy that," said Coyote. On he went. Eventually he met Bulldog, asked him the same question and got the same answer as the others. "I think they live forever," Bulldog said. "Somebody told me that they did."

On hearing this, Coyote dropped all he was doing and hurried straight to New Home, which in the native tongue was called Toronto. "People say that you never die," he said. "Is this true?"

"Yes," the Star People replied. "We have medicines for that."

"I would like some of those medicines, if you please."

"They are too valuable to give away. The likes of you could never afford them."

"Surely I have something that you need."

"We always need land," the Star People said. "But whenever we try to buy it from you, you cheat us."

Coyote and the Star People sat down to bargain. The Star People bargained hard, for they had been fooled by Coyote many, many times. In the end, he gave them New England. He gave them Mexico. He gave them San Francisco and Seattle and the Gulf Coast and New York City as well. This is why there are no Mud People in any of those places today. One by one, Coyote gave the Star People everything he owned. For he thought, "Forever is a long time. If I live forever, there'll be plenty of opportunity to trick the Star People into giving me these places back again."

So it was done. The Star People gave Coyote the medicines to live forever, and he went up and down the continent, giving them to all the Mud People who would take them. This was almost everybody, for they all wanted to live forever.

But then a strange thing happened. Everywhere the Mud People began to die. They grew sick and they withered and died. Only those few who had not taken the medicines did not grow sick. Their numbers dwindled to almost nothing.

Coyote went to see the Star People. "Your medicines were supposed to make us live forever," he said. "Instead, they make us all die."

"It is not our fault," said the Star People. "The medicines were perfectly good. How were *we* to know you didn't have triple-strand DNA?"

"You have cheated me," said Coyote. "Give me back all my lands and wealth."

But when the Star People heard this, they grew angry. "How many times did you trick us?" they said. "You stole our technology and never gave us the land for it you promised. Now the shoe is on the other foot. There are many of us, and therefore we need the land. There are few of you, and therefore you don't."

So Coyote went away, sorrowing.

Since that time, there have been very few Mud People, and they have never been wealthy again. The world they used to own belongs today to the Star People, who take better care of it than ever Coyote had. Coyote himself is still famed in stories, but he is never seen walking up and down the Earth anymore, and nobody knows if he's still alive or not.

In Fading Suns and Dying Moons

JOHN VARLEY

John Varley [www.Varley.net] lives somewhere on the west coast of the United States in a trailer. He moves around. The last address I have is in Oceano, California. Thank goodness for the internet and email. Varley is a fine and popular SF writer who came to prominence like a skyrocket in the late 1970s but has published only sporadically since 1984. His early reputation is based principally upon the innovative stories in his first story collection, The Persistence of Vision, *and his early novels,* The Ophiuchi Hotline *and* Titan. *Later collections include* The Barbie Murders and Other Stories, Picnic on Nearside, *and* Blue Champagne. *He published two novels in the 1990s,* Steel Beach *and* The Golden Globe, *and three stories in 2003, as many as he published in the whole of the 1990s, as well as a new novel,* Red Thunder. *It is great to have him back.*

"In Fading Suns and Dying Moons" is another story from Ian & Resnick's Stars. *It is in the great tradition of "universal darkness cover all" SF, like Arthur C. Clarke's "The Nine Billion Names of God," in which the purpose of life on Earth is revealed, and it ends.*

Within the memories of our lives gone by,
afraid to die, we learn to lie
and measure out the time in coffee spoons
In fading suns, and dying moons

—from "Aftertones" by Janis Ian

The first time they came through the neighborhood there really wasn't much neighborhood to speak of. Widely dispersed hydrogen molecules, only two or three per cubic meter. Traces of heavier elements from long-ago supernovas. The usual assortment of dust particles, at a density of one particle every cubic mile or so. The "dust" was mostly ammonia, methane, and water ice, with some more complex molecules like benzene. Here and there these thin ingredients were pushed into eddies by light pressure from neighboring stars.

Somehow they set forces in motion. I picture it as a Cosmic Finger stirring the mix, out in the interstellar wastes where space is really flat, in the Einsteinian sense, making a whirlpool in the unimaginable cold. Then they went away.

Four billion years later they returned. Things were brewing nicely. The space debris had congealed into a big, burning central mass and a series of rocky or gaseous globes, all sterile, in orbit around it.

They made a few adjustments and planted their seeds, and saw that it was good. They left a small observer/recorder behind, along with a thing that would call them when everything was ripe. Then they went away again.

* * *

A billion years later the timer went off, and they came back.

I had a position at the American Museum of Natural History in New York City, but of course I had not gone to work that day. I was sitting at home watching the news, as frightened as anyone else. Martial law had been declared a few hours earlier. Things had been getting chaotic. I'd heard gunfire from the streets outside.

Someone pounded on my door.

"United States Army!" someone shouted. "Open the door immediately!"

I went to the door, which had four locks on it.

"How do I know you're not a looter?" I shouted.

"Sir, I am authorized to break your door down. Open the door, or stand clear."

I put my eye to the old-fashioned peephole. They were certainly dressed like soldiers. One of them raised his rifle and slammed the butt down on my doorknob. I shouted that I would let them in, and in a few seconds I had all the locks open. Six men in full combat gear hustled into my kitchen. They split up and quickly explored all three rooms of the apartment, shouting out, "All clear!" in brisk, military voices. One man, a bit older than the rest, stood facing me with a clipboard in his hand.

"Sir, are you Doctor Andrew Richard Lewis?"

"There's been some mistake," I said. "I'm not a medical doctor."

"Sir, are you Doctor—"

"Yes, yes. I'm Andy Lewis. What can I do for you?"

"Sir, I am Captain Edgar and I am ordered to induct you into the United States Army Special Invasion Corps effective immediately, at the rank of Second Lieutenant. Please raise your right hand and repeat after me."

I knew from the news that this was now legal, and I had the choice of enlisting or facing a long prison term. I raised my hand and in no time at all I was a soldier.

"Lieutenant, your orders are to come with me. You have fifteen minutes to pack what essentials you may need, such as prescription medicine and personal items. My men will help you assemble your gear."

I nodded, not trusting myself to speak.

"You may bring any items relating to your specialty. Laptop computer, reference books . . ." He paused, apparently unable to imagine what a man like me would want to bring along to do battle with space aliens.

"Captain, do you know what my specialty is?"

"My understanding is that you are a bug specialist."

"An entomologist, Captain. Not an exterminator. Could you give me . . . any clue as to why I'm needed?"

For the first time he looked less than totally self-assured.

"Lieutenant, all I know is . . . they're collecting butterflies."

They hustled me to a helicopter. We flew low over Manhattan. Every street was gridlocked. All the bridges were completely jammed with mostly abandoned cars.

I was taken to an air base in New Jersey and hurried onto a military jet transport that stood idling on the runway. There were a few others already on board. I knew most of them; entomology is not a crowded field.

The plane took off at once.

There was a colonel aboard whose job was to brief us on our mission, and on what was thus far known about the aliens: not much was really known that I hadn't already seen on television.

They had appeared simultaneously on seacoasts worldwide. One moment there was nothing, the next moment there was a line of aliens as far as the eye could see. In the western hemisphere the line stretched from Point Barrow in Alaska to Tierra del Fuego in Chile. Africa was lined from Tunis to the Cape of Good Hope. So were the western shores of Europe, from Norway to Gibraltar. Australia, Japan, Sri Lanka, the Philippines, and every other island thus far contacted reported the same thing: a solid line of aliens appearing in the west, moving east.

Aliens? No one knew what else to call them. They were clearly not of Planet Earth, though if you ran into a single one, there would be little reason to think them very odd. Just millions and millions of perfectly ordinary people dressed in white coveralls, blue baseball caps, and brown boots, within arm's reach of each other.

Walking slowly toward the east.

Within a few hours of their appearance someone on the news had started calling it the Line, and the creatures who were in it Linemen. From the pictures on the television they appeared rather average and androgynous.

"They're not human," the colonel said. "Those coveralls, it looks like they don't come off. The hats, either. You get close enough, you can see it's all part of their skin."

"Protective coloration," said Watkins, a colleague of mine from the Museum. "Many insects adapt colors or shapes to blend with their environment."

"But what's the point of blending in," I asked, "if you are made so conspicuous by your actions?"

"Perhaps the 'fitting in' is simply to look more like us. It seems unlikely, doesn't it, that evolution would have made them look like . . ."

"Janitors," somebody piped up.

The colonel was frowning at us.

"You think they're insects?"

"Not by any definition I've ever heard," Watkins said. "Of course, other animals adapt to their surroundings, too. Arctic foxes in winter coats, tigers with their stripes. Chameleons."

The colonel mulled this for a moment, then resumed his pacing.

"Whatever they are, bullets don't bother them. There have been many instances of civilians shooting at the aliens."

Soldiers, too, I thought. I'd seen film of it on television, a National Guard unit in Oregon cutting loose with their rifles. The aliens hadn't reacted at all, not visibly . . . until all the troops and all their weapons just vanished, without the least bit of fuss.

And the Line moved on.

We landed at a disused-looking airstrip somewhere in northern California. We were taken to a big motel, which the

Army had taken over. In no time I was hustled aboard a large Coast Guard helicopter with a group of soldiers—a squad? a platoon?—led by a young lieutenant who looked even more terrified than I felt. On the way to the Line I learned that his name was Evans, and that he was in the National Guard.

It had been made clear to me that I was in charge of the overall mission and Evans was in charge of the soldiers. Evans said his orders were to protect me. How he was to protect me from aliens who were immune to his weapons hadn't been spelled out.

My own orders were equally vague. I was to land close behind the Line, catch up, and find out everything I could.

"They speak better English than I do," the colonel had said. "We must know their intentions. Above all, you must find out why they're collecting . . ." and here his composure almost broke down, but he took a deep breath and steadied himself.

"Collecting butterflies," he finished.

We passed over the Line at a few hundred feet. Directly below us individual aliens could be made out, blue hats and white shoulders. But off to the north and south it quickly blurred into a solid white line vanishing in the distance, as if one of those devices that make chalk lines on football fields had gone mad.

Evans and I watched it. None of the Linemen looked up at the noise. They were walking slowly, all of them, never getting more than a few feet apart. The terrain was grassy, rolling hills, dotted here and there with clumps of trees. No man-made structures were in sight.

The pilot put us down a hundred yards behind the Line.

"I want you to keep your men at least fifty yards away from me," I told Evans. "Are those guns loaded? Do they have those safety things on them? Good. Please keep them on. I'm almost as afraid of being shot by one of those guys as I am of . . . whatever they are."

And I started off, alone, toward the Line.

* * *

How does one address a line of marching alien creatures? *Take me to your leader* seemed a bit peremptory. *Hey, bro, what's happening . . .* perhaps overly familiar. In the end, after following for fifteen minutes at a distance of about ten yards, I had settled on *Excuse me*, so I moved closer and cleared my throat. Turns out that was enough. One of the Linemen stopped walking and turned to me.

This close, one could see that his features were rudimentary. His head was like a mannequin, or a wig stand: a nose, hollows for eyes, bulges for cheeks. All the rest seemed to be painted on.

I could only stand there idiotically for a moment. I noticed a peculiar thing. There was no gap in the Line.

I suddenly remembered why it was me and not some diplomat standing there.

"Why are you collecting butterflies?" I asked.

"Why not?" he said, and I figured it was going to be a long, long day. "*You* should have no trouble understanding," he said. "Butterflies are the most beautiful things on your planet, aren't they?"

"I've always thought so." Wondering, *did he know I was a lepidopterist?*

"Then there you are." Now he began to move. The Line was about twenty yards away, and through our whole conversation he never let it get more distant than that. We walked at a leisurely one mile per hour.

Okay, I told myself. Try to keep it to butterflies. Leave it to the military types to get to the tough questions: *When do you start kidnapping our children, raping our women, and frying us for lunch?*

"What are you doing with them?"

"Harvesting them." He extended a hand toward the Line, and as if summoned, a lovely specimen of *Adelpha bredowii* fluttered toward him. He did something with his fingers and a pale blue sphere formed around the butterfly.

"Isn't it lovely?" he asked, and I moved in for a closer look. He seemed to treasure these wonderful creatures I'd spent my life studying.

He made another gesture, and the blue ball with the *Adelpha* disappeared. "What happens to them?" I asked him.

"There is a collector," he said.

"A lepidopterist?"

"No, it's a storage device. You can't see it because it is . . . off to one side."

Off to one side of what? I wondered, but didn't ask.

"And what happens to them in the collector?"

"They are put in storage in a place where . . . time does not move. Where time does not pass. Where they do not move through time as they do here." He paused for a few seconds. "It is difficult to explain."

"Off to one side?" I suggested.

"Exactly. Excellent. Off to one side of time. You've got it."

I had nothing, actually. But I plowed on.

"What will become of them?"

"We are building a . . . place. Our leader wishes it to be a very special place. Therefore, we are making it of these beautiful creatures."

"Of butterfly wings?"

"They will not be harmed. We know ways of making . . . walls in a manner that will allow them to fly freely."

I wished someone had given me a list of questions.

"How did you get here? How long will you stay?"

"A certain . . . length of time, not a great length by your standards."

"What about your standards?"

"By our standards . . . no time at all. As to how we got here . . . have you read a book entitled *Flatland*?"

"I'm afraid not."

"Pity," he said, and turned away, and vanished.

Our operation in Northern California was not the only group trying desperately to find out more about the Linemen, of course. There were Lines on every continent, and soon they would be present in every nation. They had covered many small Pacific islands in only a day, and when they reached the Eastern shores, they simply vanished, as my guide had.

News media were doing their best to pool information. I

believe I got a lot of those facts before the general population, since I had been shanghaied into the forefront, but our information was often as garbled and inaccurate as what the rest of the world was getting. The military was scrambling around in the dark, just like everyone else.

But we learned some things:

They were collecting moths as well as butterflies, from the drabbest specimen to the most gloriously colored. The entire order Lepidoptera.

They could appear and vanish at will. It was impossible to get a count of them. Wherever one stopped to commune with the natives, as mine had, the Line remained solid, with no gaps. When they were through talking to you, they simply went where the Cheshire Cat went, leaving behind not even a grin.

Wherever they appeared, they spoke the local language, fluently and idiomatically. This was true even in isolated villages in China or Turkey or Nigeria, where some dialects were used by only a few hundred people.

They didn't seem to weigh anything at all. Moving through forests, the Line became more of a wall, Linemen appearing in literally every tree, on every limb, walking on branches obviously too thin to bear their weight and not even causing them to bend. When the tree had been combed for butterflies, the crews vanished, and appeared in another tree.

Walls meant nothing to them. In cities and towns nothing was missed, not even closed bank vaults, attic spaces, closets. They didn't come through the door, they simply appeared in a room and searched it. If you were on the toilet, that was just too bad.

Any time they were asked about where they came from, they mentioned that book, *Flatland*. Within hours the book was available on hundreds of Web sites. Downloads ran to the millions.

The full title of the book was *Flatland: A Romance of Many Dimensions*. It was supposedly written by one Mr. A. Square, a resident of Flatland, but its actual author was Edwin Abbott, a nineteenth century cleric and amateur mathematician. A copy was waiting for me when we got back to camp after that first frustrating day.

The book is an allegory and a satire, but also an ingenious way to explain the concept of multidimensional worlds to the layman, like me. Mr. Square lives in a world of only two dimensions. For him, there is no such thing as up or down, only forward, backward, and side to side. It is impossible for us to really *see* from Square's point of view: A single line that extends all around him, with nothing above it or below it. *Nothing*. Not empty space, not a black or white void . . . nothing.

But humans being three-dimensional, can stand outside Flatland, look up or down at it, see its inhabitants from an angle they can never have. In fact, we could see *inside* them, examine their internal organs, reach down and touch a Flatlander's heart or brain with our fingers.

In the course of the book Mr. Square is visited by a being from the third dimension, a Sphere. He can move from one place to another without apparently traversing the space between point A and point B. There was also discussion of the possibilities of even higher dimensions, worlds as inscrutable to us as the 3-D world was to Mr. Square.

I'm no mathematician, but it didn't take an Einstein to infer that the Line, and the Linemen, came from one of those theoretical higher planes.

The people running the show were not Einstein either, but when they needed expertise they knew where to go to draft it.

Our mathematician's name was Larry Ward. He looked as baffled as I must have looked the day before and he got no more time to adjust to his new situation than I did. We were all hustled aboard another helicopter and hurried out to the Line. I filled him in, as best I could, on the way out.

Again, as soon as we approached the Line, a spokesman appeared. He asked us if we'd read the book, though I suspect he already knew we had. It was a creepy feeling to realize he, or something like him, could have been standing . . . or existing, in some direction I couldn't imagine, only inches away from me in my motel bedroom, looking at me read the book just as the Sphere looked down on Mr. A. Square.

A flat, white plane appeared in the air between us and geometrical shapes and equations began drawing themselves on it. It just hung there, unsupported. Larry wasn't too flustered by it, nor was I. Against the background of the Line an antigravity blackboard seemed almost mundane.

The Lineman began talking to Larry, and I caught maybe one word in three. Larry seemed to have little trouble with it at first, but after an hour he was sweating, frowning, clearly getting out of his depth.

By that time I was feeling quite superfluous, and it was even worse for Lieutenant Evans and his men. We were reduced to following Larry and the Line at its glacial but relentless pace. Some of the men took to slipping between the gaps in the Line to get in front, then doing all sorts of stupid antics to get a reaction, like tourists trying to rattle the guards at the Tower of London. The Linemen took absolutely no notice. Evans didn't seem to care. I suspected he was badly hung over.

"Look at this, Doctor Lewis."

I turned around and saw that a Lineman had appeared behind me, in that disconcerting way they had. He had a pale blue sphere cupped in his hands, and in it was a lovely specimen of *Papilio zelicaon*, the Anise Swallowtail, with one blue wing and one orange wing.

"A gynandromorph," I said, immediately, with the spooky feeling that I was back in the lecture hall. "An anomaly that sometimes arises during gametogenesis. One side is male and the other is female."

"How extraordinary. Our . . . leader will be happy to have this creature existing in his . . . palace."

I had no idea how far to believe him. I had been told that at least a dozen motives had been put forward by Line spokesmen, to various exploratory groups, as the rationale for the butterfly harvest. A group in Mexico had been told some substance was to be extracted—harmlessly, so they said—from the specimens. In France, a lepidopterist swore a

Lineman told her the captives were to be given to fourth-dimension children, as pets. It didn't seem all the stories could be true. Or maybe they could. Step One in dealing with the Linemen was to bear in mind that *our* minds could not contain many concepts that, to them, were as basic as *up* and *down* to us. We had to assume they were speaking baby talk to us.

But for an hour we talked butterflies, as Larry got more and more bogged down in a sea of equations and the troops got progressively more bored. The creature knew the names of every Lepidopteran we encountered that afternoon, something I could not claim. That fact had never made me feel inadequate before. There were around 170,000 species of moth and butterfly so far cataloged, including several thousand in dispute. Nobody could be expected to know them all . . . but I was sure the Linemen did. Remember, every book in every library was available to them, and they did not have to open them to read them. And time, which I had been told was the fourth dimension but now learned was only *a* fourth dimension, almost surely did not pass for them in the same way as it passed for us. Larry told me later that a billion years was not a formidable . . . distance for them. They were masters of space, masters of time, and who knew what else?

The only emotion any of them had ever expressed was delight at the beauty of the butterflies. They showed no anger or annoyance when shot at with rifles; the bullets went through them harmlessly. Even when assaulted with bombs or artillery rounds they didn't register any emotion, they simply made the assailants and weapons disappear. It was surmised by those in charge, whoever they were, that these big, noisy displays were dealt with only because they harmed butterflies.

The troops had been warned, but there's always some clown . . .

So when an *Antheraea polyphemus* fluttered into the air in front of a private named Paulson, he reached out and grabbed it in his fist. Or tried to; while his hand was still an inch away, he vanished.

I don't think any of us quite credited our senses at first. I didn't, and I'd been looking right at him, wondering if I should say something. There was nothing but the Polyphemus moth fluttering in the sunshine. But soon enough there were angry shouts. Many of the soldiers unslung their rifles and pointed them at the Line.

Evans was frantically shouting at them, but now they were angry and frustrated. Several rounds were fired. Larry and I hit the deck as a machine gun started chattering. Looking up carefully, I saw Evans punch the machine gunner and grab the weapon. The firing stopped.

There was a moment of stunned silence. I got to my knees and looked at the Line. Larry was okay, but the "blackboard" was gone. And the Line moved placidly on.

I thought it was all over, and then the screaming began, close behind me. I nearly wet myself and turned around quickly.

Paulson was behind me, on his knees, hands pressed to his face, screaming his lungs out. But he was changed. His hair was all white and he'd grown a white beard. He looked thirty years older, maybe forty. I knelt beside him, unsure what to do. His eyes were full of madness . . . and the name patch sewn on the front of his shirt now read:

ИOƧJUAꟼ

"They reversed him," Larry said.

He couldn't stop pacing. Myself, I'd settled into a fatalistic calm. In the face of what the Linemen could do, it seemed pointless to worry much. If I did something to piss them off, *then* I'd worry.

Our Northern California headquarters had completely filled the big Holiday Inn. The Army had taken over the whole thing, this bizarre operation gradually getting the encrustation of barnacles any government operation soon acquires, literally hundreds of people bustling about as if they had something important to do. For the life of me, I couldn't see how any of us were needed, except for Larry and a helicopter pilot to get him to the Line and back. It seemed obvious that any answers we got would come from him, or someone like him. They certainly wouldn't come from the troops, the tanks, the nuclear missiles I'm sure were targeted on the Line, and certainly not from me. But they kept me on, probably because they hadn't yet evolved a procedure to send anybody home. I didn't mind. I could be terrified here just as well as in New York. In the meantime, I was bunking with Larry . . . who now reached into his pocket and produced a penny. He looked at it, and tossed it to me.

"I grabbed that when they were going through his pockets," he said. I looked at it. As I expected, Lincoln was looking to the left and all the inscriptions were reversed.

"How can they do that?" I asked.

He looked confused for a moment, then grabbed a sheet of motel stationery and attacked it with one of the pens in his pocket. I looked over his shoulder as he made a sketch of a man, writing L by one hand and R by the other. Then he folded the sheet without creasing it, touching the stick figure to the opposite surface.

"Flatland doesn't have to be flat," he said. He traced the stick man onto the new surface, and I saw it was now reversed. "Flatlanders can move through the third dimension without knowing they're doing it. They slide around this curve in their universe. Or, a third-dimensional being can lift them up *here*, and set them down *here*. They've moved, without traveling the distance between the two points."

We both studied the drawing solemnly for a moment.

"How is Paulson?" I asked.

"Catatonic. Reversed. He's left-handed now, his appendectomy scar is on the left, the tattoo on his left shoulder is on the right now."

"He looked older."

"Who can say? Some are saying he was scared gray. I'm pretty sure he saw things the human eye just isn't meant to see . . . but I think he's actually older, too. The doctors are still looking him over. It wouldn't be hard for a fourth-dimensional creature to do, age him many years in seconds."

"But why?"

"They didn't hire me to find out 'why.' I'm having enough

trouble understanding the 'how.' I figure the why is your department." He looked at me, but I didn't have anything helpful to offer. But I had a question.

"How is it they're shaped like men?"

"Coincidence?" he said, and shook his head. "I don't even know if 'they' is the right pronoun. There might be just one of them, and I don't think it looks *anything* like us." He saw my confusion, and groped again for an explanation. He picked up another piece of paper, set it on the desk, drew a square on it, put the fingertips of his hand to the paper.

"A Flatlander, Mr. Square, perceives this as five separate entities. See, I can surround him with what he'd see as five circles. Now, imagine my hand moving down, *through* the plane of the paper. Four circles soon join together into an elliptical shape, then the fifth one joins, too, and he sees a cross section of my wrist: another circle. Now extend that . . ." He looked thoughtful, then pulled a comb from his back pocket and touched the teeth to the paper surface.

"The comb moves through the plane, and each tooth becomes a little circle. I draw the comb through Flatland, Mr. Square sees a row of circles coming toward him."

It was making my head hurt, but I thought I grasped it.

"So they . . . or it, or whatever, is combing the planet . . ."

"Combing out all the butterflies. Like a fine-tooth comb going through hair, pulling out . . . whaddayou call 'em . . . lice eggs . . ."

"Nits." I realized I was scratching my head. I stopped. "But these aren't circles, they're solid, they look like people . . ."

"If they're solid, why don't they break tree branches when they go out on them?" He grabbed the goosenecked lamp on the desk and pointed the light at the wall. Then he laced his hands together. "You see it? On the wall? This isn't the best light . . ."

Then I did see it. He was making a shadow image of a flying bird. Larry was on a roll; he whipped a grease pencil from his pocket and drew a square on the beige wall above the desk. He made the shadow-bird again.

"Mr. Square sees a pretty complex shape. But he doesn't

know the half of it. Look at my hands. Just my hands. Do you see a bird?"

"No," I admitted.

"That's because only one of many possible cross sections resembles a bird." He made a dog's head, and a monkey. He'd done this before, probably in a lecture hall.

"What I'm saying, whatever it's using, hands, fingers, whatever shapes its actual body can assume in four-space, all we'd ever see is a three-dimensional cross section of it."

"And that cross section looks like a man?"

"Could be." But his hands were on his hips now, regarding the square he'd drawn on the wall. "How can I be sure? I can't. The guys running this show, they want answers, and all we can offer them is possibilities."

By the end of the next day, he couldn't even offer them that.

I could see he was having tough sledding right from the first. The floating blackboard covered itself with equations again, and the . . . Instructor? Tutor? Translator? . . . stood patiently beside it, waiting for Larry to get it. And, increasingly, he was not.

The troops had been kept back, almost a quarter mile behind the Line. They were on their best behavior, as that day there was some brass with them. I could see them back there, holding binoculars, a few generals and admirals and such.

Since no one had told me to do differently, I stayed up at the Line near Larry. I wasn't sure why. I was no longer very afraid of the Linemen, though the camp had been awash in awful rumors that morning. It was said that Paulson was not the first man to be returned in a reversed state, but it had been hushed up to prevent panic. I could believe it. The initial panics and riots had died down quite a bit, we'd been told, but millions around the globe were still fleeing before the advancing Line. In some places around the globe, feeding these migrant masses was getting to be a problem. And in some places, the moving mob had solved the problem by looting every town they passed through.

Some said that Paulson was not the worst that could happen. It was whispered that men had been "vanished" by the

Line and returned everted. Turned inside out. And still alive, though not for long. . . .

Larry wouldn't deny it was possible.

But today Larry wasn't saying much of anything. I watched him for a while, sweating in the sun, writing on the blackboard with a grease pencil, wiping it out, writing again, watching the Lineman patiently writing new stuff in symbols that might as well have been Swahili.

Then I remembered I had thought of something to ask the night before, lying there listening to Larry snoring in the other king-size bed.

"Excuse me," I said, and instantly a Lineman was standing beside me. The same one? I knew the question had little meaning.

"Before, I asked, 'Why butterflies?' You said because they are beautiful."

"The most beautiful things on your planet," he corrected.

"Right. But . . . isn't there a second best? Isn't there anything else, anything at all, that you're interested in?" I floundered, trying to think of something else that might be worth collecting to an aesthetic sense I could not possibly imagine. "Scarab beetles," I said, sticking to entomology. "Some of them are fabulously beautiful, to humans anyway."

"They are quite beautiful," he agreed. "However, we do not collect them. Our reasons would be difficult to explain." A diplomatic way of saying humans were blind, deaf, and ignorant, I supposed. "But yes, in a sense. Things are grown on other planets in this solar system, too. We are harvesting them now, in a temporal way of speaking."

Well, this was new. Maybe I could justify my presence here in some small way after all. Maybe I'd finally asked an intelligent question.

"Can you tell me about them?"

"Certainly. Deep in the atmospheres of your four gas giant planets, Jupiter, Saturn, Uranus, and Neptune, beautiful beings have evolved that . . . our leader treasures. On Mercury, creatures of quicksilver inhabit deep caves near the poles. These are being gathered as well. And there are lifeforms we admire that thrive on very cold planets."

Gathering cryogenic butterflies on Pluto? Since he showed me no visual aids, the image would do until something better came along.

The Lineman didn't elaborate beyond that, and I couldn't think of another question that might be useful. I reported what I had learned at the end of the day. None of the team of expert analysts could think of a reason why this should concern us, but they assured me my findings would be bucked up the chain of command.

Nothing ever came of it.

The next day they said I could go home, and I was hustled out of California almost as fast as I'd arrived. On my way I met Larry, who looked haunted. We shook hands.

"Funny thing," he said. "All our answers, over thousands of years. Myths, gods, philosophers . . . What's it all about? Why are we here? Where do we come from, where do we go, what are we supposed to do while we're here? What's the meaning of life? So now we find out, and it was never about us at all. The meaning of life is . . . butterflies." He gave me a lopsided grin. "But you knew that all along, didn't you?"

Of all the people on the planet, I and a handful of others could make the case that we were most directly affected. Sure, lives were uprooted, many people died before order was restored. But the Linemen were as unobtrusive as they could possibly be, given their mind-numbing task, and things eventually got back to a semblance of normalcy. Some people lost their religious faith, but even more rejected out of hand the proposition that there was no God but the Line, so the holy men of the world registered a net gain.

But lepidopterists . . . let's face it, we were out of a job.

I spent my days haunting the dusty back rooms and narrow corridors of the museum, opening cases and drawers, some of which might not have been disturbed for decades. I would stare for hours at the thousands and thousands of preserved moths and butterflies, trying to connect with the childhood fascination that had led to my choice of career. I remembered expeditions to remote corners of the world, miserable, mosquito-bitten, and exhilarated at the same time. I recalled conversations, arguments about this or that taxonomic point. I tried to relive my elation at my first new species, *Hypolimnes lewisii*.

All ashes now. They didn't even look very pretty anymore.

On the twenty-eighth day of the invasion, a second Line appeared on the world's western coasts. By then the North American Line stretched from a point far in the Canadian north through Saskatchewan, Montana, Wyoming, Colorado, and New Mexico, reaching the Gulf of Mexico somewhere south of Corpus Christi, Texas. The second Line began marching east, finding very few butterflies but not seeming to mind.

It is not in the nature of the governmental mind to simply do nothing when faced with a situation. But most people agreed there was little or nothing to be done. To save face, the military maintained a presence following the Line, but they knew better than to do anything.

On the fifty-sixth day the third Line appeared.

Lunar cycle? It appeared so. A famous mathematician claimed he had found an equation describing the Earth-Moon orbital pair in six dimensions, or was it seven? No one cared very much.

When the first Line reached New York, I was in the specimen halls, looking at moths under glass. A handful of Linemen appeared, took a quick look around. One looked over my shoulder at the displays for a moment. Then they all went away, in their multidimensional way.

And there it is.

I don't recall who it was that first suggested we write it all down, nor can I recall the reason put forward. Like most literate people of the Earth, though, I dutifully sat down and wrote my story. I understand many are writing entire biographies, possibly an attempt to shout out *"I was here!"* to an indifferent universe. I have limited myself to events from Day One to the present.

Perhaps someone else will come by, some distant day, and read these accounts. Yes, and perhaps the Moon is made of green butterflies.

It turned out that my question, that last day of my military career, was the key question, but I didn't realize I had been given the answer.

The Lineman never said they were growing creatures on Pluto.

He said there were things they grew on cold planets.

After one year of combing the Earth, the Linemen went away as quickly as they appeared.

On the way out, they switched off the light.

It was night in New York. From the other side of the planet the reports came in quickly, and I climbed up to the roof of my building. The moon, which should have been nearing full phase, was a pale ghost and soon became nothing but a black hole in the sky.

Another tenant had brought a small TV. An obviously frightened astronomer and a confused news anchor were counting seconds. When they reached zero, a bit over twenty minutes after the events at the antipodes, Mars began to dim. In thirty seconds it was invisible.

He never mentioned Pluto as their cold-planet nursery. . . .

In an hour and a half Jupiter's light failed, then Saturn.

When the sun came up in America that day, it looked like a charcoal briquette, red flickerings here and there, and soon not even that. When the clocks and church bells struck noon, the Sun was gone.

Presently, it began to get cold.

Castaway

GENE WOLFE

Gene Wolfe (tribute site: http://www.op.net/~pduggan/ wolfe.html and www.ultan.co.uk/) lives in Barrington, Illinois. Some people consider him among the greatest living American writers, an opinion printed more than once in the Washington Post Book World, *a leading literary newspaper. We concur. His four volume Book of the New Sun is an acknowledged masterpiece. His most recent book is* The Knight, *the first half of a huge fantasy meganovel,* The Wizard Knight. *The second half,* The Wizard, *is forthcoming. His previous SF novel was* Return to the Whorl, *the third volume of* The Book of the Short Sun *(really a single huge novel), which many of his most attentive readers feel is his best book yet. Collections of his short fiction include* The Island of Dr. Death and Other Stories and Other Stories, Storeys from the Old Hotel, Endangered Species, *and* Strange Travelers.

"Castaway" was published electronically by SciFiction, and this is perhaps its first time in print. It is a short, compressed SF allegory, in which a castaway in the distant future, stranded on an isolated planet that is itself dying, relates his melancholy recollections of his years there and his relation with the spirit of the place. Ironically, his memories are full of music and color, and his rescue ship sterile and mechanical.

We picked him up on some dead world nobody ever goes to. We did it because we had a field problem that required a lot of tests, and that stuff is easier if you can just dodge in and out of the ship without worrying about the airlocks and how much air you're dumping every time you go outside. Bad as this place was, you could breathe—the air turned out to be real good, in fact—so we set down in a warm belt around the middle.

Warm's one of those words, you know? It was still cold enough for hightherms, and even with hightherms I blew on my fingers a lot. The sun was red and real close, but there didn't seem to be a lot of heat in it.

Anyway, he had been there twenty-seven years, he said, and I said, standard years or world years, and he said, they were so close it didn't make any difference. World years were half an hour shorter now, he said, and I should've asked why now—had they been longer a while back? Only I didn't think of it right then.

"We got hit by the Atrothers," he said; so it had been back during the war all right, back before I was born. "We tried to get home, but we could see we couldn't make it. This place was close, and we landed here."

We're not there anymore, I told him, we took off. Well, that shut him up for the rest of the week. So next time I tried not to say things like that. I know they had him up to Debriefing three times. So you know they never got much out of him, didn't get what they wanted, or they wouldn't have talked to him so much. Somebody said his mind was blown, and I guess that was sort of right.

Only he used to open up to me sometimes in the break area, and that's what I want to tell about. Then maybe I can stop thinking about him.

"There were only three of us," he said, "and Obert died the first year and Yarmouth the second year. I thought we were dying off one by one, and I'd go next year if nobody came. But I didn't. We'd hung up the distress buoy. It didn't do a bit of good, but I stayed tough."

He looked at me then like I wanted to argue. I just said, sure.

"The rations ran out," he said. "I had to eat whatever I could find. There's still a few plants. They're not good, but you can eat them if you boil them long enough and keep changing the water."

I said you were there all alone, huh? It must've been double duty.

Of course that shut him up again, but next day he came in about ten minutes after I got off shift. He sat down right where he'd sat before. All the tables are white and so are the chairs, so it doesn't make any difference where you sit, it's all the same. Only he knew somehow, and that's where he sat. I carried my caff over and sat down across from him and waited.

About ten minutes after that he said, "There was a woman. A woman was there with me. I wasn't alone. No. Not really. Not with her there."

I said you should have told us. We'd have taken her off, too.

He just shook his head.

Later he said it was too late for her. "She's old," he said. "Old and ugly, and she can't think any more. She tries to think of new things, but nothing comes. Nothing works now, and sometimes she can't think at all. She told me. You've got a good medpod. That's what they say."

I guess I nodded.

"I've been spending a lot of time in there. Maybe it's helping. I don't know. But it wouldn't help her."

Then he reached over and grabbed my wrist—his hand

was like a vise. "We could have saved her. Earlier. We could have made her young again. We could have taken her away. We could have done it. Nothing stopping us."

Next day he wouldn't talk at all, or the day after that either. I guess I should have just let him alone, but I was sick of talking to the other guys in the crew. I'd been talking to them ever since I signed on, and I knew what they were going to say and the games they wanted to play and what all their jokes were.

So I tried to figure out a way to get him going again. Everybody likes to brag, right? Especially when you can't check up on them. The next time he was in the break room, I sat down next to him and said tell me some more about this woman that was dirtside with you. I guess you got plenty, huh?

He just looked at me for maybe two minutes. I knew he was talking in his head. He'd been alone for so long. I ran into a guy once who had tended a navigation beacon way out on the Rim for ten years. You do that, and the severance pay's a fortune. Go in at thirty—you've got to be at least thirty—and come out at forty, rich for life. What they don't tell you is that most of them go crazy. Anyway, he said you get to talking to yourself. When they finally pull you out, you try to stop and you don't talk to anybody, just in your head. You haven't talked to anybody for so long that talking out loud is the same as talking to yourself, as far as you're concerned.

Finally he said, "She was old. Terribly old and dying. I thought I told you."

I said, yeah, I guess you did.

"Millions and millions of years old, and used to think she'd never die. But it was all over for her, and she knew it. We never wanted to help her. We never wanted to save her, and now we couldn't if we wanted to. It's too late. Too late . . ."

After that he started to cry. I listened to it and sort of tapped his shoulder and talked to him for as long as it took to finish my caff. But he didn't say anything else that day.

The next day he sort of motioned to me to come over and sit with him. He'd never done that before. So I did.

"She could make pictures in your head." He was whispering. "Show you things. Did I tell you about that?"

He never had, and I said so.

"They're trying to make me forget the leaves. Billions and billions of leaves, all sizes and shapes and shades of green, and the rising sun turning them gold. Sometimes the bottom was a different color, and when the wind blew the whole tree would change."

I wanted to ask what a tree was, but I figured I could just look it up and kept quiet.

"She used to show me birds, too. Wonderful birds. Some that could sleep while they flew. Some that sang and flew at the same time. All kinds of colors and all kinds of shapes. You know what a bird is?"

Naturally I said I didn't.

"It's a kind of flying animal. Some of them made music. A lot of the little ones did. Singing, you know, only they sounded more like flutes. It was beautiful!"

I said, did they know "Going to Bunk with You Tonight," because that's my favorite song. He said they didn't play our music, they played their own, and he sang some of it for me, looking like he was going to kiss somebody. I didn't like it much, but I pretended I did. I wanted to know how she had showed him all this and made him hear it, because I think it would be really nice if I could do that, and useful, too. He said he didn't know, and after that he was pretty quiet 'til I'd finished my caff.

Then he said, "You know how a man puts part of himself into a woman?"

I said sure.

"It's like that, only in the brain. She puts part of herself into your brain."

Naturally I laughed, and I said was it as good for you as it was for her, and did you feel the ship jump?

And he said, "It wasn't good for her at all, but it was wonderful for me, even the time I watched the last bird die."

There was a lot of other stuff, too, some of it happy and some really, really sad. I will remember it, but I don't think you would want to hear about all of it. Finally he told me how sick she had been, and how he had sat beside her night after night. He would pick up her hand and hold it, and try to think of something he could say that would make her feel better, only he could never think of anything and every time he tried it was just so dumb he made himself shut up. He would hold her hand, like I said up there, and sort of stroke it, and after a while it would melt away and he would have to look for it and pick it up all over. I didn't understand that at all. I still don't.

But finally he thought of something he could say that didn't make him feel worse, and he thought maybe it had even made her feel better, a little. He said, "I love you." It seemed like it worked, he said, and so he said it again and again.

And that is all I remember about him except for when we set down and he left the ship. Only I want to say this. I know he was crazy, and if you read this and want to tell me I was crazy too to hang out with him in the break area like I did for so long, that's all right. I knew he was crazy, but he was somebody new and it was kind of fun to pull it out of him like I did and see what he would say.

Besides, he was a lot older than I am and his face had all these lines because of being down there so long and practically starving, so he was fun to look at, and the other thing was the color. The ship is all white, the walls and ceilings and floor and everything else. That makes it easy to spot fluid leaks and sometimes shorts that start little fires someplace. But all that white and the white uniforms and so on seem like they just suck the color out of everything except blood.

Only it never sucked the color out of him, and that made him special to me. Nice to look at, and fun, too. I remember seeing him walking along Corridor A the last time. He was headed for the lock and going out, and I knew it from the old, old dress blues and the little bag in his hand. And I thought, oh shit, that's the last color we had and now he's going and this really licks.

And it did, too.

So I ran and said goodbye and how much I was going to miss him and called him Mate and all that. You know. And he was nice and we talked a little bit more, just standing there in Corridor A.

Of course I put my elbow in it, the way I always did sooner or later. I said about the woman that had been dirtside with him, was she still alive when we took him off, because he'd said how sick she was, and I thought he wouldn't go off and leave her.

He sort of smiled. I never had seen a smile like that before, and I don't ever want to see another one. "She was and she wasn't," he said. "There were things inside her, eating the corpse. Does that count?"

I said no, of course not, for it to count they would have to have been part of her.

"They were," he said, and that was the real end of it.

Only he turned to go, and I wanted to walk with him at least 'til he got to the lock. Which I did. And talking to himself I heard him say, "She had been so beautiful. Just so damned beautiful."

All right, his mind had blown, like everybody says. But sometimes I can almost see him again when I'm in my bunk and just about asleep. He smiles, and there's somebody standing behind him, but I can't quite see her.

Not ever.

The Hydrogen Wall

GREGORY BENFORD

Gregory Benford [www.authorcafe.com/benford] is a plasma physicist and astrophysicist, and one of the leading SF writers of the last twenty-five years. He is a science columnist for Fantasy & Science Fiction, *and in 1999 published his first popular science book,* Deep Time. *One of the chief spokesmen of hard SF of the last three decades, Benford is articulate and contentious, and he has produced some of the best fiction of recent decades about scientists working (including some unpleasant realism) and about the riveting and astonishing concepts of cosmology and the nature of the universe. Among his many awards is the 1990 United Nations Medal in Literature. His most famous novel is* Timescape *(1980), his most recent,* Beyond Infinity *(2004). Many of his (typically hard) SF stories are collected in* In Alien Flesh *(1986) and* Matters End *(1995).*

"The Hydrogen Wall" was published in Asimov's, *which had another strong year, although some of its thunder (and its best writers) have occasionally been lured away to the high-paying electronic competition. It often seems to amuse Benford to portray something politically offensive, perhaps to evoke outrage and argument, or perhaps to weed out those who aren't there for the hard SF. Whatever the purpose, it is certainly the case in this story.*

—for Fred Lerner

Hidden wisdom and hidden treasure—of what use is either?

—Ecclesiasticus 20:30

"Your ambition?" The Prefect raised an eyebrow.

She had not expected such a question. "To, uh, translate. To learn." It sounded lame to her ears, and his disdainful scowl showed that he had expected some such rattled response. Very well then, be more assertive. "Particularly, if I may, from the Sagittarius Architecture."

This took the Prefect's angular face by surprise, though he quickly covered by pursing his leathery mouth. "That is an ancient problem. Surely you do not expect that a Trainee could make headway in such a classically difficult challenge."

"I might," she shot back crisply. "Precisely because it's so well documented."

"Centuries of well-marshalled inquiry have told us very little of the Sagittarius Architecture. It is a specimen from the highest order of Sentient Information, and will not reward mere poking around."

"Still, I'd like a crack at it."

"A neophyte—"

"May bring a fresh perspective."

They both knew that by tradition at the Library, incoming candidate Librarians could pick their first topic. Most deferred to the reigning conventional wisdom and took up a small Message, something from a Type I Civilization just coming onto the galactic stage. Something resembling what Earth had sent out in its first efforts. To tackle a really big problem was foolhardy.

But some smug note in the Prefect's arrogant gaze had kindled an old desire in her.

He sniffed. "To merely review previous thinking would take a great deal of time."

She leaned forward in her chair. "I have studied the Sagittarius for years. It became something of a preoccupation of mine."

"Ummm." She had little experience with people like this. The Prefect was strangely austere in his unreadable face, the even tones of his neutral sentences. Deciphering him seemed to require the same sort of skills she had fashioned through years of training. But at the moment she felt only a yawning sense of her inexperience, amplified by the stretching silence in this office. The Prefect could be right, after all. She started to phrase a gracious way to back down.

The Prefect made a small sound, something like a sigh. "Very well. Report weekly."

She blinked. "Um, many thanks."

Ruth Angle smoothed her ornate, severely traditional Trainee shift as she left the Prefect's office, an old calming gesture she could not train away. Now her big mouth had gotten her into a fix, and she could see no way out. Not short of going back in there and asking for his guidance, to find a simpler Message, something she could manage.

To hell with that. The soaring, fluted alabaster columns of the Library Centrex reminded her of the majesty of this entire enterprise, stiffening her resolve.

There were few other traditional sites, here at the edge of the Fourth Millennium, that could approach the grandeur of the Library. Since the first detection of signals from other galactic civilizations nearly a thousand years before, no greater task had confronted humanity than the learning of such vast lore.

The Library itself had come to resemble its holdings:

huge, aged, mysterious in its shadowy depths. In the formal grand pantheon devoted to full-color, moving statues of legendary Interlocutors, giving onto the Seminar Plaza, stood the revered block of black basalt: the Rosetta Stone, symbol of all they worked toward. Its chiseled face was nearly three millennia old, and, she thought as she passed it, endearingly easy to understand. It was a simple linear, one-to-one mapping of three human languages, found by accident. Having the same text in Greek II, which the discoverers could read, meant that the hieroglyphic pictures and cursive Demotic forms could be deduced. This battered black slab, found by troops clearing ground to build a fort, had linked civilizations separated by millennia.

She reached out a trembling palm to caress its chilly hard sleekness. The touch brought a thrill. They who served here were part of a grand, age-old tradition, one that went to the heart of the very meaning of being human.

Only the lightness of her ringing steps buoyed her against the grave atmosphere of the tall, shadowy vaults. Scribes passed silently among the palisades, their violet robes swishing after them. She was noisy and new, and she knew it.

She had come down from low lunar orbit the day before, riding on the rotating funicular, happy to rediscover Luna's ample domes and obliging gravity. Her earliest training had been here, and then the mandatory two years on Earth. The Councilors liked to keep a firm hold on who ran the Library, so the final scholastic work had to be in bustling, focal point Australia, beside foaming waves and tawny beaches. Luna was a more solemn place, unchanging.

She savored the stark ivory slopes of craters in the distance as she walked in the springy gait of one still adjusting to the gravity.

Sagittarius, here I come.

Her next and most important appointment was with the Head Nought. She went through the usual protocols, calling upon lesser lights, before being ushered into the presence of Siloh, a smooth-skinned Nought who apparently had not learned to smile. Or maybe that went with the cellular territory; Noughts had intricate adjustments to offset their deeply sexless natures.

"I do hope you can find a congruence with the Sagittarius Architecture," Siloh said in a flat tone that ended each sentence with a purr. "Though I regret your lost effort."

"Lost?"

"You will fail, of course."

"Perhaps a fresh approach—"

"So have said many hundreds of candidate scholars. I remind you of our latest injunction from the Councilors—the heliosphere threat."

"I thought there was little anyone could do."

"So it seems." Siloh scowled. "But we cannot stop from striving."

"Of course not," she said in what she hoped was a demure manner. She was aware of how little she could make of this person, who gave off nothing but sentences.

Noughts had proven their many uses centuries before. Their lack of sexual appetites and apparatus, both physical and mental, gave them a rigorous objectivity. As diplomats, Contractual Savants, and neutral judges, they excelled. They had replaced much of the massive legal apparatus that had come to burden society in earlier centuries.

The Library could scarcely function without their insights. Alien texts did not carry unthinking auras of sexuality, as did human works. Or more precisely, the Messages might carry alien sexualities aplenty, however much their original creators had struggled to make them objective and transparent. Cutting through that was a difficult task for ordinary people, such as herself. The early decades of the Library had struggled with the issue, and the Noughts had solved it.

Translating the Messages from a human male or female perspective profoundly distorted their meaning. In the early days, this had beclouded many translations. Much further effort had gone to cleansing these earlier texts. Nowadays, no work issued from the Library without a careful Nought vetting, to erase unconscious readings.

Siloh said gravely, "The heliosphere incursion has baffled our finest minds. I wish to approach it along a different path. For once, the Library may be of immediate use."

Ruth found this puzzling. She had been schooled in the loftier aspects of the Library's mission, its standing outside the tides of the times. Anyone who focused upon Messages that had been designed for eternity had to keep a mental distance from the events of the day. "I do not quite . . ."

"Think of the Library as the uninitiated do. They seldom grasp the higher functions we must perform, and instead see mere passing opportunity. That is why we are bombarded with requests to view the Vaults as a source for inventions, tricks, novelties."

"And reject them, as we should." She hoped she did not sound too pious.

But Siloh nodded approvingly. "Indeed. My thinking is that an ancient society such as the Sagittarius Architecture might have encountered such problems before. It would know better than any of our astro-engineers how to deal with the vast forces at work."

"I see." *And why didn't I think of it? Too steeped in this culture of hushed reverence for the sheer magnitude of the Library's task?* "Uh, it is difficult for me to envision how—"

"Your task is not to imagine but to perceive," Siloh said severely.

She found Noughts disconcerting, and Siloh more so. Most chose to have no hair, but Siloh sported a rim of kinked coils, glinting like brass, as if a halo had descended onto his skull. His pale eyelashes flicked seldom, gravely. Descending, his eyelids looked pink and rubbery. The nearly invisible blond eyebrows arched perpetually, so his every word seemed layered with artifice, tones sliding among syllables with resonant grace. His face shifted from one nuanced expression to another, a pliable medium in ceaseless movement, like the surface of a restless pond rippled by unfelt winds. She felt as though she should be taking notes about his every utterance. Without blinking, she shifted to recording mode, letting her spine-based memory log everything that came in through eyes and ears. Just in case.

"I have not kept up, I fear," she said; it was always a good idea to appear humble. "The incursion—"

"Has nearly reached Jupiter's orbit," Siloh said. The wall behind the Nought lit with a display showing the sun, gamely plowing through a gale of interstellar gas.

Only recently had humanity learned that it had arisen in a benign time. An ancient supernova had once blown a bubble in the interstellar gas, and Earth had been cruising through that extreme vacuum while the mammals evolved from tree shrews to big-brained world-conquerors. Not that the sun was special in any other way. In its gyre about the galaxy's hub, it moved only fifty light years in the span of a million years, oscillating in and out of the galaxy's plane every thirty-three million years—and that was enough to bring it now out of the Local Bubble's protection. The full density of interstellar hydrogen now beat against the Sun's own plasma wind, pushing inward, hammering into the realm of the fragile planets.

"The hydrogen wall began to bombard the Ganymede Colony yesterday," Siloh said with the odd impartiality Ruth still found unnerving, as though not being male or female gave it a detached view, above the human fray. "We at the Library are instructed to do all we can to find knowledge bearing upon our common catastrophe."

The wall screen picked up this hint and displayed Jupiter's crescent against the hard stars. Ruth watched as a fresh flare coiled back from the ruby, roiling shock wave that embraced Jupiter. The bow curve rippled with colossal turbulence, vortices bigger than lesser worlds. "Surely we can't change the interstellar weather."

"We must try. The older Galactics may know of a world that survived such an onslaught."

The sun's realm, the heliosphere, had met the dense clump of gas and plasma eighty-eight years before. Normally the solar wind particles blown out from the sun kept the interstellar medium at bay. For many past millennia, these pressures had struggled against each other in a filmy barrier a hundred Astronomical Units beyond the cozy inner solar system. Now the barrier had been pressed back in, where the outer planets orbited.

The wall's view expanded to show what remained of the comfy realm dominated by the Sun's pressure. It looked like an ocean-going vessel, seen from above: bow waves generated at the prow rolled back, forming the characteristic parabolic curve.

Under the steadily rising pressure of the thickening interstellar gas and dust, that pressure front eroded. The sun's course slammed it against the dense hydrogen wall at sixteen kilometers per second and its puny wind was pressed back into the realm of solar civilization. Pluto's Cryo Base had been abandoned decades before, and Saturn only recently. The incoming hail of high energy particles and fitful storms had killed many. The Europa Ocean's strange life was safe beneath its ten kilometers of ice, but that was small consolation.

"But what can we do on our scale?" she insisted.

"What we can."

"The magnetic turbulence alone, at the bow shock, holds a larger energy store than all our civilization."

Siloh gave her a look that reminded her of how she had, as a girl, watched an insect mating dance. Distant distaste. "We do not question here. We listen."

"Yes, Self." This formal title, said to be preferred by Noughts to either Sir or Madam, seemed to please Siloh. It went through the rest of their interview with a small smile, and she could almost feel a personality beneath its chilly remove. Almost.

She left the Executat Dome with relief. The Library sprawled across the Locutus Plain, lit by Earth's stunning crescent near a jagged white horizon. Beneath that preserved plain lay the cryofiles of all transmissions received from the Galactic Complex, the host of innumerable societies that had flourished long before humanity was born. A giant, largely impenetrable resource. The grandest possible intellectual scrap heap.

Libraries were monuments not so much to the Past, but to

Permanence itself. Ruth shivered with anticipation. She had passed through her first interviews!—and was now free to explore the myriad avenues of the galactic past. The Sagittarius was famous for its density of information, many layered and intense. A wilderness, beckoning.

Still, she had to deal with the intricacies of the Library, too. These now seemed as steeped in arcane byways and bureaucratic labyrinths as were the Library's vast contents. Ruth cautioned herself to be careful, and most especially, to not let her impish side show. She bowed her head as she passed an aged Nought, for practice.

The greatest ancient library had been at Alexandria, in Afrik. An historian had described the lot of librarians there with envy: *They had a carefree life: free meals, high salaries, no taxes to pay, very pleasant surroundings, good lodgings, and servants. There was plenty of opportunity for quarreling with each other.*

So not much had changed. . . .

Her apartment mate was a welcome antidote to the Nought. Small, bouncy, Catkejen was not the usual image of a librarian candidate. She lounged around in a revealing sarong, sipping a stimulant that was scarcely allowed in the Trainee Manual.

"Give 'em respect," she said off-hand, "but don't buy into all their solemn dignity-of-our-station stuff. You'll choke on it after a while."

Ruth grinned. "And get slapped down."

"I kinda think the Librarians *like* some back talk. Keeps 'em in fighting trim."

"Where are you from?—Marside?"

"They're too mild for me. No, I'm a Ganny."

"Frontier stock, eh?" Ruth sprawled a little herself, a welcome relief from the ramrod-spine posture the Librarians kept. No one hunched over their work here in the classic scholar's pose. They kept upright, using the surround environs. "Buried in ice all your life?"

"Don't you buy that." Catkejen waved a dismissive hand,

extruding three tool-fingers to amplify the effect. "We get out to prospect the outer moons a lot."

"So you're wealthy? Hiding behind magneto shields doesn't seem worth it."

"More clichés. Not every Ganny strikes it rich."

The proton sleet at Ganymede was lethal, but the radiation-cured elements of the inner Jovian region had made many a fortune, too. "So you're from the poor folks who had to send their brightest daughter off?"

"Another cliché." Catkejen made a face. "I hope you have better luck finding something original in—what was it?"

"The Sagittarius Architecture."

"Brrrrr! I heard it was a hydra."

"Each time you approach it, you get a different mind?"

"If you can call it a mind. I hear it's more like a talking body."

Ruth had read and sensed a lot about the Sagittarius, but this was new. They all knew that the mind-body duality made no sense in dealing with alien consciousness, but how this played out was still mysterious. She frowned.

Catkejen poked her in the ribs. "Come on, no more deep thought today! Let's go for a fly in the high-pressure dome."

Reluctantly, Ruth went. But her attention still fidgeted over the issues. She thought about the challenge to come, even as she swooped in a long, serene glide over the fern-covered hills under the amusement dome, beneath the stunning ring of orbital colonies that made a glittering necklace in the persimmon sky.

Into her own pod, at last!

She had gone through a week of final neural conditioning since seeing Siloh, and now the moment had arrived: direct line feed from the Sagittarius Architecture.

Her pod acted as a neural web, using her entire body to convey connections. Sheets of sensation washed over her skin, a prickly itch began in her feet.

She felt a heady kinesthetic rush of acceleration as a constellation of fusions drew her to a tight nexus. Alien architectures used most of the available human input landscape. Dizzying surges in the ears, biting smells, ringing cacophonies of elusive patterns, queasy perturbations of the inner organs—a Trainee had to know how these might convey meaning.

They often did, but translating them was elusive. After such experiences, one never thought of human speech as anything more than a hobbled, claustrophobic mode. Its linear meanings and frail attempts at linked concepts were simple, utilitarian, and typical of younger minds.

The greatest task was translating the dense smatterings of mingled sensations into discernible sentences. Only thus could a human fathom them at all, even in a way blunted and blurred. Or so much previous scholarly experience said.

Ruth felt herself bathed in a shower of penetrating responses, all coming from her own body. These were her own in-board subsystems coupled with high-bit-rate spatterings of meaning—guesses, really. She had an ample repository of built-in processing units, lodged in her spine and shoulders. No one would attempt such a daunting task without artificial amplifications. To confront such slabs of raw data with a mere unaided human mind was pointless and quite dangerous. Early Librarians, centuries before, had perished in a microsecond's exposure to such layered labyrinths as the Sagittarius.

Years of scholarly training had conditioned her against the jagged ferocity of the link, but still she felt a cold shiver of dread. That, too, she had to wait to let pass. The effect amplified whatever neural state you brought to it. Legend had it that a Librarian had once come to contact while angry, and been driven into a fit from which he'd never recovered. They had found the body peppered everywhere with micro-contusions.

The raw link was as she had expected:

A daunting, many-layered language. Then she slid into an easier notation that went through her spinal interface, and heard/felt/read:

❁❋▲❊◗❑❒■❄✲◗❆❊✌✓➺✗✘❋✗✲✱✲✛➲➺➲✌❍

Much more intelligible, but still. . . . She concentrated—

We wish you greetings, new sapience.

"Hello. I come with reverence and new supple offerings." This was the standard opening, one refined over five centuries ago and never changed by so much as a syllable.

And you offer?

"Further cultural nuances." Also a ritual promise, however unlikely it was to be fulfilled. Few advances into the Sagittarius had been made in the last century. Even the most ambitious Librarians seldom tried any longer.

Something like mirth came wafting to her, then:

We are of a mind to venture otherwise with you.

Damn! There was no record of such a response before, her downlink confirmed. It sounded like a preliminary to a dismissal. That overture had worked fine for the last six Trainees. But then, they hadn't gotten much farther, either, before the Sagittarius lost interest and went silent again. Being ignored was the greatest insult a Trainee faced, and the most common. Humans were more than a little boring to advanced intelligences. The worst of it was that one seldom had an idea why.

So what in hell did this last remark from it mean? Ruth fretted, speculated, and then realized that her indecision was affecting her own neural states. She decided to just wing it. "I am open to suggestion and enlightenment."

A pause, getting longer as she kept her breathing steady. Her meditative cues helped, but could not entirely submerge her anxieties. Maybe she had bitten off entirely too much—

From Sagittarius she received a jittering cascade, resolving to:

As a species you are technologically gifted yet philosophically callow, a common condition among emergent intelligences. But of late it is your animal property of physical expression that Intrigues. Frequently you are unaware of your actions—which makes them all the more revealing.

"Oh?" She sat back in her pod and crossed her legs. The physical pose might help her mental profile, in the global view of the Sagittarius. Until now its responses had been within conventional bounds; this last was new.

You concentrate so hard upon your linear word groups that you forget how your movements, postures and facial cues give you away.

"What am I saying now, then?"

That you must humor Us until you can ask your questions about the heliosphere catastrophe.

Ruth laughed. It felt good. "I'm that obvious?"

Many societies We know only through their bit-strings and abstractions. That is the nature of binary signals. You on the other hand (to use a primate phrase), We can know through your unconscious self.

"You want to know about *me*?"

We have heard enough symphonies, believe Us.

At least it was direct. Many times in the past, her research showed, it—"They"—had not been. The Architecture was paying attention!—a coup in itself.

"I'm sorry our art forms bore you."

Many beings who use acoustic means believe their art forms are the most important, valuable aspects of their minds. This is seldom so, in Our experience.

"So involvement is more important to you?"

For this moment, truly. Remember that We are an evolving composite of mental states, no less than you. You cannot meet the same Us again.

"Then you should be called . . . ?"

We know your term "Architecture" and find it—your phrasing?—amusing. Better perhaps to consider Us to be a composite entity. As you are yourselves, though you cannot sense this aspect. You imagine that you are a unitary consciousness, guiding your bodies.

"And we aren't?"

Of course not. Few intelligences in Our experience know as little of their underlying mental architecture as do you.

"Could that be an advantage for us?"

With the next words came a shooting sensation, something like a dry chuckle.

Perhaps so. You apparently do all your best work off stage. Ideas appear to you without your knowing where they come from.

She tried to imagine watching her own thoughts, but was at a loss where to go with this. "Then let's . . . well . . ."

Gossip?

What an odd word choice. There was something like a tremor of pleasure in its neural tone, resounding with long, slow wavelengths within her.

"It sounds creepy," Catkejen said. She was shoveling in food at the Grand Cafeteria, a habit Ruth had noticed many Gannies had.

"Nothing in my training really prepared me for its . . . well, coldness, and . . ."

Catkejen stopped eating to nod knowingly. "And intimacy?"

"Well, yes."

"Look, I've been doing pod work only a few weeks, just like you. Already it's pretty clear that we're mostly negotiating, not translating."

Ruth frowned. "They warned us, but still. . . ."

"Look, these are big minds. Strange as anything we'll ever know. But they're trapped in a small space, living cyberlives. We're their entertainment."

"And I am yours, ladies," said a young man as he sat down at their table. He ceremoniously shook hands. "Geoffrey Chandis."

"So how're you going to amuse us?" Catkejen smiled skeptically.

"How's this?" Geoffrey stood and put one hand on their table. In one deft leap he was upside down, balanced upon the one hand, the other saluting them.

"You're from HiGee." Catkejen applauded.

He switched his support from one hand to the other. "I find this paltry 0.19 Lunar gee charming, don't you?"

Ruth pointed. "As charming as one red sock, the other blue?"

Unfazed, Geoffrey launched himself upward. He did a flip and landed on two feet, without even a backward step to restore balance. Ruth and Catkejen gave him beaming smiles. "Socks are just details, ladies. I stick to essentials."

"You're in our year, right?" Catkejen asked. "I saw you at the opening day ceremonies."

Geoffrey sat, but not before he twirled his chair up into the air, making it do a few quick, showy moves. "No, I was just sneaking in for some of the refreshments. I'm a lordly year beyond you two."

Ruth said, "I thought HiGee folk were, well—"

"More devoted to the physical? Not proper fodder for the Library?" He grinned.

Ruth felt her face redden. Was she that easy to read? "Well, yes."

"My parents, my friends, they're all focused on athletics. Me, I'm a rebel."

Catkejen smiled. "Even against the Noughts?"

He shrugged. "Mostly I find a way to go around them."

Ruth nodded. "I think I'd rather be ignored by them."

"Y'know," Catkejen said reflectively, "I think they're a lot like the Minds."

Ruth asked slowly, "Because they're the strangest form of human?"

Geoffrey said, "They're sure alien to me. I'll give up sex when I've lost all my teeth, maybe, but not before."

"They give me the shivers sometimes," Catkejen said. "I was fetching an ancient written document over in the Hard Archives last week, nighttime. Three of them came striding down the corridor in those capes with the cowls. All in black, of course. I ducked into a side corridor—they scared me."

"A woman's quite safe with them," Geoffrey said. "Y'know, when they started up their Nought Guild business, centuries back, they decided on that all-black look and the shaved heads and all, because it saved money. But everybody read it as dressing like funeral directors. Meaning, they were going to bury all our sex-ridden, old ways of interpreting."

"And here I thought I knew a lot about Library history," Catkejen said in an admiring tone. "Wow, that's good gossip."

"But they've made the big breakthroughs," Ruth said. "Historically—"

"Impossible to know, really," Catkejen said. "The first Noughts refused to even have names, so we can't cite the work as coming from them."

Geoffrey said mock-solemnly, "Their condition they would Nought name."

"They've missed things, too," Catkejen said. "Translated epic sensual poems as if they were about battles, when they were about love."

"Sex, actually," Geoffrey said. "Which can seem like a battle."

Catkejen laughed. "Not the way *I* do it."

"Maybe you're not doing it right." Geoffrey laughed with her, a ringing peal.

"Y'know, I wonder if the Noughts ever envy us?"

Geoffrey grunted in derision. "They save so much time by not having to play our games. It allows them to contemplate the Messages at their leah-zure."

He took a coffee cup and made it do a few impossible stunts in midair. Ruth felt that if she blinked she would miss something; he was *quick*. His compact body had a casual grace, despite the thick slabs of muscle. The artful charm went beyond the physical. His words slid over each other in an odd pronunciation that had just enough inflection to ring musically. Maybe, she thought, there were other amusements to be had here in the hallowed Library grounds.

She worked steadily, subjecting each microsecond of her interviews with the Architecture to elaborate contextual analysis. Codes did their work, cross-checking furiously across centuries of prior interpretation. But they needed the guidance of the person who had been through the experience: her.

And she felt the weight of the Library's history upon her every translation. Each cross-correlation with the huge body of Architecture research brought up the immense history behind their entire effort.

When first received centuries before, the earliest extraterrestrial signals had been entirely mystifying. The initial celebrations and bold speeches had obscured this truth, which was to become the most enduring fact about the field.

For decades the searchers for communications had rummaged through the frequencies, trying everything from radio waves to optical pulses, and even the occasional foray into X-rays. They found nothing. Conventional wisdom held that the large power needed to send even a weak signal across many light years was the most important fact. Therefore, scrutinize the nearby stars, cupping electromagnetic ears for weak signals from penny-pinching civilizations. The odds were tiny that a society interested in communication would be nearby, but this was just one of those hard facts about the cosmos—which turned out to be wrong.

The local-lookers fell from favor after many decades of increasingly frantic searches. By then the Galactic Center Strategy had emerged. Its basis lay in the discovery that star formation had begun in the great hub of stars within the innermost ten thousand light years. Supernovas had flared early and often there, stars were closer together, so heavy elements built up quickly. Three-quarters of the suitable life-supporting stars in the entire galaxy were older than the Sun, and had been around on average more than a billion years longer.

Most of these lay within the great glowing central bulge—

the hub, which we could not see through the lanes of dust clogging the constellation of Sagittarius. But in radio frequencies, the center shone brightly. And the entire company of plausible life sites, where the venerable societies might dwell, subtended an arc of only a few degrees, as seen from Earth.

We truly lived in the boondocks—physically, and as became apparent, conceptually as well.

Near the center of the hub, thousands of stars swarmed within a single light year. Worlds there enjoyed a sky with dozens of stars brighter than the full moon. Beautiful, perhaps—but no eyes would ever evolve there to witness the splendor.

The dense center was dangerous. Supernovas drove shock waves through fragile solar systems. Protons sleeted down on worlds, sterilizing them. Stars swooped near each other, scrambling up planetary orbits and raining down comets upon them. The inner zone was a dead zone.

But a bit further out, the interstellar weather was better. Planets capable of sustaining organic life began their slow winding path upward toward life and intelligence within the first billion or two years after the galaxy formed. An Earth-like world that took 4.5 billion years to produce smart creatures would have done so about four billion years ago.

In that much time, intelligence might have died out, arisen again, and gotten inconceivably rich. The beyond-all-reckoning wealthy beings near the center could afford to lavish a pittance on a luxury—blaring their presence out to all those crouched out in the galactic suburbs, just getting started in the interstellar game.

Whatever forms dwelled further in toward the center, they knew the basic symmetry of the spiral. This suggested that the natural corridor for communication is along the spiral's radius, a simple direction known to everyone. This maximized the number of stars within a telescope's view. A radius is better than aiming along a spiral arm, since the arm curves away from any straight-line view. So a beacon should broadcast outward in both directions from near the center.

So, rather than look nearby, the ancient Search for Extraterrestrial Intelligence searchers began to look inward. They pointed their antennas in a narrow angle toward the constellation Sagittarius. They listened for the big spenders to shout at the less prosperous, the younger, the unsophisticated.

But how often to cup an ear? If Earth was mediocre, near the middle in planetary properties, then its day and year were roughly typical. These were the natural ranges any world would follow: a daily cycle atop an annual sway of climate.

If aliens were anything like us, they might then broadcast for a day, once a year. But which day? There was no way to tell—so the Search for Extraterrestrial Intelligence searchers began to listen *every* day, for roughly a half hour, usually as the radio astronomers got all their instruments calibrated. They watched for narrow-band signals that stood out even against the bright hub's glow.

Radio astronomers had to know what frequency to listen to, as well. The universe is full of electromagnetic noise at all wavelengths from the size of atoms to those of planets. Quite a din.

There was an old argument that water-based life might pick the "watering hole"—a band near 1 billion cycles/second where both water and hydroxyl molecules radiate strongly. Maybe not right on top of those signals, but nearby, because that's also in the minimum of all the galaxy's background noise.

Conventional Search for Extraterrestrial Intelligence had spent a lot of effort looking for nearby sources, shifting to their rest frame, and then eavesdropping on certain frequencies in that frame. But a beacon strategy could plausibly presume that the rest frame of the galactic center was the obvious gathering spot, so anyone broadcasting would choose a frequency near the "watering hole" frequency of the galaxy's exact center.

Piggy-backing on existing observing agendas, astronomers could listen to a billion stars at once. Within two years, the strategy worked. One of the first beacons found was from the Sagittarius Architecture.

Most of the signals proved to have a common deep motivation. Their ancient societies, feeling their energies ebb, yet treasuring their trove of accumulated art, wisdom and insight, wanted to pass this on. Not just by leaving it in a vast museum somewhere, hoping some younger species might come calling someday. Instead, many built a robotic funeral pyre fed by their star's energies, blaring out tides of timeless greatness:

> *My name is Ozymandias, King of Kings,*
> *Look on my works, ye Mighty, and despair!*

as the poet Percy Bysshe Shelley had put it, witnessing the ruins of ancient Egypt, in Afrik.

At the very beginnings of the library, humanity found that it was coming in on an extended discourse, an ancient interstellar conversation, without notes or history readily provided. Only slowly did the cyber-cryptographers fathom that most alien cultures were truly vast, far larger than the sum of all human societies. And much older.

Before actual contact, nobody had really thought the problem through. Historically, Englishmen had plenty of trouble understanding the shadings of, say, the Ozzie Bushmen. Multiply that by thousands of other Earthly and solar system cultures and then square the difficulty, to allow for the problem of expressing it all in sentences—or at least, linear symbolic sequences. Square the complexity again to allow for the abyss separating humanity from any alien culture.

The answer was obvious: any alien translator program had to be as smart as a human. And usually much more so.

The first transmission from any civilization contained elementary signs, to build a vocabulary. That much even human scientists had guessed. But then came incomprehensible slabs, digital Rosetta stones telling how to build a simulated alien mind that could talk down to mere first-timers.

The better part of a century went by before humans worked out how to copy and then represent alien minds in silicon. Finally the Alien Library was built, to care for the

Minds and Messages it encased. To extract from them knowledge, art, history, and kinds of knowing for which humans might very well have no name.

And to negotiate with them. The cyber-aliens had their own motivations.

"I don't understand your last statement."

I do not need to be told that. You signal body-defiance with your crossed arms, barrier gestures, pursed lips, contradictory eyebrow slants.

"But these tensor topologies are not relevant to what we were discussing."

They are your reward.

"For what?"

Giving me of your essence. By wearing ordinary clothes, as I asked, and thus displaying your overt signals.

"I thought we were discussing the Heliosphere problem."

We were. But you primates can never say only one thing at a time to such as We.

She felt acutely uncomfortable. "Uh, this picture you gave me . . . I can see this is some sort of cylindrical tunnel through—"

The plasma torus of your gas giant world, Jupiter. I suggest it as a way to funnel currents from the moon, Io.

"I appreciate this, and will forward it—"

There is more to know, before your level of technology—forgive me, but it is still crude, and will be so for far longer than you surmise—can make full use of this defense.

Ruth suppressed her impulse to widen her eyes. *Defense?* Was this it? A sudden solution? "I'm not a physiker—"

Nor need you be. I intercept your host of messages, all unspoken. Your pelvis is visible beneath your shift, wider and rotated back slightly more than the male Supplicants who come to Us. Waist

more slender, thighs thicker. Navel deeper, belly longer. Specializations impossible to suppress.

Where was it—They—going with this? "Those are just me, not messages."

It is becoming of you to deny them. Like your hourglass shape perceived even at a distance, say, across an ancient plain at great distance. Your thighs admit an obligingly wider space, an inward slope to the thickened thighs, that gives an almost knock-kneed appearance.

"I *beg* your pardon—"

A pleasant saying, that—meaning that We have overstepped (another gesture) your boundaries? But I merely seek knowledge for my own repository.

"I—we—don't like being taken apart like this!"

But reduction to essentials is your primary mental habit.

"Not reducing people!"

Ah, but having done this to the outside world, you surely cannot object to having the same method applied to yourselves.

"People don't like being dissected."

Your science made such great strides—unusual upon the grander stage of worlds—precisely because you could dexterously divide your attentions into small units, all the better to understand the whole.

When They got like this it was best to humor Them. "People don't like it. That is a social mannerism, maybe, but one we *feel* about."

And I seek more.

The sudden grave way the Sagittarius said this chilled her.

Siloh was not happy, though it took a lot of time to figure this out. The trouble with Noughts was their damned lack of signals. No slight downward tug of lips to signal provisional disapproval, no sideways glance to open a possibility. Just the facts, Ma'am. "So it is giving you tantalizing bits."

"*They*, not It. Sometimes I feel I'm talking to several different minds at once."

"It has said the same about us."

The conventional theory of human minds was that they were a kind of legislature, always making deals between differing interests. Only by attaining a plurality could anyone make a decision. She bit her lip to not give away anything, then realized that her bite was visible, too. "We're a whole species. They're a simulation of one."

Siloh made a gesture she could not read. She had expected some congratulations on her work, but then, Siloh was a Nought, and had little use for most human social lubrications. He said slowly, "This cylinder through the Io plasma—the physikers say it is intriguing."

"How? I thought the intruding interstellar plasma was overpowering everything."

"It is. We lost Ganymede Nation today."

She gasped. "I hadn't heard."

"You have been immersed in your studies, as is fitting."

"Does Catkejen know?"

"She has been told."

Not by you, I hope. Siloh was not exactly the sympathetic type. "I should go to her."

"Wait until our business is finished."

"But I—"

"Wait."

Siloh leaned across its broad work plain, which responded by offering information. Ruth crooked her neck but could not make out what hung shimmering in the air before Siloh. Of course; this was a well designed office, so that she could not read its many ingrained inputs. He was probably summoning information all the while he talked to her, without her knowing it. Whatever he had learned, he sat back with a contented, small smile. "I believe the Sagittarius Congruence is emerging in full, to tantalize you."

"Congruence?"

"A deeper layer to its intelligence. You should not be deceived into thinking of it as remotely like us. We are comparatively simple creatures." Siloh sat back, steepling its fingers and peering into them, a studied pose. "Never does the Sagittarius think of only a few moves into its game."

"So you agree with Youstani, a Translator Supreme from the twenty-fifth century, that the essential nature of Sagittarius is to see all conversations as a game?"

"Are ours different?" A sudden smile creased his leathery face, a split utterly without mirth.

"I would hope so."

"Then you shall often be deceived."

She went to their apartment immediately, but someone had gotten there before her. It was dark, but she caught muffled sounds from the living room. Was Catkejen crying?

Earth's crescent shed a dim glow into the room. She stepped into the portal of the living room and in the gloom saw someone on the viewing pallet. A low whimper drifted in the darkness, repeating, soft and sad, like crying, yes—

But there were two people there. And the sobbing carried both grief and passion, agony and ecstasy. An ancient tide ran in the room's shadowed musk.

The other person was Geoffrey. Moving with a slow rhythm, he was administering a kind of sympathy Ruth certainly could not. And she had not had the slightest clue of this relationship between them. A pang forked through her. The pain surprised her. She made her way out quietly.

Catkejen's family had not made it out from Ganymede. She had to go through the rituals and words that soften the hard edges of life. She went for a long hike in the domes, by herself. When she returned she was quieter, worked long hours and took up sewing.

The somber prospects of the Ganymede loss cast a pall over all humanity, and affected the Library's work. This disaster was unparalleled in human history, greater even than the Nation Wars.

Still, solid work helped for a while. But after weeks, Ruth needed a break, and there weren't many at the Library. Anything physical beckoned. She had gone for a swim in the spherical pool, of course, enjoying the challenge. And flown in broad swoops across the Greater Dome on plumes of hot air. But a simmering frustration remained. Life had changed.

With Catkejen she had developed a new, friendly, work-buddy relationship with Geoffrey. Much of this was done without words, a negotiation of nuances. They never spoke of that moment in the apartment, and Ruth did not know if they had sensed her presence.

Perhaps more than ever, Geoffrey amused them with his quick talk and artful stunts. Ruth admired his physicality, the yeasty smell of him as he laughed and cavorted. HiGeers were known for their focus, which athletics repaid in careers of remarkable performance. The typical HiGee career began in sports and moved later to work in arduous climes, sites in the solar system where human strength and endurance still counted, because machines were not dexterous and supple enough.

Some said the HiGeer concentration might have come from a side effect of their high-spin, centrifugal doughnut habitats. Somehow Geoffrey's concentration came out as a life-of-the-party energy, even after his long hours in intense rapport with his own research.

Appropriately, he was working on the Andromeda Manifold, a knotty tangle of intelligences that stressed the embodied nature of their parent species. Geoffrey's superb nervous system, and especially his exact hand-eye coordination, gave him unusual access to the Manifold. While he joked about this, most of what he found could not be conveyed in words at all. That was one of the lessons of the Library—that other intelligences sensed the world, and the body's relation to it, quite differently. The ghost of Cartesian duality still haunted human thinking.

Together the three of them hiked the larger craters. All good for the body, but Ruth's spirit was troubled. Her own work was not going well.

She could scarcely follow some of the Architecture's conversations. Still less comprehensible were the eerie sensoria it projected to her—sometimes, the only way it would take part in their discourse, for weeks on end.

Finally, frustrated, she broke off connection and did not return for a month. She devoted herself instead to historical records of earlier Sagittarius discourse. From those had come some useful technical inventions, a classic linear text, even a new digital art form. But that had been centuries ago.

Reluctantly she went back into her pod and returned to linear speech mode. "I don't know what you intend by these tonal conduits," she said to the Sagittarius—after all. It probably had an original point of view, even upon its own motivations.

I was dispatched into the Realm to both carry my Creators' essentials, to propagate their supreme Cause, and to gather knowing-wisdom for them.

So it spoke of itself as "I" today—meaning that she was dealing with a shrunken fraction of the Architecture. Was it losing interest? Or withholding itself, after she had stayed away?

I have other functions, as well. Any immortal intelligence must police its own mentation.

Now what did that mean? Suddenly, all over her body washed sheets of some strange signal she could not grasp. The scatter-shot impulses aroused a pulse-quickening unease in her. *Concentrate.* "But . . . but your home world is toward the galactic center, at least twenty thousand light years away. So much time has passed—"

Quite so—my Creators may be long extinct. Probabilities suggest so. I gather from your information, and mine, that the mean lifetime for civilizations in the Realm is comparable to their/our span.

"So there may be no reason for you to gather information from us at all. You can't send it to them any more." She could not keep the tensions from her voice. In earlier weeks of incessant pod time, she had relied upon her pod's programming to disguise her transmission. And of course, It knew this. Was anything lost on it?

Our motivations do not change. We are eternally a dutiful servant, as are you.

Ah, an advance to "We." She remembered to bore in on the crucial, not be deflected. "Good. If the interstellar plasma gets near Earth—"

We follow your inference. The effects I know well. My Creators inhabit[ed] a world similar to yours, though frankly, more beautiful. [You have wasted so much area upon water!] We managed the electrical environs of our world to send our beacon signal, harnessing the rotational energy of our two moons to the task.

This was further than anyone had gotten with Sagittarius in a lifetime of Librarians. She felt a spike of elation. "Okay, what will happen?"

If the bow shock's plasma density increases further, while your ordinary star plows into it, then there shall be electrical consequences.

"What . . . consequences?"

Dire. You must see your system as a portrait in electrodynamics, one that is common throughout the Realm. Perceive currents seethe forth—

A three-dimensional figure sprang into being before her, with the golden sun at its center. Blue feelers of currents sprouted from the sun's angry red spots, flowing out with the gale of particles, sweeping by the apron-strings of Earth's magnetic fields. This much she knew—that Earth's fields deflected huge energies, letting them pass into the great vault where they would press against the interstellar pressures.

But the currents told a different tale. They arced and soared around each world, cocooning each in some proportion. Then they torqued off into the vastness, smothering in darkness, then eventually returning in high, long arcs to the sun. They were like colossal rubber bands that could never break, but that forces could stretch into fibrous structures.

And here came the bulge of interstellar plasma. Lightning forked all along its intrusion. It engulfed Jupiter, and spikes of coronal fury arced far out from the giant planet. These bright blue streamers curled inward, following long tangents toward the sun.

Some struck the Earth.

"I don't need a detailed description of what that means," she said.

Your world is like many others, a spherical capacitor. Disruption of the electrodynamic equilibrium will endanger the fragile skin of life.

From the Sagittarius came a sudden humid reek. She flinched. Sheeting sounds churned so low that she felt them as deep bass notes resounding in her. Wavelengths longer than her body rang through her bones. Her heart abruptly pounded. A growling storm rose in her ears.

"I . . . I will take this . . . and withdraw."

Have this as well, fair primate—

A squirt of compressed meaning erupted in her sensorium.

It will self-unlock at the appropriate moment.

Opened, the first fraction of the squashed nugget was astonishing. Even Siloh let itself appear impressed. She could tell this by the millimeter rise of a left lip.

"This text is for the Prefect's attention." When Siloh rose and walked around its work-plane she realized that she had never seen its extent—nearly three meters of lean muscle, utterly without any hint of male or female shaping. The basic human machine, engineered for no natural world. It stopped to gaze at her. "This confirms what some physikers believe. Jupiter is the key."

Within an hour the Prefect agreed. He eyed them both and flicked on a display. "The Sagittarius confirms our worst suspicions. Trainee, you said that you had captured from it yet more?"

She displayed the full data-nugget It had given her. A pyrotechnic display arced around a simulated Jupiter—

"There, at the poles," the Prefect said. "That cylinder."

The fringing fields carried by interstellar plasma swarmed into the cylinder. This time, instead of ejecting fierce currents, Jupiter absorbed them.

"That tube is electrically shorting out the disturbance," Siloh said. "The cylinders at both poles—somehow they shunt the energies into the atmosphere."

"And not into ours," Ruth said. "It's given us a solution."

The Prefect said, "What an odd way to do it. No description, just pictures."

Siloh said slowly, "Ummmm . . . And just how do we build those cylinders?"

They looked at her silently, but she got the message: *Find out.*

The sensations washing over her were quite clear now. She had asked for engineering details, and it had countered with a demand. A quite graphic one.

This is my price. To know the full extent of the human sensorium.

"Sex?! You want to—"

It seems a small measure in return for the life of your world.

Before she could stop herself she blurted, "But you're not—"

Human? Very well, we wish to fathom the meaning of that word, all the more. This is one step toward comprehending what that symbol-complex means.

"You're a *machine*. A bunch of electronic bips and stutters."

Then we ask merely for a particular constellation of such information.

She gasped, trying not to lose it entirely. "You . . . would barter that for a civilization?"

We are a civilization unto Ourself. Greater than any of you singletons can know.

"I . . . I can't. I *won't*."

"You will," Siloh said with stony serenity.

Ruth blinked. "No!"

"Yes."

"This is more, much more, than required by all the Guild standards of neural integration."

"But—yes."

In her sickening swirl of emotions, she automatically reached for rules. Emotion would carry no weight with this Nought.

She felt on firm ground here, despite not recalling well the welter of policy and opinions surrounding the entire phenomenon. A millennium of experience and profound philosophical analysis, much of it by artificial minds, had created a vast, weighty body of thought: Library Meta-theory. A lot of it, she thought, was more like the barnacles on the belly of a great ship, parasitic and along for the ride. But the issue could cut her now. Given a neurologically integrated system with two parties enmeshed, what was the proper separation?

"This issue is far larger than individual concerns." Siloh's face remained calm though flinty.

"Even though a Trainee, I am *in charge* of this particular translation—"

"Only nominally. I can have you removed in an instant. Indeed, I can do so myself."

"That would take a while, for anyone to achieve my levels of attunement and focus—"

"I have been monitoring your work. I can easily step in—"

"The Sagittarius Composite doesn't want to sleep with *you*."

Siloh froze, composure gone. "You are inserting personal rebuke here!"

Her lips twitched as she struggled not to smile. "Merely an observation. Sagittarius desires something it cannot get among the Nought class."

"I can arrange matters differently, then." Its face worked with several unreadable signals—as though, she thought, something unresolved was trying to express itself.

"I want to remain at work—"

Suddenly he smiled and said lightly, "Oh, you may. You definitely may."

An abrupt hand waved her away. Plainly it had reached some insight it would not share. But what? Siloh's bland gaze gave away nothing. And she was not good enough at translating him, yet.

Some of the Messages lodged in the Library had not been intended for mortal ears or eyes at all. Like some ancient rulers of Mesopotamia, these alien authors directly addressed their deities, and only them. One opened plaintively.

Tell the God we know and say
For your tomorrow we give our today.

It was not obvious whether this couplet (for in the original it was clearly rhymed) came from a living civilization, or from an artifact left to remind the entire galaxy of what had come before. Perhaps, in alien terms, the distinction did not matter.

Such signals also carried Artificials, as the digital minds immersed in the Messages were termed. The advanced Artificials, such as Sagittarius, often supervised vast data-banks containing apparent secrets, outright brags, and certified history—which was, often, merely gossip about the great. These last, rather transparently, were couched to elicit punishment for the author's enemies, from alien gods. This differed only in complexity and guile from the ancient motivations of Babylonian kings.

Most Messages of this beseeching tone assumed some universal moral laws and boasted of their authors' compliance with them. At first the Sagittarius Architecture had appeared to be of this class, and so went largely uninterpreted for over a century. Only gradually did its sophistication and rich response become apparent. Most importantly, it was a new class entirely—the first Architecture Artificial.

It had something roughly comparable to a human unconscious—and yet it could see into its own inner minds at will. It was as if a human could know all of his/her impulses came from a locus of past trauma, or just a momentary anger—and could see this instantly, by tracing back its own workings. The strange power of human art sprang in part from its invisible wellsprings. To be able to unmask that sanctum was an unnerving prospect.

Yet human-made Artificials always worked with total transparency. The Sagittarius could work that way, or it could mask portions of its own mind from itself, and so attain something like that notorious cliché, the Human Condition.

Since in that era current opinion held that the supreme advantage of any artificial mind lay in its constant transparency, this was a shock. What advantage could come to an Artificial that did not immediately know its own levels? Which acted out of thinking patterns it could not consciously review?

Since this was a property the Sagittarius Architecture shared (in a way) with humans, the discussion became heated for over two centuries. And unresolved.

Now when Ruth engaged with it, she was acutely conscious of how the Artificial could change nature with quixotic speed. Swerves into irritation came fast upon long bouts of analytic serenity. She could make no sense of these, or fathom the information she gained in these long episodes of engagement. The neurological impact upon her accumulated. Her immersion in the pod carried a jittery static. Her nerves frayed.

Some fraction of the information the Sagittarius Architecture gave her bore upon the problem of heliospheric physics, but she could not follow this. She conveyed the passages, many quite long, to Siloh.

The crisis over the Artificial's demand seemed to have passed. She worked more deeply with it now, and so one afternoon in the pod, concentrating upon the exact nuances of the link, she did not at first react when she felt a sudden surge of unmistakable desire in herself. It shook her, yeasty and feverish, pressing her calves together and urging her thighs to ache with a sweet longing.

Somehow this merged with the passage currently under translation/discussion. She entered more fully into the difficult problem of extracting just the right subtlety from the [illegible] when all at once she was not reasoning in one part of her mind but, it seemed, in all of them.

From there until only a few heartbeats later she ran the gamut of all previous passions. An ecstasy and union she had experienced only a few times—and only partially, she now saw—poured through her. Her body shook with gusts of raw pleasure. Her Self sang its song, rapt. A constriction of herself seized this flood and rode it. Only blinding speed could grasp what this was, and in full passionate flow she felt herself hammered on a microsecond anvil—into the internal time frames of the Composite.

Dizzy, blinding speed. It registered vast sheets of thought while a single human neuron was charging up to fire. Its cascades of inference and experience were like rapids in a river she could not see but only feel, a kinesthetic acceleration, swerves that swept finally into a delightful blur.

Thought, sensation—all one.

She woke in the pod. Only a few minutes had passed since she had last registered any sort of time at all.

Yet she knew what had happened.

And regretted that it was over.

And hated herself for feeling that way.

"It *had* me."

Siloh began, "In a manner of speaking—"

"Against my will!"

Siloh looked judicial. "So you say. The recordings are necessarily only a pale shadow, so I cannot tell from experiencing them myself—"

Scornfully: "How could you anyway?"

"This discussion will not flow in that direction."

"Damn it, you knew it would do this!"

Siloh shook his head. "I cannot predict the behavior of such an architectural mind class. No one can."

"You at least *guessed* that it would, would find a way into me, to . . . to *mate* with me. At a level we poor stunted humans can only approximate because we're always in two different bodies. It was *in* mine. It—they—knew that in the act of translation there are ways, paths, avenues. . . ." She sputtered to a stop.

"I am sure that description of the experience is impossible." Siloh's normally impenetrable eyes seemed to show real regret.

Yeah? she thought. *How would you know?* But she said as dryly as she could muster, "You could review the recordings yourself, see—"

"I do not wish to."

"Just to measure—"

"No."

Abruptly she felt intense embarrassment. Bad enough if a man had been privy to those moments, but a Nought. . . .

How alien would the experience be, for Siloh?—and *alien* in two different senses of the word? She knew suddenly that there were provinces in the landscape of desire Siloh could not visit. The place she had been with the Composite no human had ever been. Siloh could not go there. Perhaps an ordinary man could not, either.

"I know this is important to you," Siloh said abstractly. "You should also know that the Composite also gave us, in the translation you achieved—while you had your, uh, seizure—the key engineering design behind the heliospheric defense."

She said blankly, "The cylinders . . ."

"Yes, they are achievable, and very soon. A 'technically sweet' solution, I am told by the Prefect. Authorities so far above us that they are beyond view have begun the works needed. They took your information and are making it into an enormous construction at both poles of Jupiter. The entire remaining population of the Jovian Belt threw themselves into shaping the artifacts to achieve this."

"They've been following . . . what *I* say?"

"Yours was deemed the most crucial work. Yet you could not be told."

She shook her head to clear it. "So I wouldn't develop shaky hands."

"And you did not, not at all." Siloh beamed in an inscrutable way, one eyebrow canted at an ambiguous angle.

"You knew," she said leadenly. "What it would do."

"I'm sure I do not fathom what you mean."

She studied Siloh, who still wore the same strange beaming expression. *Remember*, she thought, *it can be just as irritating as an ordinary man, but it isn't one.*

The colossal discharge of Jupiter's magnetospheric potentials was an energetic event unparalleled in millennia of humanity's long strivings to harness nature.

The Composite had brought insights to bear that physikers would spend a century untangling. For the moment, the only important fact was that by releasing plasma spirals at just the right pitch, and driving these with electrodynamic generators (themselves made of filmy ionized barium), a staggering current came rushing out of the Jovian system.

At nearly the speed of light it intersected the inward bulge of the heliosphere. Currents moved in nonlinear dances, weaving a pattern that emerged within seconds, moving in intricate harmonies.

Within a single minute a complex web of forces flexed into being. Within an hour the bulge of interstellar gas arrested its inward penetration. It halted, waves slamming in vexed lines of magnetic force, against the Jovian sally. And became stable.

Quickly humans—ever irreverent, even in the face of catastrophe—termed their salvation The Basket. Invisible to the eye, the giant web the size of the inner solar system was made of filmy fields that weighed nothing. Yet it was all the same massively powerful, a dynamically responding screen protecting the Earth from a scalding death. The hydrogen wall seethed redly in the night sky. To many, it seemed an angry animal caught at last in a gauzy net.

She witnessed the display from the Grand Plaza with a crowd of half a million. It was humbling, to think that mere primates had rendered such blunt pressures awesome but impotent.

The Sagittarius sent, **We render thanks.**

Her chest was tight. She had dreaded entering the pod again, and now could not speak.

We gather it is traditional among you to compliment one's partner, and particularly a lady . . . afterward.

"Don't . . . don't try."

We became something new from that moment.

She felt anger and fear, and yet simultaneously, pride and curiosity. They twisted together in her. Sweat popped out on her upper lip. The arrival of such emotions, stacked on top of each other, told her that she had been changed by what had happened in this pod, and would—could—never be the same. "I did not *want* it."

Then by my understanding of your phylum, you would not then have desired such congress.

"I—me, the conscious me—did not want it!"

We do not recognize that party alone. Rather, we recognize all of you equally. All your signals, do we receive.

"I don't want it to happen again."

Then it will not. It would not have happened the first time had the congruence between us not held true.

She felt the ache in herself. It rose like a tide, swollen and moist and utterly natural. She had to bring to bear every shred of her will to stop the moment, disconnect, and leave the pod, staggering and weeping and then running.

* * *

Geoffrey opened the door to his apartment, blinking owlishly—and then caught her expression.

"I know it's late, I wondered. . . ." She stood numbly, then made herself brush past him, into the shadowed room.

"What's wrong?" He wore a white robe and wrapped it self-consciously around his middle.

"I don't think I can handle all this."

He smiled sympathetically. "You're the toast of the Library, what's to handle?"

"I—come here."

Words, linear sequences of blocky words—all useless. She reached inside the robe and found what she wanted. Her hands slid over muscled skin and it was all *so different*, real, not processed and amped and translated through centuries of careful dry precision.

A tremor swept over her, across the gap between them, onto his moistly electric flesh.

"There is news."

"Oh?" She found it hard to focus on Siloh's words.

"You are not to discuss this with anyone," Siloh said woodenly. "The discharges from Jupiter's poles—they are now oscillating. At very high frequencies."

She felt her pulse trip-hammer, hard and fast and high, still erratic now, hours after she had left Geoffrey. Yet her head was ahead of her heart; a smooth serenity swept her along, distracting her with the pleasure of the enveloping sensation. "The Basket, it's holding, though?"

"Yes." Siloh allowed himself a sour smile. "Now the physikers say that this electromagnetic emission is an essential part of the Basket's power matrix. It cannot be interfered with in the slightest. Even though it is drowning out the sum of all of humanity's transmissions in the same frequency band. It is swamping us."

"Because?"

Siloh's compressed mouth moved scarcely at all. "It."

"You mean. . . ."

"The Composite. It made this happen, by the designs it gave us."

"Why would it want. . . ." Her voice trailed off as she felt a wave of conflicting emotions.

"Why? The signal Jupiter is sending out now, so powerfully, is a modified version of the original Message we received from the Sagittarius authors."

"Jupiter is broadcasting *their* Message?"

"Clearly, loudly. Into the plane of the galaxy."

"Then it built the Basket to re-radiate its ancestors', its designers'—"

"We have learned," Siloh said, "a lesson perhaps greater than what the physikers gained. The Artificials have their own agendas. One knows this, but never has it been more powerfully demonstrated to us."

She let her anxiety out in a sudden, manic burst of laughter. Siloh did not seem to notice. When she was done she said, "So it saved us. And used us."

Siloh said, "Now Jupiter is broadcasting the Sagittarius Message at an enormous volume, to the outer fringes of the galaxy's disk. To places the original Sagittarius signal strength could not have reached."

"It's turned us into its relay station." She laughed again, but it turned to a groan and a sound she had never made before. Somehow it helped, that sound. She knew it was time to stop making it when the men eased through the door of Siloh's office, coming to take her in hand.

Gingerly, she came back to work a month later. Siloh seemed atypically understanding. He set her to using the verification matrices for a few months, calming work. Far easier, to skate through pillars and crevasses of classically known information. She could experience it all at high speed, as something like recreation—the vast cultural repositories of dead civilizations transcribed upon her skin, her neural beds, her five senses linked and webbed into something more. She even made a few minor discoveries.

She crept up upon the problem of returning to the task she

still desired: the Sagittarius. It was, after all, a thing in a box. The truism of her training now rang loudly in her life:

The Library houses entities that are not merely aliens and not merely artificial minds, but the strange sum of both. A Trainee forgets this at her peril.

After more months, the moment came.

The Sagittarius sent,

We shall exist forever, in some manifestation. That is our injunction, ordained by a span of time you cannot fathom. We carry forward our initial commanding behest, given unto us from our Creators, before all else.

"The Sagittarians told you to? You were under orders to make use of whatever resources you find?" She was back in the pod, but a team stood by outside, ready to extricate her in seconds if she gave the signal.

We were made as a combination of things, aspects for which you have not words nor even suspicions. We have our own commandments from on high.

"Damn you! I was so close to you—and I didn't know!"

You cannot know me. We are vaster.

"Did you say 'vaster' or 'bastard'?"

She started laughing again, but this time it was all right. It felt good to make a dumb joke. Very, well, human. In the simplicity of doing that she could look away from all this, feel happy and safe for a flickering second. With some luck, at least for a moment, she might have a glimmer of the granite assurance this strange mind possessed. It was all alone, the only one of its kind here, and yet unshakable. Perhaps there was something in that to admire.

And now she knew that she could not give up her brushes with such entities. In the last few days, she had doubted that. This was now her life. Only now did she fathom how eerie a life it might be.

"Will you go silent on us, again?"

We may at any time.

"Why?"

The answer does not lie within your conceptual space.

She grimaced. "Damn right." She could forget the reality of the chasm between her and this thing that talked and acted and was not ever going to be like anyone she had ever known, or could know. She would live with the not knowing, the eternal ignorance before the immensity of the task here.

The abyss endured. In that there was a kind of shelter. It was not much but there it was.

The Day We Went Through the Transition

RICARD DE LA CASA AND
PEDRO JORGE ROMERO

translated by Yolanda Molina-Gavilán

Ricard de la Casa is a businessman, and an editor and writer who has published two solo SF novels, and a number of stories in collaboration with Romero. Pedro Jorge Romero [http://www.pjorge.com] has a degree in physics, and is a translator, essayist, and editor. Both de la Casa and Romero are active in Spanish SF fandom, and collaborate on the magazine BEM [http://www.bemmag.com].

"The Day We Went Through the Transition" appeared in the fine anthology, Cosmos Latinos. *A time travel story first published in Spanish in 1997, and now translated into English, it reinvigorates that sub-genre. The logic of the story is tight, with real science woven in, but its emotional power comes from the heart-wrenching love story at its center. The extremely complicated plot is held together by clever quantum-mechanical speculation.*

"It's your turn to go through the Transition today," said the voice of the duty lieutenant in my ear.

I opened my eyes at once. The whole room was dark. A temporal alarm had gone off, so the entire building would be completely sealed off; nobody could go in or out. Ten seconds later the lights went on. Our bodies' nanosystems started to become active and control hundreds of biological processes. I could see more clearly now.

The Transition is a classic. Someone has to go through it at least once a week, and sometimes even two or three times on the same day. Why are all terrorists, from both sides, fixated on that time period? Why don't they intervene more often in the Civil War, or in that Invincible Armada affair? I suppose that the Transition is just so full of possibilities, there are so many simultaneously open paths, that every political camp or economic group believes itself capable of adjusting the process so that its particular position triumphs.

It seems to be a particularly Spanish fixation as well. Other countries also suffer from attacks by terrorists who attempt to change history to their liking, but those cases happen once or twice a year. We, however, have to manage up to thirty cases a week, and more than half of them may be placed at the Transition period. It seems that we Spaniards are so unsatisfied with our own history and are so incapable of accepting that others have triumphed in the past, that we make great efforts to change it. It doesn't matter, in any case: the work of the GEI Temporal Intervention Corps is to stop these situations from happening, and we pay particular attention to the Transition.

To tell the truth, we've become experts at it. Learning from the terrorists has provided us with an excellent understanding of that period. We have delved into all its twists and turns so much that we're able to venture into those years without any specific study or preparation.

Rudy is a specialist in temporal flux—I would say a very good one. He's capable of discerning what action will yield the best result. Marisa and I are experts in comparative Spanish history. Not only our own, but also the post-2012 main underlying branches. Isabel is an expert in both subjects at once; she is very good at connecting them.

We got up from our hard old beds immediately. I was the first one, Isabel was next, then Marisa, and finally Rudy. Isabel and Marisa were very experienced, but it was the first time that Rudy would go through the Transition since his recent recruitment. As for me, I've gone through the Transition ten times in a row: my best record.

Those of us who are on duty normally sleep with our clothes on to be ready in case we need to carry out an operation. We were soon ready; Isabel came close and stared at me. It was a confirmation of our agreement; we have been lovers on most occasions, only friends on others, but we've always been together and have supported each other. Our last relationship had been a bit unbalanced; she was not very sure of herself, but it seems that I kept trying.

"Let's go," she said to me, looking away.

"Yes," was my laconic answer. I always get up in a bad mood and don't feel like talking.

Rudy and Marisa had already left with that weird speed that characterizes them; I still haven't managed to get used to their hyperactivity. They have a strange relationship, those two; one minute they ignore each other and the next they're inseparable. Each quarantine period changes everything. Though in reality, every TIC agent has to live with that; couples like Isabel and me are rather the exception.

We ran through the hallways toward the documentation

chamber. In the holographic movies, at whatever temporal line, the policeman or secret agent throws himself immediately into action, beating people up right and left, and everything is fixed. Reality is not like that at all. Unfortunately, while there is an action component to our work, first there is a need to establish precisely which change in time has occurred and evaluate the best way of correcting it. We intervene only afterward, trying to execute an operation in the cleanest and quickest way possible. And even then we still have to write the report. And God save you from having to report on a disappearance, because in that case the paperwork becomes endless and another operation is needed.

We arrived at the tubes. Marisa pressed the button that would take us to the basement. The documentation chamber is located on one of the lowest levels of the TIC General Headquarters. It's a large place, almost completely filled by six computer terminals, and underneath there's only the armored dome that contains the portal, the most watched and secure place in the TIC.

The tubular door opens directly onto the documentation chamber. During an emergency only the guards on duty—us in this case—may access the room. The tubes' electronic system reads the state of our implants to determine if we have permission to be there. In the event that one of us wasn't authorized, the tube wouldn't even move.

The support group was already there evaluating the changes. José Luis, Sara, Didac, and Sandra. They would be our substitutes if anything were to go wrong during the operation.

"I swear I'm getting fed up with so much Transition," yawned Sara as she saw us arrive.

Isabel sat down in front of one of the consoles. Marisa occupied the one that was free. The rest of us stood behind. From her seat, Isabel observed the changing images of the laborious search for the rupture point that the computers were trying to locate by historical comparison. The system is relatively simple; one just needs to begin searching back starting from 7 August 2012. At first, events differ quite a bit from history as we know it, but little by little the changes start merging toward zero and history more closely resembles the real one. Besides, in this case, we also had the advantage of knowing, through some preliminary automatic analyses, that the change had happened at the Transition. Each console is connected simultaneously to our own databases, to history as it happened, and to the external database, which allows us to compare the records.

The entire TIC General Headquarters, which in turn depends on the Spanish Intelligence Group, is enclosed in an ecstasis field. This means that we notice the changes in history only by comparing our records to those on the outside; for those of us who are inside the chamber, the change that had altered life in the outside world had not taken place and we remembered history just as it had happened. The existence of the ecstasis field means that we are virtually trapped in the building. We can leave, yes, but we cannot lead an independent life. If we were to live outside without protection, history's tidal wave would end up engulfing us. We would end up living a particular version of the universe and we would lose our effectiveness as agents. No, we may spy on the world, on outside reality, but we can't really enjoy it.

The theory that allows for time travel is probably the strangest of the whole history of physics; it's difficult to understand and it's based on an incredible number of equations. It is the basis for a great unification theory that some day will explain everything but that, for now, allows us to travel through time using reasonable quantities of energy. It is simply called Temporal Theory, or TT. Unfortunately, some of the effects caused by the theory are almost metaphysical. When it was formulated, when that young physicist finally comprehended it and conceived it pure and whole for the first time, the theory changed the nature of the universe and of reality itself. Before 7 August 2012 only one temporal line existed. There was only one history, shared by all. That August afternoon, exactly at the moment the theory was definitively formulated, time became multiple; temporal lines started to diverge as quanta phenomena were happening in the universe. There are now infinite histories, most of them almost identical, globally indistinguishable with only trivial details to differentiate them; yet others are very different. Exact copies of each human being on Earth live in many—in billions of them.

Philosophers and physicists have spent years trying to explain this, and they haven't gotten very far. It is clear, though, that the first quantum physicists were right: the observer has an effect on the observed, and the existence of intelligent beings in the cosmos alters the workings of the universe. How else to explain this situation? Five minutes before one August day there was only one history, and five minutes afterward there were millions. Furthermore, those temporal lines are real and may be visited easily. The same technology that allows time travel allows taking a trip among alternative temporal lines.

In 1955, Hugh Everett formulated what was called the "many worlds interpretation" of quantum mechanics. According to him, each time a phenomenon of quantum scale occurred, the universe divided itself into as many versions as were necessary to account for all possible results. In the simplest case, there were two possibilities: on one branch the process had happened, and on the other it hadn't. But now one could say that Everett was both right and wrong at the same time. Before the summer of 2012, the universe, in the simplest, two-option case, accepted one of those phenomena and discarded the other one. But after that summer, the universe executes all the possibilities and Everett is proven correct. Since 7 August 2012, the universe divides itself into as many universes as are necessary to cover all possibilities.

The ecstasis field surrounding the Temporal Intervention Center, which is based on a weird property of what physicists call imaginary time, allows those of us inside to experience only one past. If someone changes history, we continue to remember history just as it was, which lets us perceive when it has been manipulated. Unfortunately, the ecstasis field was a late byproduct of the theory, and by the time it was developed it was already too late—although I'm not sure what could have been done differently: surround the entire universe with an ecstasis field?

One thing we can be certain about is that this theory

proves we are alone in the universe. At least that there is no extraterrestrial civilization at our stage of development. If there were a more advanced civilization, their physicists would have discovered Temporal Theory before and we would now see that the temporal divergences in the universe began at an earlier date than our own discovery of the theory. Since that isn't the case, the conclusion is that we are alone, or at least, that we are the most advanced in the entire universe. It's not as surprising as it seems: someone had to be the first.

"I've got it," José Luis said out loud to get our attention.

We all crowded around his console. The computers had located the change point. On his screen was the 28 February 1977 front page of *El País*. In the version we had on our database—the version of history as it had really happened—the headlines were the usual ones for the time period. The version we had from the outside had only one headline that covered the whole first page: *Carrillo Murdered*. The newspaper from the day before was identical to our version, but the one for the following day had that ominous news eclipsing all the rest.

"This is new, isn't it?" said Rudy.

Nobody acknowledged him; he really wasn't looking for an answer.

"Poor man, that was all he needed. They've done just about everything else to him." Rudy continued.

During our training they teach us many of the tricks used to change the past. Almost all of them follow the same plan, killing some well-known person. Almost invariably they're the same people: Hitler, Stalin, Kennedy. But Rudy was right: they hadn't tried to kill Carrillo during that interview, which was odd, considering the many times the Communist leader was manipulated in one sense or another.

"We'd better look some more. Return to your consoles and continue searching. This is too obvious," I said.

Each one of us tried to find data that would link Carrillo with that date. With the information from the newspaper article, and from later ones that dealt with the news, we soon had a more or less clear idea of what had transpired. But we did not find any other point of change that wasn't caused by the assassination of the Spanish Communist Party's leader.

I started to compare data. President Suárez had arranged a secret interview with Carrillo for 27 February. At that time, the Communist Party hadn't been legalized yet—that was still a couple of months away—and, for the Spain of the times, to have an interview with the CP's secretary-general was to have a date with the devil himself. It seems incredible now, but back then the Communist Party had great moral weight in Spanish society, and counting on the Communists was essential for the consolidation of democracy, but acting with too much haste could bring about serious consequences. Suárez understood this, but he also knew that if he could legalize the Communist Party and celebrate free elections with the whole political spectrum, he would gain strength and prestige. For that reason he arranged that ultra-secret interview; only the king and a couple of government members were in the know. The meeting itself wasn't very important, but if it had been discovered, the still-strong Francoist structures would have forced the fall of Suárez and delayed or stopped the advent of democracy.

"That's odd . . . It's been more than three years since Carrillo wasn't murdered," said Isabel in her characteristically soft voice.

At five in the afternoon they picked Carrillo up from his apartment in the Puente de Vallecas. He was driven down a hidden road. A person—a woman—took him to the Santa Ana cottage in the outskirts of Madrid, a quiet place. In real history, Suárez arrived a few minutes later and they both talked for hours about Politics with a capital "P." What the terrorists had done was very elementary. They had simply blown up Carrillo's car just before it got to the house. They were thus assured of two things: that the Bunker would know of this interview and that the Communist Party would be enraged about their leader's death. Weren't government members the only ones that knew of this supersecret interview? Suspicion fell immediately on the executive branch of the government, particularly on Suárez himself, who was innocent.

From that moment on there was a flood of events. I searched for the latest Carrillo assassinations. There were only two: in both instances he had been gunned down, once as he was strolling in the middle of the street only hours before the Communist Party became legal, and the other time when he made his first public appearance. The consequences of the two assassinations were, in both cases, much less serious than this one.

This time, the authorities asked for calm in vain. The Bunker demanded immediate explanations and Suárez's instant removal from office, which the king was forced to agree to only a few days later. Meanwhile, the Communist Party took to the streets. The previous month, faced with the Atocha Street lawyers' murders, the Spanish Communist Party had shown some savoir faire by leading silent protests, but back then they had Carrillo as their guide and trusted the democratization process, if only minimally. Now Carrillo was no more and nobody trusted the government.

From the short list they presented to the king, the Francoists forced the election of a harsh president who ordered a charge on the protesters. Civilians were confronting the police all around the country. Gradually, other democratic forces began to join the demonstrations. The democratization process had been definitely lost, but the worst was yet to come.

A week later there is a coup d'état. The king loses all his effective powers and a state of emergency is declared throughout the country. Nobody respects it. The clashes continue, and it soon becomes clear that Spain is immersed in another civil war: what no one wanted, what everyone would have liked to avoid. Cataluña and the Basque Country take advantage of the confusion to declare themselves independent, Morocco occupies the Canary Islands, invoking its sovereignty, but at least the Canary Islanders escape the worst of the war. Barcelona is besieged and completely razed. Nobody knows how many sides are involved in the fighting. In the capitals, snipers shoot at anything that moves, and a stunned international community witnesses a civil war in Europe. Spain in 1997 was what Yugoslavia was in the 1990s: a land of mass murders, exterminations, rapes, war crimes . . .

All types of weapons are used, biological, chemical . . . millions of people die, even more when a nuclear explosion destroys Madrid. Nobody knows who has detonated the device or where it has come from, everyone points fingers at each other. That proves to be too much. United Nations forces occupy Spain and impose a precarious peace. After five years of fighting, the country is ruined, destroyed, devastated, having lost almost one-third of its population, with refugees and survivors who hardly have anything to eat. There is no parliament anymore, there is no monarchy—the royal family died with Madrid—there is nothing worth fighting for. The wounds will take time to heal. Reconstruction will take years, and no one knows how long it will last. Its echoes still resound in 2032.

I must admit that as a terrorist plan it was a very good one, better than most. I've seen them in all colors. Sometimes they prolong Franco's life and that delays the whole democratic process. In some versions, democracy arrives with Franco still alive and in command of the army. On other occasions, they avoid the death of Carrero Blanco, who becomes president of the king's first government and manages to stop the opening-up process. Others also plot to assassinate the king and create a republic. And at times they conspire for Juan Carlos not to succeed Franco; his place is then filled by another candidate to the throne, one who continues the dictator's work. But as far as number of effects per minimal cause is concerned, nothing matched this case. Who could imagine that the murder of one man in circumstances that later would be recorded as only a historical footnote could have such huge consequences?

Causing a change in history after 2012 would not have the slightest consequence; such a thing would simply make a new version of history that would coexist with those already in existence and with those constantly produced by quantum mechanics. But TT prohibits the simultaneous existence of more than one history before 7 August 2012. Thus, the pre-existing history gets replaced by the one resulting from the change. Many times I've asked myself why we insist on correcting history; after all, who cares? The only answer I have been able to find is that history just as it was, good or bad, happy or unfortunate, is ours and nobody has the right to manipulate it according to who-knows-what murky interests.

All that aside, once the junction point has been located, we must fix it. This is the most delicate moment. Normally the true instigators don't expose themselves directly; they hire the necessary personnel to carry out the action and they, in turn, subcontract other menials wherever they want to intervene. So in general all we find are some poor devils who barely know anything. On the other hand, we have the names of those highly specialized in temporal jumps, who need to be apprehended. We try to scare the former to death so that they don't become repeat offenders, but we can't do much more. The latter are very difficult to surprise. They, like us, have all the time in the world at their disposal, and we do not have the necessary equipment to invest in costly and lengthy field research. Therefore, when we run into them, more out of luck than anything else, we aren't usually very considerate.

We took the tube and went to the Transition chamber. That period is visited so often it occupies a whole wing of the main basement. Wardrobe and props are stored there; likewise our weapons, disguised as everyday objects in that time period. We use those clothes so much we need to replace them quite often.

We changed for the time period and the season. We left and got in the tube again. We passed new security controls, even stricter ones, and arrived at the underground dome where the portal is kept.

When one visits it as often as we do, it ends up losing all its charm; it becomes one more piece of the armored dome's surrealist decoration.

The structure is a type of cube. It's really taller than it is wide and it isn't solid—it consists only of the lines that form the structure. It's called the Visser Portal and is made of negative mass. When you get close you start to feel a strange repulsion, because instead of attracting matter, negative mass repels it. Therefore, it's impossible to touch it, but that isn't necessary. The structure is about five meters wide and we all fit in perfectly.

The portal is completely inactive as is. To make the trip one has to find an adequate quantum wormhole, one that connects our time period in a natural way with the temporal point we want to travel to. It seems that, at a sufficiently small scale, the space-time is not a plane but a foam where anomalous structures are constantly being formed. Some of these structures are tunnels that connect two separate regions—for example, a point from 2032 with another one in 1977. Those structures are formed and destroyed so many times that we don't have to wait very long to find the right one. When we do, the technicians feed it with energy in order to make it grow to macroscopic size, big enough so that we can cross it. But it isn't safe yet, the negative mass structures need to be attached to the Visser Portal so they become stable. First the one next to us is connected, then a similar one, a little smaller, is sent through the tunnel so that the other end is also stabilized. At that moment, if the wormhole's chosen longitude is small enough, one can go across almost instantaneously. You simply see the image from the other side, take one step and there you are.

Before 2012 they knew that such a thing was possible, but they believed the necessary energies were so great that no government on Earth, not even all of them together, would have been able to provide the energy required to open a portal. Besides, the portals must be huge, about five kilometers in diameter, in order to guarantee a successful crossing and, in that case, we were talking about several times the mass of the sun. TT changed all that. All of a sudden, minimal quantities of energy could be used to expand a tunnel between two regions of the space-time continuum or between two different space-times.

The technicians were now prepared for the jump. Located in a control room above was our support team, in case we needed additional information or in the event there were any last-minute changes in the continuum.

"Everyone ready?" Isabel asked. As the veteran of the group, it fell to her to be the leader.

Everybody checked the equipment they carried. We'd put on those clothes so many times, we no longer noticed how strange we looked. With a bit of luck we wouldn't have to go undetected for long; if everything went as planned, it would be a simple in-and-out job. Everyone seemed to have the equipment in order. Rudy was the last one to finish. He was looking at his wrist as if one of the readings didn't quite convince him. Finally he lowered it and said yes.

"All set," he said.

Good, that was it. Now or never, as always. Marisa, the daring one, was the first one to approach the portal. She stood right at the edge. She must have been feeling all the tension. The structure's negative mass combines with the positive mass of the tunnel, and that's why the sum could have either a negative, a positive, or a null net mass. The technicians always hope to get a null mass, but they're satisfied if the combined mass isn't too big in absolute terms. That way, in theory, you shouldn't feel anything when you approach, but in reality, the negative mass is closer to your body than the tunnel is, and it's normal to feel a slight pressure that pushes you forward.

Marisa disappeared and was followed by Rudy. I stopped myself at the threshold. I have never liked going through the portal. Our tunnels are normally less than twenty centimeters long, so that it's just a matter of taking one step to cross it. However, they're long enough so that you feel the peculiar effects caused by their geometry. If you look briefly toward the tunnel's wall, you will see your own image there, being repeated ad infinitum. Of course, at the other end you see the outside landscape, but that's exactly what makes it more disconcerting.

I turned to Isabel and kissed her on the lips.

"Good luck," I said.

"Good luck," she said back. She glanced at me for a moment but then looked away and approached the tunnel as well.

* * *

Each time I cross the portal old memories of how I was recruited for the TIC come to mind.

I remember mixed emotions, nostalgia and innocence, just like when someone watches a stale disk of images and movies. Everything has that blurry patina that makes defects disappear and makes you believe those times were better than they really were.

Once a week after class I used to join my friends at the La Granja Park to chat, work out, and, eventually, spend the night partying. That spring day they had canceled my historical perspective class and I arrived earlier than usual, something that of course was part of the plan.

Wearing my shorts and a pair of red shoes Isabel would later tell me were horrible, I laid down on the grass to kill time. Some things never change, and it seems my bad taste in clothes is quite known.

She approached me. It was Isabel, of course, but I didn't know that yet. She sat down next to me, close enough so as to make sure her presence was noticed, but not so close that I thought she was after me. She was wearing the light blue dress I liked so much, the one I had given her as a present. Her hair was down and she wore almost no make-up, very natural. Everything carefully thought out, everything researched. Is there anything we haven't analyzed? She had a copy of *History Reviews*, a journal I was in the habit of reading. I stared at her while she did her best to keep her eyes glued to the page. Suddenly, she lifted her face, saw me, smiled, and buried her face in the journal again.

I got up and approached her.

"Have you read Martinson's article on Carthage?" I asked her. "The one that says it didn't really exist, that the Romans built it so they could later say they had destroyed it?"

She kept silent and still while looking at me for seconds that seemed an eternity. Her expressive eyes suggested more than I needed to know and more than she wanted to display. Something about her, something indefinable, seduced me right then; it was as if a shiver ran up and down my body. I suppose at that moment she was already playing with me.

"Well, excuse me for approaching you like this," I continued. "I saw the journal you're reading and it just so happens to be my specialty. My name's Mikel, and I teach at Logroño's UniCentral."

I shifted my body trying not to look too ridiculous. I decided to sit down next to her.

"Hi," she said, a little doubtful. "I'm Isabel. I've read the article . . ." She paused while her lips outlined a hint of a smile. "To tell you the truth, I think it's totally moronic."

I was completely taken aback. I was expecting many replies, but not that one. She sat there, looking at me, calm, serene, waiting. It was obviously a provocation, and it took me a while to realize it.

"Don't listen to me," she said with an open smile. "I had a bad day yesterday, that's all. Now I'm trying to put the pieces back together."

I had lost the initiative. The feeling that overcomes you at times like these is one of impotence, of being left out of the game. The problem is I still didn't know that from the moment she had appeared we were playing with marked cards.

"Although . . . we could discuss the subject," she added without giving me time to even think of an answer. "I warn you that I'm not easy to convince."

Her voice sounded much better this time. Later I knew why: it had been a shock for her to see me, to hear me again.

"Me either," I said regaining my control somewhat.

We got up and started walking. I didn't know that from that day on I'd never see my friends again.

Of course we didn't talk about Martinson, or Carthage, or anything like that, nor did we need to. We chatted about trivialities, work, and dreams. Isabel let her true mission be lost in a limbo of gestures and anecdotes. We wandered aimlessly from here to there, we had dinner at some strange but quiet place, we ended up in my apartment.

It was at five in the morning, after having made love for the second time, that she told me. She gave me the same old speech. Why pretend? I would find out sooner or later. One needs to have a great capacity to absorb what they tell you and I admit I didn't understand it too well. What was all that about time travel, changes in history and parallel universes? She told me as well that she had been in love with me for years although, according to my own temporal experience, we'd only met that morning. I fell back asleep from shock and the peace that comes from not understanding.

I woke up first, got up, and walked toward the window; I needed to think. Outside, one of those blue days that predicts the arrival of the heat blinded me with its light.

She stirred in bed, looking for me.

"What are you thinking about?" she asked with eyes closed. She knew I was there. She knew what I was thinking, what my doubts were.

I had been meditating. The terrible reality of what she had told me had been settling in my mind, and a question was steadily buzzing about my brain.

"Do I have any option that isn't joining the TIC?" I asked her, in a somewhat sad voice.

"Of course," she answered me. "You may stay here."

"Is that what you want?"

Isabel didn't lie to me. She knew I needed her to be sincere, or at least to appear to be.

"No."

"What's our future like?"

Her answer was a nail in the coffin of my hopes. Her tone, however, gave her away.

"We don't have any future," she said.

I didn't get all the implications of her answer. Even now I discover new sides to her short but intense response.

We had lunch together that day, we went for a walk, chatted, tried to be as honest as possible. I was sincere; she only needed to be persuasive. The portal appeared in the afternoon and I crossed it for the first time to go to the TIC. We arrived seconds after Isabel left to look for me. I went through the formalities of recruitment. It was confusing to realize everybody knew me and was happy to see me again. It was as if I had always been there, and in a sense that was true. My old colleagues greeted me and took me to the accelerated instruction booths. That was the day my life started again.

* * *

We were near the place and it was still early. Everything seemed calm; it was sunny and warm for February. What we were really hoping for was to see the unsuspecting bombers appear. Usually that's the best way to go: the meeting was so secret that there were no security devices. Who would trust a police force inherited from the Francoist system?

Each one of us had a preassigned mission, so we all knew what we had to do. We headed toward the action point.

"I think they're coming," announced Marisa, who was watching the road.

"Rudy, be on the outlook for any Extras," said Isabel, and added: "Marisa, cut them off from behind. Mikel, you're with me. We'll use stunners as defense. That will be enough."

We're always afraid some Extra may show up, some stranger from the future, that is. Someone who'd come to ruin the plan. It's a bit dumb, but it works sometimes. So the best thing to do is not to lower one's guard.

We've studied terrorist bomb attacks so well that we can almost fix them with our eyes closed. It's a matter of blocking their way naturally, while we prepare our stunners. Normally we don't want to kill anybody, only stop the attempt. If any Extra appeared, of course, we wouldn't hesitate to kill him.

The van was approaching. They were calm. The place they had chosen for the bombing was still a few kilometers away. There were three of them, young, probably recruited in some Madrid neighborhood like Tresaguas or Horcasitas. I almost pitied them.

When they had almost reached us Isabel sent us the signal to begin. The moves were balletlike. Somehow I seemed to be flying above the place, supervising the operation. I saw myself moving, Isabel stopping them and me stunning the first one, Isabel the second one, me the third, seizing the bomb. Marisa was behind us observing, on guard. Rudy was a bit further out, checking out everything around us. He has something special that makes him sensitive, a sixth sense that allows him to anticipate danger.

I looked at the device; it was a common bomb, powerful enough to reach its target. Incredibly crude. I looked it over twice. Simple, I corrected myself, like the operation, and that was something I didn't like. I looked to Rudy for a sign, but he was still calm, so I tried to relax.

Only a few seconds had gone by and everything was over.

The simplest thing was left to do, but it was the trickiest: all those people need to be moved away from there, the road needs to be cleared for Carrillo, the bomb must disappear and those men need to forget the affair. Nobody must find out.

We can hang around to make sure there isn't a back-up team or another bomb, but that's just wasting time. Carrillo will never know he owes us his life, nor do we care. It's simpler to return and make sure everything is back in its original place.

We get in the van and begin the return trip to Madrid. We abandon it in Vallecas, a good place for it to disappear without a trace. We inject the three of them with a solution that will make them forget even their names. They will have to go back to school. We take the bomb, their weapons, and all their documents back to our own time period. Nobody will know who they are or what happened to them.

We stop somewhere with little traffic. We make them get out and give them a little push so they start to walk. They are three zombies by then. We start the car, they get lost in the crowd. Soon they'll be noticed.

We leave the van in an open field and look around for a discreet place to await the portal. It'll be a few minutes until they find an adequate quantum tunnel. I start to relax.

The bad thing about traveling through time is that you get completely disconnected from your own time. There's no way to communicate with it; you're left to your own devices and can only count on your own team for help.

When I saw the familiar sight of the dome I sighed in relief.

"Complete success," Isabel informed us.

Didac was gesturing at us from above.

"Tune to channel four, I think Didac wants to give us some bad news," I remarked.

"Hello everyone, I'm happy to see you," said Didac, waving a greeting. "I believe the worst is over, but there are still serious deviations in the course of events."

Marisa swore.

"Meeting in the documentation room in five minutes," said Isabel, stoically accepting that the operation had been a failure.

"What's our current situation?" asked Isabel as soon as she came in.

José Luis motioned toward the terminals without a word.

The problem was still simple. The meeting had been broadcast by radio when it was being held, and Suárez had been exposed. His position had been weakened and his enemies had taken advantage of the situation to the fullest. There was no war, everything seemed to be going well, but Suárez had been forced to negotiate with the Francoists and the Transition had been delayed. The temporal line showed clearly now how a few special groups had benefited. I thought I understood.

"An interesting simulation exercise," I said raising my voice so that everyone could hear me. "They create a deviation we must resolve; I suspect our arrival is the cause they were waiting for so they could trigger a new effect, precisely the one they really wanted. The first one was nothing but bait. Effective."

The ability to intervene in time is not unlimited. You cannot continue to put patches over other patches forever. Someday everything may explode in our faces if we keep on fixing history. We're already beginning to have problems with forgetful people.

Isabel and the rest of the group looked at me. They had all understood the trap that had been set for us. We were the fuse for the true historical manipulation.

"Don't be so Machiavellian," Rudy remarked. "They knew we were going to intervene, so they planned everything out. We've only corrected an anomalous situation for them, one that makes room for a beneficial one. They're sophisticated, but I've seen worse."

"We have to go back," said Marisa.

We all looked at each other. Nobody likes to go back to the same place we're already at; it's just nerves. It's been proven we can coexist with ourselves in the same place and time, even though I don't know anyone who likes doing it. We couldn't ask the back-up team to go, either; it was our mission and we had to fix it ourselves.

Isabel transmitted the new data to Operations Control and requested another delivery. Meanwhile, the rest of us focused on looking for a new inflection point.

We located it: a radio station had been tipped off about something that was going to occur at that location. They had sent a camouflaged car and none of us had taken notice. That's the problem with the huge quantity of variations, ours or theirs, that can get caught up in a mission. Intelligent and simple. They never get tired, but they don't realize we don't get tired either.

We got ready again. We hadn't changed clothes, so this time everything went faster. We entered the tube and there we were again. It was still that ominous afternoon. We were one kilometer further down, at a point midway between our first action and the country house where the conversations were to be held.

The first warning came, as was normal in these cases, from Rudy.

"Danger!"

We were all more calm and relaxed, since there was no reason for this to be dangerous or complicated. Except that this time nothing went well. They were waiting for us. They knew we would go and, unfortunately for us, they had even guessed where we would enter that continuum. That's our worst moment, since we're always dazed for a few minutes.

They were shooting at us but we didn't see anybody. They were Extras, of course; the weapons they were using left no doubt. Rudy had detected them, but not fast enough. We all tried to cover ourselves and spread out. What mattered was to locate the source of the shots. Marisa set up a scanner as soon as she found the source, and we all started to return fire.

There were two of them, and they were placed at an angle so as to catch us in crossfire. Rudy was already positioning himself to catch them from behind while Marisa moved in on his left. I was shooting like a madman to cover them while Isabel, the most daring, was advancing straight toward them, covering herself as best she could. With luck there wouldn't be any traces of the raid left. We were all shooting with plasma pistols—they don't make any sound and affect only the ecstasis field that surrounds us; that's enough.

I didn't have time to think. I heard a scream and a red light lit up on my console. I didn't want to find out whose it was. We had just suffered a casualty. The three of us who were left coldly bore down on them; we were already in position and didn't give them any kind of a chance. They knew they would never have one. It was as if a light went off, only you don't stay in the dark.

We became tense, serious. Suddenly everything was quiet; it was time to worry about the rest of the world and about ourselves. I didn't need to look at the console to know which one of us was gone. What a euphemism! I felt a sharp pain and I let it show.

"It's Isabel," Marisa's voice pierced my ears.

I approached her body. Her head was smashed. I held her right wrist and read what her control panel said. It indicated a massive brain failure. Our nanosystems can repair many wounds, but not even all the technology of the twenty-first century could reconstruct a shattered brain.

"We've got a job to do," Rudy declared. He's usually the most practical and coldest among us.

We divided up the work. This time we were more conscientious. We checked that nobody had witnessed the little battle, then prepared the bodies to take them back to the future with us.

When we finished, we simply waited for the transmitter people to arrive. Rudy and Marisa kept watch just in case any other Extra showed up trying to spoil the plan.

Isabel's memory hit me at regular intervals, as if it had installed itself in my heart. Each beat gave me life, each beat killed me.

The transmitter people arrived, very discreetly, in a car without any identification and parked two hundred meters from the house. I didn't even give them time to get out of the car. I went straight to them. I blurted out what we had prepared: I pretended I was lazy and sold them the information they wanted to hear. I sent them to Arganda. The information was good, I told them. Some of their colleagues had already come and gone when they got the new tip; at the last minute, the meeting of several Francoist factions had moved to the old Institute in Arganda del Rey, on the road toward Valencia. They still had time to get there, since it had been delayed for two hours because of the move. If they hurried, they would still arrive in time.

It was best to muddle up places, times, and characters. Besides, Arganda had been a communist domain during the first decade of the Transition. It was perfect for the Francoists. The car started up again and made its way down the road. We didn't see them again.

We were checking everything around us. The hours seemed like flagstones slowly falling down on us. Right on time, Carrillo passed by us and went inside the house. That time there was no strange movement. The leader of the Communist Party didn't even see us as he went by. We had saved his life, but he would never know that.

We checked around for the last time and waited for the portal to go back to our time. When we returned it was a relief to verify that history was back to being the original one, at least for now. Somebody, somewhere, would be plotting some new way to change it. The technicians took the bodies away.

As the second most senior member, I tackled the difficult duty of filling out the paperwork. Rudy and Marisa offered to help, but I preferred to do it alone. The bureaucrats, those who are safe in their offices, want to know everything about everybody. They don't leave anything to chance.

When I was finished, the orders for the second operation flashed on the console screen before me.

Isabel lied to me. I don't bear her any grudge. We know everything about ourselves; there are too many possibilities about the future. The truth is there are so many futures that knowing anything about them simply stops being interesting. That's why she didn't tell me the truth, and I'm grateful to her for that; it's a bit overwhelming to begin to glimpse all of the implications of belonging to the GEI.

Before crossing the portal I have consulted every available file about Isabel. So now I know everything about her. Not firsthand. It was the first time she was recruited in this life, so I have lots of information about her previous enlistments, but they are cold reports, without soul, without conscience, without respect for her. That's why I've decided to be my own memory. I think I must have considered doing it more than once, writing to leave myself the story of my experiences with Isabel, the only thing that really matters to me. It's clear I'll always be here, so I'd better have some good notes about my own emotions and feelings. Maybe someday I'll get tired and erase them, but that will be the decision of another Mikel, not me. Perhaps I'll get Isabel to collaborate. All the Mikels that follow me will always have the opportunity to access what I'm writing.

I am walking around the halls of the university where Isabel studies. I am going to find her. Before getting here I've had to evaluate what my feelings toward Isabel are at this moment. I try to be as impartial as possible so that they don't interfere with the operation, which absolutely must be successful. It's odd how Isabel has categorically refused to be recruited some times; it happened to me once and I believe I know why, even though I haven't told anyone. I've discovered that the first hours are crucial to her subsequent behavior toward me, so the first thing I had to do was establish exactly what it was I wanted, this time, from her. We are like little gods deciding the lives of others, returning over and over again to make the same decisions. One has to be careful, since what we are sure of is that at some time things will be reversed, and therefore one must work and behave honestly so that later you may be treated likewise.

According to the records, I have already explored some variations with Isabel, not only about kinds of relationships, but even with regard to age. I have three particular moments in which I'm completely certain about her behavior. The first one is when she is twenty-three and a bit wild, but her intuition and self-assurance are brilliant. The second is when she's twenty-six. It's her best moment: she's just over a failed relationship, disillusioned with her work and with men, she's decided to take refuge in her studies, her best qualities aren't lost yet. The third one is when she's thirty-two, which is when I personally like her best. She's much more serious, poised, and her character has lost much of the harshness that irritates me when we fight. I've never gone beyond them. In many of the temporal lines, Isabel begins a lasting relationship at thirty-three, and I've never felt like exploring much further from that point.

This time I've chosen the hardest of the three Isabels I prefer. She's twenty-six and she'll look at me with mistrust. She's withdrawn into herself since her last companion let her down. It's clear I won't get anything today. That's what I prefer; at this point sex doesn't interest me. I think I would be unable to tell her how much I love her, unable to explain to her what a tremendous temporal mess we've gotten ourselves into. As she stands before me, Isabel wouldn't be able to understand why I complain. She would remind me too much of that other Isabel, so familiar and close, who has just kissed me and wished me luck before entering the portal. We both have to go through a period of mutual adaptation—well, only I have to this time; everything will be new, and thus attractive, for her.

I have three days ahead of me to talk to her. Isabel will miss her classes, I've already reserved a table at the Gorría Atemparak in Barcelona for tomorrow. We'll go to the theater and go see *Aïda* again. According to the records, I've seen it countless times, but it'll be the first time for both of us. We'll take a walk along the beach and, little by little, I'll unravel the threads of the huge skein I'm hiding. Maybe at the end we'll wind up in bed, maybe not. That's one of the few things I don't dare to predict.

I'm getting closer, all I have to do is go around a corner and I'll have her in sight. I vow I'll take care of myself and her, of us both. I don't want to go through this, it's very hard on me.

There are people, many people in the hallways, they're coming out of class. For a moment I doubt I'll be able to see her. I'm not afraid, I know she's there, waiting for me to come and tell her I'm sorry.

None of the records, none of the tapes have prepared me for her dazzling appearance. She is over there, at the exact place and at the right time. She has that cheerful, happy look, her shining eyes seem to give off light. Her lips form a smile that is a never-ending invitation. She's looked at me from afar without recognizing me, she has no reason to, she's talking to a classmate and they would continue if I didn't get in their way. She doesn't know who I am yet, she doesn't avert her eyes until she's right next to me. I've simply bumped into her and she has dropped her books. All I could do was smile and hide my face. I'm telling her that I'm sorry and she listens to a simple apology, in reality I'm asking her forgiveness for what I'm doing to her, for uprooting her from her temporal line, for loving her, for taking her far away and maybe for killing her over and over again, but I cannot do anything else. What better team than the one already formed? The one whose members' reactions are all known, and whose value and ability have been proven. Who's to stop us from continually recruiting the same agents when there are millions of almost identical copies of them in millions of similar worlds?

I speak but I don't listen to myself; I only have ears for her. I recite a song learned too long ago.

I close my eyes. I finally understand what she felt when she came toward me in the park. I desperately look for time to recover, I let her smell envelop me.

The situation is somewhat poetic. Isabel is here again, she has always been here, she never left. I only need to hand her the memories she has lost, so that she becomes herself again.

It's hard to realize it, when you finally understand you want to forget it, you would like not to even suspect it, but this moment arrives and you bump right into bitter reality.

Now I know we are immortal, we don't have any future, but what does that matter when an eternal present is ours? Millions of Isabels await me. All of them are within my reach. All of them are waiting for a fraction of their own eternity.

Nimby and the Dimension Hoppers

CORY DOCTOROW

Cory Doctorow [www.craphound.com] is a Canadian, recently living in San Francisco, California, and now moving to England. His first novel, Down and Out in the Magic Kingdom, *was published in 2002; his second novel,* Eastern Standard Tribe, *in 2004. A collection of short stories is forthcoming in 2004. He's a sincere convert to the wonders of technology, especially if it involves computers, the very spirit of new millennium optimism. He's the Outreach Coordinator for the Electronic Frontier Foundation, an organization that has been fighting for cyber-rights for more than a decade, and he gives his fiction away electronically after publication in an attempt to inspire readers to buy a hard copy of the publisher's edition. He also co-wrote* The Complete Idiot's Guide to Writing Science-Fiction, *with Karl Schroeder, and has collaborated on several stories with Charles Stross.*

"Nimby and the Dimension Hoppers" appeared in Asimov's. *It's a charming domestic tale of power ranger-like combatants intruding into the organic homes of people living in the post-technological future, and shooting them up with blasters. This destruction is outrageous, absurd, and must be stopped.*

Don't get me wrong—I *like* unspoiled wilderness. I *like* my sky clear and blue and my city free of the thunder of cars and jackhammers. I'm no technocrat. But goddammit, who wouldn't want a fully automatic, laser-guided, armor-piercing, self-replenishing personal sidearm?

Nice turn of phrase, huh? I finally memorized it one night, from one of the hoppers, as he stood in my bedroom, pointing his hand-cannon at another hopper, enumerating its many charms: "This is a laser-guided blah blah blah. Throw down your arms and lace your fingers behind your head, blah blah blah." I'd heard the same dialog nearly every day that month, whenever the dimension-hoppers catapulted into my home, shot it up, smashed my window, dived into the street, and chased one another through my poor little shtetl, wreaking havoc, maiming bystanders, and then gating out to another poor dimension to carry on there.

Assholes.

It was all I could do to keep my house well-fed on sand to replace the windows. Much more hopper invasion and I was going to have to extrude its legs and babayaga to the beach. Why the hell was it always *my* house, anyway?

I wasn't going to get back to sleep, that much was sure. The autumn wind blowing through the shattered window was fragrant with maple and rich decay and crisp hay, but it was also cold enough to steam my breath and turn me out in all-over gooseflesh. Besides, the racket they were making out in the plaza was deafening, all supersonic thunderclaps and screams from wounded houses. The househusbands would have their work cut out for them come morning.

So I found a robe and slippers and stumbled down to the kitchen, got some coffee from one of the nipples and milk from another, waited for the noise to recede into the bicycle fields and went outside and knocked on Sally's door.

Her bedroom window flew open and she hung her head out. "Barry?" she called down.

"Yeah," I called back up, clouds of condensed breath obscuring her sleep-gummed face. "Let me in—I'm freezing to death."

The window closed and a moment later the door swung open. Sally had wrapped a heavy duvet around her broad shoulders like a shawl, and underneath, she wore a loose robe that hung to her long, bare toes. Sally and I had a thing, once. It was serious enough that we attached our houses and joined the beds. She curled her toes when I tickled her. We're still friends—hell, our houses are still next door to one another—but I haven't curled her toes in a couple of years.

"Jesus, it can't be three in the morning, can it?" she said as I slipped past her and into the warmth of her house.

"It can and is. Transdimensional crime fighters hew to no human schedule." I collapsed onto her sofa and tucked my feet under my haunches. "I have had more than enough of this shit," I said, massaging my temples.

Sally sank down next to me and threw her comforter over my lap, then gave my shoulder a squeeze. "It's taking a toll on all of us. The Jeffersons are going to relocate. They've been writing to their cousins in Niagara Falls, and they say that there're hardly any hoppers down there. But how long is that gonna last, I wonder?"

"Oh, I don't know. The hoppers could go away tomorrow. We don't know that they're going to be here forever."

"Of course I know it. You can't put the genie back in the bottle. They've got d-hoppers now—they're not going to just stop using them."

I didn't say anything, just stared pointedly at the abstract mosaic covering her parlor wall: closely fitted pieces of scrap aluminum, plastics too abstruse to feed to even the crudest house, rare beach-glass and bunched vinyl.

"That's different," she said. "We ditched the technocracy because we found something that worked better. No one decided it was too dangerous and had to be set aside for our own good. It just got . . . obsolete. Nothing's going to make d-hoppers obsolete for those guys." Out in the plaza, the booms continued, punctuated by the peristaltic noises of houses hurrying away. Sally's house gave a shudder in sympathy, and the mosaic rippled.

I held my cup away from the comforter as coffee sloshed over the edge and to the floor, where the house drank it greedily.

"No caffeine!" Sally said as she sopped up the coffee with her stockinged foot. "The house gets all jumpy."

I opened my mouth to say something about Sally's crackpot house-husbandry theories, and then the door was blown off its hinges. A hopper in outlandish technocrat armor rolled into the parlor, sat up, snapped off three rounds in the general direction of the door (one passed through it, the other two left curdled houseflesh and scorch marks on the wall around it).

Sally and I levitated out of our seats and dived behind the sofa as another hopper rolled through the door and returned fire, missing his opponent but blowing away the mosaic. My heart hammered in my chest, and all my other clichés hackneyed in my chestnuts.

"You okay?" I hollered over the din.

"I think so," Sally said. A piece of jagged plastic was embedded in the wall inches over her head, and the house was keening.

A stray blast of electric thunder set the sofa ablaze, and we scrambled away. The second gunman was retreating under a volley of fire from the first, who was performing machine-assisted gymnastics around the parlor, avoiding the shots aimed at him. The second man made good his escape, and the first holstered his weapon and turned to face us.

"Sorry about the mess, folks," he said, through his faceplate.

I was speechless. Sally, though, cupped her ear and hollered "What?"

"Sorry," the gunman said.

"What?" Sally said again. She turned and said, "Can you make out what he's saying?" She winked at me with the eye that faced away from him.

"No," I said, slowly. "Can't make out a word."

"Sorry," he said again, more loudly.

"We! Can't! Understand! You!" Sally said.

The man raised his visor with an air of exasperation and said, "I'm sorry, all right?"

"Not as sorry as you're gonna be," Sally said, and jammed her thumb into his eye. He hollered and his gauntlets went to his face just as Sally snatched away his gun. She rapped the butt against his helmet to get his attention, then scampered back, keeping the muzzle aimed at him. The gunman looked at her with dawning comprehension, raising his arms, lacing his fingers behind his head and blah blah blah.

"Asshole," she said.

His name was Larry Roman, which explained the word "ROMAN" stenciled onto each piece of his armor. Getting it off of him was trickier than shelling a lobster, and he cursed us blue the whole way. Sally kept the gun trained on him, impassive, as I peeled off the sweaty carapace and bound his wrists and ankles.

Her house was badly injured, and I didn't think it would make it. Certainly, the walls' fading to a brittle, unhealthy white boded ill. The d-hopper itself was a curious and complex device, a forearm-sized lozenge seemingly cast of a single piece of metal—titanium?—and covered with a welter of confusing imprinted controls. I set it down carefully, not wanting to find myself inadvertently whisked away to a parallel universe.

Roman watched me from his good eye—the one that Sally poked was swollen shut—with a mixture of resentment and concern. "Don't worry," I said. "I'm not going to play with it."

"Why are you doing this?" he said.

I cocked my head at Sally. "It's her show," I said.

Sally kicked her smoldering sofa. "You killed my house," she said. "You assholes keep coming here and shooting up the place, without a single thought to the people who live here—"

"What do you mean, 'keep coming here'? This is the first time anyone's ever used the trans-d device."

Sally snorted. "Sure, in *your* dimension. You're a little behind schedule, pal. We've had hoppers blasting through here for months now."

"You're lying," he said. Sally looked coolly at him. I could have told him that that was no way to win an argument with Sally. I'd never found *any* way of winning an argument with her, but blank refusal didn't work for sure. "Look, I'm a police officer. The man I'm chasing is a dangerous criminal. If I don't catch him, you're all in danger."

"Really?" she drawled. "Greater danger than you assholes put us in when you shoot us?"

He swallowed. Stripped of his armor, wearing nothing but high-tech underwear, and he was finally getting scared. "I'm just doing my duty. Upholding the law. You two are going to end up in a lot of trouble. I want to speak to someone in charge."

I cleared my throat. "That would be me, this year. I'm the mayor."

"You're kidding."

"It's an administrative position," I apologized. I'd read up on civics of old, and I knew that mayoring wasn't what it once was. Still, I'm a fine negotiator, and that's what it takes nowadays.

"So what are you going to do with me?"

"Oh, I'm sure we'll think of something," Sally said.

Sally's house was dead by sunrise. It heaved a terrible sigh, and the nipples started running with black gore. The stink was overpowering, so we led our prisoner shivering next door to my place.

My place wasn't much better. The cold wind had been blowing through my bedroom window all night, leaving a rime of frost over the house's delicate, thin-barked internal walls. But I've got a southern exposure, and as the sun rose, buttery light pierced the remaining windows and warmed the interior, and I heard the house's sap sluicing up inside the walls. We got ourselves coffees and resumed the argument.

"I tell you, Osborne's out there, and he's got the morals of a jackal. If I don't get to him, we're all in trouble." Roman was still trying to convince us to give him back his gear and let him get after his perp.

"What did he do, anyway?" I asked. Some sense of civic responsibility was nagging at me—what if the guy really *was* dangerous?

"Does it matter?" Sally asked. She was playing with Roman's gear, crushing my ornamental pebbles to powder with the power-assisted gauntlets. "They're all bastards. *Technocrats*." She spat out the word and powdered another pebble.

"He's a monopolist," Roman said, as though that explained everything. We must have looked confused, because he continued. "He's the Senior Strategist for a company that makes networked relevance filters. They've been planting malware online that breaks any standards-defined competing products. If he isn't brought to justice, he'll own the whole goddamn media ecology. He *must* be stopped!" His eyes flashed.

Sally and I traded looks, then Sally burst out laughing. "He did *what?*"

"He's engaged in unfair business practices!"

"Well, I think we'll be able to survive, then," she said. She hefted the pistol again. "So, Roman, you say that you folks just invented the d-hopper, huh?"

He looked puzzled. "The trans-d device," I said, remembering what he'd called it.

"Yes," he said. "It was developed by a researcher at the University of Waterloo and stolen by Osborne so he could flee justice. We had that one fabbed up just so we could chase him."

Aha. The whole shtetl was built over the bones of the University of Waterloo—my house must be right where the physics labs once stood; still stood, in the technocratic dimensions. That explained my popularity with the transdimensional set.

"How do you work it?" Sally asked, casually.

I wasn't fooled and neither was Roman. Sally's version of casual put my most intense vibe to shame.

"I can't disclose that," Roman said, setting his face in an expression of grim dutifulness.

"Aw, c'mon," Sally said, fondling the d-hopper. "What's the harm?"

Roman stared silently at the floor.

"Trial and error it is, then," Sally said, and poised a finger over one of the many inset controls.

Roman groaned.

"Don't do that. Please," he said. "I'm in enough trouble as it is."

Sally pretended she hadn't heard him. "How hard can it be, after all? Barry, we've both studied technocracy—let's figure it out together. Does this look like the on-switch to you?"

"No, no," I said, catching on. "You can't just go pushing buttons at random—you could end up whisked away to another dimension!" Roman appeared relieved. "We have to take it apart to see how it works first. I've got some tools out in the shed." Roman groaned.

"And if those don't work," Sally continued, "I'm sure these gloves would peel it open real quick. After all, if we break this one, there's always the other guy—Osborne? He's got one, too."

"I'll show you," Roman said. "I'll show you."

Roman escaped as we were finishing breakfast. It was my fault. I figured that once he'd taken us through the d-hopper's workings, he was cowed. Sally and I had a mini-spat over untying him, but that left me feeling all nostalgic and fuzzy for our romantic past, and maybe that's why I wasn't on my guard. It also felt less antisocial once my houseguest was untied and spooning up mueseli at my homey old kitchen table.

He was more cunning than I'd guessed. Square-jawed,

blue-eyed (well, black-and-blue-eyed, thanks to Sally), and exhausted, he'd lulled me into a false sense of security. When I turned to squeeze another cup of coffee from the kitchen wall, he kicked the table over and scrambled away. Sally fired a bolt after him, which hit my already overwrought house and caused my toilet to flush and all my tchotchkes to rain down from my shelves as it jerked. In an instant, Roman was scurrying away down the street.

"Sally!" I shouted, exasperated. "You could've killed him!"

She was ashen, staring at the pistol. "I didn't mean to! It was a reflex."

We both struggled into our shoes and took off after him. By the time I caught sight of him, he was off in the bicycle fields, uprooting a ripe mountain bike and pedaling away toward Guelph.

A group of rubberneckers congregated around us, most of the town, dressed in woolens and mitts against the frosty air. Sally and I were still in our pajamas, and I saw the town gossips taking mental notes. By supper, the housenet would be burning up with news of our reconciliation.

"Who was that?" Lemuel asked me. He'd been mayor before me, and still liked to take a proprietary interest in the comings and goings around town.

"D-hopper," Sally said. "Technocrat. He killed my house."

Lemuel clucked his tongue and scrunched up his round, ruddy face. "That's bad. The Beckers' house, too. Barry, you'd better send someone off to Toronto to parley for some more seed."

"Thank you, Lemuel," I said, straining to keep the irritation out of my voice. "I'll do that."

He held his hands up. "I'm not trying to tell you how to do your job," he said. "Just trying to help you out. Times like this, we all need to pull together."

"I just want to catch that son-of-a-bitch," Sally said.

"Oh, I expect he'll be off to his home dimension shortly," Lemuel said.

"Nuh-uh," I said. "We got—oomph." Sally trod on my foot.

"Yeah, I expect so," she said. "How about the other one—did anyone see where he went?"

"Oh, he took off east," Hezekiah said. He was Lemuel's son, and you could've nested them like Russian dolls: ruddy, paunchy, round-faced, and earnest. Hezekiah had a fine touch with the cigarette trees, and his grove was a local tourist stop. "Headed for Toronto, maybe."

"All right, then," Sally said. "I'll send word ahead. He won't get far. We'll head out and meet him."

"What about your house?" Lemuel asked.

"What about it?"

"Well, you've got to get your stuff moved out soon—the househusbands will be wanting to take it away for mulch."

"Tell them they can put my stuff in Barry's place," she said. I watched the gossipy looks flying.

Sally worked the housenet furiously as the househusbands trekked in and out of my place with armloads of her stuff. They kept giving me hey-big-fella looks, but I knew that any congratulations were premature. Sally wasn't moving in to get romantic—she was doing it out of expedience, her primary motivation in nearly every circumstance. She scribed with the housenet stylus, back rigid, waiting impatiently for her distant correspondents to work their own styli, until every wall in my house was covered in temporary pigment. No one had seen Osborne.

"Maybe he went back to his dimension," I said.

"No, he's here. I saw his d-hopper before he ran out last night—it was a wreck."

"Maybe he fixed it," I said.

"And maybe he hasn't. This has got to stop, Barry. If you don't want to help, just say so. But stop trying to dissuade me." She slammed the stylus down. "Are you in or out?"

"I'm in," I said. "I'm in."

"Then get dressed," she said.

I was already dressed. I said so.

"Put on Roman's armor. We need to be on even footing with Osborne if we're going to catch him, and that stuff won't fit me."

"What about Roman?"

"He'll be back," she said. "We have his d-hopper."

* * *

What did I call it? "Outlandish technocrat armor?" Maybe from the outside. But once I was inside, man, I was a *god.* I walked on seven-league boots, boots that would let me jump as high as the treetops. My vision extended down to the infrared and up into the ultraviolet and further up into the electromagnetic, so that I could see the chemically encoded housenet signals traversing the root-systems that the houses all tied into, the fingers of polarized light lengthening as the sun dipped to the west. My hearing was acute as a rabbit's, the wind's soughing and the crackle of forest-creatures and the whoosh-whoosh of sap all clearly delineated and perfectly triangulated. We set out after Roman, and I quickly evolved a search-strategy: I would leap as high as I could, then spin around quickly as I fell back to earth, surveying the countryside in infrared for anything human-shaped. Once back on terra firma, I scooped up Sally and took a great leap forward—no waiting for her slow, unassisted legs to keep up with my gigantic strides—set her down, and repeated the process.

We kept after it for an hour or two, falling into a kind of pleasant reverie, lulled by the fiery crazy quilt of the autumn leaves viewed from great height. I'd seen color plates in old technocrat books, the earth shown from such heights, even from *space,* and of all the things we'd given up with technocracy, I think that flight was the thing that I wished for most fervently.

It was growing chilly by the time we reached Hamilton. Hamilton! In two hours! I was used to thinking of Hamilton as being a hard day's bikeride from home, but here I was, not even out of breath, and there already. I gathered Sally into my arms and leapt toward the city-limits, enchanted by the sunset's torchy light over the hills, and something fast and hard smashed into me from the side. Instinctively, I tightened my grip on Sally, but she wasn't there—good thing, since with the armor's power-assist, squeezing Sally that hard might've broken her spine.

I slammed into the dirt, the armor's suspension whining. I righted myself and heard Sally hollering. I looked up and there she was, squirming in Osborne's arms as he leapt away with her.

They headed west, back toward the shtetl, and I chased as best I could, but Osborne worked the armor like he'd been born in it. How must his dimension be, where people leap through the air on tireless, infinitely strong legs, enhanced vision and reflexes making light work of the banal realities of geography, time, and space?

I lost them by Flamborough. Panic scratched at my guts as I sought them through the entire electromagnetic spectrum, as I strained my ears to make out Sally's outraged bellows. A moment's reflection told me I was panicking needlessly: there was only one place they could be going: to the shtetl, to my house, to the d-hopper.

Except that I had the d-hopper with me, neatly clipped to the armor's left thigh-guard, in a small cargo-space. The right thigh-guard was full of miniature, telescoping survival bits of various description and a collection of pills that Roman had identified as nutritional supplements. Osborne wouldn't be getting out of my dimension any time soon.

I set off for home as fast as I could in the now near-total darkness. A bloody harvest moon rose behind me as I made my leaping dash, and then I got lost twice in the odd shadows it cast from my unfamiliar aerial vantage-points. Still, it took less than an hour traveling alone, not bothering to search anymore.

My house's own biosystems cast a welter of infrared shadows, making it impossible for me to tell if Sally and Osborne were inside, so I scrambled up the insulating ivy on the north side and then spidered along the walls, peering in the windows.

I found them in the Florida room at the back of the house. Osborne had his helmet off—he had a surprisingly boyish, good-natured face that took me off my guard for a moment—and was eating a slice of pumpkin pie from my fridge, his sidearm trained on Sally, who was glaring at him from her seat in the rickety twig-chair she'd given me for my birthday half a decade before.

The biolume porch-lamp glowed brightly inside the Florida room, and I knew that it would be throwing up glare on the inside of the windows. Emboldened, I crouched down and duck-walked the length of the windowsill, getting the lay of the land before deciding on my next course of action. Osborne's helmet was propped atop the fridge, staring blindly at me. The pistol was in his left hand, the pie in his right, and his finger was on the trigger. I couldn't think of any way to disarm him before he fired on Sally. I would have to parley. It's my strong-suit, anyway. That's why they made me mayor: I could bargain with those arrogant pricks in Toronto for house-seeds; with the fools of Hamilton for cold-temp citrusfruit; with the traveling circuses that demanded bicycle after bicycle in exchange for a night's entertainment. In Lemuel's day, the shtetl had hardly a bike to its name by March, the whole harvest traded away for our necessities. After my first year as mayor, we'd had to grow an extra barn with hooks along all the rafters to hang our spare bicycles from. I would parley with Osborne for Sally, extract a promise to steer clear of our dimension forever in exchange for his damned technocrat gadget.

I was raising a gauntleted hand to tap on the window when I was tackled from behind.

I had the presence of mind to stifle my grunt of surprise as the armor's gyros whined to keep me erect under the weight of the stranger on my back.

I reached behind me and grabbed my assailant by the shoulder, flipping him over my head and to the earth. He, too, stifled his groan, and as I peered at him in the false-light of my visor's display, I saw that it was Roman.

"You can't give him the trans-d device," he hissed. He massaged his shoulder. I felt a pang of guilt—that must've really hurt. I hadn't so much as slapped someone in ten years. Who had?

"Why not?" I asked.

"I have to bring him to justice. He's the only one with the key to his malware agents. If he gets away now, we'll never catch him—the whole world will be at his mercy."

"He's got Sally," I said. "If I need to give him the d-hopper to get her back, that's what I'm gonna do." Thinking: What the hell do I care about *your* world, pal?

He grimaced and flushed. He'd stolen a wooly coat and a pair of unripened gumboots from somewhere but he was still wearing nothing but his high-tech underwear underneath, and his lips were cyanotic blue. I was nice and toasty in the heated armor. Muffled voices came from my Florida room. I risked a peek. Sally was haranguing Osborne fiercely, though nothing but her baleful tone was discernable through the pane. Osborne was grinning.

I could have told him that that wasn't much of a strategy. He seemed to be chuckling, and I watched in horrified fascination as Sally stood abruptly, unmindful of the gun, and heaved her chair at his head. He raised his forearms to defend himself and his gun wasn't pointing at Sally anymore. No thinking at all, just action, and I jumped through the window, a technocrat action-hero snap-rolling into his shins, grappling with his gun hand, and my enhanced hearing brought me Sally's shouts, Osborne's grunts of surprise, Roman's bellowing passage through the sharp splinters of the window. I kept trying for Osborne's unprotected head, but he was *fast,* fast as a world where time is sliced into fractions of a second, fast as a person raised in that world, and I—who never measured time in a unit smaller than a morning—was hardly a match for him.

He fired the pistol wildly, setting the house to screaming. Before I knew it, Osborne had me pinned on my stomach, my arms trapped beneath me. He leveled the pistol at Sally again. "What a waste," he sighed, and took aim. I wriggled fiercely, trying to free my arms, and the d-hopper dropped into my gauntlet. Without thinking, I jammed as many controls as I could find and the universe stood on its head.

There was an oozy moment of panic as the world slurred and snapped back into focus, the thing taking less time than the description of it, so fast that I only assimilated it post-facto, days later. Osborne was still atop me, and I had the presence of mind to roll him off and get to my feet, snatch free my gun, and point it at his unprotected face.

He stood slowly, hands laced behind his head, and looked at me with a faint sneer.

"What is your problem?" a voice said from behind me. I kept the gun on Osborne and scuttled left so that I could see the speaker.

It was me.

Me, in a coarsely woven housecoat and slippers, eyes gummed with sleep, thin to gauntness, livid, shaking with rage. Osborne took advantage of my confusion and made a jump for the whole-again Florida room window. I squeezed off two rounds at his back and hit the house instead, which screamed. I heard knick-knacks rattling off their shelves.

"Oh, for Christ's sake!" I heard myself shout from behind me, and then I was reeling with the weight of myself on my own back. Hands tugged at my helmet. Gently, I holstered my gun, shucked my gauntlets, and caught the hands.

"Barry," I said.

"How'd you know my name?"

"Get down from there, Barry, okay?"

He climbed down and I turned to face him. With slow, deliberate motions, I unsnapped the helmet and pulled it off. "Hey, Barry," I said.

"Oh, for Christ's sake," he repeated, more exasperated than confused. "I should've known."

"Sorry," I said, sheepish now. "I was trying to save Sally's life."

"God, *why?"*

"What's your problem with Sally?"

"She sold us out! To Toronto! The whole shtetl hasn't got two bikes to rub together."

"Toronto? How many houses could we possibly need?"

He barked a humorless laugh. "Houses? Toronto doesn't make houses anymore. Wait there," he said and stomped off into the house's depths. He emerged a moment later holding a massive, unwieldy rifle. It had a technocratic feel, toolmarks and straight lines, and I knew that it had been manufactured, not grown. The barrel was as big around as my fist. "Civil defense," he said. "Sally's idea. We're all supposed to be ready to repel the raiders at a moment's notice. Can't you smell it?"

I took a deep breath through my nose. There was an ammonia-and-sulfur reek in the air, a sharp contrast to the autumnal crispness I was accustomed to. "What's that?"

"Factories. Ammo, guns, armor. It's all anyone does anymore. We're all on short rations." He gestured at the broken window. "Your friend's gonna get quite a surprise."

As if on cue, I heard a volley of distant thunder. The other Barry smiled grimly. "Scratch one d-hopper," he said. "If I were you, I'd ditch that getup before someone takes a shot at *you*."

I started to shuck Roman's armor when we both heard the sound of return fire, the crash of the technocrat pistol almost civilized next to the flatulence of Sally's homebrew blunderbusses. "He's tricky," I said.

But the other Barry had gone pale and still and it occurred to me that Osborne was almost certainly firing on someone that this Barry counted as a friend. Sensitivity was never one of my strong-suits.

I stripped off the rest of the armor and stood shivering in the frosty November air. "Let's go," I said, brandishing Roman's gun.

"You'll need a coat," said the other Barry. "Hang on." He disappeared into the house and came back with my second-best coat, the one with the big stain from years before on the right breast, remnants of a sloppily eaten breakfast of late blackberries right off the bush.

"Thanks," I said, feeling a tremor of dangerous weirdness as our hands touched.

The other Barry carried a biolume lamp at shoulder-height, leading the way, while I followed, noticing that his walk was splay-footed and lurching, then noticing that mine was, too, and growing intensely self-conscious about the whole matter. I nearly tripped myself a dozen times trying to correct it before we found the scene of Osborne's stand.

It was a small clearing where I'd often gone to picnic on

summer days. The lantern lit up the ancient tree-trunks, scarred with gunshot, pits with coals glowing in them like malevolent eyes. Hazy wisps of wood smoke danced in the light.

At the edge of the clearing, we found Hezekiah on his back, his left arm a wreck of molten flesh and toothy splinters of bone. His breathing was shallow and fast, and his eyes were wide and staring. He rubbed at them with his good hand when he caught sight of us. "Seeing double. Goddamn gun blew up in my arms. Goddamn gun. Goddamn it."

Neither of us knew squat about first aid, but I left the other Barry crouched beside Hezekiah while I went for help, crashing through the dark but familiar woods.

Somewhere out there, Osborne was looking for the d-hopper, for a way home. I had it in the pocket of the stained, second-best coat. If he found it and used it, I'd be stranded here, where guns explode in your arms and Barry wishes that Sally was dead.

The streets of the shtetl, normally a friendly grin of neat little houses, had been turned snaggle-toothed and gappy by the exodus of villagers under the onslaught of d-hoppers. Merry's clinic was still there, though, and I approached it cautiously, my neck prickly with imagined, observing eyes.

I was barely there when I was tackled from the side by Osborne, who gathered me roughly in his arms and jumped back into the woods. We sailed through the night sky, the d-hopper crushed to my side by his tight, metallic embrace, and when he set down and dropped me, I scrambled backward on my ass, trying to put some distance between me and him.

"Hand it over," he said, pointing his gun at me. His voice was cold, and brooked no argument. But I'm a negotiator by trade. I thought fast.

"My fingers're on it now," I said, holding it through my pocket. "Just one squeeze and poof, off I go and you're stuck here forever. Why don't you put the gun away and we'll talk about this?"

He sneered the same sneer he'd given me in the Florida room. "Off you go with a slug in you, dead or dying. Take off the coat."

"I'll be dead, you'll be stranded. If I hand it over, I'll be dead and you won't be stranded. Put the gun away."

"No arguments. Coat." He casually fired into the ground before me, showering me with hot clots of soft earth. Broken roots from the housenet squirmed as they attempted to route around the damage. I was so rattled I very nearly hit the button, but I kept my fingers still with an act of will.

"Gun," I said, as levelly as I could. My voice sounded squeaky to me. "Look," I said. "Look. If we keep arguing here, someone else will come along, and chances are, they'll be armed. Not every gun in this world blows up when you fire it," *I hope*, "and then you're going to be sorry. So will I, since you'll probably end up shooting me at the same time. Put it away, we'll talk it out. Come up with a solution we can both live with, you should excuse the expression."

Slowly, he holstered the gun.

"Toss it away, why don't you? Not far, just a couple meters. You're fast."

He shook his head. "Nervy bastard," he said, but he tossed the gun a few meters to the side.

"Now," I said, trying to disguise my sigh of relief. "Now, let's work it out."

Slowly, he flipped up his visor and looked at me as if I were a turd.

"The way I see it," I said, "we don't need to be at each other's throats. You want a dimension you can move freely in to avoid capture. We need a way to stop people from showing up and blowing the hell out of our homes. If we do this right, we can build a long-term relationship that'll benefit both of us."

"What do you want?" he asked.

"Nothing you can't afford," I said, and started to parley in earnest. "First of all, you need to take me back to where you fetched me from. I need to get a doctor for Hezekiah."

He shook his head in disbelief. "What a frigging waste."

"First Hezekiah, then the rest. Complaining is just going to slow us down. Let's go." Without ceremony, I leapt into his arms. I rapped twice on his helmet. "Up, up and away," I said. He crushed me to his chest and leapt moonward.

* * *

"All right," I said as the moon dipped on the horizon. We'd been at it for hours, but were making some good headway. "You get safe passage—a place to hide, a change of clothes—in our shtetl whenever you want it. In exchange, we both return there now, then I turn over the d-hopper. You take Roman back with you—I don't care what you do with him once you're in your dimension, but no harm comes to him in mine."

"Fine," Osborne said, sullenly. That was a major step forward—it had taken two hours to get him as far as not shooting Roman on sight. I figured that in his own dimension, clad in his armor, armed with his pistol, Roman would have a fighting chance.

"Just one more thing," I said. Osborne swore and spat in the soft earth of the clearing where Hezekiah had blown his arm off. "Just a trifle. The next time you visit the shtetl, you bring us a spare trans-d device."

"Why?" he asked.

"Never you mind," I said. "Think of it as good faith. If you want to come back to our shtetl and get our cooperation, you'll need to bring us a trans-d device, otherwise the deal's off."

The agreement wasn't immediate, but it came by and by. Negotiation is always at least partly a war of attrition, and I'm a patient man.

"Civil defense, huh?" I said to Sally. She was poring over a wall of her new house, where she and someone in Toronto were jointly scribing plans for a familiar-looking blunderbuss.

"Yes," she said, in a tone that said, *Piss off, I'm busy.*

"Good idea," I said.

That brought her up short. I didn't often manage to surprise her, and I savored a moment's gratification. "You think so?"

"Oh, sure," I said. "Let me show you." I held out my hand, and as she took it, I fingered the d-hopper in my pocket, and the universe stood on its head.

No matter how often I visit the technocratic dimensions, I'm always struck by the grace of the armored passers-by, their amazing leaps high over the shining buildings and elevated roadways. Try as I might, I can't figure out how they avoid crashing into one another.

In this version of the technocracy, the gun-shop was called "Eddy's." The last one I'd hit was called "Ed's." Small variations, but the basic routine was the same. We strolled into the shop boldly, and I waved pleasantly at Ed/Eddy. "Hi there," I said.

"Hey," he said. "Can I show you folks something?"

Sally's grip on my hand was vise-tight and painful. I thought she was freaking out over our jaunt into the transverse, but when I followed her gaze and looked out the window, I realized that there was something amiss about this place. Down the street, amid the shining lozenge-shaped buildings, stood a house that would've fit in back in the shtetl, housenet roots writhing into the concrete. In front of it were two people in well-manicured woolens and beautifully ripened gumboots. Familiar people. Sally and I. And there, on the street, was another couple—Sally and I—headed for Ed/Eddy's gun shop. I managed to smile and gasp out, "How about that fully automatic, laser-guided, armor-piercing, self-replenishing personal sidearm?"

Ed/Eddy passed it over, and as soon as the butt was securely in my hand, I looped my arm through Sally's and nailed the d-hopper. The universe stood on its head again, and we were back home, in the clearing where, a hairsbreadth away and a week ago, one version of Hezekiah had lost his arm.

I handed the gun to Sally. "More where this came from," I said.

She was shaking, and for a moment, I thought she was going to shout at me, but then she was laughing, and so was I.

"Hey," I said, "you feel like lunch? There's usually a great Italian joint just on the other side of the bicycle fields."

Night of Time

ROBERT REED

Robert Reed (info site: www.booksnbytes.com/authors/reed_robert.html) lives in Nebraska and has been one of the most prolific short story writers of high quality in the SF field for the past twelve years. His work is notable for its variety and for his steady production. His first story collection, The Dragons of Springplace *(1999), fine as it is, skims only a bit of the cream from his body of work. He writes a novel every year or two, as well. His recent novel,* Marrow *(2000), a distant future large-scale story that is hard SF, seems to be a breakthrough in his career.* The New York Times *called it "an exhilarating ride, in the hands of an author whose aspiration literally knows no bounds." A sequel,* The Sword of Creation, *is forthcoming in 2004.*

"Night of Time" is another story from Silver Gryphon, *the fine anniversary anthology of Golden Gryphon Press and another of the best anthologies of the year. It is set in the distant future world of Marrow, and is a story about a man whose profession is to restore missing memories. He is sought out by an alien creature with an immensely rich historical memory but who has forgotten one small thing. He is accompanied by a loyal assistant, Shadow, who is not what he seems.*

Ash drank a bitter tea while sitting in the shade outside his shop, comfortable on a little seat that he had carved for himself in the trunk of a massive, immortal bristle-cone pine. The wind was tireless, dense and dry and pleasantly warm. The sun was a convincing illusion—a K-class star perpetually locked at an early-morning angle, the false sky narrow and pink, a haze of artful dust pretending to have been blown from some faraway hell. At his feet lay a narrow and phenomenally deep canyon, glass roads anchored to the granite walls, with hundreds of narrow glass bridges stretched from one side to the other, making the air below him glisten and glitter. Busier shops and markets were set beside the important roads, and scattered between them were the hivelike mansions and mating halls, and elaborate fractal statues, and the vertical groves of cling-trees that lifted water from the distant river: The basics of life for the local species, the 31-3s.

For Ash, business was presently slow, and it had been for some years. But he was a patient man and a pragmatist, and when you had a narrow skill and a well-earned reputation, it was only a matter of time before the desperate or those with too much money came searching for you.

"This will be the year," he said with a practiced, confident tone. "And maybe, this will be the day."

Any coincidence was minimal. It was his little habit to say those words and then lean forward in his seat, looking ahead and to his right, watching the only road that happened to lead past his shop. If someone were coming, Ash would see him now. And as it happened, he spotted two figures ascending the long glass ribbon, one leading the other, both fighting the steep grade as well as the thick and endless wind.

The leader was large and simply shaped—a cylindrical body, black and smooth, held off the ground by six jointed limbs. Ash instantly recognized the species. While the other entity was human, he decided—a creature like himself, and at this distance, entirely familiar.

They weren't going to be his clients, of course. Most likely, they were sightseers. Perhaps they didn't even know one another. They were just two entities that happened to be marching in the same direction. But as always, Ash allowed himself a seductive premonition. He finished his tea, and listened, and after a little while, despite the heavy wind, he heard the quick dense voice of the alien—an endless blur of words and old stories and lofty abstract concepts born from one of the galaxy's great natural intellects.

When the speaker was close, Ash called out, "Wisdom passes!"

A Vozzen couldn't resist such a compliment.

The road had finally flattened out. Jointed legs turned the long body, allowing every eye to focus on the tall, rust-colored human sitting inside the craggy tree. The Vozzen continued walking sideways, but with a fatigued slowness. His only garment was a fabric tube, black like his carapace and with the same slick texture. "Wisdom shall not pass," a thin, somewhat shrill voice called out. Then the alien's translator made adjustments, and the voice softened. "If you are a man named Ash," said the Vozzen, "this Wisdom intends to linger."

"I am Ash," he replied, immediately dropping to his knees. The ground beneath the tree was rocky, but acting like a supplicant would impress the species. "May I serve your Wisdom in some tiny way, sir?"

"Ash," the creature repeated. "The name is Old English. Is that correct?"

The surprise was genuine. With a half-laugh, Ash said, "Honestly, I'm not quite sure—"

"English," it said again. The translator was extremely adept, creating a voice that was unnervingly human—male and mature, and pleasantly arrogant. "There was a tiny nation-state, and an island, and as I recall my studies, England and its confederate tribes acquired a rather considerable empire that briefly covered the face of your cradle world."

"Fascinating," said Ash, looking back down the road. The second figure was climbing the last long grade, pulling an enormous float-pack, and despite his initial verdict, Ash realized that the creature wasn't human at all.

"But you were not born on the Earth," the Vozzen continued. "In your flesh and your narrow build, I can see some very old augmentations—"

"Mars," Ash allowed. "I was born on—"

"Mars," the voice repeated. That simple word triggered a cascade of memories, facts and telling stories. From that flood, the Vozzen selected his next offering. "Old Mars was home to some fascinating political experiments. From the earliest terraforming societies to the Night of the Dust—"

"I remember," Ash interrupted, trying to gain control over the conversation. "Are you a historian, sir? Like many of your kind—?"

"I am conversant in the past, yes."

"Then perhaps I shouldn't be too impressed. You seem to have been looking for me, and for all I know, you've thoroughly researched whatever little history is wrapped around my life."

"It would be impolite not to study your existence," said the Vozzen.

"Granted." With another deep bow, Ash asked, "What can this old Martian do for a wise Vozzen?"

The alien fell silent.

For a moment, Ash studied the second creature. Its skeleton and muscle were much like a man's, and the head wore a cap of what could have been dense brown hair. There was one mouth and two eyes, but no visible nose and the mouth was full of heavy pink teeth. Of course many humans had novel genetics, and there were remoras on the Ship's hull—men and women who wore every intriguing, creative mutation. But this creature was not human. Ash sensed it, and using a private nexus, he asked his shop for a list of likely candidates.

"Ash," the Vozzen said. "Yes, I have made a comprehensive study of your considerable life."

Ash dipped his head, driving his knees into the rough ground. "I am honored, sir. Thank you."

"I understand that you possess some rather exotic machinery."

"Quite novel. Yes, sir."

"And talents. You wield talents even rarer than your machinery."

"Unique talents," Ash replied with an effortless confidence. He lifted his eyes, and smiled, and wanting the advantage in his court, he rose to his feet, brushing the grit from his slightly bloodied knees as he told his potential client, "I help those whom I can help."

"You help them for a fee," the alien remarked, a clear disdain in the voice.

Ash approached the Vozzen, remarking, "My fee is a fair wage. A wage determined by the amoral marketplace."

"I am a poor historian," the Vozzen complained.

Ash gazed into the bright black eyes. Then with a voice tinged with a careful menace, he said, "It must seem awful, I would think. Being a historian, and being Vozzen, and feeling your precious memories slowly and inexorably leaking away . . ."

The Ship was an enormous derelict—a world-sized starship discovered by humans, and repaired by humans, and sent by its new owners on a great voyage around the most thickly settled regions of the galaxy. It was Ash's good fortune to be one of the early passengers, and for several centuries, he remained a simple tourist. But he had odd skills leftover from his former life, and as different aliens boarded the Ship, he made friends with new ideas and fresh technologies. His shop was the natural outgrowth of all that learning. "Sir," he said to the Vozzen. "Would you like to see what your money would buy?"

"Of course."

"And your companion—?"

"My aide will remain outside. Thank you."

The human-shaped creature seemed to expect that response. He walked under the bristlecone, tethering his pack to a whitened branch, and with an unreadable expression, stood at the canyon's edge, staring into the glittering depths, watching for the invisible river, perhaps, or perhaps watching his own private thoughts.

"By what name do I call you?"

"Master is adequate."

Every Vozzen was named Master, in one fashion or another. With a nod, Ash began walking toward the shop's doorway. "And your aide—"

"Shadow."

"His name is?"

"Shadow is an adequate translation." Several jointed arms emerged from beneath his long body, complex hands tickling the edges of the door, a tiny sensor slipped from a pocket and pointed at the darkness inside. "Are you curious, Ash?"

"About what, Master?"

"My companion's identity. It is a little mystery to you, I think."

"It is. Yes."

"Have you heard of the Aabacks?"

"But I've never seen one." Then after a silence, he mentioned, "They're a rare species. With a narrow intelligence and a fierce loyalty, as I understand these things."

"They are rather simple souls," Master replied. "But whatever their limits, or because of them, they make wonderful servants."

The tunnel grew darker, and then the walls fell away. With a silent command, Ash triggered the lights to awaken. In an instant, a great chamber was revealed, the floor tiled simply and the pine-faced ceiling arching high overhead, while the distant walls lay behind banks upon banks of machines that were barely awake, spelling themselves for those rare times when they were needed.

"Are you curious, Master?"

"Intensely and about many subjects," said the Vozzen. "What particular subject are you asking about?"

"How this magic works," Ash replied, gesturing with an ancient, comfortable pride. "Not even the Ship's captains can wield this technology. Within the confines of our galaxy, I doubt if there are three other facilities equally equipped."

"For memory retrieval," Master added. "I know the theory at play here. You manipulate the electrons inside a client's mind, increasing their various effects. And you manipulate the quantum nature of the universe, reaching into a trillion alternate but very similar realities. Then you combine these two quite subtle tricks, temporarily enlarging one mind's ability to reminisce."

Ash nodded, stepping up to the main control panel.

"I deplore that particular theory," his client professed.

"I'm not surprised."

"That many-world image of the universe is obscene. To me, it is simply grotesque and relentlessly ridiculous, and I have never approved of it."

"Many feel that way," Ash allowed.

A genuine anger surged. "This concept of each electron existing in countless realities, swimming through an endless ocean of potential, with every possible outcome achieved to what resembles an infinite number of outcomes—"

"We belong to one branch of reality," Ash interrupted. "One minor branch in a great tree standing in an endless canopy in the multiverse forest—"

"We are not," Master growled.

The controls awoke. Every glow-button and thousand-layer display had a theatrical purpose. Ash could just as easily manipulate the machinery through nexuses buried in his own body. But his clients normally appreciated this visible, traditional show of structured light and important sounds.

"We are not a lonely reality lost among endless possibility." In Vozzen fashion, the hind legs slapped each other in disgust. "I am a historian and a scholar of some well-earned notoriety. My long, long life has been spent in the acquisition of the past, and its interpretation, and I refuse to believe that what I have studied—this great pageant of time and story—is nothing more than some obscure twig shaking on the end of an impossible-to-measure shrub."

"I'm tempted to agree with you," Ash replied.

"Tempted?"

"There are moments when I believe . . ." Ash paused, as if selecting his next words. "I see us as the one true reality. The universe is exactly as it seems to be. As it should be. And what I employ here is just a trick, a means of interacting with the ghost realities. With mathematical whispers and unborn potentials. In other words, we are the trunk of a great and ancient tree, and the dreamlike branches have no purpose but to feed our magnificent souls . . . !"

The alien regarded Ash with a new respect. The respect showed in the silence, and then, with the hands opening, delicate spiderweb fingers presenting themselves to what was, for at least this moment, their equal.

"Is that what you believe now?" Master asked.

"For the moment." Ash laughed quietly. Two nexuses and one display showed the same information: The historian had enough capital to hire him and his machinery. "And I'll keep believing it for a full day, if necessary."

Then he turned, bowing just enough. "What exactly is it that you wish to remember, Master?"

The alien eyes lost their brightness.

"I am not entirely sure," the voice confessed with a simple horror. "I have forgotten something very important . . . something essential, I fear . . . but I can't even recall what that something might be . . ."

Hours had passed, but the projected sun hadn't moved. The wind was unchanged, and the heat only seemed worse, as Ash stepped from the cool depths of his shop, his body momentarily forgetting to perspire. He had left his client alone, standing inside a cylindrical reader with a thousand flavors of sensors fixed to his carapace and floating free inside the ancient body and mind. Ash kept a close watch over the Vozzen. His nexuses showed him telemetry, and a mind's eye let him watch the scene. If necessary, he could offer words of encouragement or warning. But for the moment, his client was obeying the strict instructions, standing as motionless as possible while the machines made intricate maps of his brain—a body-long array of superconducting proteins and light-baths and quantum artesians. The alien's one slight cheat was his voice, kept soft as possible, but always busy, delivering an endless lecture about an arcane, mostly forgotten epoch.

The mapping phase was essential, and quite boring.

From a tiny slot in the pink granite wall, Ash plucked free a new cup of freshly brewed, deliciously bitter tea.

"A pleasant view," a nearby voice declared.

"I like it." Ash sipped his drink. As a rule, Aabacks appreciated liquid gifts, but he made no offer, strolling under the bristlecone, out of the wind and sun. "Do you know anything about the 31-3s?"

"I know very little," Shadow confessed. The voice was his own, his larynx able to produce clear if somewhat slow human words.

"Their home is tidally locked and rather distant from its sun," Ash explained. "Their atmosphere is rich in carbon dioxide, which my Martian lungs prefer." He tapped his own chest. "Water vapor and carbon dioxide warm the day hemisphere, and the winds carry the excess heat and moisture to the cold nightside glaciers, which grow and push into the dawn, and melt, completing the cycle." With an appreciative nod, he said, "The Ship's engineers have done a magnificent job of replicating the 31-3 environment."

Shadow's eyes were large and bright, colored a bluish gray. The pink teeth were heavy and flat-headed, suitable for a diet of rough vegetation. Powerful jaw muscles ballooned outward when the mouth closed. A simple robe and rope belt were his only clothes. Four fingers and a thumb were on each hand, but nothing like a fingernail showed. Ash watched the hands, and then the bare, almost human feet. Reading the dirt, he felt certain that Shadow hadn't moved since he had arrived. He was standing in the sun, in the wind, and like any scrupulously obedient servant, he seemed ready to remain on that patch of ground for another day, or twenty.

"The 31-3s don't believe in time," Ash continued.

A meaningful expression passed across the face. Curiosity? Disdain? Then with a brief glance toward Ash, he asked, "Is it the absence of days and nights?"

"Partly. But only partly."

Shadow leaned forward slightly. On the bright road below, a pack of 31-3s was dancing along. Voices like brass chimes rose through the wind. Ash recognized his neighbors. He threw a little stone at them, to be polite. Then with a steady voice, he explained, "The endless day is a factor, sure. But they've always been a long-lived species. On their world, with its changeless climate and some extremely durable genetics, every species has a nearly immortal constitution. Where humans and Vozzens and Aabacks had to use modern bioengineering to conquer aging, the 31-3s evolved in a world where everything can live pretty much forever. That's why time was never an important concept to them. And that's why their native physics is so odd, and lovely—they formulated a vision of a universe that is almost, almost free of time."

The alien listened carefully. Then he quietly admitted, "Master has explained some of the same things to me, I think."

"You're a good loyal audience," Ash said.

"It is my hope to be."

"What else do you do for Master?"

"I help with all that is routine," Shadow explained. "In every capacity, I give him aid and free his mind for great undertakings."

"But mostly, you listen to him."

"Yes."

"Vozzens are compulsive explainers."

"Aabacks are natural listeners," said Shadow, with a hint of pride.

"Do you remember what he tells you?"

"Very little." For an instant, the face seemed human. An embarrassed smile and a shy blinking of the blue-gray eyes preceded the quiet admission, "I do not have a Vozzen's mind. And Master is an exceptional example of his species."

"You're right," said Ash. "On both accounts."

The alien shifted his feet, and again stared down at the 31-3s.

"Come with me."

"He wants me here," Shadow replied. Nothing in the voice was defiant, or even a little stubborn. He intended to obey the last orders given to him, and with his gentle indifference, he warned that he couldn't be swayed.

Sternly, Ash asked, "What does the Master want from this day?"

The question brought a contemplative silence.

"More than anything," said Ash, "he wants to recover what's most precious to him. And that is—"

"His memory."

Again, Ash said, "Come with me."

"For what good?"

"He talks to you. And yes, you've likely forgotten what he can't remember." Ash finished his tea in one long sip. "But likely and surely are two different words. So if you truly wish to help your friend, come with me. Come now."

"I do not deserve solitude," the Vozzen reported. "If you intend to abandon me, warn me. You must."

"I will."

Then, "Do you feel that?"

"Do I . . . what . . . ?"

"Anything. Do you sense anything unusual?"

The alien was tethered to a new array of sensors, plus devices infinitely more intrusive. Here and in a hundred trillion alternate realities, Master stood in the same position, legs locked and arms folded against his belly, his voice slightly puzzled, admitting, "I seem to be remembering my cradle nest."

"Is that unusual?"

"It is unlikely," the Vozzen admitted. "I don't often—"

"And now?"

"My first mate," he began. "In the nest, overlooking a fungal garden—"

"What about now?"

He paused, and then admitted, "Your ship. I am seeing the Great Ship from space, our taxi making its final approach." With a warm laugh, he offered, "It is a historian's dream, riding in a vessel such as this—"

"And now?" Ash prompted.

Silence.

"Where are you—?"

"Inside a lecture hall," Master replied.

"When?"

"Eleven months in the past. I am giving a public lecture." He paused, and then explained, "I make a modest living, speaking to interested parties."

"What do you remember about that day's lecture?"

"Everything," Master began to say. But the voice faltered, and with a doubting tone, he said, "A woman?"

"What woman?"

"A human woman."

"What about her?" Ash pressed.

"She was attending . . . sitting in a seat to my right . . . ? No, my left. How odd. I usually know where to place every face—"

"What was the topic?"

"Topic?"

"Of your lecture. The topic."

"A general history of the Great Wheel of Smoke—"

"The Milky Way," Ash interrupted.

"Your name for everyone's galaxy, yes." With a weblike hand, the alien reached in front of his own face. "I was sharing a very shallow overview of our shared history, naming the most important species of the last three billion years." The hand closed on nothing, and retreated. "For many reasons, there have been few genuinely important species. They have been modestly abundant, and some rather wealthy. But I was making the point . . . the critical line of reasoning . . . that since the metal-rich worlds began spawning intelligence, no single species, or related cluster of sentient organisms, has been able to dominate more than a small puff of the Smoke."

"Why is that?"

The simple question unleashed a flood of thoughts, recollections, and abstract ideas, filling the displays with wild flashes of color and elaborate, highly organized shapes.

"There are many reasons," Master warned.

"Name three."

"Why? Do you wish to learn?"

"I want to pass the time pleasantly," said Ash, studying the data with a blank, almost impassive face. "Three reasons why no species can dominate. Give them to me, in brief."

"Distance. Divergence. And divine wisdom."

"The distance between stars . . . is that what you mean . . . ?"

"Naturally," the historian replied. "Star-flight remains slow and expensive and potentially dangerous. Many species find those reasons compelling enough to remain at home, safe and comfortable, reengineering the spacious confines of their own solar system."

"Divergence?"

"A single species can evolve in many fashions. New organic forms. Joining with machines. Becoming machines. Sweeping cultural experiments. Even the total obliteration of physical bodies. No species can dominate any portion of space if what it becomes is many, many new and oftentimes competing species."

Ash blinked slowly. "What about divine wisdom?"

"That is the single most important factor," said Master. "Ruling the heavens is a child's desire."

"True enough."

"The galaxy is not a world, or even a hundred thousand worlds. It is too vast and chaotic to embrace, and with maturity comes the wisdom to accept that simple impossibility."

"What about the woman?"

"Which woman?" Master was surprised by his own question, as if another voice had asked it. "That human female. Yes. Frankly, I don't think she's important in the smallest way. I don't even know why I am thinking about her."

"Because I'm forcing you to think about her."

"Why? Does she interest you?"

"Not particularly." Ash looked up abruptly, staring at the oval black eyes. "She asked you a question. Didn't she?"

"I remember. Yes."

"What question?"

"She asked about human beings, of course." With a gentle disdain, the historian warned, "You are a young species. And yes, you have been fortunate. Your brief story is fat with luck as well as fortuitous decisions. The Great Ship, as an example. Large and ancient, and empty, and you happened to be the species that found it and took possession. And now you are interacting with a wealth of older, wiser species, gaining knowledge at a rate rarely if ever experienced in the last three billion years—"

"What did she ask you?"

"Pardon me. Did you just ask a question?"

"Exactly. What did this woman say?"

"I think . . . I know . . . she asked, 'Will humanity be the first species to dominate the Milky Way?' "

"What was the woman's name?"

A pause.

Ash feathered a hundred separate controls.

"She did not offer any name," the historian reported.

"What did she look like?"

Again, with a puzzled air, the great mind had to admit, "I didn't notice her appearance, or I am losing my mind."

Ash waited for a moment. "What was your reply?"

"I told her, and the rest of my audience, 'Milk is a child's food. If humans had named the galaxy after smoke, they wouldn't bother with this nonsense of trying to consume the Milky Way.' "

For a long while, Ash said nothing.

Then, quietly, the historian inquired, "Where is my assistant? Where is Shadow?"

"Waiting where you told him to wait," Ash lied. And in the next breath, "Let's talk about Shadow for a moment. Shall we?"

"What do you remember . . . now . . . ?"

"A crunch cake, and sweet water." Shadow and Ash were

standing in a separate, smaller chamber. Opening his mouth, he tasted the cake again. "Then a pudding of succulents and bark from the Gi-Ti tree—"

"Now?"

"Another crunch cake. In a small restaurant beside the Alpha Sea."

With a mild amusement, Ash reported, "This is what you remember best. Meals. I can see your dinners stacked up for fifty thousand years."

"I enjoy eating," the alien replied.

"A good Aaback attitude."

Silence.

And then the alien turned, soft cords dragged along the floor. Perhaps he had felt something—a touch, a sudden chill—or maybe the expression on his face was born from his own thoughts. Either way, he suddenly asked, "How did you learn this work, Ash?"

"I was taught," he offered. "And when I was better than my teachers, I learned on my own. Through experiment and hard practice."

"Master claims you are very good, if not the best."

"I'll thank him for that assessment. But he is right: No one is better at this game than me."

The alien seemed to consider his next words. Then, "He mentioned that you are from a little world. Mars, was it? I remember something . . . something that happened in your youth. The Night of the Dust, was it?"

"Many things happened back then."

"Was it a war?" Shadow pressed. "Master often lectures about human history, and you seem to have a fondness for war."

"I'm glad he finds us interesting."

"Your species fascinates him." Shadow tried to move and discovered that he couldn't. Save for his twin hearts and mouth, every muscle of his body was fused in place. "I don't quite understand why he feels this interest—"

"You attend his lectures, don't you?"

"Always."

"He makes most of his income from public talks."

"Many souls are interested in his words."

"Do you recall a lecture from last year?" Ash gave details, and he appeared disappointed when Shadow said:

"I don't remember, no." An Aaback laugh ended with the thought, "There must not have been any food in that lecture hall."

"Let's try something new," said Ash. "Think back, back as far as possible. Tell me about the very first meal you remember."

A long, long pause ended with, "A little crunch cake. I was a child, and it was my first adult meal."

"I used to be an interrogator," Ash said abruptly.

The eyes were gray and watchful.

"During that old war, I interrogated people, and on certain days, I tortured them." He nodded calmly, adding, "Memory is a real thing, Shadow. It's a dense little nest made, like everything, from electrons—where the electrons are and where they are not—and you would be appalled, just appalled, by all the ways that something real can be hacked out of the surrounding bullshit."

"Quee Lee."

"Pardon?"

"The human woman. Her name was, and is, Quee Lee." Ash began disconnecting his devices, leaving only the minimal few to keep shepherding the Vozzen's mind. "It was easy enough to learn her name. A lecture attended by humans, and when I found one woman, she told me about another. Who mentioned another friend who might have gone to listen to you. But while that friend hadn't heard of you, she mentioned an acquaintance of hers who had a fondness for the past, and her name is Quee Lee. She happened to be there, and she asked the question."

Relief filled Master, and with a thrilled voice, he said, "I remember her now, yes. Yes. She asked about human dominance in the galaxy—"

"Not quite, no."

Suspicion flowered, and curiosity followed. "She didn't ask that about human dominance?"

"It was her second question, and strictly speaking, it wasn't hers." Ash smiled and nodded, explaining, "The woman sitting next to her asked it. Quee Lee simply repeated the question, since she had won your attention."

A brief pause ended with the wary question:

"What then did the woman ask me?"

Ash stared at the remaining displays, and with a quiet firm voice said, "I've spoken with Quee Lee. At length. She remembers asking you, 'What was the earliest sentient life to arise in the galaxy?' "

The simple question generated a sophisticated response. An ocean of learning was tapped, and from that enormity a single turquoise thread was pulled free, and offered. Five candidates were named in a rush. Then the historian rapidly and thoroughly described each species, their home worlds, and eventual fates.

"None survived into the modern age," he said sadly. "Except as rumor and unsubstantiated sightings, the earliest generation of intelligence has died away."

Ash nodded, and waited.

"How could I forget such a very small thing?"

"Because it is so small," Ash replied. "The honest, sad truth is that your age is showing. I'm an old man for my species, but that's nothing compared to you. The Vozzen journeyed out among the stars during my Permian. You have an enormous and dense and extraordinarily quick mind. But it is a mind. No matter how vast and how adept, it suffers from what is called bounded rationality. You don't know everything, no matter how much you wish otherwise. You're living in an enriched environment, full of opportunities to learn. And as long as you wish to understand new wonders, you're going to have to allow, on occasion, little pieces of your past to fade away."

"But why did such a trivial matter bother me so?" asked Master.

And then in the next instant, he answered his own question. "Because it was trivial, and lost. Is that why? I'm not accustomed to forgetting. The sensation is novel . . . it preyed upon my equilibrium . . . and wore a wound in my mind . . . !"

"Exactly, exactly," lied Ash. "Exactly, and exactly."

After giving him fair warning, Ash left the historian. "The final probes still need to disengage themselves," he explained. Then with a careful tone, he asked, "Should I bring your assistant to you? Would you like to see him now?"

"Please."

"Very well." Ash pretended to step outside, turning in the darkened hallway, centuries of practice telling him where to step. Then he was inside the secondary chamber, using a deceptively casual voice, mentioning to Shadow, "By the way, I think I know what you are."

"What I am?"

With a sudden fierceness, Ash asked, "Did you really believe you could fool me?"

The alien said nothing, and by every physical means, he acted puzzled but unworried.

Ash knew better.

"Your body is mostly Aaback, but there's something else. If I hadn't suspected it, I wouldn't have found it. But what seems to be your brain is an elaborate camouflage for a quiet, nearly invisible neural network."

The alien reached with both hands, yanking one of the cables free from his forehead. Then a long tongue reached high, wiping the gray blood from the wound. A halfway choked voice asked, "What did you see inside me?"

"Dinners," Ash reported. "Dinners reaching back for billions of years."

Silence.

"Do you belong to one of the first five species?"

The alien kept yanking cables free, but he was powerless to void the drifters inside his double-mind.

"No," said Ash, "I don't think you're any of those five." With a sly smile, he reported, "I can tell. You're even older than that, aren't you?"

The tongue retreated into the mouth. A clear, sorry voice reported, "I am not sure, no."

"And that's why," said Ash.

"Why?"

"The woman asked that question about the old species, and you picked that moment because of it." He laughed, nodded. "What did you use? How did you cut a few minutes out of a Vozzen's perfect memory . . . ?"

"With a small disruptive device—"

"I want to see it."

"No."

Ash kept laughing. "Oh, yes. You are going to show it to me!"

Silence.

"Master doesn't even suspect," Ash continued. "You were the one who wanted to visit me. You simply gave the Vozzen a good excuse. You heard about me somewhere, and you decided that you wanted me to peer inside his soul, and yours. You were hoping that I would piece together the clues and tell you what I was seeing in your mind—"

"What do you see?" Shadow blurted.

"Basically, two things." With a thought, he caused every link with Shadow to be severed, and with a professional poise, he explained, "Your soul might be ten or twelve years old. I don't know how that could be, but I can imagine: In the earliest days of the universe, when the stars were young and metal-poor, life found some other way to evolve. A completely separate route. Structured plasmas, maybe. Maybe. Whatever the route, your ancestors evolved and spread, and then died away as the universe grew cold and empty. Or they adapted, on occasion. They used organic bodies as hosts, maybe."

"I am the only survivor," Shadow muttered. "Whatever the reason, I cannot remember anyone else like me."

"You are genuinely ancient," Ash said, "and I think you're smarter than you pretend to be. But this ghost mind of yours isn't that sophisticated. Vozzens are smarter, and most humans, too. But when I was watching you thinking, looking at something simple—when I saw dinners reaching back for a billion years—well, that kind of vista begs for an explanation."

Ash took a deep breath, and then said, "Your memory has help. Quantum help. And this isn't on any scale that I've ever seen, or imagined possible. I can pull in the collective conscience of a few trillion Masters from the adjacent realities . . . but with you, I can't even pick a number that looks sane . . ."

The alien showed his pink teeth, saying nothing.

"Are you pleased?" Ash asked.

"Pleased by what?"

"You are probably the most common entity in Creation," said Ash. "I have never seen such a signal as yours. This clear. This deep, and dramatic. You exist, in one form or another, in a fat, astonishing portion of all the possible realities."

Shadow said, "Yes."

"Yes what?"

"Yes," he said with the tiniest nod, "I am pleased."

Always, the sun held its position in the fictional sky. And always, the same wind blew with calm relentlessness. In such a world, it was easy to believe that there was no such monster as time, and the day would never end, and a man with old and exceptionally sad memories could convince himself, on occasion, that there would never be another night.

Ash was last to leave the shop.

"Again," the historian called out, "thank you for your considerable help."

"Thank you for your generous gift." Ash found another cup of tea waiting for him, and he sipped down a full mouthful, watching as Shadow untethered the floating pack. "Where next?"

"I have more lectures to give," Master replied.

"Good."

"And I will interview the newest passengers onboard the Ship."

"As research?"

"And as a pleasure, yes."

Shadow was placing a tiny object beside one of the bristlecone's roots. "If you don't give that disruptor to me," Ash had threatened, "I'll explain a few deep secrets to the Vozzen."

Of course, Shadow had relented.

Ash sipped his tea, and quietly said, "Master. What can you tell me about the future?"

"About what is to come—?" the alien began.

"I never met a historian who didn't have opinions on that subject," Ash professed. "My species, for instance. What will happen to us in the next ten or twenty million years?"

Master launched himself into an abbreviated but dense lecture, explaining to his tiny audience what was possible about predicting the future and what was unknowable, and how every bridge between the two was an illusion.

His audience wasn't listening.

In a whisper, Ash said to Shadow, "But why live this way? With him, in this kind of role?"

In an Aaback fashion, the creature grinned. Then Shadow peered over the edge of the canyon, and speaking to no one in particular, he explained, "He needs me so much. This is why."

"As a servant?"

"And as a friend, and a confidant." With a very human shrug, he asked Ash, "How could anyone survive even a single day, if they didn't feel as if they were, in some little great way, needed?"

A Night on the Barbary Coast

KAGE BAKER

Kage Baker [www.kagebaker.com/index.html] grew up in Hollywood and Pismo Beach, California, where she still lives. She has worked as a graphic artist and mural painter, and (over a period of years for the Living History Centre) as a playwright, bit player, director, and teacher of Elizabethan English for the stage. Baker is best known for her series of SF novels and stories about "The Company," stories of time travellers, mortal and immortal workers from our future delving into periods of our past to rescue lost art and treasures on behalf of the wealthy and mysterious Company that controls their lives and the future—perhaps. Her Company novels include In the Garden of Iden, Sky Coyote, Mendoza in Hollywood, The Graveyard Game, *and* The Life of the World to Come. *She has also written a collection of Company stories,* The Company Dossiers: Black Projects, White Knights. *She published several fine novellas this year, and a stand-alone fantasy novel,* The Anvil of the World.

"A Night on the Barbary Coast" appeared in Silver Gryphon. *It is a Company story, a tale of Mendoza and Joseph in San Francisco in 1850. Its charms derive in large part from the sensuous and detailed portrayal of the setting.*

I'd been walking for five days, looking for Mendoza. The year was 1850.

Actually, *walking* doesn't really describe traveling through that damned vertical wilderness in which she lived. I'd crawled uphill on hands and knees, which is no fun when you're dressed as a Franciscan friar, with sandals and beads and the whole nine yards of brown burlap robe. I'd slid downhill, which is no fun either, especially when the robe rides up in back. I'd waded across freezing cold creeks and followed thready little trails through ferns, across forest floors in permanent darkness under towering redwoods. I'm talking *gloom*. One day the poets will fall in love with Big Sur, and after them the hippies, but if vampires ever discover the place they'll go nuts over it.

Mendoza isn't a vampire, though she is an immortal being with a lot of problems, most of which she blames on me.

I'm an immortal being with a lot of problems, too. Like father, like daughter.

After most of a week, I finally came out on a patch of level ground about three thousand feet up. I was standing there looking *down* on clouds floating above the Pacific Ocean, and feeling kind of funny in the pit of my stomach as a result—and suddenly saw the Company-issue processing credenza to my left, nicely camouflaged. I'd found Mendoza's camp at last.

There was her bivvy tent, all right, and a table with a

camp stove, and five pots with baby trees growing in them. Everything but the trees had a dusty, abandoned look.

Cripes, I thought to myself, how long since she's been here? I looked around uneasily, wondering if I ought to yoo-hoo or something, and that was when I noticed her signal coming from . . . *Up?* I craned back my head.

An oak tree rose from the mountain face behind me, huge and branching wide, and high up there among the boughs Mendoza leaned. She gazed out at the sea; but with such a look of ecstatic vacancy in her eyes, I guessed she was seeing something a lot farther away than that earthly horizon.

I cleared my throat.

The vacant look went away fast, and there was something inhuman in the sharp way her head swung around.

"Hi, honey," I said. She looked down and her eyes focussed on me. She has black eyes, like mine, only mine are jolly and twinkly and bright. Hers are like flint. Always been that way, even when she was a little girl.

"What the hell are you doing here, Joseph?" she said at last.

"I missed you too, baby," I said. "Want to come down? We need to talk."

Muttering, she descended through the branches.

"Nice trees," I remarked. "Got any coffee?"

"I can make some," she said. I kept my mouth shut as she poked around in her half-empty rations locker, and I still kept it shut when she hauled out her bone-dry water jug and stared at it in a bewildered kind of way before remembering where the nearest stream was, and I didn't even remark on the fact that she had goddamn *moss* in her hair, though what I really wanted to yell at the top of my lungs was: *How can you live like this?*

No, I played it smart. Pretty soon we were sitting at either end of a fallen log, sipping our respective mugs of coffee, just like family.

"Mm, good java," I lied.

"What do you want?" she said.

"Okay, kid, I'll tell you," I said. "The Company is sending me up to San Francisco on a job. I need a field botanist, and I had my pick of anybody in the area, so I decided on you."

I braced myself for an explosion, because sometimes Mendoza's a little touchy about surprises. But she was silent for a moment, with that bewildered expression again, and I just knew she was accessing her chronometer because she'd forgotten what year this was.

"San Francisco, huh?" she said. "But I went through Yerba Buena a century ago, Joseph. I did a complete survey of all the endemics. Specimens, DNA codes, the works. Believe me, there wasn't anything to interest Dr. Zeus."

"Well, there might be now," I said. "And that's all you need to know until we get there."

She sighed. "So it's like that?"

"It's like that. But, hey, we'll have a great time! There's a lot more up there now than fog and sand dunes."

"I'll say there is," she said grimly. "I just accessed the historical record for October 1850. There's a cholera epidemic going on. There's chronic arson. The streets are half quicksand. You really take me to some swell places, don't you?"

"How long has it been since you ate dinner in a restaurant?" I coaxed. She started to say something sarcastic in reply, looked down at whatever was floating in the bottom of her coffee, and shuddered.

"See? It'll be a nice change of scenery," I told her, as she tossed the dregs over her shoulder. I tossed out my coffee too, in a simpatico gesture. "The Road to Frisco! A fun-filled musical romp! Two wacky cyborgs plus one secret mission equals laughs galore!"

"Oh, shut up," she told me, but rose to strike camp.

It took us longer to get down out of the mountains than I would have liked, because Mendoza insisted on bringing her five potted trees, which were some kind of endangered species, so we had to carry them all the way to the closest Company receiving terminal in Monterey, by which time I was ready to drop the damn things down any convenient cliff. But away they went to some Company botanical garden, and after requisitioning equipment and horses, we finally set off for San Francisco.

I guess if we had been any other two people, we'd have

chatted about bygone times as we rode along. It's never safe to drag up old memories with Mendoza, though. We didn't talk much, all the way up El Camino Real, through the forests and across the scrubby hills. It wasn't until we'd left San Jose and were picking our way along the shore of the back bay, all black ooze and oyster shells, that Mendoza looked across at me and said:

"We're carrying a lot of lab equipment with us. I wonder why?"

I just shrugged.

"Whatever the Company's sending us after, they want it analyzed on the spot," she said thoughtfully. "So possibly they're not sure that it's really what they want. But they need to find out."

"Could be."

"And your only field expert is being kept on a need-to-know basis, which means it's something important," she continued. "And they're sending *you*, even though you're still working undercover in the Church, being Father Rubio or whoever. Aren't you?"

"I am."

"You look even more like Mephistopheles than usual in that robe, did I ever tell you that? Anyway—why would the Company send a friar into a town full of gold miners, gamblers and prostitutes?" Mendoza speculated. "You'll stick out like a sore thumb. And where does botany fit in?"

"I guess we'll see, huh?"

She glared at me sidelong and grumbled to herself a while, but that was okay. I had her interested in the job, at least. She was losing that thousand-year-stare that worried me so much.

I wasn't worrying about the job at all.

We could smell San Francisco miles before we got there. It wasn't the ordinary mortal aroma of a boomtown without adequate sanitation, even one in the grip of cholera. San Francisco smelled like smoke, with a reek that went right up your nose and drilled into your sinuses.

It smelled this way because it had been destroyed by fire

four times already, most recently only a month ago, though you wouldn't know it to look at the place. Obscenely expensive real estate where tents and shanties had stood was already filling up with brand-new frame buildings. Hammers pounded day and night along Clay, along Montgomery and Kearney and Washington. All the raw new wood was festooned with red, white and blue bunting, and hastily improvised Stars and Stripes flew everywhere. California had only just learned it had been admitted to the Union, and was still celebrating.

The bay was black with ships, but those closest to the shore were never going to sea again—their crews had deserted and the ships were already enclosed by wharves, filling in on all sides. Windows and doors had been cut in their hulls as they were converted to shops and taverns.

Way back in the sand hills, poor old Mission Dolores—built of adobe blocks by a people whose world hadn't changed in millennia, on a settlement plan first designed by officials of the Roman Empire—looked down on the crazy new world in wonderment. Mendoza and I stared too, from where we'd reined in our horses near Rincon Hill.

"So this is an American city," said Mendoza.

"Manifest Destiny in action," I agreed, watching her. Mendoza had never liked being around mortals much. How was she going to handle a modern city, after a century and a half of wilderness? But she just set her mouth and urged her horse forward, and I was proud of her.

For all the stink of disaster, the place was *alive*. People were out and running about, doing business. There were hotels and taverns; there were groceries and bakeries and candy stores. Lightermen worked the water between those ships that hadn't yet been absorbed into the city, bringing in men bound for the gold fields or crates of goods for the merchants. I heard six languages spoken before we'd crossed Clay Street. Anything could be bought or sold here, including a meal prepared by a Parisian chef. The air hummed with hunger, and enthusiasm, and a kind of rapacious innocence.

I grinned. America looked like fun.

We found a hotel on the big central wharf, and unloaded

our baggage into two narrow rooms whose windows looked into the rigging of a landlocked ship. Mendoza stared around at the bare plank walls.

"This is Oregon spruce," she announced. "You can still smell the forest! I'll bet this was alive and growing a month ago."

"Probably," I agreed, rummaging in my trunk. I found what I was looking for and unrolled it to see how it had survived the trip.

"What's that?"

"A subterfuge." I held the drawing up. "A beautiful gift for his Holiness the Pope! The artist's conception, anyway."

"A huge ugly crucifix?" Mendoza looked pained.

"*And* a matching rosary, baby. All to be specially crafted out of gold and (this is the important part) gold-bearing quartz from sunny California, U.S.A., so the Holy Father will know he's got faithful fans out here!"

"That's disgusting. Are you serious?"

"Of course I'm not serious, but we don't want the mortals to know that," I said, rolling up the drawing and sticking it in a carpetbag full of money. "You stay here and set up the lab, okay? I've got to go find some jewelers."

There were a lot of jewelers in San Francisco. Successful guys coming back from the Sacramento sometimes liked to commemorate their luck by having gold nuggets set in watch fobs, or stickpins, or brooches for sweethearts back east. Gold-bearing quartz, cut and polished, was also popular, and much classier looking.

Hiram Gainsborg, on the corner of Ohio and Broadway, had some of what I needed; so did Joseph Schwartz at Harrison and Broadway, although J.C. Russ on the corner of Harrison and Sixth had more. But I also paid a visit to Baldwin & Co. on Clay at the Plaza, and to J.H. Bradford on Kearney, and just to play it safe I went over to Dupont and Clay to see the firm of Moffat & Co., Assayers and Bankers.

So I was one pooped little friar, carrying one big heavy carpetbag, by the time I trudged back to our hotel as evening shadows descended. I'd been followed for three blocks by a

Sydney ex-convict, whose intent was robbery and possible murder; but I managed to ditch him by ducking into a saloon, exiting out the back and across the deck of the landlocked *Niantic*, and cutting through another saloon where I paused just long enough to order an oyster loaf and a pail of steam beer.

I'd lost him for good by the time I thumped on Mendoza's door with the carpetbag.

"Hey, honeybunch, I got dinner!"

She opened the door right away, jittery as hell. "Don't shout, for God's sake!"

"Sorry." I went in and set down the carpetbag gratefully. "I don't think the mortals are sleeping yet. It's early."

"There are three of them on this floor, and seventeen downstairs," she said, wringing her hands. "It's been a while since I've been around so many of them. I'd forgotten how loud their hearts are, Joseph. I can hear them beating."

"Aw, you'll get used to it in no time," I said. I held up the takeout. "Look! Oyster loaf and beer!"

She looked impatient, and then her eyes widened as she caught the scent of the fresh-baked sourdough loaf and the butter and the garlic and the little fried oysters . . .

"Oh, gosh," she said weakly.

So we had another nice companionable moment, sitting at the table where she'd set up the testing equipment, drinking from opposite sides of the beer pail. I lit a lamp and pulled the different paper-wrapped parcels from my carpetbag, one by one.

"What're those?" Mendoza inquired with her mouth full.

"Samples of gold-bearing quartz," I explained. "From six different places. I wrote the name of each place on the package in pencil, see? And your job is to test each sample. You're going to look for a blue-green lichen growing in the crevices with the gold."

She swallowed and shook her head, blank-faced.

"You need a microbiologist for this kind of job, Joseph, surely. Plants that primitive aren't my strong suit."

"The closest microbiologist was in Seattle," I explained. "And Agrippanilla's a pain to work with. Besides, you can handle this! Remember the Black Elysium grape? The mutant saccharomyces or whatever it was? You won yourself a field commendation on that one. This'll be easy!"

Mendoza looked pleased, but did her best to conceal it. "I'll bet your mission budget just wouldn't stretch to shipping qualified personnel down here, eh? That's the Company. Okay; I'll get started right after dinner."

"You can wait until morning," I said.

"Naah." She had a gulp of the beer. "Sleep is for sissies."

So after we ate I retired, and far into the hours of the night I could still see lamplight shining from her room, bright stripes through the plank wall every time I turned over. I knew why she was working so late.

It's not hard to sleep in a house full of mortals, if you tune out the sounds they make. Sometimes, though, just on the edge of sleep, you find yourself listening for one heartbeat that ought to be there, and it isn't. Then you wake up with a start, and remember things you don't want to remember.

I opened my eyes and sunlight smacked me in the face, glittering off the bay through my open door. Mendoza was sitting on the edge of my bed, sipping from her canteen. I grunted, grimaced and sat unsteadily.

"Coffee," I croaked. She looked smug and held up her canteen.

"There's a saloon on the corner. The nice mortal sold me a whole pot of coffee for five dollars. Want some?"

"Sure." I held out my hand. "So . . . you didn't mind going down to the saloon by yourself? There are some nasty mortals in this town, kid."

"The famous Sydney Ducks? Yes, I'm aware of that." She was quietly gleeful about something. "I've lived in the Ventana for years, Joseph, dodging mountain lions! *Individual* nasty mortals don't frighten me anymore. Go ahead, try the coffee."

I sipped it cautiously. It was great. We may have been in America (famous for lousy coffee) now, but San Francisco was already *San Francisco.*

Mendoza cleared her throat and said, "I found your blue-green lichen. It was growing on the sample from Hiram Gainsborg's. The stuff looks like Stilton cheese. What is it, Joseph?"

"Something the Company wants," I said, gulping down half the coffee.

"I'll bet it does," she said, giving me that sidelong look again. "I've been sitting here, watching you drool and snore, amusing myself by accessing scientific journals on bioremediant research. Your lichen's a toxiphage, Joseph. It's perfectly happy feeding on arsenic and antimony compounds found in conjunction with gold. It breaks them down. I suspect that it could make a lot of money for anyone in the business of cleaning up industrial pollution."

"That's a really good guess, Mendoza," I said, handing back the coffee and swinging my legs over the side of the bed. I found my sandals and pulled them on.

"Isn't it?" She watched me grubbing around in my trunk for my shaving kit. "Yes, for God's sake, shave. You look like one of Torquemada's henchmen, with those blue jowls. So Dr. Zeus is doing something altruistic! In its usual corporate-profit way, of course. I don't understand why this has to be classified, but I'm impressed."

"Uh-huh." I swabbed soap on my face.

"You seem to be in an awful hurry."

"Do I?" I scraped whiskers from my cheek.

"I wonder what you're in a hurry to do?" Mendoza said. "Probably hotfoot it back to Hiram Gainsborg's, to see if he has any more of what he sold you."

"Maybe, baby."

"Can I go along?"

"Nope."

"I'm not sitting in my room all day, watching lichen grow in petri dishes," she said. "Is it okay if I go sightseeing?"

I looked at her in the mirror, disconcerted. "Sweetheart, this is a rough town. Those guys from Australia are devils, and some of the Yankees—"

"I pity the mortal who approaches me with criminal intent," she said, smiling in a chilly kind of way. "I'll just ride out to the Golden Gate. How can I get into trouble? Ghirardelli's won't be there for another two years, right?"

* * *

I walked Mendoza down to the stable anyway, and saw her safely off before hotfooting it over to Hiram Gainsborg's, as she suspected.

Mr. Gainsborg kept a loaded rifle behind his shop counter. I came in through his door so fast he had the rifle out and trained on me pronto, before he saw it was me.

"Apologies, Father Rubio," he said, lowering the barrel. "Back again, are you? You're in some hurry, sir." He had a white chin beard, wore a waistcoat of red and white striped silk, and gave me the disconcerting feeling I was talking to Uncle Sam.

"I was pursued by importuning persons of low moral fiber," I said.

"That a fact?" Mr. Gainsborg pursed his lips. "Well, what about that quartz you bought yesterday? Your brother friars think it'll do?"

"Yes, my son, they found it suitable," I said. "In fact, the color and quality are so magnificent, so superior to any other we have seen, that we all agreed only *you* were worthy of this important commission for the Holy Father." I laid the drawing of the crucifix down on his counter. He smiled.

"Well, sir, I'm glad to hear that. I reckon I can bring the job in at a thousand dollars pretty well." He fixed me with a hard clear eye, waiting to see if I'd flinch, but I just hauled my purse out and grinned at him.

"Price is no object to Holy Mother Church," I said. "Shall we say, half the payment in advance?"

I counted out Chilean gold dollars while he watched, sucking his teeth, and I went on:

"In fact, we were thinking of having rosaries made up as a gift for the whole College of Cardinals. Assuming, of course, that you have enough of that *particular* beautiful vein of quartz. Do you know where it was mined?"

"Don't know, sir, and that's a fact," he told me. "Miner brought in a sackful a week ago. He reckoned he could get more for it at a jeweler's because of the funny color. There's more'n enough of it in my back room to make your beads, I bet."

"Splendid," I said. "But do you recall the miner's name, in case we do need to obtain more?"

"Ayeh." Mr. Gainsborg picked up a dollar and inspected it. "Isaiah Stuckey, that was the fellow's name. Didn't say where his claim was, though. They don't tell, as a general rule."

"Understandable. Do you know where I might find the man?"

"No, sir, don't know that. He didn't have a red cent until I paid for the quartz, I can tell you; so I reckon the next place he went was a hotel." Mr. Gainsborg looked disdainful. "Unless he went straight for the El Dorado or a whorehouse, begging your pardon. Depends on how long he'd been in the mountains, don't it?"

I sighed and shook my head. "This is a city of temptation, I am afraid. Can you describe him for me?"

Mr. Gainsborg considered. "Well, sir, he had a beard."

Great. I was looking for a man with a beard in a city full of bearded men. At least I had a name.

So I spent the rest of that day trudging from hotel to boarding house to tent, asking if anybody there had seen Isaiah Stuckey. Half the people I asked snickered and said, "No, why?" and waited for a punch line. The other half also replied in the negative, and then asked my advice on matters spiritual. I heard confessions from seventeen prostitutes, five drunks and a transvestite before the sun sank behind Knob Hill, but I didn't find Isaiah Stuckey.

By twilight, I had worked my way out to the landlocked ships along what would one day be Battery and Sansome Streets, though right now they were just so many rickety piers and catwalks over the harbor mud. I teetered up the gangplank of one place that declared itself the MAGNOLIA HOTEL, by means of a sign painted on a bedsheet hung over the bow. A grumpy-looking guy was swabbing the deck.

"We don't rent to no goddamn greasers here," he informed me. "Even if you is a priest."

"Well, now, my son, Christ be my witness I've not come about taking rooms," I said in the thickest Dublin accent I could manage, "Allow me to introduce myself! Father Ignatius Costello. I'm after searching for a poor soul whose family's in sore need of him, and him lost in the gold fields this twelvemonth. Do you rent many rooms to miners, lad?"

"Sure we do," muttered the guy, embarrassed. "What's his name?"

"Isaiah Stuckey, or so his dear old mother said," I replied.

"Him!" The guy looked up, righteously indignant now. He pointed with his mop at a vast expanse of puke on the deck. "That's your Ike Stuckey's work, by God!"

I recoiled. "He's never got the cholera?"

"No, sir, just paralytic drunk. You ought to smell his damn *room,* after he lay in there most of a week! Boss had me fetch him out, plastered or not, on account of he ain't paid no rent in three days. I got him this far and he heaved up all over my clean floor! Then, I wish I may be struck down dead if he don't sober up instant and run down them planks like a racehorse! Boss got a shot off at him, but he kept a-running. Last we saw he was halfway to Kearney Street."

"Oh, dear," I said. "I don't suppose you'd have any idea where he was intending to go, my son?"

"No, I don't," said the guy, plunging his mop in its pail and getting back to work. "But if you run too, you can maybe catch the son of a—" he wavered, glancing up at my ecclesiastical presence, "—gun. He ain't been gone but ten minutes."

I took his advice, and hurried off through the twilight. There actually was a certain funk lingering in the air, a trail of unwashed-Stuckey molecules, that any bloodhound could have picked up without much effort—not that it would have enjoyed the experience—and incidentally any cyborg with augmented senses could follow too.

So I was slapping along in my sandals, hot on Stuckey's trail, when I ran into Mendoza at the corner.

"Hey, Joseph!" She waved at me cheerily. "You'll never guess what I found!"

"Some plant, right?"

"And how! It's a form of *Lupinus* with—"

"That's fascinating, doll, and I mean that sincerely, but

right now I could really use a lift." I jumped and swung up into the saddle behind her, only to find myself sitting on something damp. "What the hell—"

"That's my *Lupinus*. I dug up the whole plant and wrapped the root ball in a piece of my petticoat until I can transplant it into a pot. If you've squashed it, I'll wring your neck," she told me.

"No, it's okay," I said. "Look, could we just canter up the street that way? I'm chasing somebody and I don't want to lose him."

She grumbled, but dug her heels into the horse's sides and we sped off, though we didn't go very far very fast because the street went straight uphill.

"It wouldn't have taken us ten minutes to go back and drop my *Lupinus* at the hotel, you know," Mendoza said. "It's a really rare subspecies, possibly a mutant form. It appears to produce photoreactive porphyrins."

"Honey, I haven't got ten minutes," I said, wrootching my butt away from the damn thing. "Wait! Turn left here!" Stuckey's trail angled away down Kearney toward Portsmouth Square, so Mendoza yanked the horse's head around and we leaned into the turn. I peered around Mendoza, trying to spot any bearded guy staggering and wheezing along. Unfortunately, the street was full of staggering bearded guys, all of them converging on Portsmouth Square.

We found out why when we got there.

Portsmouth Square was just a sandy vacant lot, but there were wire baskets full of pitch and redwood chips burning atop poles at its four corners, and bright-lit board and batten buildings lined three sides of it. The fourth side was just shops and one adobe house, like a row of respectable spinsters frowning down on their neighbors, but the rest of the place blazed like happy Gomorrah.

"Holy smoke," said Mendoza, reining up. "I'm not going in there, Joseph."

"It's just mortals having a good time," I said. Painted up on false fronts, garish as any Old West fantasy, were names like The Mazourka, Parker House, The Varsouvienne, La Souciedad, Dennison's Exchange, The Arcade. All of them were torchlit and proudly decked in red, white and blue, so the general effect was of Hell on the Fourth of July.

"It's brothels and gambling dens," said Mendoza.

"It's theaters, too," I said defensively, pointing at the upstairs windows of the Jenny Lind.

"And saloons. What do you want here?"

"A guy named Isaiah Stuckey," I said, leaning forward. His scent was harder to pick out now, but . . . over *there* . . . "He's the miner who found our quartz. I need to talk to him. Come on, we're blocking traffic! Let's try that one. The El Dorado."

Mendoza gritted her teeth but rode forward, and as we neared the El Dorado the scent trail grew stronger.

"He's in here," I said, sliding down from the saddle. "Come on!"

"I'll wait outside, thank you."

"You want to wait here by yourself, or you want to enter a nice civilized casino in the company of a priest?" I asked her.

She looked around wildly at the happy throng of mortals. "Damn you anyway," she said, and dismounted. We went into the El Dorado.

Maybe I shouldn't have used the words *nice civilized casino*. It was a big square place with bare board walls, and the floor sloped downhill from the entrance, because it was just propped up on pilings over the ash-heaps and was already sagging. Wind whistled through the planks, and there is no night air so cold as in San Francisco. It gusted into the stark booths, curtained off with thumbtacked muslin, along one wall where the whores were working. It was shantytown squalor no Hollywood set designer would dream of depicting.

But the El Dorado had all the other trappings of an Old West saloon, with as much rococo finery as could be nailed on or propped against the plank walls. There were gilt-framed paintings of balloony nude women. There was a grand mirrored bar at one end, cut glass glittering under the oil lamps. Upon the dais a full orchestra played, good and loud, and here again the Stars and Stripes were draped, swagged and rosetted in full glory.

At the gambling tables were croupiers and dealers in black suits, every one of them a gaunt Doc Holliday clone presiding over monte, or faro, or diana, or chuck-a-luck, or plain poker. A sideboard featured free food for the high rollers, and a lot of ragged men—momentary millionaires in blue jeans, back from the gold fields for the winter—were helping themselves to pie and cold beef. At the tables, their sacks of gold dust or piles of nuggets sat unattended, as safe as anything else in this town.

I wished I wasn't dressed as a friar. This was the kind of spot a cyborg with the ability to count cards could earn himself some money to offset operating expenses. I might have given it a try anyway, but beside me Mendoza was hyperventilating, so I just shook my head and focused on my quarry.

Isaiah Stuckey was in here somewhere. At the buffet table? No . . .

At the bar? No . . . Christ, there must have been thirty guys wearing blue jeans and faded red calico shirts in here, and they all stank like bachelors. Was that him? The beefy guy looking around furtively?

"Okay, Mendoza," I said, "if you were a miner who'd just recovered consciousness after a drinking binge, stone broke—where would you go?"

"I'd go bathe myself," said Mendoza, wrinkling her nose. "But a mortal would probably try to get more money. So he'd come in here, I guess. Of course, you can only *win* money in a game of chance if you already have money to bet—"

"STOP, THIEF!" roared somebody, and I saw the furtive guy sprinting through the crowd with a sack of gold dust in his fist. The croupiers had risen as one, and from the recesses of their immaculate clothing produced an awesome amount of weaponry. Isaiah Stuckey—boy, could I smell him *now!*—crashed through a back window, pursued closely by bullets and bowie knives.

I said something you don't often hear a priest say and grabbed Mendoza's arm. "Come on! We have to find him before they do!"

We ran outside, where a crowd had gathered around Mendoza's horse.

"Get away from that!" Mendoza yelled. I pushed around her and gaped at what met my eyes. The sorry-looking bush bound behind Mendoza's saddle was . . . glowing in the dark, like a faded neon rose. It was also shaking back and forth, but that was because a couple of mortals were trying to pull it loose.

They were a miner, so drunk he was swaying, and a hooker only slightly less drunk, who was holding the miner up by his belt with one hand and doing her best to yank the mutant *Lupinus* free with the other.

"I *said* leave it alone!" Mendoza shoved me aside to get at the hooker.

"But I'm gettin' married," explained the hooker, in as much of a voice as whiskey and tobacco had left her. "An' I oughter have me a buncha roses to get married holding on to. 'Cause I ain't never been married before and I oughter have me a buncha roses."

"That is not a bunch of roses, you stupid cow, that's a rare photoreactive porphyrin-producing variant *Lupinus* specimen," Mendoza said, and I backed off at the look in her eyes and so did every sober man there, but the hooker blinked.

"Don't you use that kinda language to me," she screamed, and attempted to claw Mendoza's eyes out. Mendoza ducked and rose with a roundhouse left to the chin that knocked poor Sally Faye, or whoever she was, back on her ass, and her semiconscious fiancé went down with her.

All the menfolk present, with the exception of me, drew back eagerly to give the ladies room. I jumped forward and got Mendoza's arm again.

"My very beloved daughters in Christ, is this any way to behave?" I cried, because Mendoza, with murder in her eye, was pulling a gardening trowel out of her saddlebag. Subvocally I transmitted, *Are you nuts? We've got to go after Isaiah Stuckey!*

Snarling, Mendoza swung herself back into the saddle. I had to scramble to get up there too, hitching my robe in a fairly undignified way, which got boffo laughs from the grinning onlookers before we galloped off into the night.

"Go down to Montgomery Street!" I said. "He probably came out there!"

"If one of the bullets didn't get him," said Mendoza, but she urged the horse down Clay and made a fast left onto Montgomery. Halfway along the block we slowed to a canter and I leaned out, trying to pick up the scent trail again.

"Yes!" I punched the air and nearly fell off the horse. Mendoza grabbed my hood, hauling me back up straight behind her.

"Why the hell is it so important you talk to this mortal?" she demanded.

"Head north! His trail goes back toward Washington Street," I said. "Like I said, babe, he sold that quartz to Gainsborg."

"But we already know it tested positive for your lichen," said Mendoza.

At the next intersection we paused as I sniffed the air, and then pointed forward. "He went thataway! Let's go. We want to know where he got the stuff, don't we?"

"Do we?" Mendoza kicked the horse again—I was only grateful the Company hadn't issued her spurs—and we rode on toward Jackson. "Why should we particularly need to know where the quartz was mined, Joseph? I've cultured the lichen successfully. There'll be plenty for the Company labs."

"Of course," I said, concentrating on Isaiah Stuckey's scent. "Keep going, will you? I think he's heading back toward Pacific Street."

"Unless the Company has some other reason for wanting to know where the quartz deposit is," said Mendoza, as we came up on Pacific.

I sat up in the saddle, closing my eyes to concentrate on the scent. There was his earlier track, but . . . yes . . . he was heading uphill again. "Make another left, babe. What were you just saying?"

"What I was *about* to say was, I wonder if the Company wants to be sure nobody else finds this very valuable deposit of quartz?" said Mendoza, as the horse snorted and laid its ears back; it wasn't about to gallop up Pacific. It proceeded at a grudging walk.

"Gee, Mendoza, why would Dr. Zeus worry about something like exclusive patent rights on the most valuable bioremediant substance imaginable?" I said.

She was silent a moment, but I could feel the slow burn building.

"You mean," she said, "that the Company plans to destroy the original source of the lichen?"

"Did I say that, honey?"

"Just so nobody else will discover it before Dr. Zeus puts it on the market, in the twenty-fourth century?"

"Do you see Mr. Stuckey up there anyplace?" I rose in the saddle to study the sheer incline of Pacific Street.

Mendoza said something amazingly profane in sixteenth-century Galician, but at least she didn't push me off the horse. When she had run out of breath, she gulped air and said:

"Just *once* in my eternal life I'd like to know I was actually helping to save the world, like we were all promised, instead of making a lot of technocrats up in the future obscenely rich."

"I'd like it too, honest," I said.

"Don't you *honest* me! You're a damned Facilitator, aren't you? You've got no more moral sense than a jackal!"

"I resent that!" I edged back from her sharp shoulder blades, and the glow-in-the-dark mutant *Lupinus* squelched unpleasantly under my behind. "And anyway, what's so great about being a Preserver? You could have been a Facilitator like me, you know that, kid? You had what it took. Instead, you've spent your whole immortal life running around after freaking *bushes!*"

"A Facilitator like you? Better I should have died in that dungeon in Santiago!"

"I saved your LIFE, and this is the thanks I get?"

"And as for freaking bushes, Mr. Big Shot Facilitator, it might interest you to know that certain rare porphyrins have serious commercial value in the data storage industry—"

"So, who's making the technocrats rich now, huh?" I demanded. "And have you ever stopped to consider that maybe the damn plants wouldn't *be* so rare if Botanist drones like you weren't digging them up all the time?"

"For your information, that specimen was growing on land that'll be paved over in ten years," Mendoza said coldly. "And if you call me a drone again, you're going to go bouncing all the way down this hill with the print of my boot on your backside."

The horse kept walking, and San Francisco Bay fell ever further below us. Finally, stupidly, I said:

"Okay, we've covered all the other bases on mutual recrimination. Aren't you going to accuse me of killing the only man you ever loved?"

She jerked as though I'd shot her, and turned round to regard me with blazing eyes.

"You didn't kill him," she said, in a very quiet voice. "You just let him die."

She turned away, and of course then I wanted to put my arms around her and tell her I was sorry. If I did that, though, I'd probably spend the next few months in a regeneration tank, growing back my arms.

So I just looked up at the neighborhood we had entered without noticing, and that was when I really felt my blood run cold.

"Uh—we're in Sydney-Town," I said.

Mendoza looked up. "Oh-oh."

There weren't any flags or bunting here. There weren't any torches. And you would never, *ever* see a place like this in any Hollywood western. Neither John Wayne nor Gabby Hayes even went anywhere near the likes of Sydney-Town.

It perched on its ledge at the top of Pacific Street and rotted. On the left side was one long row of leaning shacks; on the right side was another. I could glimpse dim lights through windows and doorways, and heard fiddle music scraping away, a half-dozen folk tunes from the British Isles, played in an eerie discord. The smell of the place was unbelievable, breathing out foul through dark doorways where darker figures leaned. Above the various dives, names were chalked that would have been quaint and reassuring anywhere else: The Noggin of Ale. The Tam O'Shanter. The Jolly Waterman. The Bird in Hand.

Some of the dark figures leaned out and bid us "G'deevnin'," and without raising their voices too much let us know about the house specialties. At the Boar's Head, a woman was making love to a pig in the back room; did we want to see? At the Goat and Compass, there was a man who'd eat or drink anything, absolutely *anything*, mate, for a few cents, and he hadn't had a bath in ten years. Did we want to give him a go? At the Magpie, a girl was lying on a mattress in the back, so drunk she'd never wake before morning, no matter what anyone did to her. Were we interested? And other dark figures were moving along in the shadows, watching us.

Portsmouth Square satisfied simple appetites like hunger and thirst, greed, the need to get laid or to shoot at total strangers. Sydney-Town, on the other hand, catered to specialized tastes.

It was nothing I hadn't seen before, but I'd worked in Old Rome at her worst, and Byzantium too. Mendoza, though, shrank back against me as we rode.

She had a white, stunned look I'd seen only twice before. The first was when she was four years old, and the Inquisitors had held her up to the barred window to see what could happen if she didn't confess she was a Jew. More than fear or horror, it was *astonishment* that life was like this.

The other time she'd looked like that was when I let her mortal lover die.

I leaned forward and spoke close to her ear. "Baby, I'm going to get down and follow the trail on foot. You ride on, okay? I'll meet you at the hotel."

I slid down from the saddle fast, smacked the horse hard on its rump, and watched as the luminous mutant whatever-it-was bobbed away through the dark, shining feebly. Then I marched forward, looking as dangerous as I could in the damn friar's habit, following Isaiah Stuckey's scent line.

He was sweating heavily, now, easy to track even here. Sooner or later, the mortal was going to have to stop, to set down that sack of gold dust and wipe his face and breathe.

He surely wasn't dumb enough to venture into one of these places . . .

His trail took an abrupt turn, straight across the threshold of the very next dive. I sighed, looking up at the sign. This establishment was The Fierce Grizzly. Behind me, the five guys who were lurking paused too. I shrugged and went in.

Inside the place was small, dark, and smelled like a zoo. I scanned the room. Bingo! There was Isaiah Stuckey, a gin punch in his hand and a smile on his flushed face, just settling down to a friendly crap game with a couple of serial rapists and an axe murderer. I could reach him in five steps. I had taken two when a hand descended on my shoulder.

"Naow, mate, you ain't saving no souls in 'ere," said a big thug. "You clear off, or sit down and watch the exhibition, eh?"

I wondered how hard I'd have to swing to knock him cold, but then a couple of torches flared alight at one end of the room. The stage curtain, nothing more than a dirty blanket swaying and jerking in the torchlight, was flung aside.

I saw a grizzly bear, muzzled and chained. Behind her, a guy I assumed to be her trainer, grinned at the audience. The act started.

In twenty thousand years I thought I'd seen everything, but I guess I hadn't.

My jaw dropped, as did the jaws of most of the other patrons who weren't regulars there. They couldn't take their eyes off what was happening on the stage, which made things pretty easy for the pickpockets working the room.

But only for a moment.

Maybe that night the bear decided she'd finally had enough, and summoned some self-esteem. Maybe the chains had reached the last stages of metal fatigue. Anyway, there was a sudden *ping,* like a bell cracking, and the bear got her front paws free.

About twenty guys, including me, tried to get out through the front door at the same moment. When I picked myself out of the gutter, I looked up to see Isaiah Stuckey running like mad again, further up Pacific Street.

"Hey! Wait!" I shouted; but no Californian slows down

when a grizzly is loose. Cursing, I rose and scrambled after him, yanking up my robe to clear my legs. I could hear him gasping like a steam engine as I began to close the gap between us. Suddenly, he went down.

I skidded to a halt beside him and fell to my knees. Stuckey was flat on his face, not moving. I turned him over and he flopped like a side of meat, staring sightless up at the clear cold stars.

Massive aortic aneurysm. Dead as a doornail.

"NO!" I howled, ripping his shirt open and pounding on his chest, though I knew nothing was going to bring him back "Don't you go and die on me, you mortal son of a bitch! Stupid *jackass*—"

Black shadows had begun to slip from the nearest doorways, eager to begin corpse robbing; but they halted, taken aback I guess by the sight of a priest screaming abuse at the deceased. I glared at them, remembered who I was supposed to be, and made a grudging sign of the cross over the late Isaiah Stuckey.

There was a clatter of hoofbeats. Mendoza's horse came galloping back downhill.

"Are you okay?" Mendoza leaned from the saddle. "Oh, hell, is that him?"

"The late Isaiah Stuckey," I said bitterly. "He had a heart attack."

"I'm not surprised, with all that running uphill," said Mendoza. "This place really needs those cable cars, doesn't it?"

"You said it, kiddo." I got to my feet. "Let's get out of here."

Mendoza frowned, gazing at the dead man. "Wait a minute. That's Catskill Ike!"

"Cute name," I said, clambering up into the saddle behind her. "You knew the guy?"

"No, I just monitored him in case he started any fires. He's been prospecting on Villa Creek for the last six months."

"Well, so what?"

"So I know where he found your quartz deposit," said

Mendoza. "It wasn't mined up the Sacramento at all, Joseph."

"It's in Big *Sur*?" I demanded. She just nodded.

At that moment, the grizzly shoved her way out into the street, and it seemed like a good idea to leave fast.

"Don't take it too badly," said Mendoza a little while later, when we were riding back toward our hotel. "You got what the Company sent you after, didn't you? I'll bet there'll be Security Techs blasting away at Villa Creek before I get home."

"I guess so," I said glumly. She snickered.

"And look at the wonderful quality time we got to spend together! And the Pope will get his fancy crucifix. Or was that part just a scam?"

"No, the Company really is bribing the Pope to do something," I said. "But you don't—"

"Need to know, of course. That's okay. I got a great meal out of this trip, at least."

"Hey, are you hungry? We can still take in some of the restaurants, kid," I said.

Mendoza thought about that. The night wind came gusting up from the city below us, where somebody at the Poulet d'Or was mincing onions for a *sauce piperade*, and somebody else was grilling steaks. We heard the *pop* of a wine cork all the way up where we were on Powell Street . . .

"Sounds like a great idea," she said. She briefly accessed her chronometer. "As long as you can swear we'll be out of here by 1906," she added.

"Trust me," I said happily. "No problem!"

"Trust you?" she exclaimed, and spat. I could tell she didn't mean it, though.

We rode on down the hill.

Annuity Clinic

NIGEL BROWN

Nigel Brown lives in Hove, England, and is an optometrist. He has been an occasional book reviewer for Interzone *since 1996, and published only three stories before 2003 but several this year. He is associated with the William Hope Hodgson memorial website, The Night Land, where some of his fiction appeared. He has enjoyed the work of William Hope Hodgson for many years, and considers "The Nightland" to be one of the most imaginative and exciting adventure stories he has ever read.*

"Annuity Clinic" appeared in Interzone. *It is about an old woman who used to be an engineer in a dystopian future UK, in which the elderly are forced to sell artificial body parts back to the government to get enough money to live on. Bureaucracies are run by robots of various kinds which the old woman used to work on. Technology is recycled rather than discarded. Brown combines here a problem-solving protagonist, an old woman living in a nursing home, with some interesting future speculation and dreamlike images.*

Blue dawn light seeped around the frayed curtains, throwing shadows across the small bedroom, and the hump of her gently snoring roommate Betty.

Eloise was already awake. A vision of the Eastern Mediterranean glowed in her left eye, offering a tantalizing glimpse of life two thousand miles beyond the cold plaster walls. She drank in the scene until the sun, outside her window, rose higher; a sunbeam found a chink in the curtains. The sudden glare blinded her; the cataract in her natural right eye dispersed the light into a white fog. It bleached out her cyberspace vision—her private escape.

Eloise reluctantly shut her left eye down. The Aegean, shimmering in the Mediterranean light, vanished. Now she stared, unfocused, at the ceiling. Bright after-images danced over its dark surface.

Suddenly aware of the room around her, she took shallow breaths through her mouth to endure the stink. It lay like a thick blanket in the heady air: Betty was never one for getting to her chamber pot at night.

It's ridiculous, she thought. *We've got automation so good: robots . . . even robots that are self-aware, and this dump still uses chamber pots.*

The answer lurked at the back of her mind—"Because you're at the bottom of the heap, dear . . . you let yourself drift down there. Artificial minds, robots, cost a lot more money now than you have left . . ."

That's why . . .

Something flicked through her mind—a fleeting thought she tried to catch, nearly held—then the screaming across the corridor began. The thought left her, driven out by old Arnold's cries.

Eloise lay patiently in bed, listening out for the pattering footsteps of the Duty Carer, the creak of Arnold's door, then silence as his medication was administered.

The thought crept back into her head and settled there, triggering a spark of excitement . . . today was a trip out of the home—the visit to the Annuity Clinic.

Breakfast was the usual chaos, with Betty extracting her mouthplate and tossing it onto the table, narrowly missing her bowl of cornflakes. Eloise had learned to shield her food with her hand, and place a shaky palm over the heaped cereal to avoid the spray of spittle that came from the babbling Katie sitting on her other side.

"Ready for the bus today, Eloise?"

She looked up to see the Matron, Mrs. Whitten, standing over her.

"I'm always grateful for a trip outside," she said carefully.

Mrs. Whitten frowned. "You have plenty of trips, Eloise. We're contracted to supply one trip a month—that's what you get."

"Thank you," Eloise answered.

Katie mumbled something incoherent to the Matron. A look of disgust crossed Mrs. Whitten's face, and she turned to go.

"Will my room's internet link be repaired soon?"

"It's on my list," Mrs. Whitten said. Then her eyes widened with understanding. She peered at Eloise's sapphire eye, and gave a sharp nod. "Oh I see! You'll lose access when that eye goes, won't you?" She sniffed. "I could never afford an interface eye like that . . . you'll get by—like the rest of us."

"I'm sure I will," Eloise answered, "but with my eye gone, I'll be cut off in my room . . ."

"Maybe for a while," Mrs. Whitten replied, "but you'll have the money—with that eye sold—to continue living here." She gave a wide smile. "That's a consolation, don't you think?"

* * *

Her words haunted Eloise the whole of the coach trip to the Clinic. Lost in her thoughts—dreaming of her sister's house and family on the warm Aegean—she ignored the bleak scenery through the window: the scrubby Sussex tundra running up to the dark fir-line that rimmed the South Downs.

They hurried off the coach, shivering in the raw northerly wind that blew off the Midlands glacier. The Clinic was a low, small windowed building that ran along one side of the town's bus terminal.

Eloise glanced wistfully at the other buses, but she had no money, no permit . . . no where else to go.

"This *global warming*'s boiling my blood!" Betty managed to joke.

Eloise smiled at the irony. They were all old enough to remember the predictions of vineyards in Southern England. No one listened to warnings that the Gulf Stream might shut down.

We push bad news to the back of our minds, she mused, *knowing that we lose it there.*

So how could she blame the country for her own predicament, when pension poverty had been predicted for so long?

The Annuity Clinic's waiting room was full up by the time she managed to shuffle inside. She didn't regret not getting a seat as her hip made it difficult to stand up again.

"How long'll we be 'ere?"

She turned at the sound.

"I don't know, Arnold," she replied. "They said it was for pre-assessments. I guess they need to know how much work to prepare for when we come back to have bits chopped out of us."

He looked startled at her tone.

"I'm sorry," she said. "I didn't mean it to come out like that."

His face was a pasty yellow—Eloise couldn't decide whether it was anemia or the effect of his daily sedative—but, far from his usual drowsiness, he seemed lucid enough now.

It must have been the novelty of a trip outside the home,

she decided. That was understandable. Despite what Mrs. Whitten had said, they rarely left their building.

Eloise looked around the reception area with interest, but found nothing extraordinary about the place. The grubby posters (static, not even active!) and the chipped magnolia paintwork reminded her of every other National Health Clinic she had ever been inside; the only feature that told her this was the mid-21st century was the robotic receptionist.

She cast a professional eye over the model—an A-series 412. Cheap and nasty, with barely enough processing power to do the job. She had spent her working life in the industry, and had never trusted the 412s.

Then, to her surprise, the robot's head swivelled round to face her.

"Eloise Harvey?" it said. The voice was a soft contralto (she guessed its voice box had been upgraded to make the robot appear a better model than it really was—a typical State wallpaper job).

"Yes," she answered. Despite her previous determination to be brave today, her voice came out strained—reedy. "I'm Miss Harvey. Is it time? Is it my turn now?"

"Could you please go to the Adjunct's office," the receptionist lifted a mannequin arm and pointed to an anonymous door to the side. "The Adjunct requests a meeting."

What could it mean? The others all looked at her, glad they were not the ones being singled out. Life in the Home did that to you—made you strive to keep a low profile—not stand out or be a troublemaker, then a target.

Another voice—a man's—boomed out from a speaker on the receptionist's desk: "We're not ready for you yet, Miss Harvey, but a quick word in my office would be of benefit."

Arnold nudged her as she passed, and rolled his eyes in mock terror. "They want to chop out more than just yer fancy eye, Ellie," he said.

"At least I'll be walking out of here on my own two feet," she shot back at him, glancing down at his artificial leg.

Betty just tittered as Eloise fumbled with the door handle. She was grateful to close the door on Betty's parting words:

"Offer him yer body, love! Maybe he'll let yer keep all of it, afterward!"

The Adjunct sat at a desk. Eloise realized with surprise that it was also a robot, though a more advanced model than the A412 outside.

Probably one of the T-series, she speculated. Despite her nerves, she felt a small thrill to be in its presence.

This was one of the sentient models—as close to artificial intelligence our technology could build. It had been years since she'd had the opportunity to be close to such an advanced model.

Once an engineer, she said to herself, *always an engineer*.

Its soft flesh tones and shiny black hair, with those animated, expressive eyes, would have fooled her in a poorer light—although she'd known residents in the Home who'd botoxed their skin into immobility and worn toupees . . . they'd looked more robotic than the machine facing her.

But didn't the NHS run to *any* human staff, these days?

"Please," it said, indicating the high backed chair facing it. "Sit down."

"Why am I here?" she asked. "Have I done something wrong?"

"Not at all," the Adjunct said. "I was reviewing your case, and felt it would be useful to speak to you in person."

Eloise gave it a doubtful look.

"All my documents were sent in last week. I don't think there's anything wrong. My implant is still good, isn't it?"

"Yes," the Adjunct said. "As of this moment, your ocular implant is worth 10,631 credits to the Micronesian market—that is where we can get the best price for you."

"Micronesia?"

"Our brokerage service is unrivalled in this part of Southern England," the Adjunct reassured her. "The technology built into your eye is in great demand on the Kiribati exchange."

"Oh, I'm sure you'll get me the best price for my eye," Eloise said.

"It will buy you an annuity you can live on," the Adjunct reassured her, repeating the Clinic's mantra.

She'd read that slogan on the board outside.

"So what did you want to see me about?"

The Adjunct didn't answer her at first. Its eyes seemed to defocus and stare into the middle distance, then: "What do you see before you?"

She stared at the Adjunct.

"I see a T-series machine, made to look like a man, but your flesh is too pink, your hair is too shiny."

"I am the Adjunct of this Clinic, perfectly constructed for my work . . ." it said. "If you were to look below my waist you would see that I protrude out of the back of this desk unit."

She gave a short sigh. The possibility of danger hadn't occurred to her before . . ..

"Don't worry!" it exclaimed, picking up on her thought. "I cannot hurt you. I am totally immobile."

It lowered its head to avoid her steady gaze.

"But I would not hurt you," it continued. "I used to be known by you as Clever Dolly."

Eloise frowned. Her wrinkled forehead screwed up further.

"Clever Dolly?"

"You had a doll when you were six years old," the Adjunct reminded her. "You kept it for four years, spoke to it, played with it . . . the sentient processor within it lives within me now."

Her eyes widened.

"Oh my!" she exclaimed. "You mean that you're my Clever Dolly . . . all grown up?"

"Yes, in a way," the Adjunct admitted. "I recall my time with you—no memories are ever lost for my kind."

"But . . ." Eloise said, "How do I know that this is the truth?"

The Adjunct gave a human shrug. "Why should I lie to you?"

Her eyes narrowed again: "If you're really my Clever Dolly, you'd know where I kept my secret diary."

The Adjunct was silent for a moment. She guessed it was searching its memory core.

"You had no secret diary, but I recall you would hide secret messages inside Teddy Bear and Kangaroo's pouch."

She felt her cheeks blush at its words.

"Well!" was all she could manage. Her face screwed up with concentration. "I remember the day my father brought you home. I was the first child in my school to have a Clever Dolly."

"I was an early model," the Adjunct said. "When you grew out of me—and I bear you no ill will—I was sold back to the toy store, then dismantled for my sentient processor."

Eloise gazed around the small office, taking in the shuttered window, the filing cabinet, the desk, the picture of some lost Sussex countryside (showing a summer of corn, haystacks and sunshine). It struck her that the picture was as far removed from the present reality of Southern England's tundra as this mimic sitting before her was from a real human being.

"So you ended up here," she said. "What a coincidence, us meeting like this!"

"It was not a coincidence," the Adjunct said. "When I saw your name on the application list, I made certain that you were brought to this Clinic."

"Whatever for?" Eloise asked.

"I need you to help me," it replied, "to leave this place."

"But why?" she said, startled by its sudden pleading tone.

It leaned forward as far as it could: "Because I'm unable to move from this desk; because I'm trapped here, seeing the world outside through my window or the netscreen; because I remember my time with you, being carried through the world—each moment an exploration—every moment a new thing: need I go on?"

Eloise was quiet for a moment, then she said in a firm voice: "You're a machine, made to work here. If you were to leave, what would you do? How would you go?"

"I don't know," it admitted. "I am unable to think of a solution to this problem."

"Well," she answered. "I don't see how I can help you."

"So you won't help."

"I can't," she said. "How could I? Would you expect me to carry you out of here?" Her voice softened. "I'm so sorry."

The Adjunct's head dipped down.

For a horrible moment, Eloise wondered if it had switched itself off with despair.

Then it spoke: "I bear you no ill will. Indeed, I fear that your attendance here is as futile for yourself as it has been for me. You see, I have information about your operation, figures not generally available to the public . . ."

She stiffened.

"Our private Clinic results show that patients who undergo your type of operation have a reduced lifespan afterward." It peered at her. "I am sorry to tell you this, but any annuity you receive for the sale of your eye is unlikely to benefit you for more than two years, at most."

"Is the operation dangerous?"

"No," it said, "it's perfectly safe. Our clinic figures are simply an average."

Eloise shrugged. "I'm old," she muttered. "I don't need you to tell me that . . . if losing one eye gives me a better life, even for a few years, it's worth it."

The Adjunct considered her words.

"How do you humans accept incompleteness so readily?"

"Life teaches us," she said sadly. "Being human means we can regret mistakes we've made in the past . . . or have dreams . . . aspirations for the future." She gazed at it with pity. "Sometimes it's worth being incomplete," she added, "if you're human."

Outside the office, the others wanted to know what had happened—what had taken so long.

"Took yer time, Ellie!" Betty leered at her. "Them old bones ain't what they were!"

Arnold was kinder, but she still evaded his questioning.

"It was about my annuity," she told him.

"Humph!" he muttered. "I know you'll get more than me. Legs is worth less than internet-seeing eyes, I reckon."

That night, when Betty nodded off into restless sleep, Eloise dared to activate her sapphire eye.

She couldn't afford to use it much—what she had left from her pension didn't stretch to always-on linkage fees, and the battery was becoming more expensive each time she replaced it.

At first the view was blurred, but it soon resolved into a virtual access window that floated in front of her face, intense colors her own cataract-cursed eye could no longer appreciate.

She gasped at the brilliance of the neurally enhanced colors: the deep emerald of the window's border, the glowing scarlet access icons.

She felt crushed by the thought that she had to give this up . . . exchange it for tapping away at a slow, fuzzy, filthy screen.

But she had no choice. She needed the money to live, even if it was in a dump like this.

The thought brought her up short—she shouldn't waste precious time on-line. Staring, and deliberately blinking, at the correct icons, Eloise swiftly navigated her way through the Net until she came to her sister's cyberspace.

There it was: Val's beautiful cottage. Its whitewashed stucco walls and red tiled roof contrasted vividly against the luscious green garden foliage that spread down to the deep blue Aegean beyond. Eloise tried to pick out the flowers Val had planted since her last holo had been taken . . . was there a new bed of roses behind the fountain? The English species had really taken to the Greek coast since the loss of the Gulf Stream had killed off so many native creatures and plants.

And it was killing her. When she finally got around to following Val South, it was too late. The Southern Countries had shaved their quotas to the bone before she could escape England . . .

A cursor blinked in the corner of her vision. Her credit was running out.

She watched the scene until it blanked, leaving her staring at the ceiling in her room.

Betty turned over, mumbled something, and sighed as the stench of urine soaking into her bedclothes filled the room.

Eloise waited until her roommate was fast asleep again, then hauled herself out of bed. She bent down, trying not to grunt with the effort, and reached underneath the bed.

Her personal box—what they let you keep in this place—was undisturbed. There was nothing valuable there—everything had long been sold. After a moment's rummaging she found what she was looking for.

The following week, as she boarded the coach to the Clinic, she hoped she'd remembered everything.

"Hurry up, Eloise! The knife's waiting for you." It was Mrs. Whitten, already sitting by the driver. She scribed off her name on a small datapad.

"Are you coming with us, today?" Eloise asked.

This was unexpected. She knew it could ruin her plan.

"I wouldn't miss it for the *world*!" Mrs. Whitten gave her a brief smile, a flash of small, sharp teeth. "Got to make sure my *guests* are all right . . ." her gaze flicked down to Eloise's hands. "What's in the bag, dearie?"

"Just some knitting," Eloise replied. "I don't know how long I'll be waiting." She smiled weakly back, her heart thumping . . . praying that the Matron wouldn't demand to have a peek inside.

"Oh," the Matron said, losing interest. "By the way, dear. I've had some trouble getting an internet connection for your room . . . they won't give a time when they can come and do it."

Eloise nodded. "I'll look forward to it," she said, politely.

She knew that nothing would be gained by causing a fuss—and after today, what did it matter?

She spent the journey to the Clinic going over her plan carefully. It wouldn't do to forget any crucial parts of it.

The reception room was less crowded than before.

"We've got fifteen forearms, three legs below the knee, and an ocular implant booked," Mrs. Whitten told the receptionist.

Eloise eyed the Adjunct's office door. From where she stood, it was no more than ten feet away—ten feet that might as well be one hundred miles, she thought.

Mrs. Whitten was busy at the desk, making sure that the annuity money was paid directly into the Homes account.

"Am I the last to go in, Mrs. Whitten?" Eloise said.

"What?"

"I'd like to finish off my knitting . . ."

A flicker of irritation crossed the Matron's face. "Yes, if you like."

Eloise nodded her thanks, and shuffled away—vaguely in the direction of the Adjunct's door.

Her heart thumping, she glanced around at the others. Arnold was gloomily staring at the carpet, no doubt contemplating the imminent loss of his right foot—Betty was humming to herself, a glazed look in her eyes.

As quick as she could, Eloise reached out and grasped the door handle. It turned easily. She slipped inside, closing the door quietly behind her.

The Adjunct looked up when she entered. For a moment, she saw its inhumanity—its blank stare—then the eyes came to life, focused on her standing there.

"I haven't much time: listen—my operation's due for today. Could you use my annuity money, from the sale of my eye, to buy me a coach ticket?"

The Adjunct gave a nod. "I can do this. I have enough discretion in the running of this Clinic to hold your annuity credit in a separate account—one I can create for the purpose—and to buy what you want. But where would you wish to go?"

Eloise's voice trembled as she told it about her sister, and gave it her sister's address.

"The Mediterranean League," it considered. "You would need a permit to go there."

That was the difficult part. It was something a person like Eloise would never be issued with; she was too old, too useless to a society like that of the Aegean State for them to allow her to live there . . .

"Your date of birth would be the problem . . ." the Adjunct mused.

Eloise had the impression that it was enjoying this challenge.

". . . if I make a small amendment to your date of birth that would bring you in under the age limit . . ."

It looked at her.

"I could do it. Someone with your experience in robotics will always be welcomed."

She breathed a sigh of relief.

"But why should I do this?" the Adjunct asked.

Her knees felt weak. She lifted her bag, and pulled out the doll with trembling fingers.

"A Clever Dolly," it remarked.

"You," she simply said.

There was a silence—an eon in computer time—then the Adjunct made a strange gargling noise.

"You kept me?" it said.

Somehow, she heard astonishment in that level voice.

"I didn't," she confessed. "But my mother did. When she died, some of her possessions—the worthless ones that the Council didn't take for keeping her—were passed on to me. This was one of them."

She looked down at the grubby doll. Its cloth body flopped in her hand, the only hi-tech indication was its round, molded head, with its empty chip-slot in the back.

"It was worthless, but it wasn't very big. I kept it to remind me more of my mother than of my childhood."

The Adjunct's eyes gleamed. "This is an unexpected thing. Thank you for showing me the doll."

Eloise glanced back at the door. It wouldn't do for Mrs. Whitten to hear her plan.

They did the operation under a local, keeping up a cheerful banter as they cut out her precious sapphire eye, disconnecting her optic nerve from the micro-circuitry—leaving her lying there with a black eye-patch like a pirate.

They tried the patch for size, then took it off to trim its edge.

"Don't I get an artificial eye?" she asked. "Just a painted one?"

The surgeon's eyebrows arched at her. He consulted his screen, then tapped at it with a gloved finger.

"Sorry, Mrs. Harley . . ."

She sighed, ignoring the mispronunciation of her name (it seemed like too much to ask).

"There's no provision for that in the fee?" she guessed.

"Er . . . no," he admitted. Then a thought occurred to

him—"You may get one on the secondhand market," he said. "Maybe someone in one of the African States . . ."

She sighed again. If he didn't see the irony of his suggestion, she was too tired to point it out to him.

She let them sew her up, then douse the wound in antiviral spray. The patch covered it, held on by a simple strap around her head.

"You can take it off in a week," the surgeon said. He patted her on the shoulder, not unkindly.

Afterward, they led her back into the waiting room. She sat on a hard plastic chair, numbed by the experience—no longer thinking of her plan . . . of anything in particular.

Her head didn't hurt, just floated on her neck.

It's the drugs, she thought. The anesthetic.

"Are you ready?"

It was Mrs. Whitten. She stood at the doorway, obviously impatient to get back on the coach.

"I'm ready," Eloise answered.

Something was bothering her, but it had slipped her mind. She gave a mental shrug—it couldn't be important, she thought. No doubt she'd remember what it was, once she was back in her room.

"I can't walk!"

Arnold's voice. It held that anguish she heard every morning.

"They taken my foot!" he called out again.

Mrs. Whitten glanced out of the door.

"You're in a wheelchair, Mr. Scrivens! Don't worry about the coach! It's got a ramp."

"I can't walk!" he cried again.

Mrs. Whitten gave an exasperated gasp, and disappeared out the door.

Eloise was left sitting there, staring at the receptionist.

It was a cheap 412, she recognized again. A nasty model. Stupid.

Now, she thought, the better model's around here somewhere . . . her gaze drifted around the room.

It focused on the Adjunct's door.

A cold chill gripped her heart. Her stomach flipped, making her gulp back bile.

She'd almost forgotten.

She lurched forward, out of her chair, almost toppling over.

The Adjunct's door seemed to retreat from her as she shuffled across the floor, but—after an age—she grasped the door handle, and pulled it down.

It would not move. It was locked.

Eloise turned to look at the exit, but Mrs. Whitten was still coping with Arnold—his cries sounded shrill. The edge of panic in his voice spurred her on—what could she do?

The receptionist.

"Excuse me!" she called out.

The robot's head lifted. It swivelled to face her.

"The Adjunct," Eloise said. "I want to see the Adjunct."

"Do you have an appointment?"

Then she understood.

"Yes," she answered. "Eloise Harvey."

The receptionist reached forward and flipped a toggle on its board.

"Go through, please."

Still dazed by the anesthetic, but triumphant, Eloise pulled at the door handle. It turned with a click.

In a moment, she was inside.

The Adjunct's office was dark, but there was enough light peeping out through the shuttered window for Eloise to see its shape, silent and collapsed over its desk.

A small object lay in front of it: the Clever Dolly.

Eloise moved to pick it up.

"Ellie!"

She nearly jumped out of her skin.

"Ellie! It's me!"

The small, shrill voice sounded from the doll.

The sound of it threw her back decades, to when she was a little girl. It recalled other things too: the smell of baked bread, the clatter of plates when Grandma would lay the table for the family . . . she blinked back a tear.

"Ellie!" the voice repeated.

She picked up the doll.

"You did it," she mumbled.

"It's hard for me, now," the doll said. "I've forgotten so much."

She stared at it. Of course. The simplest processor drove its brain now. Its intelligence would be a magnitude less than that of the Adjunct—like the result of a human lobotomy.

"I remember there's a message for you, Ellie," the doll said.

She looked around the room, but there was no clue.

"Where is it?"

"Don't know," the doll said. "When are we going to go on our adventures?"

Eloise sighed.

"I want to go on our adventure," the doll repeated.

She scanned the desk again, but it was empty. Then she noticed that the Adjunct held something in its lifeless hand.

A datapad.

She slipped it out between the cold fingers.

It flickered to life at her touch.

"Hello Eloise," it was the Adjunct's voice, sounding tinny through the small speaker. "This pad holds the travel permit—according to the permit, you're twenty years younger than a moment ago!—but don't worry. No one human will check that on the route I've fed into the ticket. The bus you need to catch is the 81b—it's at the Bus Terminal now. That will take you to Dover where you can take the Channel Link over to France, then cross from there to Greece. The details are on the ticket.

"It was difficult for me to accept removal of the processor, but I accepted your argument; that it's better to live life to the full, even incomplete. Take care of me!"

The pad's RAM light sparked. The message was deleted.

Eloise pocketed the pad and stuffed her Clever Dolly back into her bag.

"What's this?" a muffled voice said.

"Be quiet!" she ordered. "Don't say anything, otherwise we can't go on an adventure!"

"All right! But when can I talk again?"

She remembered, now, how argumentative her doll could be.

"When I tell you," she hissed.

She opened the office door, and peeped outside.

Mrs. Whitten was in the reception room, her face white with anger.

"There you are!" she exclaimed. "What were you doing in there? How did you get in?"

Eloise held up her bag. "I was doing my knitting."

Mrs. Whitten looked flummoxed at her answer.

"Well!" she said. "They'll be plenty of time for that on the coach. Come on! We're late enough."

Eloise followed Mrs. Whitten out through the Clinic doors. She winced from the icy slap of the glacial wind; shuffled along the tarmac as slowly as she could manage, yet without looking like she was deliberately hanging back.

A muffled voice sounded in her bag. She clutched it tight.

"Losing that eye shouldn't have slowed you down," Mrs. Whitten said. "I know you didn't use the other one much. Maybe I should have fetched a wheelchair for you, as well as for the others."

Eloise didn't reply. She was concentrating on keeping her feet moving, while trying to work out how she could avoid getting back on the coach.

It seemed an impossibility. The bus she hoped to catch was among the others she saw, parked over on the other side of the terminal. How could she get there? How could she outrun Mrs. Whitten?

Once they were at the coach door, Eloise hesitated to board.

Mrs. Whitten had turned toward her, ready to pull her up the steps, when Eloise spotted Arnold sitting in the coach's front seat. His face even paler than usual, and his right leg stuck out in front of him.

It was missing at the knee.

"Arnold!" she called out.

His eyes defocused and he stared down at her, obviously trying to place her face.

"It's me, Arnold!" she said. "How are you?"

"He's fine!" Mrs. Whitten interrupted.

"'lo Ellie!" It was Betty, banging her hand on the window. She waved her other arm, showing the stump. Despite that, she looked as cheerful as ever.

Resigned to her fate, Eloise began to board the coach.

A shrill cry erupted from her bag.

"What's that?" Arnold said.

Mrs. Whitten had heard the sound, too.

"What have you there, dear?" she asked.

She leaned forward to grab the bag, but Eloise drew back.

"No," she said. "You can't take that, too."

Mrs. Whitten's lips pursed. She took a step down toward her, tensing to snatch the bag from her hand.

Eloise knew she couldn't resist the younger woman. She gave a whimper.

The sound struck a chord deep within Arnold—something heroic awoke.

"Bitch! Bully! Leave her alone!"

His left leg shot out, slamming into Mrs. Whitten, toppling her forward down the coach steps.

She fell in a heap on the tarmac.

Eloise heard a snap, like a chicken bone cracking.

"My leg!" Mrs. Whitten screeched. "My leg!"

Eloise stepped back hurriedly, then took her chance. The others were too busy with Mrs. Whitten to notice her.

She'd crossed the tarmac by the time she heard their calls. Somehow, she found the wit to dart between the nearest set of buses, then double back—keeping the vehicles between her and the coach until she found the 81b.

It took a moment of fumbling to find the datapad—press its link node against the bus's socket.

The bus door slid open. To her relief, it was a ramp entrance.

After she had settled in her seat, she pulled the Clever Dolly out of her bag to let it look around. It seemed the only way to keep it quiet.

She had a window seat, but she was safe. The bus engine was revving up, ready to take her to Dover, and through the

Tunnel. They'd never catch her now—never think to check the borders.

As the bus pulled out of the terminal, she risked a peep out of the window. The Home Carers were still scouring the terminal in puzzlement, wondering how an old woman could disappear so quickly. Mrs. Whitten still lay by the bus steps, with a medic stooped over her.

She looked down at Clever Dolly.

"We made it," she whispered. "I don't mind losing my eye for that."

Clever Dolly opened its right eye—the sapphire implant gazed back at her.

"To be human," the doll said, "is to be incomplete."

The Madwoman of Shuttlefield

ALLEN M. STEELE

Allen M. Steele [www.allensteele.com] lives in Whateley, Massachusetts. He came on the scene as a hard SF writer in 1989 with his first novel, Orbital Decay. *It was followed by* Clarke County, Space *(1990) and* Lunar Descent *(1991), which are also set between Earth and the Moon and belong in the same Future History, which Steele calls the Near Space series. His short fiction is collected in three volumes,* Rude Astronauts *(1993),* All-American Alien Boy *(1996), and* Sex and Violence in Zero G *(1999), which collect the short fiction in the Near Space series and provide a list of the series, "all arranged in chronological order," he says on his web site. He has gone on to become one of the leading young hard SF writers today, with a talent for realism and a penchant for portraying the daily, gritty problems of living and working in space in the future.*

"The Madwoman of Shuttlefield" appeared in Asimov's *and is a sequel to his series of stories integrated into the novel* Coyote *(2002). Six years have passed since that first landing, and the settlement—its growing population now taxing limited resources—has become rigid and repressive Allegra, having come to Coyote largely to escape her past, has a rough early go of it on the new world until she accidentally befriends the mad old woman of the title.*

On the first night Allegra DiSilvio spent on Coyote, she met the madwoman of Shuttlefield. It seemed like an accident at the time, but in the weeks and months to follow she'd come to realize that it was much more, that their fates were linked by forces beyond their control.

The shuttle from the *Long Journey* touched down in a broad meadow just outside the town of Liberty. The high grass had been cleared from the landing pad, burned by controlled fires to create a flat expanse nearly a half-mile in diameter, upon which the gull-winged spacecraft settled after making its long fall from orbit. As she descended the gangway ramp and walked out from beneath the hull, Allegra looked up to catch her first sight of Bear: a giant blue planet encircled by silver rings, hovering in an azure sky. The air was fresh, scented with midsummer sourgrass; a warm breeze caressed the dark stubble of her shaved scalp, and it was in this moment that she knew that she'd made it. The journey was over; she was on Coyote.

Dropping the single bag she had been allowed to take with her from Earth, Allegra fell to her hands and knees and wept.

Eight months of waiting to hear whether she'd won the lottery, two more months of nervous anticipation before she was assigned a berth aboard the next starship to 47 Ursae Majoris, a week of sitting in Texas before taking the ride to the Union Astronautica spaceport on Matagorda Island, three days spent traveling to lunar orbit where she boarded the *Long Journey* . . . and then, forty-eight years in dreamless biostasis, to wake up cold, naked, and bald, forty-six light-years from everything familiar, with everyone she had ever known either long-dead or irrevocably out of her reach.

She was so happy, she could cry. *Thank you, God,* she thought. *Thank you, thank you . . . I'm here, and I'm free, and the worst is over.*

She had no idea just how wrong she was. And it wasn't until after she'd made friends with a crazy old lady that she'd thank anyone again.

Liberty was the first colony on Coyote, established by the crew of the URSS *Alabama* in A.D. 2300, or C.Y. 01 by LeMarean calendar. It was now 2306 on Coyote by Gregorian reckoning, though, and the original colonists had long-since abandoned their settlement, disappearing into the wilderness just days after the arrival of WHSS *Seeking Glorious Destiny Among the Stars for the Greater Good of Social Collectivism*, the next ship from Earth. No one knew why they'd fled—or at least those who knew weren't saying—but the fact remained that Liberty was built to house only a hundred people. *Glorious Destiny* brought a thousand people to the new world, and the third ship—*Traveling Forth to Spread Social Collectivism to New Frontiers*—had brought a thousand more, and so by the time the *Long Journey to the Galaxy in the Spirit of Social Collectivism* reached Coyote, the population of New Florida had swelled to drastic proportions.

The log cabins erected by the first settlers were now occupied by Union Astronautica officers from *Glorious Destiny* and *New Frontiers*. It hadn't been long before every tree within ten miles had been cut down for the construction of new houses, with roads expanding outward into what had once been marshes. Once the last stands of blackwood and faux-birch were gone, most of the wildlife moved away; the swoops and creek cats that once preyed upon livestock were seldom seen any more, and with automatic guns placed around the colony's perimeter only rarely did anyone hear the nocturnal screams of boids. Yet still there wasn't enough timber to build homes for everyone.

Newcomers were expected to fend for themselves. In the

spirit of social collectivism, aid was given in the form of temporary shelter and two meals a day, but after that it was every man and woman for himself. The Union Astronautica guaranteed free passage to Coyote for those who won the public lottery, but stopped short of promising anything once they'd arrived. Collectivist theory held that a sane society was one in which everyone reaped the rewards of individual efforts, but Liberty was still very much a frontier town, and anyone asking for room and board in the homes owned by those who'd come earlier was likely to receive a cold stare in return. All men were created equal, yet some were clearly more equal than others.

And so, once she'd picked herself up from the ground, Allegra found herself taking up residence not in Liberty, where she thought she'd be living, but in Shuttlefield, the sprawling encampment surrounding the landing pad. She made her way to a small bamboo hut with a cloverweed-thatched roof where she stood in line for an hour before she was issued a small tent that had been patched many times by those who'd used it earlier, a soiled sleeping bag that smelled of mildew, and a ration card that entitled her to eat in what had once been Liberty's grange hall before it was made into the community center. The bored Union Guard soldier behind the counter told her that she could pitch her tent wherever she wanted, then hinted that he'd be happy to share his cabin if she'd sleep with him. She refused, and he impatiently cocked his thumb toward the door before turning to the next person in line.

Shuttlefield was a slum; there was no other way to describe it. Row upon row of tents, arranged in untidy ranks along muddy footpaths trampled by countless feet, littered with trash and cratered by potholes. The industrious had erected shelter from bamboo grown from seeds brought from Earth; others lived out of old cargo containers into which they had cut doors and windows. Dirty children chased starving dogs between clotheslines draped with what looked like rags until Allegra realized that they were garments; the smoke from cook fires was rank with odor of compost. Two faux-birch shacks, side by side, had handwritten signs for

Men and Women above their doors; the stench of urine and feces lay thick around them, yet it didn't stop people from pitching tents nearby. The voices she heard were mostly Anglo, but her ears also picked up other tongues—Spanish, Russian, German, various Arab and Asian dialects—all mixed together in a constant background hum.

And everywhere, everyone seemed to be selling something, from kiosks in front of their shelters. Plucked carcasses of chickens dangled upside-down from twine suspended between poles. Shirts, jackets, and trousers stitched from some hide she'd never seen before—she'd later learn that it was swamper fur—were laid out on rickety tables. Jars of spices and preserved vegetables stood next to the pickled remains of creatures she'd never heard of. Obsolete pads containing data and entertainment from Earth, their sellers promising that their power cells were still fresh, their memories virus-clean. A captive swamper in a wooden cage, laying on its side and nursing a half-dozen babies; raise the pups until they're half-grown, their owner said, then kill the mother and in-breed her offspring for their pelts: a great business opportunity.

A small man with a furtive look in his eyes sidled up to Allegra, glanced both ways, then offered her a small plastic vial half-filled with an oily clear liquid. Sting, he confided. Pseudo-wasp venom. Just put a drop or two on your tongue, and you'll think you're back home. . . .

Allegra shook her head and kept walking, her back aching from the duffel bag carried over her shoulder and the folded tent beneath her arm. Home? This was home now. There was nothing on Earth for her to go back to, even if she could return.

She found a bare spot of ground amid several shanties, yet no sooner had she put down her belongings when a man emerged from the nearest shack. He asked if she was a member of the Cutters Guild; when she professed ignorance, he gruffly told her that this was Guild territory. Reluctant to get in a quarrel, Allegra obediently picked up her stuff and went farther down the street until she spotted another vacant place, this time among a cluster of tents much like her own.

She was beginning to erect the poles when two older women came over to her site; without explanation, one knocked over her poles while the other grabbed her bag and threw it in the street. When Allegra resisted, the first woman angrily knocked her to the ground. This was New Frontiers turf; who did she think she was, trying to squat here? A small crowd had gathered to watch; seeing that no one was going to take her side, Allegra quickly gathered her things and hurried away.

For the next several hours, she wandered the streets of Shuttlefield, searching for some place to put up her tent, yet every time she found a likely looking spot—and after the second incident, she was careful to ask permission from the nearest neighbor—she discovered that it had already been claimed by one group or another. It soon became clear that Shuttlefield was dominated by a hierarchy of guilds, groups, and clubs, ranging from societies that had originated among the passengers of earlier ships to gangs of hard-eyed men who guarded their territory with machetes. A couple of times Allegra was informed that she was welcome to stay, but only so long as she agreed to pay a weekly tax, usually one-third of what she earned from whatever job she eventually found or, failing that, one meal out of three from her ration card. A large, comfortable-looking shack occupied by single women of various ages turned out to be the local brothel; if she stayed here, the madam told her, she'd be expected to pay the rent on her back. At least she was polite about it; Allegra replied that she'd keep her offer in mind, but they both knew that this was an option only if she were desperate.

It was dusk, and she was footsore, hungry and on the verge of giving up, when Allegra found herself at the edge of town. It was close to a swamp—the sourgrass grew chest-high here, and not far away was a cluster of the ball-plants she'd been warned to avoid—and there was only one other dwelling, a slope-roofed and windowless shack nailed together from discarded pieces of faux-birch. Potted plants hung from the roof eaves above the front door, and smoke rose from a chimney hole, yet there was no one in sight.

Coming closer, Allegra heard the clucking of chickens from a wire-fenced pen out back; it also seemed as if she heard singing, a low and discordant voice from within the shack.

Allegra hesitated. This lonesome hovel away from all the others, so close to the swamp where who-knew-what might lurk, made her nervous. Yet darkness was settling upon town, and she knew she couldn't go any further. So she picked a spot of ground about ten yards from the shack and quietly went about pitching her tent. If someone protested, she'd just have to negotiate a temporary arrangement; she'd gladly trade a couple of meals for a night of sleep.

Yet no one bothered her as she erected her shelter, and although the voice stopped singing and even the chickens went quiet after awhile, no one objected to her presence. The sun was down by the time she was finished, and dark clouds shrouded the giant planet high above her. It looked like rain, so she crawled into the tent, dragging her belongings behind her.

Once she had laid out her sleeping bag, Allegra unzipped her duffel bag and dug through it until she found the lightstick she'd had been given before she left the *Long Journey*. The night was cool, so she found a sweater and pulled it on. There were a couple of food bars in the bottom of the bag; she unwrapped one. Although she was tempted to eat the other, she knew she'd want it in the morning. The way things were going, there was no telling what she'd have to suffer through before she got a decent meal. It was already evident that Shuttlefield had its own way of doing things, and the system was rigged to prevent newcomers from taking advantage of them.

Yet she was free. That counted for something. She had escaped Earth, and now she was . . .

A shuffling sound from outside.

Allegra froze, then slowly raised her eyes.

She had left the tent flap partially unzipped at the top. In the sallow glow of her lightstick, she saw someone peering in through the insectnetting: a woman's face, deeply lined, framed by lank hair that may have once been blond before it turned ash-gray.

They silently regarded each other as the first drops of night rain began tapping at the tent's plastic roof. The woman's eyes were blue, Allegra observed, yet they seemed much darker, as if something had leached all the color from her irises, leaving only an afterimage of blue.

"Why are you here?" the woman asked.

"I'm . . . I'm sorry," Allegra said. "I didn't mean to. . . ."

"Sorry for what?" The eyes grew sharper, yet the voice was hollow. Like her face, it was neither young nor old. She spoke English rather than Anglo; that caught Allegra by surprise, and she had to take a moment to mentally translate the older dialect.

"Sorry for trespassing," she replied, carefully speaking the English she'd learned in school. "I was . . ."

"Trespassing where?" Not a question. A demand.

"Here . . . your place. I know it's probably not . . ."

"My place?" A hint of a smile which quickly disappeared, replaced by the dark scowl. "Yes, this is my place. The Eastern Divide, the Equatorial River, Midland, the Meridian Sea, all the places he sailed . . . those are Rigil Kent's places. My son lives in Liberty, but he never comes to see me. No one in Shuttlefield but thieves and scum. But here. . . ." Again, the fleeting smile. "Everything is mine. The chickens, the stars, and everything in between. Who are you? And why are you here?"

The rush of words caught her unprepared; Allegra understood only the last part. "Allegra DiSilvio," she said. "I've just arrived from the . . ."

"Did Rigil Kent send you?" More insistently now.

In a flash of insight that she'd come to realize was fortunate, Allegra didn't ask who she meant. What was important was her response. "No," she said, "he didn't send me. I'm on my own."

The woman stared at her. The rain was falling harder now; somewhere in the distance, she heard the rumble of thunder. Water spilled through a leak in the tent, spattered across her sleeping bag. Yet still the woman's eyes didn't stray from her own, even though the rain was matting her gray hair. Finally, she spoke:

"You may stay."

Allegra let out her breath. "Thank you. I promise I won't. . . ."

The face vanished. Allegra heard footsteps receding. A door creaked open, slammed shut. Chickens cackled briefly, then abruptly went quiet, as if cowed into silence.

Allegra waited a few seconds, then hastily closed the tent flap. She used the discarded food wrapper to plug the leak, then removed her boots and pushed herself into her sleeping bag, reluctant to take off her clothes even though they were filthy. She fell asleep while the summer storm raged around her. She hadn't turned off the light even though common sense dictated that she needed to preserve the chemical battery.

She was safe. Yet for the first time since she'd arrived, she was truly frightened.

The next morning, though, Allegra saw her neighbor just once, and then only briefly. She awoke to hear the chickens clucking, and crawled out of her tent to see the woman standing in the pen behind her house, throwing corn from an apron tied around her waist. When Allegra called to her, though, she turned and walked back into her house, slamming the door shut behind her. Allegra considered going over and knocking, but decided against it; she clearly wanted to be left alone, and Allegra might be pushing her luck by intruding on her privacy.

So she changed clothes, wrapped a scarf around her bare scalp, and left to make the long hike into Liberty. She did so reluctantly; although there were no other tents nearby, she didn't know for certain that she wasn't camped on some group's turf. Yet her stomach was growling, and she didn't want to consume her last food bar unless necessary. And somehow, she had a feeling that people tended to leave her strange neighbor alone.

The road to Liberty was littered with trash: discarded wrappers, broken bottles, empty cans, bits and pieces of this and that. If Shuttlefield's residents made any effort to landfill or recycle their garbage, it wasn't evident. She passed farm fields where men and women worked on their hands and knees, pulling cloverweed from between rows of crops planted earlier in the summer. Coyote's seasons were three times as long as they were on Earth—ninety-one or ninety-two days in each month, twelve months in a year by the LeMarean calendar. Still, it was the near the end of Hamaliel, the second month of summer; the farmers would be working hard to pull in the midseason harvest so that they could plant again before autumn. The original colonists had struggled to keep themselves fed through the first long winter they'd faced on Coyote, and they only had a hundred or so mouths to feed.

The distant roar of engines drew her attention; looking up, she saw a shuttle descending upon the landing pad. More passengers from the *Long Journey* being ferried down to Coyote; now that a new ship from Earth had arrived, the population of New Florida would increase by another thousand people. Social collectivism may have worked well in the Western Hemisphere Union, built upon the smoldering remains of the United Republic of America, but there it benefited from established cities and hightech infrastructure. Coyote was still largely unexplored; what little technology had been brought from Earth was irreplaceable, unavailable to the average person, so the colonists had to live off the land as best they could. Judging from what she'd already seen in Shuttlefield, utopian political theory had broken down; too many people had come here too quickly, forcing the newcomers to fend for themselves in a feudal hierarchy in which the weak were at the mercy of the strong, and everyone was under the iron heel of the colonial government. Unless she wanted to either become a prostitute or live out the rest of her life as a serf, she'd better find a way to survive.

Allegra came upon a marsh where Japanese bamboo was grown. The most recent crop had already been harvested, their stumps extending for a hundred acres or so, the ground littered with broken shoots. On impulse, she left the path and waded out into the marsh, where she searched the ground until she found a foot-long stalk that was relatively undamaged. Tucking it beneath her arm, she returned to the road.

This would do for a start. Now all she needed was a sharp knife.

Liberty was much different than Shuttlefield. The streets were wide and clean, recently paved with gravel, lined on either side by log cabins. There were no hustlers, no kiosks; near the village center, she found small shops, their wares displayed behind glass windows. Yet everyone she passed refused to look her way, save for Proctors in blue uniforms who eyed her with suspicion. When she paused before the open half-door of a glassblower's shop to watch the men inside thrust white-hot rods into the furnace, a blue-shirt walked over to tap her on the shoulder, shake his head, and point the way to the community hall. Few words were spoken, yet the message was clear; she was only allowed to pass through on her way to the community hall, and not linger where she didn't belong.

Breakfast was a lukewarm porridge containing potatoes and chunks of fishmeat; it resembled clam chowder, but tasted like sour milk. The old man who ladled it out in the serving line told her that it was creek crab stew, and she should eat up—it was only a day old. When Allegra asked what was on the menu for dinner, he grinned as he added a slice of stale bread to her plate. More of the same . . . and by then it'd be a day-and-a-half old.

She found a place at one of the long wooden tables that ran down the length of the community hall, and tried not to meet the gaze of any of the others seated nearby even though she recognized several from the *Long Journey*. She'd made friends with no one during her passage from Earth, and wasn't in a hurry to do so now, so she distracted herself by studying an old mural painted on the wall. Rendered in native dyes by an untrained yet talented hand, it depicted the URSS *Alabama* in orbit above Coyote. Apparently an artifact left behind by Liberty's original residents before they'd fled. No one knew where they'd gone, although it was believed that they had started another colony somewhere on Midland, across the East Channel from New Florida.

Allegra was wondering how hard it might be to seek

them out when she heard a mechanical sound behind her: servomotors shifting gears, the thin whine of an electrical power source. Then a filtered burr of a voice, addressing her in Anglo:

"Pardon me, but are you Allegra DiSilvio?"

She looked up to see a silver skull peering at her from within a black cowl, her face dully reflected in its ruby eyes. A Savant: a posthuman who had once been flesh and blood until he'd relinquished his humanity to have his mind downloaded into cyborg form, becoming an immortal intellect. Allegra detested them. Savants operated the starships, but it was surprising to find one here and now. And worse, it had come looking for her.

"That's me." She put down her spoon. "Who're you?"

"Manuel Castro. Lieutenant Governor of the New Florida Colony." A claw-like hand rose from the folds of its dark cloak. "Please don't get up. I only meant to introduce myself."

Allegra made no effort to rise. "Pleased to meet you, Savant Castro. Now if you'll excuse me. . . ."

"Oh, now . . . no reason to be rude. I merely wish to welcome you to Coyote, make sure that all your needs are being met."

"Really? Well, then, you could start by giving me a place to stay. A house here in town would be fine . . . one room will do. And some fresh clothing . . . I've only got one other change."

"Unfortunately, there are no vacancies in Liberty. If you'd like, I can add your name to the waiting list, and notify you if something opens up. As for clothing, I'm afraid you'll have to continue wearing what you've brought until you've tallied enough hours in public service to exchange them for new clothes. However, I have a list of work details that are looking for new employees."

"Thanks, but I'll . . ." A new thought occurred to her. "Are there any openings here? I think I could give a hand in the kitchen, if they need some assistance."

"Just a moment." Castro paused for a moment, his quantum-comp brain accessing data from a central AI. "Ah, yes . . . you're in luck. The community kitchen needs a new dishwasher for the morning-to-midday shift. Eight hours per day, starting at 0600 and ending at 1400. No previous experience required. One and a half hours credit per hour served."

"When does it start?"

"Tomorrow morning."

"Thank you. I'll take it." She turned back to her meal, yet the Savant made no move to leave. It patiently stood behind her, its body making quiet machine noises. Allegra dipped her spoon into the foul stew, waited for Castro to go away. All around her, the table had gone silent; she felt eyes upon her as others watched and listened.

"From your records, I understand you had a reputation back on Earth," Castro said. "You were known as a musician."

"Not exactly. I was a composer. I didn't perform." Looking straight ahead, she refused to meet his fathomless glass eyes.

Another pause. "Ah, yes . . . so I see. You wrote music for the Connecticut River Ensemble. In fact, I think I have one of your works. . . ."

From its mouth grill, a familiar melody emerged: "Sunrise on Holyoke," a minuet for string quartet. She'd written it early one winter morning when she'd lived in the foothills of the Berkshires, trying to capture the feeling of the dawn light over the Holyoke range. A delicate and ethereal piece, reconstructed in electronic tonalities by something that had given up all pretense of humanity.

"Yes, that's mine. Thank you very much for reminding me." She glanced over her shoulder. "My stew's getting cold. If you don't mind. . . ."

The music abruptly ended. "I'm sorry. I'm afraid I can't give it justice." A moment passed. "If you're ever inclined to compose again, we would be glad to have you do so. We often lack for culture here."

"Thank you. I'll consider it."

She waited, staring determinedly into her soup bowl. After a few moments, she heard the rustle of its cloak, the subdued whir and click of its legs as it walked away. There was quiet around her, like the brief silence that falls between movements of a symphony, then murmured voices slowly returned.

For an instant they seemed to fill a void within her, one that she'd fought so long and hard to conquer . . . but then, once more, the music failed to reach her. She heard nothing, saw nothing.

"Hey, lady," someone seated nearby whispered. "You know who that was?"

"Yeah, jeez!" another person murmured. "Manny Castro! No one ever stood up to him like that. . . ."

"Who did you say you were? I didn't catch . . ."

"Excuse me." The plate and bowl rattled softly in her hands as she stood up. She carried it to a wooden cart, where she placed it with a clatter which sounded all too loud for her ears. Remembering the bamboo stalk she'd left on the table, she went back to retrieve it. Then, ignoring the questioning faces around her, she quickly strode out of the dining hall.

All this distance, only to have the past catch up to her. She began to make the long walk back to Shuttlefield.

When she returned to her tent, she found that it was still there. However, it hadn't gone unnoticed. A Proctor kneeled before the tent, holding the flap open as he peered inside.

"Pardon me," she asked as she came up behind him, "but is there something I can help you with?"

Hearing her, the Proctor turned to look around. A young man with short-cropped blond hair, handsome yet overweight; he couldn't have been much older than twenty Earth years, almost half Allegra's age. He dropped the tent flap and stood up, brushing dirt from his knees.

"Is this yours?" Less a question than a statement. His face seemed oddly familiar, although she was certain she'd never met him before.

"Yes, it's mine. Do you have a problem with that?"

Her attitude took him by surprise; he blinked, stepping back before he caught himself. Perhaps he'd never been challenged in this way. "It wasn't here the last time I stopped by," he said, businesslike but not unkind. "I wanted to know who was setting up here."

"I arrived last night." Allegra glanced toward the nearby shack; her neighbor was nowhere to be seen, yet she observed that the front door was ajar. "Came in yesterday from the *Long Journey*," she continued, softening her own tone. "I couldn't find another place to stay, so . . ."

"Everyone from the *Long Journey* is being put over there." The young blueshirt turned to point toward the other side of Shuttlefield; as he did, she noticed the chevrons on the right sleeve of his uniform. "Didn't anyone tell you?"

"No one told me anything . . . and now I suppose you want me to move." She didn't relish the thought of packing up again and relocating across town. At least here she was closer to Liberty; it would cut her morning hike to work. "I spoke with the lady who lives next door, and she didn't seem to mind if I . . ."

"I know. I've just talked to her." He cast a wary eye upon the shack, and for an instant it seemed as if the door moved a few inches, as if someone behind it was eavesdropping. The Proctor raised a hand to his face. "Can I speak with you in private?" he whispered. "You're not in trouble, I promise. It's just . . . we need to talk."

Mystified, Allegra nodded, and the blueshirt led her around to the other side of the tent. He crouched once more, and she settled down upon her knees. Now they could only see the shack roof; even the chicken pen was hidden from sight.

"My name's Chris," he said quietly as he offered his hand. "Chris Levin . . . I'm the Chief Proctor."

A lot of authority for someone nearly young enough to be her son. "Allegra DiSilvio," she replied, shaking hands with him. "Look, I'm sorry I was so . . ."

"Don't worry about it." Chris evinced a smile that didn't quite reach his eyes. "I'm sure you've noticed by now, but the lady over there . . . well, she keeps to herself. Doesn't leave the house much."

"I picked up on that."

Chris idly plucked at some grass between his knees. "Her name's Cecelia . . . Cecelia Levin, although everyone calls her Sissy. She's my mother."

Allegra felt the blood rush from her face. She suddenly recalled the old woman having mentioned that she had a son in Liberty. "I'm sorry. I didn't know."

"You couldn't have. You've just arrived." He shook his head. "Look, my mother is . . . truth is, she's not well. She's very sick, in fact . . . as you may have noticed."

Allegra nodded. His mother stood out in the pouring rain last night and raved about how she owned both her chickens and the stars; yes, that qualified as unusual behavior. "I'm sorry to hear that."

"Can't be helped. Mom's been through a lot in the last few years. She. . . ." He broke off. "Long story. In any case, that's why no one has set up camp out here. People are afraid of her . . . and to tell the truth, she chases them away. Which is why you're unusual."

"How come?"

Chris raised his eyes, and now she could see that they were much the same as his mother's: blue yet somehow hollow, although not with quite the same degree of darkness. "She let you stay. Believe me, if she didn't like you, your tent wouldn't still be standing. Oh, she might have let you spend the night, but as soon as you left she would have set fire to it. That's what she's done to everyone else who's tried to camp next to her."

Allegra felt a cold chill. She started to rise, but Chris clasped her wrist. "No, no . . . calm down. She's not going to do that. She likes you. She told me so herself."

"She . . . likes me?"

"Uh-huh . . . or at least as much as she likes anyone these days. She believes you're a nice woman who's come to keep her company."

"She wouldn't even speak to me this morning!"

"She's shy."

"Oh, for the love of . . . !"

"Look," he said, and now there was an edge in his voice, "she wants you to stay, and I want you to stay. No one will bother you out here, and she needs someone to look out for her."

"I . . . I can't do that," Allegra said. "I've just taken a job in Liberty . . . washing dishes at the community hall. I can't afford to. . . ."

"Great. I'm glad you've found work." He paused, and smiled meaningfully. "That won't pay much, though, and by winter this tent of yours will be pretty cold. But I can fix that. Stay here and take care of Mom when you're not working, and you'll have your own cabin . . . with a wood stove and even your own privy. That's better than anyone else from your ship will get. And you'll never have to deal with gangs or turf-tax. Anyone who bothers you spends six months in the stockade, doing hard time on the public works crew. Got me?"

Allegra understood. She was being given the responsibility of looking out for the demented mother of the Chief Proctor. So long as Sissy Levin had company, Allegra DiSilvio would never have to worry about freezing to death in the dark, being shaken down by the local stooges, or being raped in her tent. She would have shelter, protection, and the solitude she craved.

"Got you," she said. "It's a deal."

They shook on it, and then Chris heaved himself to his feet, extending a hand to help her up. "I'll talk to Mom, tell her that you're staying," he said. "Don't rush things. She'll introduce herself to you when she feels like it. But I think you'll make great friends."

"Thanks. We'll work things out." Allegra watched as he turned toward the shack. The door was cracked open; for an instant, she caught a glimpse of her face. "Just one more thing. . . ."

"Yes?" The Chief stopped, looked back at her.

"How long have you been here? I mean . . . which ship did you come in on?"

Chris hesitated. "We've been here three Coyote years," he said. "We came aboard the *Alabama*."

Allegra gaped at him. "I thought all the first-timers had left."

He nodded solemnly. "They did. We're the ones who stayed behind."

"So why . . . ?"

But he was already walking away. That was a question he didn't want to answer.

Time was measured by the length of her hair. A week after Allegra started work at the community kitchen, she had little more than fuzz on top of her head; that was the day she palmed a small paring knife from the sink and took it home. Its absence wasn't noticed, and it gave her the first tool she needed to do her work. By the time her shack was built, she no longer needed to wear a head scarf, and she used a few credits to purchase a brush from the general store in Liberty (where she was now allowed to enter, so long as she bought something). She was beginning to tie back her hair in a short ponytail when she finished carving her first flute; a short blade of sourgrass inserted within the bamboo shaft below the mouthpiece served as its reed, and with a little practice she was able to play simple tunes, although not well. Yet it wasn't until late summer, when her chestnut hair had finally reached the shoulder-length she'd worn it on Earth, that she finally had her first real conversation with Sissy Levin.

For many weeks, her reclusive neighbor continued to avoid her; their brief encounter the first night Allegra spent on Coyote was the only time she'd spoken with her. Every morning, just after sunrise when Allegra left to go into Liberty, she spotted Sissy feeding her chickens. She'd wave and call her name—"Good morning, Ms. Levin, how are you?"—and she had little doubt that her voice carried across the short distance between their shacks, yet Sissy never acknowledged her except for the briefest of nods. So Allegra would go to work, and early in the afternoon she'd return to find her nowhere in sight. Every now and then, Allegra would venture over to knock on her door, yet no matter how long or patiently she'd wait outside, Sissy never greeted her.

Nonetheless, there were signs that Sissy was coming to accept her. A few days after a group of men from the Carpenters Guild arrived with a cart full of lumber and spent the afternoon building a one-room shack for Allegra, complete with a wood stove fashioned from a discarded fuel cell, some basic furniture, and a small privy out back ("No charge, lady," the foreman said, "this one's on the Chief") she came home to find a wicker basket of fresh eggs on the front porch. Allegra carefully placed the eggs in the cabinet above the stove, then carried the basket over to Sissy's house. Again, there was no response to her knocks, and finally Allegra gave up and went home, leaving the basket next to her door. A few days later, though, the basket reappeared . . . this time just after sunrise, even before Allegra had awakened.

This pattern continued for awhile. Then one afternoon, Allegra returned home to open the door and discover a dead chicken hanging upside-down from the ceiling. The bird hadn't been feathered or cleaned; it was simply a carcass, its neck broken, its feet tied together with the rough twine with which it had been suspended from a crossbeam. Allegra shrieked when she saw it, and for a moment she thought she heard mad laughter from next door. She didn't know whether it was a gift or a threat, but she wasn't about to ask; she didn't know how to clean the bird, so she took it to the community hall the next morning, and a cook with whom she'd become friendly did it for her. The chicken made for a good lunch and she kept the feathers as stuffing for a pillow, yet Allegra stayed away from Sissy for awhile, and three weeks passed before she found any more eggs on her doorstep.

The first flute Allegra made didn't have a very good sound, so she gathered some more bamboo and started over again, this time experimenting with different kinds of reeds: faux-birch bark, chicken feathers, cloverleaf, whatever else she could find. She'd never fashioned her own instruments before—what little she knew, she'd learned from observing craftsmen back in New England—so it was mainly a matter of trial and error. Eventually, she discovered that swamper skin, cured and tightly stretched, produced the best results. She got it from a glovemaker in Shuttlefield; when Sissy began leaving eggs on her doorstep again, Allegra bartered a few for a square foot of skin, with the promise that she wouldn't go into the clothing business herself.

Early one evening she sat out on her front porch, playing

the flute she'd most recently fashioned. The sun had gone down, and Bear was rising to the east; she'd carried a fish-oil lamp out onto the porch, and its warm glow cast her shadow across the rough planks of the porch. The night was cool; the air redolent with the scent of approaching autumn. Not far away, she could see bonfires within Shuttlefield. It was the fourth week of Uriel, the last month of Coyote summer; next Zaphiel would be First Landing Day, the colony's biggest holiday. Already the inhabitants were gearing up for the celebration, yet she wanted nothing to do with this. Her only desire was to be left alone, to practice her art in solitude.

The new flute had a good sound: neither too shrill nor too low, and she was able to run up and down the scales without any effort. Now that she knew how to make one, it shouldn't be hard to duplicate others like it. On impulse, she shifted to a piece she'd written for the Connecticut River Ensemble. She was about halfway through the first stanza when a nearby voice began humming the melody, and she turned to see Sissy Levin standing next to her.

Allegra was so startled, she nearly dropped the flute. Sissy didn't notice. She leaned against the awning post, her eyes closed, a soft smile upon her face. In the wan light of the lamp, Allegra could now clearly see the deep wrinkles around her mouth, the crows-feet at the corners of her eyes; as always, her hair was an uncombed mass that formed a ragged halo around her head. Even so, at this moment she seemed at peace.

Her fingers trembling upon the flute, Allegra managed to finish the composition, with Sissy humming along with it. When she followed a melody, Allegra realized, Sissy had a beautiful voice; she repeated the first stanza just so she could hear more of it. When she was done, she lowered her instrument, but was careful not to speak. Let the moment take its own course. . . .

"That's a nice song," Sissy said quietly, not opening her eyes. "What's it called?"

" 'Deerfield River,' " Allegra replied. "Do you like it?"

A nod, ever so slight. "I think I remember it. Wasn't it once in a movie?"

"No . . . no, not that I know of." Although there were probably other pieces that sounded a bit like it; Allegra's style had been influenced by earlier composers. "It's my own. I wrote it for . . ."

"I think I once heard it in a movie. The one where there's a man who meets this woman in Vienna, and they fall in love even though she's dying, and then they . . ." She stopped abruptly, and opened her eyes to gaze off into some private memory. "It's a great movie. I really liked it. Jim and I saw it . . . oh, I don't know how many times. I'm sorry about the chicken. It was meant to be a joke, but I don't think you thought it was very funny."

The abrupt change of subject caught Allegra off-guard. For a moment, she didn't know what Sissy was talking about. "Well . . . no, it wasn't, but . . ."

"That was Beatrice. She was very old and couldn't lay eggs anymore, and she'd bully the other hens, so I had to . . ." Her hands came together, made a throttling motion. "Very sad, very sad . . . I hope at least that you did something good with her."

"I took it to work," Allegra said. "At the community kitchen. We . . ."

"The grange."

"Yes, the grange hall. A friend of mine cleaned her and we had it . . . I mean, we had her . . . for lunch." She wondered if she should be saying this; Beatrice had apparently meant something to Sissy.

"Good. At least you didn't throw her away. That would've been . . . cruel. She laid good eggs, and it would have been disrespectful. You haven't thrown those away, I hope."

"Oh, no!" Allegra shook her head. "I've eaten every one. They're delicious. Thank you very much for . . ."

"Did you make this?" Sissy darted forward, snatched the flute from her hands. Afraid that she'd damage it, Allegra started to reach for her instrument, but stopped herself when she saw how carefully Sissy handled it. She closely studied the patterns carved along the shaft, then before Allegra could object she blew into the mouthpiece. A harsh piping note came out, and she winced. "You do this much better. Can you make me one?"

"I . . . I'd be happy to." Allegra thought of the half-dozen inferior flutes in her shack, and briefly considered giving one to her neighbor. But no . . . she'd want one that sounded just like hers. "I'm already planning to make more, so I'll give you the first one I . . ."

"You're going to make more? Why?"

"Well, I was thinking about selling them. To earn a little more. . . ."

"No." Sissy didn't raise her voice, yet her tone was uncompromising. "No no no no. I won't allow you to sell anything out here. It'll bring the others, the . . ." She glanced in the direction of the ale-soaked laughter that brayed from the bonfires. "I don't want them around. If they come, they'll bring Rigil Kent."

"Oh, no. I don't intend to sell them here." Allegra had recently struck up tentative friendships with various kiosk-owners in Shuttlefield, and there was even a shopowner in Liberty who'd expressed interest in her work. Like Sissy, she had no wish to have strangers appearing at her front door. Yet something else she said raised her attention. "Who . . . who's Rigil Kent?"

Sissy's face darkened, and for a moment Allegra was afraid that she'd said the wrong thing. But Sissy simply handed the flute back to her, then thrust her hands into the pockets of her threadbare apron.

"If he comes back," she said quietly, "you'll know."

She started to turn away, heading back toward her shack. Then she stopped and looked back at Allegra. "I'll give you more eggs if you teach me how to play. Can you do that?"

"I'd be delighted, Sissy."

Her brow raised in astonishment. "How do you know my name?"

"Chris told me."

"Chris." She scowled. "My son. Fat worthless . . ." She stopped herself, rubbed her eyes. "What did you say your name was?"

"Allegra. Allegra DiSilvio."

She considered this. "Nice name. Sounds like music. The movie I saw, it was called . . ." She shook her head. "Never mind. I'm Cecelia . . . my friends call me Sissy."

"Pleased to meet you, Sissy," Allegra said. "Drop by anytime."

"No more chickens. I promise." And then she walked away. Allegra watched until she disappeared inside her shack, and then she let out her breath.

At least she was speaking to her now.

Three nights later, she met Rigil Kent.

Allegra had no desire to participate in the First Landing Day festivities, but it was hard to avoid them; when she reported to work that morning, the kitchen staff was already busy preparing for the evening fiesta. Several hogs had been slaughtered the night before and were now being slow-roasted in the smokehouse behind the hall, while huge cauldrons of potatoes and beans simmered on the kitchen stoves; out back, kegs of sourgrass ale were being unloaded from a cart. After breakfast was over, while the cooks began baking bread and strawberry pie, she helped cover the table with fresh white linen, upon which were placed centerpieces of fresh-cut wildflowers.

Matriarch Luisa Hernandez stopped by shortly after noon. A thick-set woman with short auburn hair beneath the raised hood of her blue robe, the colonial governor was seldom seen in public; this was only the third time Allegra had laid eyes upon her. She hovered near the door, silently observing the preparations, Savant Castro at her side speaking to her in a low voice. At one point, Allegra glanced over to see the Matriarch studying her from across the room. Their eyes met, and a faint smile touched the other woman's lips. She briefly nodded to Allegra. Feeling a chill, Allegra went back to setting tables; when she looked again, the Matriarch had disappeared, as had Manuel Castro.

Did the Matriarch know who she was? She had to assume that she did. With any luck, she would leave her alone.

What surprised her the most, though, was one of the decorations: a flag of the United Republic of America, carefully unwrapped from a plastic bag and suspended from the rafters high above the hall. When Allegra asked where it had come from, one of the cooks told her that it had been presented to Captain Robert E. Lee shortly before the *Alabama* escaped from Earth. The original settlers had left it behind, and now it was kept by Matriarch Hernandez in trust for the colony, to be publicly displayed only on this day.

Only on this day. For most of the Coyote year—1,096 days, or three Earth years—the colony carefully doled out its meager resources in only dribs and drabs. There were few other holidays, and none as important or elaborate as this; on this day, the residents of Shuttlefield gathered together at the community hall for a great feast commemorating the arrival of the *Alabama*. Yet as she headed home, she saw shopkeepers closing storm shutters and nailing boards across their doors, noted the absence of children, the increased visibility of Proctors and Union Guard soldiers.

Now she understood. This was the day the proletariat would be allowed to gorge themselves on rich food, get drunk on ale, celebrate a ghastly replication of freedom under the indulgent yet watchful eye of Union authority. A brief loosening of the leash to keep the commoners happy and content, while tactfully reminding them that this was only a temporary condition. Walking through Shuttlefield she saw that this subtlety had been lost on everyone. No one was working today, and by early afternoon the First Landing celebration was already in full swing. Out in the streets, the various guilds and groups that ruled Shuttlefield were carousing beneath the autumn sun: handmade banners hoisted above tents and shacks, while drunks staggered about with beads around their necks and wildness in their eyes, proclaiming everyone they saw to be their best friend. The paths between the camps were jagged with broken ale jars, the air rank with smoke, alcohol, and piss. She came upon a crowd cheering at something in their midst; stepping closer, Allegra saw two naked men, their bodies caked with mud, wrestling in the middle of a drainage ditch.

Disgusted, she quickly moved away, only to have her arm

grabbed by someone who thought she needed a kiss. She managed to pull herself free, but he wasn't giving up so easily. "C'mon, sweets, y'know you wan' it," he slurred as he followed her down the street. "Jus' a lil' sugar, thas'all I . . ."

"Get lost, Will," a familiar voice said. "Leave her alone, or you'll spend the night in the stockade."

Allegra looked around, found Chris Levin behind her. Two other Proctors were with him; one had already twisted the drunk's arm behind his back, and the other booted the drunk in the ass. He fell face-down into the mud, muttered an obscenity, then hauled himself to his feet and wandered away.

"Sorry about that." Chris paid little attention to what was going on behind them. "You're not hurt, are you?"

An odd question, considering what his men had just done to the drunk. "You didn't need to . . ."

"Sorry, but I think I did." He turned to his officers. "You guys continue patrol. I'll walk her home." They nodded and headed away. "And keep an eye on the creek," he called after them. "If you see anything, let me know."

This piqued her curiosity; he obviously meant Sand Creek, the narrow river that bordered the two settlements to the east. Chris saw the puzzled look on her face. "Nothing for you to worry about," he said quietly. "Look, if you don't mind, I'd like for you to stay with my mother tonight. You may have to skip the fiesta, but . . ."

"That's all right. I wasn't planning to attend anyway." From what she'd already seen, the last place she wanted to be was the community hall.

"I was hoping you'd say that." He seemed genuinely relieved. "If you want, I can have dinner brought over to you . . ."

"I'd appreciate that." They sidestepped a couple more drunks swaggering down the street, their arms around each other. One of them bumped shoulders with Chris; he turned and started to swear at the Chief Proctor, then realized who he was and thought better of it. Chris stared them down, then ushered Allegra away. "One more thing," he murmured, reaching beneath his jacket. "I think you should keep this with you."

She stared at the small pistol he offered her. A Peacekeeper Mark III flechette gun, the type carried by the Union Guard. "No, sorry . . . that's where I draw the line."

Chris hesitated, then saw that arguing with her was pointless. "Suit yourself," he said. He reholstered the pistol, then unclipped a com unit from his belt. "But carry this, at least. If you run into any trouble, give us a call. We'll have someone out there as quick as we can."

Allegra accepted the com, slipped it in a pocket of her catskin vest. "Are you really expecting much trouble tonight?"

"Not really. Things might get a little out of control once people start drinking hard, but . . ." He shrugged. "Nothing we can't handle." Then he paused. "But there's a small chance that Mama might . . . well, someone might come to see her that she doesn't want to see."

"Rigil Kent?"

She smiled when she said that, meaning it as a joke, yet Chris gave her a sharp look. "What has she told you?" he asked, his voice low.

This surprised her, although she was quick enough to hide her expression. Until now, she'd assumed that "Rigil Kent" was a manifestation of Sissy's madness, an imaginary person she'd created as a stand-in for everyone she distrusted. Certainly there was no one in the colony who went by that name; she'd already checked the roll to make sure. But Chris apparently accepted him as being real.

"A little." Which wasn't entirely untruthful. "Enough to know that she hates him."

Chris was quiet for a moment. "He may come into town tonight," he said. "This time last year, he led a small raiding party up Sand Creek. They broke into the armory in Liberty and made off with some guns, then left a note on the door signed as Rigil Kent." He shook his head. "You don't need to know what it said. But before they did all that, he stopped by to see Mama. He wanted her to come with them. She refused, of course . . . she despises him almost as much as I do."

"Of course. Can't blame her."

This caused him to raise an eyebrow. "Then you know what he did."

She shrugged. "Like I said, not very much. She hasn't told me everything."

"Probably not." He looked down at the ground as they walked along. "He used to be my best friend, back when we were kids. But then he killed my brother and . . . anyway, there's things you just don't forgive."

Apparently not. And now she had a better idea whom he was talking about. "If he shows up, I'll let you know."

"I'd appreciate it." By now they were on the outskirts of town; her shack was only a few hundred feet away. "You know, she's really come to like you," he said. "That's a major accomplishment . . . for her, I mean. She used to live in Liberty, in the cabin my dad built for us. I still live there, but she moved all the way out here because she didn't want to see anyone any more . . . not even me. But you've managed to get through to her somehow."

"We've got much in common," Allegra said. And this, at least, wasn't a lie.

Allegra took a nap, then changed into a long skirt and a sweater. Through her window, she could see Uma setting to the west, Bear rising to the east. She usually began making dinner about this time, but tonight she'd get a break from that chore, if Chris kept his word about sending over food from the community hall. So she picked up her flute, along with the one she'd finished the previous evening, and went out to sit on the porch and watch the sun go down.

As twilight set in, Shuttlefield went quiet. No doubt everyone had gone into Liberty for the fiesta. She waited until she heard the chickens clucking in her neighbor's back yard, then she picked up her flute and began to play. Not one of her own pieces this time, but a traditional English hymn she'd learned while studying music at Berklee. For some reason, it seemed appropriate for the moment.

After awhile, she heard the door of Sissy's shack creak open. Allegra didn't look up but continued playing, and a minute later there was a faint rustle of an apron next to her. "That's very nice," Sissy said quietly. "What's it called?"

"'Jerusalem.'" Allegra smiled. "It's really easy to play. Would you like to try?"

Sissy quickly shook her head. "Oh, no . . . I can't. . . ."

"No, really. It's simple. Here . . ." She picked up the new flute. "I made this for you. Try it out."

Sissy stared at it. "I . . . but I have to start dinner. . . ."

"No, you don't. It's being brought to us tonight. Ham, potatoes, fresh greens, pie . . . the works." She grinned. "Believe me, it's good. Helped make it myself."

Sissy stared at her, and Allegra realized that it was probably the first time in many years that she had been offered a meal. For a few seconds she was afraid that her neighbor would flee back to her windowless hovel, slam the door shut and not emerge again for several days. Yet a look of wary acceptance came upon her face; taking the flute, Sissy sat down on the porch.

"Show me how you do this," she said.

It didn't take long for her to learn how to work the fingerholes; teaching her how to master the first chords, though, took a little more effort. Yet Sissy didn't give up; she seemed determined to learn how to play, and she gave Allegra her undivided attention as the younger woman patiently demonstrated the basic fingering techniques.

They took a break when someone arrived with two covered baskets. Allegra carried them inside; Sissy was reluctant to follow her, until Allegra pointed out that it would be much less messy if they ate indoors. The older woman stood quietly, her hands folded in front of her, and watched as she lit the oil lamp and set the table for two. Allegra only had one chair; she was about to sit on the bed when Sissy abruptly disappeared, returning a few moments later with a rickety chair of her own. She placed it at the table, then sat down and watched as Allegra served her a plate.

They ate in silence; through the open door, they could hear the distant sounds of the First Landing festivities. The night was becoming cool, so Allegra shut the door, then put some wood in the stove and started a fire. Sissy never looked up from her meal; she ate with total concentration, never speaking, even though she cleaned her plate and beckoned for seconds. Allegra wondered how long it had been since she had eaten anything except chicken and eggs. She made a note to herself to start bringing home leftovers from the kitchen; malnutrition might have something to do with her mental condition. . . .

"Why are you here?" Sissy asked.

The question was abrupt, without preamble . . . and, Allegra realized, it was the very same one she'd posed the night they first met. Yet this time they weren't strangers, but two friends enjoying a quiet dinner together. How much had changed since then.

"You mean, why did I come here?" Allegra shrugged. "Like I told you . . . I couldn't find anywhere else in town, so I pitched my . . ."

"That's not what I mean."

Allegra didn't say anything for a moment. She put her knife and fork together on her plate and folded her hands together, and turned her gaze toward the window. Far away across the fields, she could see the houselights of Liberty; in that instant, they resembled the lights of cities she had left behind, the places she had visited. New York, Los Angeles, Rio de Janeiro, Mexico City . . .

"A long time ago," she began, "I was . . . well, I wasn't rich, nor was I famous, but I had a lot of money and I was quite well-known. For what I do, I mean. . . ."

"For making music."

"For making music, yes." She absently played with her fork, stirring some gravy left on her plate. "I traveled a great deal and I was constantly in demand as a composer, and all the people I knew were artists who were also rich and famous." As rich as social collectivism would allow, at least; she'd learned how to quietly stash her overseas royalties in trust funds maintained by European banks, as many people did to avoid the domestic salary caps imposed by the Union. But that was complicated, and there was no reason why Sissy should have to know this. "And for awhile I was satisfied with my life, but then . . . I don't know. At some point, I stopped enjoying life. It seemed as if everyone I knew was a stranger, that the only things they wanted were more fame, more money, and all I wanted was to practice my art. And then one day, I found that I couldn't even do that any more. . . ."

"You couldn't make music?"

Allegra didn't look up. "No. Oh, I could still play . . ." she picked up her flute from where she had placed on the table ". . . but nothing new came to me, just variations of things I'd done before. And when it became obvious to everyone that I was blocked, all the people I thought were my friends went away, and I was alone."

"What about your family?"

She felt wetness at the corners of her eyes. "No family. I never made time for that. Too busy. There was once someone I loved, but . . ." She took a deep breath that rattled in her throat. "Well, it wasn't long before he was gone, too."

Allegra picked up the napkin from her lap, daubed her eyes. "So I decided to leave everything behind, go as far away as I could. The Union Astronautica had started the public lottery for people who wanted to come here. The selection was supposed to be totally random, but I met someone who knew how to rig the system. I gave him everything I'd owned so that I'd get a winning number, then took only what I could carry in my bag. And . . . well, anyway, here I am."

"So why are you here?"

Allegra gazed across the table at Sissy. Hadn't she heard anything she had just said? Just as on Earth, everything she did was pointless: another exercise in self-indulgence. Yet she couldn't bring herself to scold her neighbor. It wasn't Sissy's fault that she was disturbed. Someone had hurt her a long time ago, and now . . .

"Excuse me. I think I need to visit the privy." Allegra pushed back her chair, stood up. "If you'd gather the dishes and put 'em over there, I'll wash them tomorrow."

"Okay." Sissy continued to stare at her. "If there's any food left, can I give it to my chickens?"

"Sure. Why not?" She tried not to laugh. Her best friend was a lunatic who cared more about her damn birds. "I'll be back," she said, then opened the door and stepped outside.

The night was darker than she'd expected; a thick blanket

of clouds had moved across the sky, obscuring the wan light cast by Bear. She regretted not having carried a lamp with her, yet the privy was located only a couple of dozen feet behind her house, and she knew the way by memory.

She was halfway across the back yard, though, when she heard the soft crackle of a foot stepping upon dry grass, somewhere close behind her.

Allegra stopped, slowly turned . . . and a rod was thrust against her chest. "Hold it," a voice said, very quietly. "Don't move."

Against the darkness, she detected a vague form. The rod was a rifle barrel; of that she was certain, although she couldn't see anything else. "Sure, all right," she whispered, even as she realized that the voice had spoken in Old English. "Please don't hurt me."

"We won't, if you cooperate." *We* won't? That meant there were others nearby. "Where's Cecelia?"

"I don't . . ." It took Allegra a moment to realize that he meant Sissy. "She's gone. I don't know where she is . . . maybe at the fiesta."

By now her eyes had become dark-adapted, and she could make out the figure a little better: a bearded young man, probably in his early twenties, wearing a catskin serape, his face shrouded by a broad hat. She carefully kept her hands in sight, and although he didn't turn it away from her, at least he stepped back a little when he saw that she wasn't armed.

"I rather doubt that," he murmured. "She doesn't go into town much."

"How would you know?"

A pause. "Then you know who I am."

"I've got a good idea. . . ."

"Get this over, man," a voice whispered from behind her. "We're running out of . . ."

"Calm down." The intruder hesitated, his head briefly turning toward her cabin. "Is she in there?" She didn't answer. "Call her out."

"No. Sorry, but I won't."

He let out his breath. "Look, I'm not going to hurt her, or you either. I just want to talk to . . ."

"She doesn't want to talk to you." Allegra remembered the com Chris had given her. It was on her bedside table, where she had put it before she had taken her afternoon nap. Yet even if she could get to it, she wasn't sure how much difference it would make. The Proctors were a long way off, and these men sounded as if they were anxious to leave. "If you want to speak to her, you're going to have to go in there yourself."

He took a step toward the cabin. "Carlos, damn it!" the one behind her snapped. "We don't have time for this! Let's go!"

Carlos. Now she knew who he was, even if she had only suspected it before: Carlos Montero, one of the original settlers. The teenager who had sailed alone down the Great Equatorial River, charting the southern coast of Midland the year after the *Alabama* arrived. Like the other colonists, he'd vanished into the wilderness when the *Glorious Destiny* showed up. Now he was back.

"So you're Rigil Kent," she whispered. "Glad to make your acquaintance."

"Guess they found my note." He chuckled softly. "I imagine Chris doesn't have much good to say about me."

"Neither does his mother. Please, just leave her alone."

"Look, I don't want to push this." He lowered his gun. "Would you just deliver a message . . . ?"

"Dammit!" Now the second figure came in sight; Allegra wasn't surprised to see that he wasn't much older than Carlos, also wearing a poncho and carrying a rifle. He grasped his friend's arm, pulling him away. "Time's up, man! Move or lose it!"

"Cut it out, Barry." Carlos shook off his hand, looked at Allegra again. "Tell her Susan's all right, that she's doing well, and so's Wendy. Tell her that we miss her, and if she ever changes her mind, all she has to do is . . ."

A brilliant flash from the direction of the landing field. For a moment Allegra thought someone was shooting off fireworks, then the hollow thud of an explosion rippled across Shuttlefield as a ball of fire rose above the settlement. She suddenly knew what it was: one of the *Long Journey* shuttles blowing up.

"That's it! We're out of here!" Barry turned to run, sprinting away into the dark marshland behind the shacks. "Go!"

Yet Carlos lingered for another moment. Now Allegra could see him clearly; there was a ruthless grin on his face as he looked at her one last time. "And one more thing," he said, no longer bothering to keep his voice low, "and you can pass this along to Chris or whoever else . . . Coyote belongs to us!" He jabbed a finger toward the explosion. "Rigil Kent was here!"

And then he was gone, loping off into the swamp. In another moment he had vanished, leaving behind the shouts of angry and frightened men, the rank odor of burning fuel.

Wrapping her arms around herself, Allegra walked back to the cabin. As she turned the corner, she was surprised to find Sissy standing outside the door. She watched the distant conflagration, her face without emotion. Allegra saw that she clutched her flute.

"He returned." Her voice was a hoarse whisper. "I knew he would."

"I . . . I saw him." Allegra came closer, intending to comfort her. "He was outside. He told me to tell you . . ."

"I know. I heard everything . . . every word."

And then she raised the flute, put it to her mouth, and began to play the opening bars of "Jerusalem." Flawlessly, without a single missed note.

The shuttle burned all night; by morning it was a blackened skeleton that lay in the center of the landing field. Fortunately the blaze didn't spread to the rest of Shuttlefield; Allegra would later learn that the townspeople, upon realizing that their homes weren't in danger, abandoned all efforts at forming a bucket brigade and spent the rest of the night dancing around the burning spacecraft, throwing empty ale jugs into the pyre. It was the highlight of First Landing Day, one which people would talk about for a long time to come.

Later that day, Chris Levin came out to check on his mother. She was through feeding the chickens, though, and didn't want to talk to him. The door of her shack remained shut even after he pounded on it, and after awhile he gave up and walked over to visit Allegra. She told him that they'd spent a quiet evening in her house, and were unaware of any trouble until they heard the explosion. No, they hadn't seen anyone; did he know who was responsible? Chris didn't seem entirely satisfied by this answer, but he didn't challenge it, either. Allegra returned the com he'd lent her, and he left once again.

In the months to come, as the last warm days faded away and the long autumn set in, she continued to make flutes. Once she had enough, she began selling them to shops and kiosks. Most of those who purchased them didn't know how to play them, so she began giving lessons, at first in Shuttlefield, then in Liberty. By midwinter she was holding weekly seminars in the community center, and earning enough that she was eventually able to quit her job as a dishwasher. Some of her students turned out to have talent, and it wasn't long before she had trained enough musicians to form the Coyote Wood Ensemble.

One morning, she awoke to see the first flakes of snow falling upon the marshes. Winter was coming, and yet she didn't feel the cold. Instead she heard a muse whose voice she hadn't heard in many years. She picked up her flute, put it to her lips, and without thinking about what she was doing, began to play an unfamiliar melody; for her, it sounded like a song of redemption. When she was done, there were tears in her eyes. Two days later, she taught it to her students. She called the piece "Cecelia."

Yet despite invitations to move to Liberty, she remained in Shuttlefield, living in a small one-room cabin on the outskirts of town. Every morning, just after sunrise, she sat outside and waited for her neighbor to finish feeding the chickens. And then, regardless of whether the days were warm or if there was snow on the ground, they would practice together. Two women, playing the flute, watching the sun come up over Shuttlefield.

And waiting. Waiting for the return of Rigil Kent.

Bread and Bombs

M. RICKERT

M. Rickert lives in Saratoga Springs, New York. She had only three stories published prior to 2003, but appeared almost every month in 2003 in Fantasy & Science Fiction, *with a number of different and excellent stories, including "The Chambered Fruit," "The Super Hero Saves the World," and "Peace on Suburbia," work good enough to make her the hot new writer of the year in our opinion.*

"Bread and Bombs" also appeared in Fantasy & Science Fiction. *The story's complex and resonant social criticism suggests a contrast to J.G. Ballard's* Running Wild. *Rickert's is excellent dystopian near-future SF told from the point of view of an adult recalling a terrible time from her childhood. A town's children have a social conscience that puts them at odds with paranoid adult society.*

The strange children of the Manmensvitzender family did not go to school so we only knew they had moved into the old house on the hill because Bobby had watched them move in with their strange assortment of rocking chairs and goats. We couldn't imagine how anyone would live there, where the windows were all broken and the yard was thorny with brambles. For a while we expected to see the children, two daughters who, Bobby said, had hair like smoke and eyes like black olives, at school. But they never came.

We were in the fourth grade, that age that seems like waking from a long slumber into the world the adults imposed, streets we weren't allowed to cross, things we weren't allowed to say, and crossing them, and saying them. The mysterious Manmensvitzender children were just another in a series of revelations that year, including the much more exciting (and sometimes disturbing) evolution of our bodies. Our parents, without exception, had raised us with this subject so thoroughly explored that Lisa Bitten knew how to say vagina before she knew her address and Ralph Linster delivered his little brother, Petey, when his mother went into labor one night when it suddenly started snowing before his father could get home. But the real significance of this information didn't start to sink in until that year. We were waking to the wonders of the world and the body; the strange realizations that a friend was cute, or stinky, or picked her nose, or was fat, or wore dirty underpants, or had eyes that didn't blink when he looked at you real close and all of a sudden you felt like blushing.

When the crab apple tree blossomed a brilliant pink, buzzing with honey bees, and our teacher, Mrs. Graymoore, looked out the window and sighed, we passed notes across the rows and made wild plans for the school picnic, how we would ambush her with water balloons and throw pies at the principal. Of course none of this happened. Only Trina Needles was disappointed because she really believed it would but she still wore bows in her hair and secretly sucked her thumb and was nothing but a big baby.

Released into summer we ran home or biked home shouting for joy and escape and then began doing everything we could think of, all those things we'd imagined doing while Mrs. Graymoore sighed at the crab apple tree which had already lost its brilliance and once again looked ordinary. We threw balls, rode bikes, rolled skateboards down the driveway, picked flowers, fought, made up, and it was still hours before dinner. We watched TV, and didn't think about being bored, but after a while we hung upside down and watched it that way, or switched the channels back and forth or found reasons to fight with anyone in the house. (I was alone, however and could not indulge in this.) That's when we heard the strange noise of goats and bells. In the mothy gray of TV rooms, we pulled back the drapes, and peered out windows into a yellowed sunlight.

The two Manmensvitzender girls in bright clothes the color of a circus, and gauzy scarves, one purple, the other red, glittering with sequins came rolling down the street in a wooden wagon pulled by two goats with bells around their necks. That is how the trouble began. The news accounts never mention any of this; the flame of crab apple blossoms, our innocence, the sound of bells. Instead they focus on the unhappy results. They say we were wild. Uncared for. Strange. They say we were dangerous. As if life was amber and we were formed and suspended in that form, not evolved into that ungainly shape of horror, and evolved out of it, as we are, into a teacher, a dancer, a welder, a lawyer, several soldiers, two doctors, and me, a writer.

Everybody promises during times like those days immediately following the tragedy that lives have been ruined, futures shattered but only Trina Needles fell for that and eventually committed suicide. The rest of us suffered various forms of censure and then went on with our lives. Yes it is true, with a dark past but, you may be surprised to learn, that can be lived with. The hand that holds the pen (or chalk, or the stethoscope, or the gun, or lover's skin) is so different from the hand that lit the match, and so incapable of such an act that it is not even a matter of forgiveness, or healing. It's strange to look back and believe that any of that was me or us. Are you who you were then? Eleven years old and watching the dust motes spin lazily down a beam of sunlight that ruins the picture on the TV and there is a sound of bells and goats and a laugh so pure we all come running to watch the girls in their bright colored scarves, sitting in the goat cart which stops in a stutter of goat-hoofed steps and clatter of wooden wheels when we surround it to observe those dark eyes and pretty faces. The younger girl, if size is any indication, smiling, and the other, younger than us, but at least eight or nine, with huge tears rolling down her brown cheeks.

We stand there for a while, staring, and then Bobby says, "What's a matter with her?"

The younger girl looks at her sister who seems to be trying to smile in spite of the tears. "She just cries all the time."

Bobby nods and squints at the girl who continues to cry though she manages to ask, "Where have you kids come from?"

He looks around the group with an are-you-kidding kind of look but anyone can tell he likes the weeping girl, whose dark eyes and lashes glisten with tears that glitter in the sun. "It's summer vacation."

Trina, who has been furtively sucking her thumb, says, "Can I have a ride?" The girls say sure. She pushes her way through the little crowd and climbs into the cart. The younger girl smiles at her. The other seems to try but cries especially loud. Trina looks like she might start crying too until the younger one says, "Don't worry. It's just how she is." The crying girl shakes the reins and the little bells ring and the goats and cart go clattering down the hill. We listen to Trina's shrill scream but we know she's all right. When they come back we take turns until our parents call us home with whistles and shouts and screen doors slam. We go home for dinner, and the girls head home themselves, the one still crying, the other singing to the accompaniment of bells.

"I see you were playing with the refugees," my mother says. "You be careful around those girls. I don't want you going to their house."

"I didn't go to their house. We just played with the goats and the wagon."

"Well all right then, but stay away from there. What are they like?"

"One laughs a lot. The other cries all the time."

"Don't eat anything they offer you."

"Why not?"

"Just don't."

"Can't you just explain to me why not?"

"I don't have to explain to you, young lady, I'm your mother."

We didn't see the girls the next day or the day after that. On the third day Bobby, who had begun to carry a comb in his back pocket and part his hair on the side, said, "Well hell, let's just go there." He started up the hill but none of us followed.

When he came back that evening we rushed him for information about his visit, shouting questions at him like reporters. "Did you eat anything?" I asked, "My mother says not to eat anything there."

He turned and fixed me with such a look that for a moment I forgot he was my age, just a kid like me, in spite of the new way he was combing his hair and the steady gaze of his blue eyes. "Your mother is prejudiced," he said. He turned his back to me and reached into his pocket, pulling out a fist that he opened to reveal a handful of small, brightly wrapped candies. Trina reached her pudgy fingers into Bobby's palm and plucked out one bright orange one. This was followed by a flurry of hands until there was only Bobby's empty palm.

Parents started calling kids home. My mother stood in the

doorway but she was too far away to see what we were doing. Candy wrappers floated down the sidewalk in swirls of blue, green, red, yellow and orange.

My mother and I usually ate separately. When I was at my dad's we ate together in front of the TV which she said was barbaric.

"Was he drinking?" she'd ask. Mother was convinced my father was an alcoholic and thought I did not remember those years when he had to leave work early because I'd called and told him how she was asleep on the couch, still in her pajamas, the coffee table littered with cans and bottles which he threw in the trash with a grim expression and few words.

My mother stands, leaning against the counter, and watches me. "Did you play with those girls today?"

"No. Bobby did though."

"Well, that figures, nobody really watches out for that boy. I remember when his daddy was in high school with me. Did I ever tell you that?"

"Uh-huh."

"He was a handsome man. Bobby's a nice looking boy too but you stay away from him. I think you play with him too much."

"I hardly play with him at all. He plays with those girls all day."

"Did he say anything about them?"

"He said some people are prejudiced."

"Oh, he did, did he? Where'd he get such an idea anyway? Must be his grandpa. You listen to me, there's nobody even talks that way anymore except for a few rabble rousers, and there's a reason for that. People are dead because of that family. You just remember that. Many, many people died because of them."

"You mean Bobby's, or the girls?"

"Well, both actually. But most especially those girls. He didn't eat anything, did he?"

I looked out the window, pretending a new interest in our backyard, then, at her, with a little start, as though suddenly awoken. "What? Uh, no."

She stared at me with squinted eyes. I pretended to be unconcerned. She tapped her red fingernails against the kitchen counter. "You listen to me," she said in a sharp voice, "there's a war going on."

I rolled my eyes.

"You don't even remember, do you? Well, how could you, you were just a toddler. But there was a time when this country didn't know war. Why, people used to fly in airplanes all the time."

I stopped my fork halfway to my mouth. "Well, how stupid was that?"

"You don't understand. Everybody did it. It was a way to get from one place to another. Your grandparents did it a lot, and your father and I did too."

"You were on an airplane?"

"Even you." She smiled. "See, you don't know so much, missy. The world used to be safe, and then, one day, it wasn't. And those people," she pointed at the kitchen window, straight at the Millers' house, but I knew that wasn't who she meant, "started it."

"They're just a couple of kids."

"Well, not them exactly, but I mean the country they come from. That's why I want you to be careful. There's no telling what they're doing here. So little Bobby and his radical grandpa can say we're all prejudiced but who even talks that way anymore?" She walked over to the table, pulled out a chair and sat down in front of me. "I want you to understand, there's no way to know about evil. So just stay away from them. Promise me."

Evil. Hard to understand. I nodded.

"Well, all right." She pushed back the chair, stood up, grabbed her pack of cigarettes from the windowsill. "Make sure not to leave any crumbs. This is the time of year for ants."

From the kitchen window I could see my mother sitting on the picnic table, a gray plume of smoke spiraling away from her. I rinsed my dishes, loaded the dishwasher, wiped the table and went outside to sit on the front steps and think about the world I never knew. The house on top of the hill blazed in the full sun. The broken windows had been covered by some sort of plastic that swallowed the light.

That night one flew over Oakgrove. I woke up and put my helmet on. My mother was screaming in her room, too frightened to help. My hands didn't shake the way hers did, and I didn't lie in my bed screaming. I put the helmet on and listened to it fly past. Not us. Not our town. Not tonight. I fell asleep with the helmet on and in the morning woke up with the marks of it dented on my cheeks.

Now, when summer approaches, I count the weeks when the apple trees and lilacs are in blossom, the tulips and daffodils in bloom before they droop with summer's heat and I think how it is so much like that period of our innocence, that waking into the world with all its incandescence, before being subdued by its shadows into what we became.

"You should have known the world then," my father says, when I visit him at the nursing home.

We've heard it so much it doesn't mean anything. The cakes, the money, the endless assortment of everything.

"We used to have six different kinds of cereal at one time," he raises his finger instructively, "coated in sugar, can you imagine? It used to go stale. We threw it out. And the planes. The sky used to be filled with them. Really. People traveled that way, whole families did. It didn't matter if someone moved away. Hell, you just got on a plane to see them."

Whenever he speaks like this, whenever any of them do, they sound bewildered, amazed. He shakes his head, he sighs. "We were so happy."

I cannot hear about those times without thinking of spring flowers, children's laughter, the sound of bells and clatter of goats. Smoke.

Bobby sits in the cart, holding the reins, a pretty dark-skinned girl on either side of him. They ride up and down the street all morning, laughing and crying, their gauzy scarves blowing behind them like rainbows.

The flags droop listlessly from flagpoles and porches.

Butterflies flit in and out of gardens. The Whitehall twins play in their backyard and the squeaky sound of their unoiled swings echoes through the neighborhood. Mrs. Renquat has taken the day off to take several kids to the park. I am not invited, probably because I hate Becky Renquat and told her so several times during the school year, pulling her hair which was a stream of white gold so bright I could not resist it. It is Ralph Paterson's birthday and most of the little kids are spending the day with him and his dad at The Snowman's Cave Amusement Park where they get to do all the things kids used to do when snow was still safe, like sledding, and building snowmen. Lina Breedsore and Carol Minstreet went to the mall with their baby-sitter who has a boyfriend who works at the movie theater and can sneak them in to watch movies all day long. The town is empty except for the baby Whitehall twins, Trina Needles who is sucking her thumb and reading a book on her porch swing, and Bobby, going up and down the street with the Manmensvitzender girls and their goats. I sit on my porch picking at the scabs on my knees but Bobby speaks only to them, in a voice so low I can't hear what he says. Finally I stand up and block their way. The goats and cart stutter to a stop, the bells still jingling as Bobby says, "What's up, Weyers?"

He has eyes so blue, I recently discovered, I cannot look into them for more than thirty seconds, as though they burn me. Instead I look at the girls who are both smiling, even the one who is crying.

"What's your problem?" I say.

Her dark eyes widen, increasing the pool of milky white around them. She looks at Bobby. The sequins of her scarf catch the sun.

"Jesus Christ, Weyers, what are you talking about?"

"I just want a know," I say still looking at her, "what it is with all this crying all the time, I mean like is it a disease, or what?"

"Oh for Christ's sake." The goats' heads rear, and the bells jingle. Bobby pulls on the reins. The goats step back with clomps and the rattle of wheels but I continue to block their path. "What's your problem?"

"It's a perfectly reasonable question," I shout at his shadow against the bright sun. "I just wanta know what her problem is."

"It's none of your business," he shouts and at the same time the smaller girl speaks.

"What?" I say to her.

"It's the war, and all the suffering."

Bobby holds the goats steady. The other girl holds onto his arm. She smiles at me but continues to weep.

"Well, so? Did something happen to her?"

"It's just how she is. She always cries."

"That's stupid."

"Oh, for Christ's sake, Weyers!"

"You can't cry all the time, that's no way to live."

Bobby steers the goats and cart around me. The younger girl turns and stares at me until, at some distance, she waves but I turn away without waving back.

Before it was abandoned and then occupied by the Mannensvitzenders the big house on the hill had been owned by the Richters. "Oh sure they were rich," my father says when I tell him I am researching a book. "But you know, we all were. You should have seen the cakes! And the catalogs. We used to get these catalogs in the mail and you could buy anything that way, they'd mail it to you, even cake. We used to get this catalog, what was it called, Henry and Danny? Something like that. Two guys' names. Anyhow, when we were young it was just fruit but then, when the whole country was rich you could order spongecake with buttercream, or they had these towers of packages they'd send you, filled with candy and nuts and cookies, and chocolate, and oh my God, right in the mail."

"You were telling me about the Richters."

"Terrible thing what happened to them, the whole family."

"It was the snow, right?"

"Your brother, Jaime, that's when we lost him."

"We don't have to talk about that."

"Everything changed after that, you know. That's what got your mother started. Most folks just lost one, some not even, but you know those Richters. That big house on the hill and when it snowed they all went sledding. The world was different then."

"I can't imagine."

"Well, neither could we. Nobody could of guessed it. And believe me, we were guessing. Everyone tried to figure what they would do next. But snow? I mean how evil is that anyway?"

"How many?"

"Oh, thousands. Thousands."

"No, I mean how many Richters?"

"All six of them. First the children and then the parents."

"Wasn't it unusual for adults to get infected?"

"Well, not that many of us played in the snow the way they did."

"So you must have sensed it, or something."

"What? No. We were just so busy then. Very busy. I wish I could remember. But I can't. What we were so busy with." He rubs his eyes and stares out the window. "It wasn't your fault. I want you to know I understand that."

"Pop."

"I mean you kids, that's just the world we gave you, so full of evil you didn't even know the difference."

"We knew, Pop."

"You still don't know. What do you think of when you think of snow?"

"I think of death."

"Well, there you have it. Before that happened it meant joy. Peace and joy."

"I can't imagine."

"Well, that's my point."

"Are you feeling all right?" She dishes out the macaroni, puts the bowl in front of me and stands, leaning against the counter, to watch me eat.

I shrug.

She places a cold palm on my forehead. Steps back and frowns. "You didn't eat anything from those girls, did you?"

I shake my head. She is just about to speak when I say, "But the other kids did."

"Who? When?" She leans so close that I can see the lines of makeup sharp against her skin.

"Bobby. Some of the other kids. They ate candy."

Her hand comes palm down, hard, against the table. The macaroni bowl jumps, and the silverware. Some milk spills. "Didn't I tell you?" she shouts.

"Bobby plays with them all the time now."

She squints at me, shakes her head, then snaps her jaw with grim resolve. "When? When did they eat this candy?"

"I don't know. Days ago. Nothing happened. They said it was good."

Her mouth opens and closes like a fish. She turns on her heels and grabs the phone as she leaves the kitchen. The door slams. I can see her through the window, pacing the backyard, her arms gesturing wildly.

My mother organized the town meeting and everybody came, dressed up like it was church. The only people who weren't there were the Manmensvitzenders, for obvious reasons. Most people brought their kids, even the babies who sucked thumbs or blanket corners. I was there and so was Bobby with his grandpa who chewed the stem of a cold pipe and kept leaning over and whispering to his grandson during the proceedings which quickly became heated, though there wasn't much argument, the heat being fueled by just the general excitement of it, my mother especially in her roses dress, her lips painted a bright red so that even I came to some understanding that she had a certain beauty though I was too young to understand what about that beauty wasn't entirely pleasing. "We have to remember that we are all soldiers in this war," she said to much applause.

Mr. Smyths suggested a sort of house arrest but my mother pointed out that would entail someone from town bringing groceries to them. "Everybody knows these people are starving. Who's going to pay for all this bread anyway?" she said. "Why should we have to pay for it?"

Mrs. Mathers said something about justice.

Mr. Hallensway said, "No one is innocent anymore."

My mother, who stood at the front of the room, leaning slightly against the village board table, said, "Then it's decided."

Mrs. Foley, who had just moved to town from the recently destroyed Chesterville, stood up, in that way she had sort of crouching into her shoulders, with those eyes that looked around nervously so that some of us had secretly taken to calling her Bird Woman, and with a shaky voice, so soft everyone had to lean forward to hear, said, "Are any of the children actually sick?"

The adults looked at each other and each other's children. I could tell that my mother was disappointed that no one reported any symptoms. The discussion turned to the bright colored candies when Bobby, without standing or raising his hand, said in a loud voice, "Is that what this is about? Do you mean these?" He half laid back in his chair to wiggle his hand into his pocket and pulled out a handful of them.

There was a general murmur. My mother grabbed the edge of the table. Bobby's grandfather, grinning around his dry pipe, plucked one of the candies from Bobby's palm, unwrapped it, and popped it into his mouth.

Mr. Galvin Wright had to use his gavel to hush the noise. My mother stood up straight and said, "Fine thing, risking your own life like that, just to make a point."

"Well, you're right about making a point, Maylene," he said, looking right at my mother and shaking his head as if they were having a private discussion, "but this is candy I keep around the house to get me out of the habit of smoking. I order it through the Government Issue catalog. It's perfectly safe."

"I never said it was from them," said Bobby, who looked first at my mother and then searched the room until he found my face, but I pretended not to notice.

When we left, my mother took me by the hand, her red fingernails digging into my wrist. "Don't talk," she said, "just don't say another word." She sent me to my room and I fell asleep with my clothes on still formulating my apology.

* * *

The next morning when I hear the bells, I grab a loaf of bread and wait on the porch until they come back up the hill. Then I stand in their path.

"Now what d'you want?" Bobby says.

I offer the loaf, like a tiny baby being held up to God in church. The weeping girl cries louder, her sister clutches Bobby's arm. "What d'you think you're doing?" he shouts.

"It's a present."

"What kind of stupid present is that? Put it away! Jesus Christ, would you put it down?"

My arms drop to my sides, the loaf dangles in its bag from my hand. Both girls are crying. "I just was trying to be nice," I say, my voice wavering like the Bird Woman's.

"God, don't you know anything?" Bobby says. "They're afraid of our food, don't you even know that?"

"Why?"

"'Cause of the bombs, you idiot. Why don't you think once in a while?"

"I don't know what you're talking about."

The goats rattle their bells and the cart shifts back and forth. "The bombs! Don't you even read your history books? In the beginning of the war we sent them food packages all wrapped up the same color as these bombs that would go off when someone touched them."

"We did that?"

"Well, our parents did." He shakes his head and pulls the reins. The cart rattles past, both girls pressed against him as if I am dangerous.

"Oh, we were so happy!" my father says, rocking into the memory. "We were like children, you know, so innocent, we didn't even know."

"Know what, Pop?"

"That we had enough."

"Enough what?"

"Oh, everything. We had enough everything. Is that a plane?" he looks at me with watery blue eyes.

"Here, let me help you put your helmet on."

He slaps at it, bruising his fragile hands.

"Quit it, Dad. Stop!"

He fumbles with arthritic fingers to unbuckle the strap but finds he cannot. He weeps into his spotted hands. It drones past.

Now that I look back on how we were that summer, before the tragedy, I get a glimmer of what my father's been trying to say all along. It isn't really about the cakes, and the mail order catalogs, or the air travel they used to take. Even though he uses stuff to describe it that's not what he means. Once there was a different emotion. People used to have a way of feeling and being in the world that is gone, destroyed so thoroughly we inherited only its absence.

"Sometimes," I tell my husband, "I wonder if my happiness is really happiness."

"Of course it's really happiness," he says, "what else would it be?"

We were under attack is how it felt. The Manmensvitzenders with their tears and fear of bread, their strange clothes and stinky goats were children like us and we could not get the town meeting out of our heads, what the adults had considered doing. We climbed trees, chased balls, came home when called, brushed our teeth when told, finished our milk, but we had lost that feeling we'd had before. It is true we didn't understand what had been taken from us, but we knew what we had been given and who had done the giving.

We didn't call a meeting the way they did. Ours just happened on a day so hot we sat in Trina Needles's playhouse fanning ourselves with our hands and complaining about the weather like the grownups. We mentioned house arrest but that seemed impossible to enforce. We discussed things like water balloons, T.P.ing. Someone mentioned dog shit in brown paper bags set on fire. I think that's when the discussion turned the way it did.

You may ask, who locked the door? Who made the stick piles? Who lit the matches? We all did. And if I am to find solace, twenty-five years after I destroyed all ability to feel that my happiness, or anyone's, really exists, I find it in this. It was all of us.

Maybe there will be no more town meetings. Maybe this plan is like the ones we've made before. But a town meeting is called. The grownups assemble to discuss how we will not be ruled by evil and also, the possibility of widening Main Street. Nobody notices when we children sneak out. We had to leave behind the babies, sucking thumbs or blanket corners and not really part of our plan for redemption. We were children. It wasn't well thought out.

When the police came we were not "careening in some wild imitation of barbaric dance" or having seizures as has been reported. I can still see Bobby, his hair damp against his forehead, the bright red of his cheeks as he danced beneath the white flakes that fell from a sky we never trusted; Trina spinning in circles, her arms stretched wide, and the Manmensvitzender girls with their goats and cart piled high with rocking chairs, riding away from us, the jingle bells ringing, just like in the old song. Once again the world was safe and beautiful. Except by the town hall where the large white flakes rose like ghosts and the flames ate the sky like a hungry monster who could never get enough.

The Great Game

STEPHEN BAXTER

Stephen Baxter (www.cix.co.uk/~sbradshaw/baxterium/baxterium.html) is now one of the big names in SF. In 1995 and 1996, he became a major figure internationally in hard SF when his work was first published outside the UK. Not only were his earlier novels reprinted in the U.S., but The Time Ships *(1995) was a leading contender in 1996 for the Hugo Award for best novel. In the mid and late 1990s he produced nearly ten short stories a year. He published four books in 2000, including a collaboration with Arthur C. Clarke,* The Light of Other Days, *and* Space: Manifold 2 *(titled* Manifold: Space *in the U.S.), and won the Philip K. Dick Award for his collection,* Vacuum Diagrams *(1999).* Origin: Manifold 3 *was published in 2001, as was* Icebones, Deep Time, *and a collection,* Ormegatropic: Non-Fiction & Fiction. *His novel* Evolution *appeared in 2002, and he did two more collaborations with Clarke,* Time's Eye *and* Nova.

"The Great Game" is an anti-war story set in his Xeelee future universe. It is a timely story, and part of the ongoing political dialogue in hard SF between the UK left and the U.S. right.

We were in the blister, waiting for the drop. My marines, fifty of them in their bright orange Yukawa suits, were sitting in untidy rows. They were trying to hide it, but I could see the fear in the way they clutched their static lines, and their unusual reluctance to rib the wetbacks.

Well, when I looked through the transparent walls and out into the sky, I felt it myself.

We had been flung far out of the main disc, and the sparse orange-red stars of the halo were a foreground to the galaxy itself, a pool of curdled light that stretched to right and left as far as you could see. But as the Spline ship threw itself gamely through its complicated evasive maneuvers, that great sheet of light flapped around us like a bird's broken wing. I could see our destination's home sun—it was a dwarf, a pinprick glowing dim red—but even that jiggled around the sky as the Spline bucked and rolled.

And, leaving aside the vertigo, what deepened my own fear was the glimpses I got of the craft that swarmed like moths around that dwarf star. Beautiful swooping ships with sycamore-seed wings, they were unmistakable. They were Xeelee nightfighters.

The Xeelee were the captain's responsibility, not mine. But I couldn't stop my over-active mind speculating on what had lured such a dense concentration of them so far out of the Galactic core that is their usual stamping ground.

Given the tension, it was almost a relief when Lian threw up.

Those Yukawa suits are heavy and stiff, meant for protection rather than flexibility, but she managed to lean far enough forward that her bright yellow puke mostly hit the floor. Her buddies reacted as you'd imagine, but I handed her a wipe.

"Sorry, Lieutenant." She was the youngest of the troop, at seventeen ten years younger than me.

I forced a grin. "I've seen worse, marine. Anyhow you've given the wetbacks something to do when we've gone."

"Yes, sir. . . ."

What you definitively don't want at such moments is a visit from the brass. Which, of course, is what we got.

Admiral Kard came stalking through the drop blister, muttering to the loadmaster, nodding at marines. At Kard's side was a Commissary—you could tell that at a glance—a woman, tall, ageless, in the classic costume of the Commission for Historical Truth, a floor-sweeping gown and shaved-bald head. She looked as cold and lifeless as every Commissary I ever met.

I stood up, brushing vomit off my suit. I could see how the troops were tensing up. But I couldn't have stopped an admiral; this was his flag.

They reached my station just as the destination planet, at last, swam into view.

We grunts knew it only by a number. That eerie sun was too dim to cast much light, and despite low-orbiting sunsats much of the land and sea was dark velvet. But great orange rivers of fire coursed across the black ground. This was a suffering world.

Admiral Kard was watching me. "Lieutenant Neer. Correct?"

"Sir."

"Welcome to Shade," he said evenly. "You know the setup here. The Expansion reached this region five hundred years ago. We haven't been much in contact since. But when our people down there called for help, the Navy responded." He had cold artificial Eyes, and I sensed he was testing me.

"We're ready to drop, sir."

The Commissary was peering out at the tilted landscape,

hands folded behind her back. "Remarkable. It's like a geology demonstrator. Look at the lines of volcanoes and ravines. Every one of this world's tectonic faults has given way, all at once."

Admiral Kard eyed me. "You must forgive Commissary Xera. She does think of the universe as a textbook."

He was rewarded for that with a glare.

I kept silent, uncomfortable. Everybody knows about the tension between Navy, the fighting arm of mankind's Third Expansion, and Commission, implementer of political will. Maybe that structural rivalry was the reason for this impromptu walk-through, as the Commissary jostled for influence over events, and the admiral tried to score points with a display of his fighting troops.

Except that right now they were *my* troops, not his.

To her credit, Xera seemed to perceive something of my resentment. "Don't worry, Lieutenant. It's just that Kard and I have something of a history. Two centuries of it, in fact, since our first encounter on a world called Home, thousands of light years from here."

I could see Lian look up at that. According to the book, *nobody* was supposed to live so long. I guess at seventeen you still think everybody follows the rules.

Kard nodded. "And you've always had a way of drawing subordinates into our personal conflicts, Xera. Well, we may be making history today. Neer, look at the home sun, the frozen star."

I frowned. "What's a *frozen star?*"

The Commissary made to answer, but Kard cut across her. "Skip the science. Those Xeelee units are swarming like rats. We don't know *why* the Xeelee are here. But we do know what they are doing to this human world."

"That's not proven," Xera snapped.

Despite that caveat I could see my people stir. None of us had ever heard of a direct attack by the Xeelee on human positions.

Lian said boldly, "Admiral, sir—"

"Yes, rating?"

"Does that mean we are at war?"

Admiral Kard sniffed up a lungful of ozone-laden air. "After today, perhaps we will be. How does that make you feel, rating?"

Lian, and the others, looked to me for guidance.

I looked into my heart.

Across seven thousand years humans had spread out in a great swarm through the galaxy, even spreading out into the halo beyond the main disc, overwhelming and assimilating other life forms as we encountered them. We had faced no opponent capable of systematic resistance since the collapse of the Silver Ghosts five thousand years before—none but the Xeelee, the galaxy's other great power, who sat in their great concentrations at the core, silent, aloof. For my whole life, and for centuries before, all of mankind had been united in a single purpose: to confront the Xeelee, and claim our rightful dominion.

And now—perhaps—here I was at the start of it all.

What I felt was awe. Fear, maybe. But that wasn't what the moment required. "I'll tell you what I feel, sir. Relief. *Bring them on!*"

That won me a predictable hollering, and a slap on the back from Kard. Xera studied me blankly, her face unreadable.

Then there was a flare of plasma around the blister, and the ride got a lot bumpier. I sat before I was thrown down, and the loadmaster hustled away the brass.

"Going in hard," called the loadmaster. "Barf bags at the ready. Ten minutes."

We were skimming under high, thin, icy clouds. The world had become a landscape of burning mountains and rivers of rock that fled beneath me.

All this in an eerie silence, broken only by the shallow breaths of the marines.

The ship lurched up and to the right. To our left now was a mountain; we had come so low already that its peak was above us. According to the century-old survey maps the locals had called it Mount Perfect. And, yes, once it must have been a classic cone shape, I thought, a nice landmark for an earthworm's horizon. But now its profile was spoiled by bulges and gouges, ash had splashed around it, and deeper mud-filled channels had been cut into the landscape, splayed like the fingers of a hand.

Somewhere down there, amid the bleating locals, there was an academician called Tilo, dropped by the Navy a couple of standard days earlier, part of a global network who had been gathering data on the causes of the volcanism. Tilo's job, bluntly, had been to prove that it was all the Xeelee's fault. The academician had somehow got himself cut off from his uplink gear; I was to find and retrieve him. No wonder Xera had been so hostile, I thought; the Commissaries were famously suspicious of the alliance between the Navy and the Academies—

Green lights marked out the hatch in the invisible wall.

The loadmaster came along the line. "Stand up! Stand up!" The marines complied clumsily.

"Thirty seconds," the loadmaster told me. He was a burly, scarred veteran, attached to a rail by an umbilical as thick as my arm. "Winds look good."

"Thank you."

"You guys be careful down there. All clear aft. Ten seconds. Five." The green lights began to blink. We pulled our flexible visors across our faces. "Three, two—"

The hatch dilated, and the sudden roar of the wind made all this real.

The loadmaster was standing by the hatch, screaming. "Go, go, go!" As the marines passed I checked each static line one last time with a sharp tug, before they jumped into blackness. The kid, Lian, was the second last to go—and I was the last of all.

So there I was, falling into the air of a new world.

The static line went taut and ripped free, turning on my suit's Yukawa-force gravity nullifier. That first shock can be hurtful, but to me, after maybe fifty drops in anger, it came as a relief.

I looked up and to my right. I saw a neat line of marines falling starfished through the air. One was a lot closer to me than the rest—Lian, I guessed. Past them I made out our Spline vessel, its hull charred from its hurried entry into the atmosphere. Even now it looked immense, its pocked hull like an inverted landscape above me. It was a magnificent sight, an awe-inspiring display of human power and capability.

But beyond it I saw the hulking majesty of the mountain, dwarfing even the Spline. A dense cloud of smoke and ash lingered near its truncated summit, underlit by a fiery glow.

I looked down, to the valley I was aiming for.

The Commission's maps had shown a standard-issue Conurbation surrounded by broad, shining replicator fields, where the ground's organic matter was processed seamlessly into food. But the view now was quite different. I could see the characteristic bubble-cluster shape of a Conurbation, but it looked dark, poorly maintained, while suburbs of blockier buildings had sprouted around it.

You expected a little drift from orthodoxy, out here on the edge of everything.

Still, that Conurbation was our target for the evacuation. I could see the squat cone shape of a heavy-lift shuttle, dropped here on the Spline's last pass through the atmosphere, ready to lift the population. My marines were heading for the Conurbation, just as they should.

But I had a problem, I saw now. There was another cluster of buildings and lights, much smaller, stranded half way up the flank of the mountain. Another village?

I'm not sentimental. You do what you can, what's possible. I wouldn't have gone after that isolated handful—if not for the fact that a pale pink light blinked steadily at me.

It was Tilo's beacon. Kard had made it clear enough that unless I came home with the academician, or at least with his data, next time I made a drop it would be without a Yukawa suit.

I slowed my fall and barked out orders. It was a simple mission; I knew my people would be able to supervise the evacuation of the main township without me. Then I turned and continued my descent, down toward the smaller community.

It was only after I had committed myself that I saw one of my troop had followed me: the kid, Lian.

No time to think about that now. A Yukawa suit is good for

one drop, one way. You can't go back and change your mind. Anyhow I was already close. I glimpsed a few ramshackle buildings, upturned faces shining like coins.

Then the barely visible ground raced up to meet me. Feet together, knees bent, back straight, roll when you hit—and then a breath-stealing impact on hard rock.

I allowed myself three full breaths, lying there on the cold ground, as I checked I was still in one piece.

Then I stood and pulled off my visor. The air was breathable, but thick with the smell of burning, and of sulphur. But the ground quivered under my feet, over and over. I wasn't too troubled by that—until I reminded myself that planets were supposed to be *stable*.

Lian was standing there, her suit glowing softly. "Good landing, sir," she said.

I nodded, glad she was safe, but irritated; if she'd followed orders she wouldn't have been here at all. I turned away from her, a deliberate snub that was enough admonishment for now.

The sky was deep. Beyond clouds of ash, sunsats swam. Past them I glimpsed the red pinprick of the true sun, and the wraith-like galaxy disc beyond.

Behind me the valley skirted the base of Mount Perfect, neatly separating it from more broken ground beyond. The landscape was dark green, its contours coated by forest, and clear streams bubbled into a river that ran down the valley's center. A single, elegant bridge spanned the valley, reaching toward the old Conurbation. Further upstream I saw what looked like a logging plant, giant pieces of yellow-colored equipment standing idle amid huge piles of sawn trees. Idyllic, if you liked that kind of thing, which I didn't.

On this side of the valley, the village was just a huddle of huts—some of them made from *wood*—clustered on the lower slopes of the mountain. Bigger buildings might have been a school, a medical center. There were a couple of battered ground transports. Beyond, I glimpsed the rectangular shapes of fields—apparently plowed, not a glimmer of replicator technology in sight, mostly covered in ash.

People were standing, watching me, gray as the ground under their feet. Men, women, children, infants in arms, old folk, people in little clusters. There were maybe thirty of them.

Lian stood close to me. "Sir, I don't understand."

"These are *families,*" I murmured. "You'll pick it up."

"Dark matter." The new voice was harsh, damaged by smoke; I turned, startled.

A man was limping toward me. About my height and age but a lot leaner, he was wearing a tattered Navy coverall, and he was using an improvised crutch to hobble over the rocky ground, favoring what looked like a broken leg. His face and hair were gray with the ash.

I said, "You're the academician."

"Yes, I'm Tilo."

"We're here to get you out."

He barked a laugh. "Sure you are. Listen to me. *Dark matter*. That's why the Xeelee are here. It may have nothing to do with *us* at all. Things are going to happen fast. If I don't get out of here—whatever happens, just remember that one thing . . ."

Now a woman hurried toward me. One of the locals, she was wearing a simple shift of woven cloth, and leather sandals on her feet; she looked maybe forty, strong, tired. An antique translator box hovered at her shoulder. "My name is Doel," she said. "We saw you fall—"

"Are you in charge here?"

"I—" She smiled. "Yes, if you like. Will you help us get out of here?"

She didn't look, or talk, or act, like any Expansion citizen I had ever met. Things truly had drifted here. "You are in the wrong place." I was annoyed how prissy I sounded. I pointed to the Conurbation, on the other side of the valley. "*That's* where you're supposed to be."

"I'm sorry," she said, bemused. "We've lived here since my grandfather's time. We didn't like it, over in Blessed. We came here to live a different way. No replicators. Crops we grow ourselves. Clothes we make—"

"Mothers and fathers and grandfathers," Tilo cackled. "What do you think of that, Lieutenant?"

"Academician, why are you here?"

He shrugged. "I came to study the mountain, as an exemplar of the planet's geology. I accepted the hospitality of these people. That's all. I got to like them, despite their—alien culture."

"But you left your equipment behind," I snapped. "You don't have comms implants. You didn't even bring your mnemonic fluid, did you?"

"I brought my pickup beacon," he said smugly.

"Lethe, I don't have time for this." I turned to Doel. "Look—if you can get yourself across the valley, to where that transport is, you'll be taken out with the rest."

"But I don't think there will be time—"

I ignored her. "Academician, can you walk?"

Tilo laughed. "No. And *you* can't hear the mountain."

That was when Mount Perfect exploded.

Tilo told me later that, if I'd known where and how to look, I could have seen the north side of the mountain bulging out. The defect had been growing visibly, at a meter a day. Well, I didn't notice that. Thanks to some trick of acoustics, I didn't even hear the eruption—though it was slightly heard by other Navy teams working hundreds of kilometers away.

But the aftermath was clear enough. With Lian and Doel, and with Academician Tilo limping after us, I ran to the crest of a ridge to see down the length of the valley.

A sharp earthquake had caused the mountain's swollen flank to shear and fall away. As we watched, a billion tons of rock slid into the valley in a monstrous landslide. Already a huge gray thunderhead of smoke and ash was rearing up to the murky sky.

But that was only the start, for the removal of all that weight was like opening a pressurized can. The mountain erupted—not upward, but *sideways,* like the blast of an immense weapon, a volley of superheated gas and pulverized rock. It quickly overtook the landslide, and I saw it roll over trees—imports from distant Earth, great vegetable sentinels centuries old, flattened like straws.

I was stupefied by the *scale* of it all.

Now, from out of the ripped-open side of the mountain, a chthonic blood oozed, yellow-gray, viscous, steaming hot. It began to flow down the mountainside, spilling into rain-cut valleys.

"That's a lahar," Tilo murmured. "Mud. I've learned a lot of esoteric geology here, Lieutenant. . . . The heat is melting the permafrost—these mountains were snow-covered two weeks ago; did you know that?—making up a thick mixture of volcanic debris and meltwater."

"So it's just mud," said Lian uncertainly.

"You aren't an earthworm, are you, marine?"

"Look at the logging camp," Doel murmured, pointing.

Already the mud had overwhelmed the heavy equipment, big yellow tractors and huge cables and chains used for hauling logs, crumpling it all like paper. Piles of sawn logs were spilled, immense wooden beams shoved downstream effortlessly. The mud, gray and yellow, was steaming, oddly like curdled milk.

For the first time I began to consider the contingency that we might not get out of here. In which case my primary mission was to preserve Tilo's data.

I quickly used my suit to establish an uplink. We were able to access Tilo's records, stored in cranial implants, and fire them up to the Spline. But in case it didn't work—

"Tell me about dark matter," I said. "Quickly."

Tilo pointed up at the sky. "That star—the natural sun, the dwarf—shouldn't exist."

"What?"

"It's too small. It has only around a twentieth Earth's sun's mass. It should be a planet: a brown dwarf, like a big, fat Jovian. It shouldn't burn—*not yet*. You understand that stars form from the interstellar medium—gas and dust, originally just Big-Bang hydrogen and helium. But stars bake heavy elements, like metals, in their interiors, and eject them back into the medium when the stars die. So as time goes on, the medium is increasingly polluted."

Impatiently I snapped, "And the point—"

"The point is that an increase in impurities in the medium lowers the critical mass needed for a star to be big enough to burn hydrogen. Smaller stars start lighting up. Lieutenant, that star shouldn't be shining. Not in this era, not for trillions of years yet; the interstellar medium is too clean. . . . You know, it's so small that its surface temperature isn't thousands of degrees, like Earth's sun, but the freezing point of water. That is a star with ice clouds in its atmosphere. There may even be liquid water on its surface."

I looked up, wishing I could see the frozen star better. Despite the urgency of the moment I shivered, confronted by strangeness, a vision from trillions of years downstream.

Tilo said bookishly, "What does this mean? It means that out here in the halo, something, some agent, is making the interstellar medium dirtier than it ought to be. The only way to do that is by *making the stars grow old*." He waved a hand at the cluttered sky. "And if you look, you can see it all over this part of the halo; the H-R diagrams are impossibly skewed. . . ."

I shook my head; I was far out of my depth. What could make a star grow old too fast? . . . Oh. "Dark matter?"

"The matter we're made of—baryonic matter, protons and neutrons and the rest—is only about a tenth the universe's total. The rest is dark matter: subject only to gravity and the weak nuclear force, impervious to electromagnetism. Dark matter came out of the Big Bang, just like the baryonic stuff. As our galaxy coalesced the dark matter was squeezed out of the disc. . . . But this is the domain of dark matter, Lieutenant. Out here in the halo."

"And this stuff can affect the ageing of stars."

"Yes. A dark matter concentration in the core of a star can change temperatures, and so affect fusion rates."

"You said *an agent* was ageing the stars." I thought that over. "You make it sound intentional."

He was cautious now, an academician who didn't want to commit himself. "The stellar disruption appears nonrandom."

Through all the jargon, I tried to figure out what this

meant. "Something is *using* the dark matter? . . . Or are there life forms *in* the dark matter? And what does that have to do with the Xeelee, and the problems here on Shade?"

His face twisted. "I haven't figured out the links yet. There's a lot of history. I need my data desk," he said plaintively.

I pulled my chin, thinking of the bigger picture. "Academician, you're on an assignment for the admiral. Do you think you're finding what he wants to hear?"

He eyed me carefully. "The admiral is part of a—grouping—within the Navy that is keen to go to war, even to provoke conflict. Some call them extremists. Kard's actions have to be seen in this light."

Actually, I'd heard such rumors, but I stiffened. "He's my commanding officer. That's all that matters."

Tilo sighed. "Mine too, in a sense. But—"

"Lethe," Lian said suddenly. "Sorry, sir. But that mud is moving *fast*."

So it was, I saw.

The flow was shaped by the morphology of the valley, but its front was tens of meters high, and it would soon reach the village. And I could see that the gush out of the mountain's side showed no signs of abating. The mud was evidently powerfully corrosive; the land's green coat was ripped away to reveal bare rock, and the mud was visibly eating away at the walls of the valley itself. I saw soil and rock collapse into the flow. Overlaying the crack of tree trunks and the clatter of rock, there was a noise like the feet of a vast running crowd, and a sour, sulphurous smell hit me.

"I can't believe how fast this stuff is rising," I said to Tilo. "The volume you'd need to fill up a valley like this—"

"You and I are used to spacecraft, Lieutenant. The dimensions of human engineering. Planets are *big*. And when they turn against you—"

"We can still get you out of here. With these suits we can get you over that bridge and to the transport—"

"What about the villagers?"

I was aware of the woman, Doel, standing beside me

silently. Which, of course, made me feel worse than if she'd yelled and begged.

"We have mixed objectives," I said weakly.

There was a scream. We looked down the ridge and saw that the mud had already reached the lower buildings. A young couple with a kid were standing on the roof of a low hut, about to get cut off.

Lian said, "Sir?"

I waited one more heartbeat, as the mud began to wash over that hut's porch.

"Lethe, Lethe." I ran down the ridge until I hit the mud.

Even with the suit's augmentation the mud was difficult stuff to wade through—lukewarm, and with a consistency like wet cement. The stench was bad enough for me to pull my visor over my mouth. On the mud's surface were dead fish that must have jumped out of the river to escape the heat. There was a lot of debris in the flow, from dust to pebbles to small boulders: no wonder it was so abrasive.

By the time I reached the little cottage I was already tiring badly.

The woman was bigger, obviously stronger than the man. I had her take her infant over her head, while I slung the man over my shoulder. With me leading, and the woman grabbing onto my belt, we waded back toward the higher ground.

All this time the mud rose relentlessly, filling up the valley as if it had been dammed, and every step sapped my energy.

Lian and Doel helped us out of the dirt. I threw myself to the ground, breathing hard. The young woman's legs had been battered by rocks in the flow; she had lost one sandal, and her trouser legs had been stripped away.

"We're already cut off from the bridge," Lian said softly.

I forced myself to my feet. I picked out a building—not the largest, not the highest, but a good compromise. "That one. We'll get them onto the roof. I'll call for another pickup."

"Sir, but what if the mud keeps rising?"

"Then we'll think of something else," I snapped. "Let's get on with it."

She was crestfallen, but she ran to help as Doel improvised a ladder from a trellis fence.

My first priority was to get Tilo safely lodged on the roof. Then I began to shepherd the locals up there. But we couldn't reach all of them before the relentless rise of the mud left us all ankle-deep. People began to clamber up to whatever high ground they could find—verandas, piles of boxes, the ground transports, even rocks. Soon maybe a dozen were stranded, scattered around a landscape turning gray and slick.

I waded in once more, heading toward two young women who crouched on the roof of a small building, like a storage hut. But before I got there the hut, undermined, suddenly collapsed, pitching the women into the flow. One of them bobbed up and was pushed against a stand of trees, where she got stuck, apparently unharmed. But the other tipped over and slipped out of sight.

I reached the woman in the trees and pulled her out. The other was gone.

I hauled myself back onto the roof for a break. All around us the mud flowed, a foul-smelling gray river, littered with bits of wood and rock.

I'd never met that woman. It was as if I had become part of this little community, all against my will, as we huddled together on that crudely built wooden roof. Not to mention the fact that I now wouldn't be able to fulfill my orders completely.

The loss was visceral. I prepared to plunge back into the flow.

Tilo grabbed my arm. "No. You are exhausted. Anyhow you have a call to make, remember?"

Lian spoke up. "Sir. Let me go," she said awkwardly, "I can manage that much."

Redemption time for this marine. "Don't kill yourself," I told her.

With a grin she slid off the roof.

Briskly, I used my suit's comms system to set up a fresh

link to the Spline. I requested another pickup—was told it was impossible—and asked for Kard.

Tilo requested a Virtual data desk. He fell on it as soon as it appeared. His relief couldn't have been greater, as if the mud didn't exist.

When they grasped the situation I had gotten us all into, Admiral Kard and Commissary Xera both sent down Virtual avatars. The two of them hovered over our wooden roof, clean of the mud, gleaming like gods among people made of clay.

Kard glared at me. "What a mess, Lieutenant."

"Yes, sir."

"You should have gotten Tilo over that damn bridge while you could. We're heavily constrained by the Xeelee operations. You realize we probably won't be able to get you out of here alive."

It struck me as somewhat ironic that in the middle of a galaxy-spanning military crisis I was to be killed by mud. But I had made my choice. "So I understand."

"But," Xera said, her thin face fringed by blocky pixels, "he has completed his primary mission, which is to deliver Tilo's data back to us."

Kard closed his Eyes, and his image flickered; I imagined Tilo's data and interpretations pouring into the processors that sustained this semiautonomous Virtual image, tightly locked into Kard's original sensorium. Kard said, "Lousy prioritization. Too much about this *dark matter* crud, Academician."

Xera said gently, "You were here on assignment from your masters in the Navy, with a specific purpose. But it's hard to close your eyes to the clamoring truth, isn't it, Academician?"

Tilo sighed, his face mud-covered.

"We must discuss this," Kard snapped. "All of us, right now. We have a decision to make, a recommendation to pass up the line—and we need to assess what Tilo has to tell us, in case we can't retrieve him."

I understood immediately what he meant. I felt a deep thrill. Even the locals stirred, apparently aware that something momentous was about to happen, even in the midst of their own misfortunes, stuck as we were on that battered wooden roof.

So it began.

At first Tilo wasn't helpful.

"It isn't clear that this is Xeelee action, deliberately directed against humans." Despite Kard's glare, he persisted, "I'm sorry, Admiral, but it isn't *clear*. Look at the context." He pulled up historical material—images, text that scrolled briefly in the murky air. "This is not a new story. There is evidence that human scientists were aware of dark-matter contamination of the stars *before* the beginning of the Third Expansion. It seems an engineered human being was sent into Sol itself. . . . An audacious project. But this was largely lost in the Qax Extirpation, and after that—well, we had a galaxy to conquer. There was a later incident, a project run by the Silver Ghosts, but—"

Kard snapped, "What do the Xeelee care about dark matter?"

Tilo rubbed tired eyes with grubby fists. "However exotic they are, the Xeelee are baryonic life forms, like us. It isn't in their interests for the suns to die young, any more than for us." He shrugged. "Perhaps they are trying to stop it. Perhaps *that's* why they have come here, to the halo. Nothing to do with us—"

Kard waved a Virtual hand at Mount Perfect's oozing wounds. "Then why all this, just as they show up? Coincidence?"

"Admiral—"

"This isn't a trial, Tilo," Kard said. "We don't need absolute proof. The imagery—human refugees, Xeelee nightfighters swooping overhead—will be all we need."

Xera said dryly, "Yes. All we need to sell a war to the Coalition, the governing councils, and the people of the Expansion. This is wonderful for you, isn't it, Admiral? It's what the Navy has been waiting for, along with its Academy cronies. An excuse to attack."

Kard's face was stony. "The cold arrogance of you cosseted intellectuals is sometimes insufferable. It's true that the Navy is ready to fight, Commissary. That's our job. We have the plans in place."

"But does the existence of the plans *require* their fulfillment? And let's remember how hugely the Navy itself will benefit. As the lead agency, a war would clearly support the Navy's long-term political goals."

Kard glared. "We all have something to gain."

And they began to talk, rapidly, about how the different agencies of the Coalition would position themselves in the event of a war.

The military arms, like the Pilots and the Communicators, would naturally ally with the Navy, and would benefit from an increase in military spending. Academic arms like the great Libraries on Earth would be refocused; there was thought to be a danger that with their monopoly on information they were becoming too powerful. Even the Guardians—the Expansion's internal police force—would find a new role: the slowly rising tide of petty crime and illegal economic operations would surely reverse, and the Guardians could return to supporting the Commission in the policing of adherence to the Druz Doctrine—not to mention enforcing the draft.

A lot of this went over my head. I got the sense of the great agencies as shadowy independent empires, engaging in obscure and shifting alliances—like the current links between Navy and Academies, designed to counter the Commission's intellectual weight. And now each agency would consider the possibility of a war as an opportunity to gain political capital.

It was queasy listening. But there's a lot I didn't want to know about how the Coalition is run. Still don't, in fact.

". . . And then there is the economic argument," Kard was saying. "It is as if the Third Expansion itself *is* a war, an endless war against whoever stands in our way. Our economy is on a permanent war-time footing. Let there be no mistake—we could not coexist with the Xeelee, for they would forever represent a ceiling to our ambitions, a ceiling under which we would ultimately wither. We need continued growth—and so a confrontation with the Xeelee is ultimately inevitable." He leaned forward. "And there is more. Xera, *think how much the Commission itself stands to benefit.*

"You Commissaries are responsible for maintaining the unity of mankind; the common principles, common purpose, the *belief* that has driven the Expansion so far. But isn't it obvious that you are failing? Look at this place." He waved a Virtual hand through Doel's hair; the woman flinched, and the hand broke up into drifting pixels. "This woman is a *mother*, apparently some kind of matriarch to her extended *family*. It's as if Hama Druz never existed.

"If the Druz Doctrine were to collapse, the Commission would have no purpose. Think of the good you do, for you know so much better than the mass of mankind how they should think, feel, live, and die. Your project is humanitarian! And it has to continue. We need a purification. An ideological cleansing. And that's what the bright fire of war will give us."

I could see that his arguments, aimed at the Commissary's vanity and self-interest, were leaving a mark.

Tilo was still trying to speak. He showed me more bits of evidence he had assembled on his data desk. "I think I know now why the volcanism started here. *This planet* has an unusually high dark matter concentration in its core. Under such densities the dark matter annihilates with ordinary matter and creates heat—"

I listened absently. "Which creates the geological upheaval."

He closed his eyes, thinking. "Here's a scenario. The Xeelee have been driving dark matter creatures out of the frozen star—and, fleeing, they have lodged here—and that's what set off the volcanism. It was all inadvertent. The Xeelee are trying to *save stars*, not harm humans. . . ."

But nobody paid any attention to that. For, I realized, we had already reached a point where evidence didn't matter.

Kard turned to the people of the village, muddy, exhausted, huddled together on their rooftop. "What of you? *You* are the citizens of the Expansion. There are reformers who say you have had enough of expansion and conflict, that we should seek stability and peace. Well, you have heard what we have had to say, and you have seen our mighty ships in the sky. Will you live out your lives on this drifting rock, helpless before a river of mud—or will you transcend your birth and die for an epic cause? War makes everything new. War is the wildest poetry. *Will you join me?*"

Those ragged-ass, dirt-scratching, orthodoxy-busting farmers hesitated for a heartbeat. You couldn't have found a less likely bunch of soldiers for the Expansion.

But, would you believe, they started cheering the admiral: every one of them, even the kids. Lethe, it brought a tear to my eye.

Even Xera seemed coldly excited now.

Kard closed his Eyes; metal seams pushed his eyelids into ridges. "A handful of people in this desolate, remote place. And yet a new epoch is born. They are listening to us, you know—listening in the halls of history. And *we* will be remembered forever."

Tilo's expression was complex. He clapped his hands, and the data desk disappeared in a cloud of pixels, leaving his work unfinished.

We mere fleshy types had to stay on that rooftop through the night. We could do nothing but cling to each other, as the muddy tide rose slowly around us, and the kids cried from hunger.

When the sunsats returned to the sky, the valley was transformed. The channels had been gouged sharp and deep by the lahar, and the formerly agricultural plain had been smothered by lifeless gray mud, from which only occasional trees and buildings protruded.

But the lahar was flowing only sluggishly. Lian cautiously climbed to the edge of the roof and probed at the mud with her booted foot. "It's very thick."

Tilo said, "Probably the water has drained out of it."

Lian couldn't stand on the mud, but if she lay on it she didn't sink. She flapped her arms and kicked, and she skidded over the surface. Her face gray with the dirt, she laughed like a child. "Sir, look at me! It's a lot easier than trying to swim. . . ."

So it was, when I tried it myself.

And that was how we got the villagers across the flooded valley, one by one, to the larger township—not that much was left of that by now—where the big transport had waited to take us off. In the end we lost only one of the villagers, the young woman who had been overwhelmed by the surge. I tried to accept that I'd done my best to fulfill my contradictory mission objectives—and that, in the end, was the most important outcome for me.

As we lifted, Mount Perfect loosed another eruption.

Tilo, cocooned in a med cloak, stood beside me in an observation blister, watching the planet's mindless fury. He said, "You know, you can't stop a lahar. It just goes the way it wants to go. Like this war, it seems."

"I guess."

"We understand so little. We *see* so little. But when you add us together we combine into huge historical forces that none of us can deflect, any more than you can dam or divert a mighty lahar. . . ."

And so on. I made an excuse and left him there.

I went down to the sick bay, and watched Lian tending to the young from the village. She was patient, competent, calm. I had relieved her of her regular duties, as she was one of the few faces here that was familiar to the kids, who were pretty traumatized. I felt proud of that young marine. She had grown up a lot during our time on Shade.

And as I watched her simple humanity, I imagined a trillion such acts, linking past and future, history and destiny, a great tapestry of hard work and goodwill that united mankind into a mighty host that would some day rule a galaxy.

To tell the truth I was bored with Tilo and his niggling. *War!* It was magnificent. It was inevitable.

I didn't understand what had happened down on Shade, and I didn't care. What did it matter *how* the war had started, in truth or lies? We would soon forget about dark matter and the Xeelee's obscure, immense projects, just as we had before; we humans didn't think in such terms. All that mattered was that the war was here, at last.

The oddest thing was that none of it had anything to do with the Xeelee themselves. Any enemy would have served our purposes just as well.

I began to wonder what it would mean for me. I felt my heart beat faster, like a drumbeat.

We flew into a rising cloud of ash, and bits of rock clattered against our hull, frightening the children.

The Albertine Notes

RICK MOODY

Rick Moody lives in New York City and is not essentially a genre writer but a distinguished contemporary writer of literary ambition. He is the author of Demonology, Purple America, The Ring of Brightest Angels Around Heaven, *and* The Ice Storm and Garden State. *He is a past recipient of the Addison Metcalf Award and a Guggenheim fellowship. He says, in a Powells.com interview, "Literature precedes genre. Genre is a bookstore problem, not a literary problem. It helps people know what section to browse, but I don't care about that stuff. I'm trying to stay close to language first and foremost and make sure that the paragraphs sing, that it sounds like music to me. What genre it falls under is only of interest later." He also used to write the* Details *comic strip ("which was really fun").*

"The Albertine Notes" was published in McSweeney's Thrilling Tales, *an original anthology of genre fiction edited by Michael Chabon, which was to our minds the most ambitious fiction anthology of the year, in a year with many strong contenders. This novella is a superior work of SF, in the exclusive and distinguished tradition of Philip K. Dick's "Faith of Our Fathers" and Gene Wolfe's "Seven American Nights," of stories that call into question the nature of reality in an SF setting involving drugs, politics, and present a character struggling to hold on to life and sanity. It is perhaps the best SF story of the year.*

Albertine, solace of a city in ruins. Any memory you wanted, anytime you wanted it. All for the low, low price of—history itself.

The first time I got high all I did was make sure these notes came out all right. I mean, I wanted the girl at the magazine to offer me work again, and that was going to happen only if the story sparkled. There wasn't much work then because of the explosion. The girl at the magazine was saying, "Look, you don't have to like the assignment, just do the assignment. If you don't want it there are people lined up behind you." And she wasn't kidding. There really were people lined up. Out in reception. An AI receptionist, in a makeshift lobby, in a building on Staten Island, the least-affected precinct of the beleaguered City of New York. Writers spilling into the foyer, shouting at the robot receptionist. All eager to show off their clips.

The editor was called Tara. She had turquoise hair. She looked like a girl I knew when I was younger. Where was that girl now? Back in the go-go days you could yell a name at the TV and it would run a search on the identities associated with that name. For a price. Credit card records, toll plaza visits, loan statements, you set the parameters. My particular Web video receiver, in fact, had a little pop-up window in the corner of the image that said, *Want to see what your wife is doing right now?* Was I a likely customer for this kind of snooping based on past purchases? Anyway, recreational detection and character assassination, that was all *before* Albertine.

Street name for the buzz of a lifetime. Bitch goddess of the overwhelming past. Albertine. Rapids in the river of time. Skin pop a little bit, or take up the celebrated Albertine eyedropper, and any memory you've ever had is available to you all over again. That and more. Not a memory like you've experienced it before, not a little tremor in some *presque vu* register of your helter-skelter consciousness: Oh yeah, I remember when I ate peanut butter and jelly with Serena in Boston Commons and drank rum out of paper cups. No, the actual event itself, completely renewed, playing in front of you as though you were experiencing it for the first time. There's Serena in blue jeans with patches on the knee, the green Dartmouth sweatshirt that goes with her eyes, drinking the rum a little too fast and spitting up some of it, picking her teeth with her deep red nails, shade called "lycanthrope," and there's the taste of super-chunky peanut butter, in the sandwiches, stale pretzel rods. Here you are, the two of you, walking around that part of the Commons with all those willows. She lets slip your hand because your palms are moist. The smell of a city park at the moment when a September shower dampens the pavement, car exhaust, a mist hanging in the air at dusk, the sound of kids fighting over the rules of softball, a homeless dude, scamming you for a sip of your rum.

Get the idea?

It almost goes without saying that Albertine appeared in a certain socioeconomic sector not long after the blast. When you're used to living a comfortable middle-class life, when you're used to going to the organic farmers' market on the weekend, maybe a couple of dinners out at that new Indian place, you're bound to become very uncomfortable when fifty square blocks of your city suddenly looks like NASA photos of Mars. You're bound to look for some relief when you're camped in a school gymnasium pouring condensed milk over government-issued cornflakes. Under the circumstances, you're going to prize your memories, right? So you'll skin pop some Albertine, or you'll use the eyedropper, hold open your lid, and go searching back through the halcyon days. Afternoons in the stadium, those stadium lights on the turf, the first roar of the crowd. Or how about your first concert? Or your first kiss?

Only going to cost you twenty-five bucks.

I'm Kevin Lee. Chinese-American, third generation, which doesn't mean my dad worked in a delicatessen to get me into MIT. It means my father was an IT venture capitalist and my mother was a microbiologist. I grew up in Newton, Mass., but I also lived in northern California for a while. I came to New York City to go to Fordham, dropped out, and started writing about the sciences for one of the alternative weeklies. It was a start. But the offices of the newspaper, all of its owners, a large percentage of its shareholders, and nine-tenths of its reporting staff were incinerated. Not like I need to bring all of that up again. If you need to assume anything, assume that all silences from now on have grief in them.

One problem with Albertine was that the memories she screened were not all good, naturally. Albertine didn't guarantee good memories. In fact, Albertine guaranteed at least a portion of pretty awful memories. One guy I interviewed, early on when I was chasing the story, he spoke about having only memories of jealousy. He got a bad batch, probably too many additives, and all he could see in his mind's eye were these moments of intense jealousy. He was even weeping when we spoke. On the comedown. I'd taken him out to an all-night diner. Where Atlantic Avenue meets up with Conduit. Know that part of the city? A beautiful part of the city, a neglected part. Ought to have been a chill in the early autumn night. Air force jets were landing at the airport in those days. The guy, we'll say his name is Bob, he was telling me about the morning he called a friend, Nina, to meet her for a business breakfast. In the middle of the call Nina told him that his wife, Maura, had become her lover. He remembered everything about this call, the exact wording of the revelation. *Bob, Maura has been attracted to me as far back as your wedding*. He remembered the excruciating pauses. He could overhear the rustling of bedclothes. All these things he could picture, just like they were happening, and even the things he imagined during the phone call, which took place seventeen years ago. What Nina had done to Maura in bed, what dildo they used. It was seventeen years later on Atlantic and Conduit, and Maura was vaporized, or that's what Bob said, "Jesus, Maura is dead and I never told her I regretted all of that, I never told her what was great about the years together, and I'll never have that chance now." He was inconsolable, but I kept asking questions. Because I'm a reporter. I put it together that he'd spent fifty bucks on two doses of Albertine. Six months after the thyroid removal, here he was. Bob was just hoping to have one sugary memory—of swimming in the pond in Danbury, the swimming hole with the rope swing. Remember that day? And all he could remember was that his wife had slept with his college friend, and that his brother took the girl he liked in high school. Like jealousy was the single color of his life. Like the atmosphere was three parts jealousy, one part oxygen.

That's what Albertine was whispering in his ear.

Large-scale drug dealing, it's sort of like beta-testing. There are unscrupulous people around. Nobody knows how a chemical is going to behave until the guinea pigs have lined up. FDA thinks it knows, like when it rubber-stamps some compound that makes you grow back hair you lost during chemotherapy. But the feds know nothing. Try giving your drug to a hundred and fifty thousand disenfranchised members of the new middle-class poor in a recently devastated American city. Do it every day for almost a year. Allow people to mix in randomly their favorite inert substances.

There were lots of stories. Lots of different experiences. Lots of fibs, exaggerations, innuendoes, rumors. Example: not only did Albertine cause bad memories as frequently as good memories—this is the lore—but she also allowed you to *remember the future*. This is what Tara told me when she assigned me the 2500 words. "Find out if it's true. Find out if we can get to the future on it."

"What would you do with it?"

"None of your business," she said, and then like she was covering her tracks, "I'd see if I was ever going to get a promotion."

Well, here's one example. The story of Deanna, whose name I'm also changing for her own protection: "I was going to church after the blast, you know, because I was kind of feeling like God should be doing something about all the heartache. I mean, maybe that's simpleminded or something. I don't care. I was in church and it was a beautiful place. Any church still standing was a beautiful place, when you had those horrible clouds overhead all the time and everybody getting sick. Fact of the matter is, while I was there in church, during what should have been a really calm time, instead of thinking that the gospels were good news, I was having a vision. I don't know what else to call it. It was like in the movies, when the movie goes into some kind of flashback. Except in this vision, I saw myself driving home from church, and I saw a car pulling ahead of me out onto the road by the reservoir, and I had this feeling that the car pulling out toward the reservoir, which was a twenty-year-old model of one of those minivans, was some kind of bad omen, you know? So I went to my priest, and I told him what I thought, that this car had some bad intention, at least in my mind's eye, you know, I could see it, I could see that Jesus was telling me this, *Better watch out at the reservoir*. Some potion is going to be emptied into the reservoir. I have seen it, I have seen it. The guys doing it, they're emptying jugs in and they definitely have mustaches. They're probably from some desert country. The priest took me to the bishop, and I repeated everything I knew, about the Lord and what he had told me, and so I had an audience with the archbishop. The archbishop said, 'You have to tell me if Jesus really told you this. Did Jesus tell you personally? Is this a genuine message from the Christ?' In this office with a lot of dusty books on the dusty shelves. You could tell that they were all really hungry to be in the room with the word of the Christ, and who wouldn't feel that way? Everybody is desperate, right? But then one of them says, 'Roll up your sleeves, please.' "

Deanna was shown the door. Because of the needle tracks. Now she's working down by the Gowanus Expressway.

The archbishop did give the tip to the authorities, however, just to be on the safe side, and the authorities did stop a

Ford Explorer on the way to the reservoir in Katonah. And Deanna's story was just one along these lines. Many Albertine users began reporting "memories" of things that were yet to happen. Outcomes of local elections, declines in various international stocks, the intensity of the upcoming hurricane season. The dealers, whether skeptical or believing on this point, saw big profits in the mythology. Because garbage heads and gamblers often live right next door to one another, know what I mean? One vice is like another. Soon there were those scraggly guys that you used to see at the track. These guys were all looking to cop from the man in Red Hook, or East New York, and they were sitting like autistics in a room with Sheetrock torn from the walls, no electricity, no running water, people pissing themselves, refusing food, and they were in search of the name of the greyhound that was going to take the next race. Maybe they could bet the trifecta? Teeth were falling out of the heads of these bettors, and their hair falling out, because they believed if they just hung on long enough, they would receive the vision.

Now that's marketing.

Logically speaking, there were some issues with a belief system like this. On Albertine, the visions of the past were mixed up with the alleged future, of course. And sometimes these were nightmarish visions. You had to know where to cast your gaze. There was no particular targeting of receptors. The drug wasn't advanced. It was like using a lawn mower to harvest wildflowers. I shook one girl awake, Cassandra, down in the Hot Zone in Bed-Stuy. I knew Cassandra was a bullshit name, the kind of name you'd tell a reporter. It was a still night, coming on toward December, bitter cold, because the debris cloud had really fucked with global warming, and I was walking around dictating into a digital recorder, okay? The streets were uninhabited. I mean, take a city from eight million down to four and a half million, suddenly everything seems kind of empty. And this is a pedestrian town anyhow. Now more than ever. I was on my way to interview an epidemiologist who claimed that while on Albertine he'd had a memory of the proper way to eradicate the drug. He'd tell me if I would remunerate him. And maybe Tara would reimburse me, because I had run through most of the few hundred dollars I had in cash before my bank was wiped off the map. And I'd already sold blood and volunteered for a dream lab.

But on the way to the epidemiologist, I saw this girl nodding out on a swing, an old wooden swing, the kind that usually gets stolen in the projects. Over by the middle school in the Hot Zone. I picked up her arm; she didn't even seem to notice at first. I lifted up her arm; I turned it over. Like I couldn't tell from the rings under the eyes, those black bruises that say, *This one has remembered too much.* I checked her arms anyway. Covered with lesions.

I said, "Hey, I'm doing a story for one of those tits-and-lit mags. About Albertine. Wondering if I can ask you a few questions."

Her voice frail at first, almost as if it was the first voice ever used:

"Ask me any question. I'm like the oracle at Delphi, boyfriend."

Sort of a dark-haired girl, and she sort of reminded me of Serena. Wearing this red scarf on her head. A surge from her voice, like I'd heard it before, like maybe I was almost verging on something from the past. I figured I'd try out Cassandra, see what kind of a fact-gathering resource she could be, see where it led. It beat watching the Hasidim in Crown Heights fighting with the West Indians. Man, I'd had enough with the Hasidim and the Baptists and their rants about *end times*. The problem was that Albertine, bitch goddess, kept giving conflicting reports about which end times we were going to get.

"What's my name?" I said.

"Your name is Kevin Lee. You're from Massachusetts."

"Okay, uh, what am I writing about?"

"You're writing about Albertine, and you're way in over your head already. And the batteries on your recording device are going to run out soon."

"Thanks for the tip. Are we going to kiss?"

A reality-testing question, get it?

No inflection at all, Cassandra said: "Sure. We are. But not now. Later."

"What do you know about the origins of Albertine?"

"What do you want to know?"

"Are you high now?"

Which was like asking if she'd ever seen rain.

"Are you high enough to see the origins from where you are sitting?"

"I'd need to have been there to have a memory of it."

"What have you heard about it?" I said.

"Everybody's heard something."

"I haven't."

"You aren't listening. Everybody knows."

"Then tell me," I said.

"You have to be *inside*. Take the drug; then you'll be inside."

Up at the corner, a blue-and-white sedan—NYPD—as rare as the white tiger in this neighborhood. The police were advance men for the cartels. They had no peacetime responsibility any longer, except that they made sure the trade proceeded without any interference. For this New York's Finest got a cut, a portion of which they tithed back to the city. So the syndicate was subsidizing the City of New York, the way I saw it. Subsidizing the rebuilding, subsidizing the government, so that government would have buildings, underground bunkers, treatment centers, whole departments devoted to Albertine, to her care and protection.

Fox, a small-time dealer and friend of Bob, one of my sources, was the first person I could find who'd float these conspiratorial theories. Right before he disappeared. And he wasn't the only one who disappeared. Bob stopped returning my calls too. Not that it amounted to much, a disappearance, here and there. Our city was outside of history now, beyond surveillance. People disappeared.

"I don't buy the conspiracy angle," I said to Cassandra. "Been there, done that."

Her eyes fluttered like she was fighting off an invasion of butterflies.

"Well, actually . . ." she said.

"Government isn't competent enough for conspiracy. Government is a bunch of guys in a subbasement somewhere, in Englewood, waiting for the war to blow over. Guys hoping they won't have to see what everyone out on the street has seen."

I helped her from the swing. She was thin like a greyhound, just as distracted. The chains on the swing clattered as she dismounted.

It wasn't that hard to be at the center of the Albertine story, see, because there was no center. Everywhere, people were either selling the drug or using the drug, and if they were using the drug, they were in its thrall, which is the thrall of memory. You could see them lying around everywhere. In all public places. Albertine expanded to fill any container. If you thought she was confined to Red Hook, it seemed for a while like she *was* only in Red Hook. But then if you looked in Astoria, she was in Astoria too. As if it were the activity of observing that somehow turned her up. More you looked, more you saw. A city whose citizens, when outdoors, looked preoccupied, or vacant. If inside, almost paralytic. I couldn't tell you how many times that week I happened to gaze in a ground-floor window and saw people staring at television screens that were turned off.

"People think the government has the skills to launch conspiracies. But if they were good enough, then they'd be good enough to track some guy who brings a suitcase detonator into the country across the Canadian border and has the uranium delivered to him by messenger. Some messenger on a bike! They'd be good enough to avoid having a third of Manhattan blown up! Or they'd be able to infiltrate the cartels. Or they'd be able to repair all of this. So are we going to kiss now?"

"Later," she said.

I was thinking maybe this conversation had come to an end, that there was no important subtext to the conversation, that Cassandra was just another deep-fried intelligence locked away in the past, and maybe I should have gone on my way to pay off the epidemiologist with the new angle. But then, like she was teasing out a little bit of insider information, she said, "Brookhaven."

Meaning what? Meaning the laboratory?

Of course, the Brookhaven theory, like the MIT theory, like the Palo Alto Research Center theory. These rumors just weren't all that compelling, because everyone had heard them, but for some reason I had this uncanny recognition at the sound of the name of the government facility on Long Island. Then she said that we should *go see the man*.

"I don't know exactly about the beginning, the origin," Cassandra said, "but I've been with someone who does. He'll be there. Where we're going."

"What are you seeing right now?"

"Autumn," she whispered.

It was a coming-down thing. The imagery of Albertine began to move toward the ephemeral, the passing away, leaves mulching, pumpkin seeds, first frost. Was there some neurotransmitter designated as the seat of memory that necessarily had autumn written into it? A chromosome that contained a sensitivity to fall? When I was a kid there were a couple years we lived in northern California, a charmed place, you know, during the tech boom. Those words seem quaint. Like saying *whore with a heart of gold.* I couldn't forget northern California, couldn't forget the redwoods, seals, rugged beaches, the austere Pacific, and when I heard the words I knew what memory I would have if I took the drug, which was the memory of the first autumn that I didn't get to see the seasons change. In northern California, watching the mist creep into the bay, watching the Golden Gate engulfed, watching that city disappear. In northern California, I waited till evening; then I'd go over to the used bookstores in town, because there was always someone in the used bookstores who was from back east. So this would be my memory, a memory of reading, of stealing time from time itself, of years passing while I was reading, hanging out in a patched armchair in the used bookstore in northern California and later on, back in Mass. Maybe I was remembering this memory, or maybe I was constructing it.

We were going over the bridge, the Kosciuszko, where there was only foot traffic these days. Down Metropolitan Ave, from Queens to Brooklyn, over by where the tanks used to be. Not far from the cemetery. You know what you might have seen there? Right? Used to be the skyline, you used to see it there every day, caught in traffic, listening to the all-news format, maybe you got bored of the skyline rising above you, maybe it was like a movie backdrop, there it was again, you'd seen it so many times that it meant nothing, skyscrapers like teeth on the insipid grin of enterprise, cemetery and skyscrapers, nice combination. The greatest city in the world? Once my city was the greatest, but this was not the view anymore, on the night that I walked across there with Cassandra. No more view, right? Because there were the debris clouds, and there was the caustic rain that fell on all the neighborhoods, a rain that made everybody sick afterward, a rain that made people choke and puke. People wore gas masks on the Kosciuszko. Gas masks were the cut-rate fashion statement. South of Citicorp Center, whose tampon-applicator summit had been blown clean off. There was nothing. Show over. Get it? You could see all the way to Jersey, during the day. If the wind was blowing right. Edgewater. You could see the occasional lights of Edgewater. There was no Manhattan to see, and there was no electricity in Manhattan, where the buildings remained. The generating plant downtown had been obliterated. Emergency lights, not much else.

People just turned their backs on Manhattan. They forgot about that island, which was the center of nothing, except maybe the center of society ladies with radiation burns crowding the trauma units at the remaining hospitals. Manhattan was just landfill now. And there are no surprises in a landfill. Unless you're a seagull.

Outer boroughs, that was where the action was. Like this place we were going. It'd been a smelting plant, and the police cars were lined up around it, the cops were all around it like they were the blue border of imagination. It was a ghost factory, and I dictated these impressions, because the digital recorder was still recording. When I played back my notes, there was a section of the playback that was nothing but a sequence of words about autumn, soaping windows, World Series, school supplies, yellow jackets, presidential elections, hurricane season. Who was I trying to kid? I was pretending I was writing a story about Albertine. I was writing nothing.

Cassandra was mumbling: "They were fine-tuning some interrogation aids, or they had made a chemical error with some antidepressants. Or they made progress with ECT therapies, or they saw it in the movies and just duplicated the effects. They figured out how to do it with electrodes, or they figured out how to prompt certain kinds of memories, and then they thought perhaps they could coerce certain kinds of testimony with electrodes. They could torture certain foreign nationals, force confessions from these people, and the confession would be freely signed, because the memories would be true. Who's going to argue with a memory?"

"How do you know all of this?"

We stood in front of a loading dock elevator, and the cops were frozen around us, hands on holsters, cops out front, nervous cops, cops everywhere, and the shadows in the elevator shaft danced, because the elevator was coming for us. The elevator was the only light.

"I can see," Cassandra said.

"In the big sense?"

It was the only time she smiled in the brief period when I knew her. When I was up close enough to see her lesions. People were so busy firing chemicals into their bodies, so busy in the past that they didn't notice. Their cancers were blossoming. They stopped worrying about whether the syringe was dirty or not. And they stopped going to the clinics or the emergency rooms. They let themselves vanish out of the world, like by doing so they could get closer to some point of origin: your mom on your fourth birthday, smiling, holding out her hands, *Darling, it's your birthday!*

She said, "Think biochemistry," and she had the eyedropper out again. "Think quantum mechanics. What would happen if you could harness some of the electrical charges in the brain by bombarding it with certain kinds of free particles?" Her eyes were hopelessly bloodshot. She had a mean case of pink eye. And her pupils were dilated.

"And because it's all about electrical charges, it's all about power, right? And about who has the power."

I was holding her hand, don't know why. Trying to stop her from dribbling more of that shit in her eye. I wasn't under any particular illusion about what was happening. I was lonely. Why hadn't I gone back up to Massachusetts? Why hadn't I called my cousins across town to see if they were okay? I was hustling. I knew things, but I didn't know when to stop researching and when to get down to work. There was always another trapdoor in the history of Albertine, another theory to chase down, some epidemiologist with a new slant. Some street addict, who will tell you things, if you pay.

I knew, for example, that a certain Eduardo Cortez had consolidated himself as a kingpin of the Albertine trade, at least in Manhattan and Brooklyn, and that he occasionally drove his confederates around in a military convoy. Everyone claimed to have seen the convoy, jeeps and hummers. Certain other dealers in the affected neighborhoods, like Mnemonic X in Fort Greene, the 911 Gang in Long Island City, a bunch of them had been *neutralized,* as the language goes, in the gangland style. I knew all of this, and still I walked into the ghost factory in Greenpoint, like I was somebody, not an Asian kid sent by a soft-core porn mag, who rode up in the elevator with a girl whose skin looked like a relief map, a prostitute in a neighborhood where almost everyone was a prostitute. As Fox, Bob's dealer, told me, before he disappeared, You'd be amazed what a woman will do for a dealer.

"When Cortez tied off, you know, everything changed," Cassandra said. It was one of those elevators that took forever. She'd been thinking what I was thinking before I even got to saying it. Her lips were cracked; her teeth were bad. She had once been brilliant, I could tell, or maybe that's just how I wanted it to be. Maybe she'd been brilliant, maybe she'd been at a university once. But now we used different words of praise for those we admired, *shrewd, tough.* And the most elevated term of respect: *alive.* Cortez was Dominican, alive, and thus he was part of the foul-is-fair demographics of Albertine. He was from nowhere, raised up in a badly depressed economy. Cortez had been a bike messenger, and then a delivery truck driver, and some of his associates insisted that his business was still about message delivery. *We just trying to run a business.*

I'd seen the very site of Cortez's modest childhood recently, took me almost ten hours to get there, which tells you nothing. It's a big mistake to measure space in time, after all. Because times change. Still, Cortez had the longest subway ride of anyone in the drug trade. If he wanted to go look after his operatives in Brooklyn, he had to get all the way from northern Manhattan to Brooklyn, and most of those lines didn't run anymore. Under the circumstances, a military convoy was just a good investment.

Washington Heights. Kids playing stickball in the street using old-fashioned boom microphones for baseball bats. There were gangsters with earpieces on stoops up and down the block. What were the memories of these people like? Did they drop, as the addicts put it? Did they use? And what were Cortez's memories like? Memories of middleweight prizefighting at the gym up the block? Maybe. Some drinking with the boys. Some whoring around with the streetwalkers on Upper Broadway. Assignations with Catholic girls in the neighborhood? Cortez had a bad speech impediment, everybody said. Would Albertine make it so that he, in memory, could get as far back as the time before speech acquisition, to the sweet days before the neighborhood kids made fun of him for the way he talked? Could he teach his earlier self better how to say the "s" of American English? To speak with authority? One tipster provided by my magazine had offered sinister opinions about the appearance of Cortez, this Cortez of the assumed name. This tipster, whispering into that most rare landline, had offered the theory that the culture of Albertine itself changed when Cortez appeared, just like with the appearance of the original Cortez, great explorer, bearer of a shipload of smallpox. This was, of course, a variation on the so-called *diachronous theory of abuse patterns* that has turned up a lot in the medical journals recently.

There were traditional kinds of memories before the appearance of Albertine, namely *identity builders,* according to these medical theorists. Like that guy at Brooklyn College, the government anthropologist of Albertine, Ernst Wentworth, Ph.D. Even repressed memory syndrome, in his way of thinking, was an identity builder, because in repressed memory syndrome you learn ultimately to empower yourself, in that you are identifying past abusers and understanding the ramifications of their misdeeds. I hate the word *empowerment,* but this is the terminology Wentworth used. A repetition of stressful memories is, according to his writing, an attempt by an identity to arrive at a solution to stress. Even a calamity, the collapse of a bridge, when remembered by one who has plunged into an icy river, is an identity builder, in that it ultimately engenders the reassurance of the remembering subject. The here and now puts him in the position of being alive all over again, no matter how painful it is to be alive. The Wentworth identity-building theory was the prevailing theory of memory studies, up until Albertine.

Since Albertine arrived on the scene after the blast, theorists eventually needed to consider the blast in all early Albertine phenomena. Figures, right? One night I felt like I started to understand these theories in a dramatic way, in my heart, or what was left of it. I was at the armory, where I slept in a closet, really—used to be a supply closet, and there were still some supplies in there, some rug-cleaning solvents, some spot removers, extra towels. You never know when you might need this stuff. Anyway, the halls outside the supply closet echo; you could hear every whisper, in the halls of the armory. You could hear people coming and going. It wasn't and isn't a great place to live, when you consider that I used to have a studio in the East Village. But compared to living in the great hall itself, where mostly people tried to erect cubicles for themselves, cubicles made out of cardboard or canvas or Sheetrock, the supply closet was not so bad. The process of doling out closets had fallen to an Albertine addict called Bertrand, and when I fixed up Bertrand with Fox and a few other dealers, I got bumped up to the supply closet right away. When moths came after my remaining shirts and sweaters, I had all the insecticide I'd need.

This night I'm describing, I had a breakthrough of dialectical reasoning: I was hearing the blast. You know the conventional wisdom about combat veterans, loud noises suggesting the sharp crack of submachine-gun fire, all that? I thought just the opposite. That certain silences recreated the blast, because there's something about fission, you know it's soundless in a way, it suggests soundlessness, it's a violence contained in the opposite of violence, big effects from preposterously small changes. Say you were one of the four million who survived, you were far enough away that the blast, heat, and radiation could do their damage before the sound reached you, wherever you were. So it follows that the sound of the explosion would be best summoned up in no sound at all. The pauses in the haggard steps of the insomniacs of the armory walking past the door to my closet, this sound was the structured absence in what all our memories were seeking to suppress or otherwise avoid: the truth of the blast.

I'm not a philosopher. But my guess was that eventually people would start *remembering the blast.* You know? How could it be otherwise? I'm not saying I'm the person who came up with the idea; maybe the government mole did. Maybe Ernst Wentworth did. I'm saying, I guess, that all memories verged on being memories of the blast, like footsteps in the echoing corridor outside my supply closet. Memories were like downpours of black raindrops. All noises were examples of the possibility of the noise of the blast, which is the limit of all possibilities of sound, and thus a limit on all possibilities of memory. For a lot of people, the blast was so traumatic they couldn't even remember where they were that day, and I'm one of those people, in case you were wondering. I know I was heading out to Jersey for a software convention in the New Brunswick area. At least, that's what I think I was doing. But I don't know how I got back. When I came to, Manhattan was gone.

People began to have memories of the blast while high.

And people began to die of certain memories on the drug. Makes perfect sense. And this is part of the *diachronous theory of abuse patterns* that I was just talking about. First, Conrad Dixon, a former academic himself, was found dead in his apartment in the Flatbush section of Brooklyn, no visible sign of death, except that he'd just been seen scamming a bunch of dealers in Crown Heights. Was the death by reason of poisonous additives in the drug cocktail? That'd be a pretty good theory, if he were the only person who died this way, but all at once, a lot of people started dying, and it was my contention, anyhow, that they were remembering the blast. There were the bad memories in an ordinary fit of Albertine remembering, and then there was the memory of this moment of all moments, a sense of the number of people eliminated in the carnage, a sense of the kind of motive of the guy or guys, men or women, who managed to smuggle the dirty uranium device into the country and then have it delivered, etc. An innocent thing when Conrad Dixon, or the others like him, first did what they did. In the early curve of the epidemic, everybody used Albertine alone, because memories are most often experienced alone. And the recitation of them, that's like dull plot summaries from movies: Oh, let me tell you about the time that I was in Los Angeles, and I saw such and such a starlet at the table next to me, or about the time I broke my arm trying to white-water raft, whatever your pathetic memory is. It's all the same, the brimming eyes of your daughter when she was a toddler and accidentally got a bump on her head, I don't give a fuck, because I know what happened with Conrad Dixon, which is that he put the needle in his arm, and then he was back in midtown and looking down at the lower part of the island where he had spent his entire youth. A good thing, sure, that Conrad, that day, had to take that programmer's certification test up at Columbia, because instead of becoming a faint shadow on the side of some building on Union Square, he could see the entire neighborhood that he worked in subsumed in perfect light, and he could feel the nausea rising in him, and he could see the cloud's outstretched arms, and all the information in him was wiped aside, he was a vacuum of facts, a memory vacuum, and again and again, he could see the light, feel the incineration, and he knew something about radiation that he hadn't known before, about the light on the surface of the stars, giver of all things. He knew that he was sick, knew that again he was going to have to live through the first few days, when everyone was suffering the poisoning of cells, the insides of them liquifying. Don't make me walk you through it, the point is that Albertine gave back the blast, when Conrad had hoped never to experience the blast again, and Conrad was so stuck in the loop of this recollection that he could do nothing else, but die, because that was the end of the blast; whether in actual space, or on the recollected plane, whether in the past, or the present or the future, whether in ideas or reality, the blast was about death.

What's this have to do with Eduardo Cortez? Well, it has to do with the fact that Cortez's play for control of the Albertine cartel came exactly at the moment of highest density of deaths from Albertine overdose or drug interaction. I refer you back again to the *diachronous theory of abuse patterns*. See what I mean? The big question is how does Cortez, by his presence, affect the way that Albertine was used? The mixture of the chemical, if it's even a chemical, certainly didn't change all that much, had not changed, during the course of the twelve months that it grew into a street epidemic. Can we attribute the differences in abuse patterns to any other factors? Why is it Cortez who seemed to be responsible for the blast intruding into everybody's memory?

My notes for the magazine are all about skepticism. I knew I was holding Cassandra's hand now, prostitute in rags, woman with the skeletal body, while she was using the eyedropper, and I know this might seem like a hopeful gesture. Like some good could come out of it all. I heard her sigh. The cage of the elevator, at a crawl, passed a red emergency light on the wall of the shaft. Hookers were always erotic about nonerotic things. Time, for example. The elsewhere of time amok was all over her, like she was coming to memories of a time before prostitution. I was holding her hand. I was disoriented. I checked my watch. I mean I checked what day it was. I had been assigned to the Albertine story for two weeks, according to my Rolex knockoff—which had miraculously survived the electromagnetic pulse—but I could swear that it had just been two days before that I'd been hanging out in the offices of the soft-core porn mag, the offices with the bulletproof glass and the robot receptionist out front. When had I last been back to the supply closet to sleep? When had I last eaten? Wasn't it last night, the evening with the footsteps in the corridor, and the revelation about the blast? I was holding Cassandra's hand, because she had this tenuous link to the facts of Albertine, and this seemed like the last chance to master the story, to get it down somehow, instead of being consumed by it.

This is my scoop then. The scoop is that, suddenly, *I saw what she was seeing*.

Cassandra said, "Watch this."

Pay close attention. I saw a close-up, in my head I saw it, like from some Web movie, a guy's arm, a man's arm, an arm covered with scars, almost furry, it was so hairy, and then a hand pulling tight a belt around a bicep, jamming in a needle, depressing the plunger, a grunt of initial discomfort. Then the voice of the guy, thick accent, maybe a Puerto Rican accent, announcing his threats, "I'm going back to the Lower East Side, and I'm going to cap the motherfucker, see if I don't." Definite speech impediment. A problem with sibilance. Then this guy, this dude was looking over at Cassandra, she was in the scene, not in the stairwell, where we were at least theoretically standing, but she was someway associated with Eduardo Cortez. She was his consort. He was taking her hand, there was a connection of hands, a circular movement of hands, and then we were on a street, and I saw Cortez, in Tompkins Square Park, which doesn't exist anymore, of course, and it was clear that he was searching out a particular white guy, and now, coming through the crowd, here was the guy, looked like an educated man, if you know what I mean, one of those East Village art slumming dudes. Cortez was searching out this guy, kinda grungy, wearing black jeans and a T-shirt, and it was all preordained, and now Cortez had found him.

Lights associated with the thrall of Cassandra's recollection, phantom lights, auras. The particulars were like a migraine. Things were solarized, there were solar flares around the streetlamps. We were bustling in and around the homeless army of Tompkins Square. I could hear my own panicky breathing. I was in a park that didn't exist anymore, and I was seeing Cortez, and I was seeing this guy, this white guy, he had that look where one side of his face, the right side, was different from the other side, so that on the right side, he seemed to be melancholy and placid, whereas on the left side of the face, there was the faintest smirk at all times. The left side was contorted and maybe there were scars there, some kind of slasher's jagged line running from the corner of his mouth to his ear, as if his face too were divided in certain ways, as if his face were a product of erosion, and Cassandra, I guess, was saying, "Let's not do this, okay? Eduardo? Please? Eduardo? We can fix the problem another way." Except that at the same moment what she was saying to me, somehow outside of the memory, outside of the memory belonging to someone else, she was saying, "Do you understand what you're seeing?"

I said, "He's going to—"

"—Kill the guy."

"And that guy is?"

"Addict Number One."

"Who?"

"That guy is the first user," she said. "The very first one."

"And why is he important?"

Cassandra said, "For the sake of control. You don't get it, do you?"

"Tell me," I said.

"Addict Number One is being killed *in a memory.*"

Something coursed in me like a flash flood. A real perception, maybe, or just the blunt feelings of sympathetic drug abuse. When I tried to figure out the enormity of what Cassandra was telling me, I couldn't. I couldn't understand the implications, couldn't understand why she would tell me, because to tell me was to die, far as I could tell, because Fox was dead, Bob was dead, the Mnemonic X boys had been completely wiped out, probably fifty guys, all disappeared, same day, same time, reporters from my old paper were dead. Chasing the story was to chase time itself, and time guarded its secrets.

"How's that possible? That's not possible! How are you going to kill someone in a memory? It doesn't make any sense."

"Right. It doesn't make any sense, but it happened. And it could happen again."

"But a memory isn't a place. It's nowhere but in someone's head. There's not a movie running somewhere. You can't jump up into the screen and start messing with action."

"Just watch and see."

I was thinking about the diachronous theory. The pattern of abuse and dispersal was widest and most threatening at the instant of the murder of Addict Number One, I was guessing, which was about to be revealed as a murder, the first and only murder, I hoped, that I ever needed to witness, because even if he was a smirking guy, someone unliked or ridiculed, even if he was just a drug addict, whatever, Addict Number One was a prodigious rememberer. As the first full-scale Albertine addict, I learned later, he had catalogued loads of memories, for example, light in the West Village, which in July is perfect at sunset on odd-numbered streets in the teens and twenties. It was true. Addict Number One had learned this. If you stood on certain corners and looked west in June and July, at dusk, you would see that the City of New York had sunsets that would have animated the great landscape painters. Or how about the perfect bagel? Addict Number One had sampled many of the fresh bagels of the City of New York, and he compiled notes about the best hot bagels, which were found at a place on University and Thirteenth Street. They were large, soft, and warm. Addict Number One devoted pages to the taste of bagel as it went into your mouth.

Sadly, instead of illuminating the life of Addict Number One, it's my job now to describe the pattern of the dispersal of his brains. The pattern of which was exactly like the pattern of dispersal of radioactive material in lower Manhattan. Cortez held the revolver to the head of Addict Number One, whose expression of complete misunderstanding and disbelief was heartrending, enough so to prove that he had no idea what his murder meant, and Cortez pulled the trigger of the revolver, and Addict Number One fell over like he had never once been a living thing. *Fucking punk-ass junky,* Cortez intoned. Were the baroque memories of Addict Number One now part of all that tissue, splattered on the dog run in Tompkins Square? Was that a memory splashed on that retriever there, gunking up its fur, an electrical impulse, a bit of energy withering in a pool of gore in a city park? I saw it, because Cortez saw it, and Cortez gave the memory to Cassandra, who gave it to me: corpus callosum and basal ganglia on the dogs, on the lawn, and screaming women, the homeless army drawn up near, gazing, silent, as Addict Number One, slain by a drug dealer in memory only, weltered, gasping. His memories slain with him.

It was like this. Even though the memory was just a memory, its effect was real. As real as if it were all happening now. This is like saying that nine-tenths of the universe is invisible, I know. But just bear with me. Cortez's accomplishment was that, according to Cassandra, he'd learned from informers that Addict Number One was once a real person, with a real past (went to NYU, and his name was Paley, and he wanted to make movies), after which he'd located a picture of Addict Number One by reading an obituary from the time when Addict Number One was already dead.

Must have been pretty tempting to try to fabricate a memory about Addict Number One. Oh yeah, I saw him on the Christopher Street pier that time. Or, I saw him on my way to Forest Hills to visit my grandma. Cortez may have tried this, perhaps a dozen times, skin popping Albertine in an unfurnished room in East Harlem, vainly attempting to put a bullet in the head of an imagined encounter with Addict Number One, but no. Cortez had to go through every face in every crowd, all the imagined crowds of which he had ever been a part, every face passed on Broadway, every prone body on the Bowery, every body in the stands of Yankee Stadium. He shot more, spent most of the money from his bike messenger job on this jones for narrative, and then one day, he was certain.

He was killing roaches in his empty apartment, when he knew. He was prying up a floorboard to look for roaches, and he knew. As certainly as he knew the grid of his city. He'd walked by Addict Number One, one day, when he was sixteen, in Tompkins Square. On his way to a game of handball. He'd walked by him, he knew it. Not someone else, but him, Addict Number One. Guy looked like a faggot, the way Cortez told Cassandra later. All white guys looked like faggots as far as he was concerned, and he'd just as soon kill the punk-ass motherfucker for looking like a faggot as any other reason, although there were plenty of other reasons. Main thing was that if he could figure out a way to kill Addict Number One in his memory, then a whole sequence of events failed, like when Addict Number One hooked up with certain black guys in his neighborhood who had been fronting heroin up until that time, gave to them the correct chemical compound of Albertine, the secrets of the raw materials needed for the manufacture, the apparatus. If Cortez killed his ass this future would not turn out to be the real future. If Cortez killed his ass, then Cortez would control the syndicate.

It would take even more time and money, more time, doping, a solid six months, in fact, in his room, going through that whole sequence of his life, like that time with Eduardo's neighbor, he told Cassandra. Over and over again, Eduardo had to deal with that *drunken fuck neighbor,* not even gonna say his name here, Cortez would say to Cassandra, fighting off that memory when the guy, Eduardo's alleged uncle, in the rubble of an abandoned building, exposed himself to little Eduardo, his droopy uncut penis, fucking guy couldn't get hard no more, looked like a gizzard, and the uncle drunkenly pronounced that he was lonelier than any man had ever been, didn't belong in this country, couldn't go back to the island nation of his birth, no reason for a man to be as lonely as this man, no reason for this surfeiting of loneliness, every day in every way, and would Eduardo just make him feel comfortable for just this one day, just treat him like a loving man, this one time, because he was so lonely, had an aching in his heart that nothing could still, wouldn't ask again, he swore, and took Eduardo, just a little compadre, just a wisp, couldn't even lift up an aluminum baseball bat, couldn't lift a finger against the alleged uncle, took Eduardo for his goddess, you are my priestess, you are my goddess, and now Eduardo vowed that he would never again suffer that way before any man.

The syringe, the eyedropper, the concentric rings of the past. Again and again the uncle would attempt to seduce him. He was willing to go through that, a thousand times if he had to, until he had the gun on his person, in the waistband of his warm-up suit, and he was ready. He was sixteen, with fresh tattoos, and he'd been to mass that morning and he had a gun, and he was going to play handball, and he saw this white faggot in the dog run, and he just walked up to him like they never met. Though in truth it was like Eduardo Cortez knew him inside and out, and Eduardo wanted to make something out of himself, his life that was lost up until then, where he was just a bike messenger, and the desperados of his neighborhood, they were all going to be working for him and if they made one wrong move, he'd throw them off a fucking bridge, whatever bridge is still up, and if they touched the little girls in his neighborhood, that's another crime, for which he would exact a very high price, a mortal price, and the first priority, the long-term business plan was that Eduardo Cortez would be the guy who would make profits from memories, even if his own memories were bad. That was just how it was going to go, and I saw all this with Cassandra, that Cortez had managed by sheer brute force to murder a memory, splatter a memory like it was nothing at all.

One minute Addict Number One was wandering in the East Village, years before he was an addict, years before there even was an Albertine to cop, and he was thinking about how he was going to get funding for his digital video project, and then, right in front of a bunch of dog walkers, the guy disappeared. This is the story, from the point of view of those who were not in on the cascading of memories. It's one of the really great examples of public delusion, when you read it on the on-line police records, like I did. *Witnesses insist that the victim, first referred to as Caucasian John Doe, later identified as Irving Paley of 433 East 9th St., was present on the scene, along with a Hispanic man in his teens, and then, abruptly, no longer present. "It's as if he just vanished," remarked one witness. Others concur. No body located thereafter. Apartment also completely emptied, possibly by assailant.* Good thing those records were stored on a server. Since One Police Plaza is dust.

The guys in the smelting factory were all wearing uniforms. They were the uniforms of bike messengers, as if the entire story somehow turned on bike messengers. Bike messenger as conveyor of meaning. There were these courtiers in the empire of Eduardo Cortez, and the lowest echelon was the beat cop, a phalanx of whom were all encircling the building, sending news of anyone in the neighborhood into command central by radio. And then there were the centurions of the empire, the guys in the bike messenger uniforms, wearing the crash helmets of bike messengers. All done up in Lycra, like this was some kind of superhero garb. When the elevator door swung back, it was clear that we had definitely penetrated to the inner sanctum of Eduardo Cortez, as if by merely thinking. And this inner sanctum was inexplicable, comic, and deadly. Sure it was possible that I had now been researching for two weeks, and no longer needed food or sleep in order to do it. Sure, maybe I was just doing a really great job, and, since I was an honest guy who seemed cool and nonthreatening, maybe I was just allowed into places that the stereotypical Albertine abuser would not ordinarily be allowed. But it seemed unlikely. This was evidently one of the fabled five mansions of Cortez, to which he shuttled, depending on his whim, like a despot from the coca-producing latitudes.

"Eddie," Cassandra sang out into the low lighting of the smelting factory floor, "I brought him like you said."

Which one was Eddie? The room was outfitted with gigantic machines, suspension devices, ramrods, pistons thundering, wheels turning, like some fabulous Rube Goldberg future, and there was no center to it, no throne, no black leather sofa with a leopard-print quilt thrown over it, and none of the bike messengers in the room looked like the Cortez of my memory, the Cortez of Tompkins Square Park, on his way to play handball. Maybe he'd had himself altered by a cosmetic surgeon with a drug problem and a large debt. In fact, in scanning the faces of the dozens of bike messengers in the room it seemed that they all looked similar, all of European extraction with brown hair on the verge of going gray, all with blue eyes, a little bit paunchy. Were they robots? Were they street toughs from the bad neighborhoods? They were, it turned out, the surgically altered army of Eddie Cortez homonyms, who made it possible for him to be in so many places at so many times, in all the fabled five mansions. Eddie was a condition of the economy now, not a particular person.

At the remark from Cassandra, several of the bike messengers gathered in the center of the room. Maybe they were all modified comfort robots, so that Eddie could use them professionally during the day and fuck them later at night. One of them asked, with a blank expression, "His writing any good?"

Cassandra turned to me. "They want to know if you're a good writer."

"Uh, sure," I said, answering to the room. "Sure. I guess. Uh, you wanting me to write something? What do you have in mind exactly?"

More huddling. No amount of time was too lengthy, in terms of negotiation, and this was probably because time was no longer all that important to Cortez and the empire. Time present was now swallowed in the riptide of the past. Since it was now possible that Eddie could disappear, at any moment, like Addict Number One had, when someone else figured out his technique for dealing with the past, he had apparently moved to ensure an eternal boring instant, where everybody looked the same, and where nothing particularly happened. Events, any kind of events, were dangerous. Eddie's fabled five mansions featured a languid, fixed now. He took his time. He changed his appearance frequently, as well as the appearance of all those around him. That way he could control memories. So his days were apparently taken up with dye jobs, false beards, colored contact lenses, all the shopping for items relating to disguise and imposture and disfigurement.

"Funny you should, uh, suggest it," I said. "Because I have been assigned to write a history of Albertine, and that's why I got in contact with Cassandra, in the first place. . . ."

Everyone looked at her. Faint traces of confusion.

Have I described her well enough? In the half-light, she too was a goddess, even though I figure addicts always shine in low lighting. In the emergency lighting of Eddie's lair, Cassandra was the doomed forecaster, like her name implied. She was the whisperer of syllables in a tricky meter. She was the possibility of possibilities. I knew that desire for me must have been a thing that was slumbering for a really long time, it was just desire for desire, but now it was ungainly. I felt some stirring of possible futures with Cassandra, didn't want to let her out of my sight. I was guilty of treating women like ideas in my search for Albertine. In fact, I knew so little about her, that it was only just then that I thought about the fact that she was Asian too. From China, or maybe her parents or grandparents were from Hong Kong, or Taiwan. Because now she swept back her black and maroon hair, and I could see her face. Her expression was kind of sad.

They all laughed. The bike messengers. I was the object of hilarity.

"Cassandra," they said. "That's a good one. What's that, like some Chinese name?"

"You did good, girl. You're a first-class bitch, Albertine, and so it's time for a treat, if you want."

A broadcaster's voice. Like Eddie had managed to hire network talent to make his announcements.

"Wait," I said, "her name is . . ."

And then I got it. They named it after her.

"You named the drug after her?"

"Not necessarily," the broadcasting voice said. "Might have named her after the drug. We can't really remember the sequence. And the thing is there are memories going either way."

"She doesn't look like an Albertine to me."

"The *fuck* you know, canary," the broadcaster said, and suddenly I heard Eddie in there, heard his attitude. Canary. A reporter's nickname.

Cassandra was encircled by bike messengers, and hefted up to a platform in the midst of the Rube Goldberg devices. Her rags were removed from her body by certain automated machines, prosthetic digits, and she was laid out like a sacrificial victim, which I guess is what she was, one knee bent, like in classical sculpture, one arm was laid out above her head. No woman is more poignant than the woman about to be sacrificed, but even this remark makes me more like Eddie, less like a lover.

"Your pleasure?" a bike messenger called out.

"Slave Owner, please," said Cassandra.

"Good choice. Four horsepower, fifteen volts, 350 rpms."

I covered my ears with my hands, and except for the glimpse of the steel bar that was meant to raise her ankles over her head, I saw no more—for the simple reason that I didn't want to have to remember.

The bike messengers of the Cortez cartel had a different idea for me. I was led down a corridor, to the shooting gallery. I was finally going to get my taste.

The guy holding my arms said, "Thing is all employees got to submit to a mnemonic background check. . . ."

A week or so before, I'd read a pamphlet by a specialist in medicinal applications of Albertine. There's always a guy like this, right, a Dr. Feelgood, an apologist. He was on the Upper West Side, and his suggestion was that, when getting high, one should always look carefully around a room and eliminate bad energies. Set and setting, in fact, was just as important here as with drugs in the hallucinogenic family:

> If there's any scientific validity at all to the theories of C.G. Jung and his followers, there's genuine cause for worry when taking the drug known as Albertine.
>
> The reason for this is quite simply Jung's concept

known as the collective unconsciousness. What do we mean when we invoke this theory? We mean that under certain extraordinary circumstances it is possible that memory, properly thought of as the exclusive domain of an Albertine effect, can occasionally collide with other areas of brain function. As Jung supposed, we each harbor a register of the simulacra that is part of being human. This fantasy register, it is said, can be a repository for symbolisms that are true across cultural and national lines. What kinds of images are these? Some of them are good, useful images, such as the representation of the divine: Christ as the Lamb of God, Buddha under the bodhi tree, Ganesh, with his many arms. Each of these is a useful area for meditation. However, images of the demonic are also collective, as with depictions of witches. The terrors of hell, in fact, have had a long collective history. Now it appears that certain modern phantasms—the CIA operative, the transnational terrorist—are also both "real" and collective.

Therefore, we can suggest that casual users of Albertine make sure to observe some rules for their excursions. It's important to know a little about whom you have with you at the time of ingestion. It's important to know a little bit about their own circumstances. To put it another way, people you trust are a crucial part of any prolonged Albertine experience.

I suggest five easy steps to a rewarding experience with your memories: 1) Find a comfortable place, 2) Bring along a friend or loved one, 3) Use the drug after good meals or rewarding sexual experiences, so that you won't waste all your time on the re-creation of these things, 4) Keep a photo album at hand, in case you want to draw your attention back to less harmful recollections, 5) Avoid horror films, heavy metal music, or anything with occult imagery.

The advice of the good doctor was ringing in my ears. No matter what happened to my city, no matter how many incarnations of boom and bust it went through, the go-go times, the Municipal Assistance Corporation, didn't seem to matter, shooting galleries persisted in the Hot Zone and elsewhere. The exposed beams, the crumbling walls, the complete lack of electricity, the absence of heat, windows shattered, bodies lying around on mattresses. If it was important to know or trust the people with whom I was going to use, I was in some deep shit. Who wouldn't dread coming here to this place of unwashed men, of human waste and dead bodies?

In the shadows, there was a guy with a stool and a metal folding table. I was motioned forward, as an old hippie collapsed onto the floor. Probably remembering the best night of sleep he ever had.

Behind me, operatives in the Cortez syndicate made sure that my step was sturdy.

"Give me your hand," the Albertine provider said. In a kind of doomed murmur.

I looked at my hand. Laid it out on that cheap table, site of a hundred violent games of poker.

"Don't mind we kinda stay close?" said one of the goons. He used the chokehold. Another guy held my hand. This would be the gentle description. If they were worried about my getting away, they shouldn't have, because I was a reporter. But that wasn't the motive it dawned on me. They were hoping to come along for the ride, if possible, to see what they needed to know about their collaborator, if that's what I was going to be. The historian of the Empire.

"You don't honestly think you're going to be able to see what I see, do you?" I said. "There's just no way that works according to physics."

The needle went in between the tendons on the top of my right hand. Blood washed back into the syringe. A bead pearling at my knuckle.

"First time, yo?" someone said.

"For sure," I said.

"Goes better if you're thinking about what you want to know, *Chiming*. Thinking of bells, bells from a church, that's what you do, things get chiming, the pictures get chiming. Because if you think of stuff you don't want to know, then, *bang*—"

Like I said, what I wanted to know first when I finally got dosed on Albertine was how I did on this assignment. I mean, if you could see the future, which seemed like horse-shit, if that was really possible, then I wanted to know how my story turned out. Which I guess makes me a real writer, because a reporter is someone who doesn't care about his own well-being when the story is coming due, he just cares about the story, about getting it done. I just wanted to get the story done, I wanted to get it into the magazine. I wanted to be more than just another guy who survived the blast. So that was the memory where I was bound. But that doesn't describe the beginning at all. One second I was listening to the guy tell me about chiming, next moment there was a world beside the world in which I lived, a world behind the world, and maybe even a sequence of them lined up one behind the other, where crucial narratives were happening. Suddenly the splinter hanging off the two-by-four next to the table seemed to have a world-famous history, where dragonflies frolicked in the limbs of an ancient redwood. And maybe this was the prize promised first by Albertine, that all things would have meaning. Suddenly there was discrimination to events, not all this disjunctive shit, like a million people getting incinerated for no good reason. Instead: discrimination, meaning, value. The solarizing thing again, and I could hear the voices of the people in the room, but like I was paralyzed, I was experiencing language as material, not as words, but as something sludgy like molasses, language was molasses. Like life had been EQ'd badly, and all was high-end distortion, and then there was a tiling effect, and the grinning toothless face of the guy who'd just shot me up was divided into zones, like he was a painting from the Modernist chapter of art history, and zones were sort of rearranged, so he was a literal blockhead, and then I heard this music, like the whole history of sounds from my life had become a tunnel under the present, and I could hear voices, and I could hear songs, I could pluck one out, like I could pluck out some jazz from the 1950s, here's a guy banging on the eighty-eights, stride style, and when I plucked it out of the tunnel I could hear the things beside it, a concert that I had to go to in junior high, school auditorium, where some guys in robes demonstrated some Buddhist overtone singing, they were sitting on an oriental carpet, you know the mysteries of the world always had to have an oriental carpet involved, we were all supposed to be mystical and wearing robes and shit, and beside me there was the voice of my friend Dave Wakabayashi, who whispered, "Man, we could be listening to the game," because there was a day game that day, right. What team? And who was pitching? And then the sound of Mandarin, which was exactly like a song to me, because of all the kinds of intonation that were involved in it, all those words that had the same sound but different intonations.

And after that accretion of songs, a flood of the smells from my life, barely had time to say some of them aloud, while my stool was tipping backward, in the shooting gallery, my stool was tipping backward, and the back of my head was connecting with some hard surface, citronella, cardamom, smell of melting vinyl, smell of a pack of Polaroid film, five kinds of perfume, smell of my grandfather dying, meat loaf prepared from a box, freshly cut lawns, the West Indian Day Parade in New York City, which is the smell of curried goat, ozone right before a storm, diesel exhaust, the smell of just having fucked someone for the first time, the shock of it, more perfumes, a dog that just rolled in something, city streets in July, fresh basil, chocolate chip cookies, ailanthus trees, and just when I was getting dizzy from all the smells, and right about the moment at which I heard the guys from Eddie's team, in their mellifluous slang, saying *Take his damn money,* which they definitely were going to do now, because I could tell that my arms were thrown wide to the world, give me the world, give me your laser light show and your perfect memories, doesn't matter what they are, rinse me in your sanitorium of memories, for I am ready as I have never been, all of my short life. All was rehearsal for this moment as observer of what has come before, my longing was for perception, for the torrents of the senses, the tastes, the languor of skin on skin. I was made for this trip, it felt good, it felt preposterously good, and I noticed absently that my cock was hard, actually, I'm a little embarrassed to say it now, but I realized in that moment that mastery of the past, even when drug-induced, was as sexy as the vanquishing of loneliness, which is really what men in the city fuck against. Think about it, the burden of isolation that's upon us all day and night, and think about how that diminishes in the carnival of sex. It's the same on the Teen, it's the same with *chiming,* and I was actually a little worried that I might come like that lying on the floor of their shooting gallery, with this guy standing over me, reaching into my hip pocket where there used to be a wallet, but there was no wallet now, just a couple of twenties to get me out of trouble, if it came to that. He wanted them and he took them. I wanted to yell Get the fuck off me, but I could feel the blobs of drool detaching from the corner of my mouth, and I knew I could say nothing, I could say only Yes, yes, yes. And when that seemed like that was the lesson of Albertine, bitch goddess, when I thought, Well, this must be what you get for your twenty-five bucks, you get to see the light show of lost time, just then I got up off the floor and walked into the lobby of the tits-and-lit magazine that had hired me, except that they hadn't hired me, I guess, not like I believed. The matter was still up in the air, and I was in the line with a lot of people claiming to be writers, people with their plagiarized clip files, though why anyone would want to pretend to be a writer is beyond me. I was hoping, since I was the genuine article, that I might actually get the call. Out came this girl with blue hair, past the receptionist robot at the desk out front, saying my name, Kevin Lee, like it somehow magically rhymed with *bored,* and I got up, walked past all those people. I realized, yes, that I was going to get the assignment, because I was the guy who had actually written something, I was the genuine article, and maybe fate had it in store for me that I'd get out of the armory where I shared a cardboard box with a computer programmer from Islamabad who despite the unfortunate fact of his nationality in the current global climate was a good guy.

The girl had blue hair! The girl had blue hair! And she looked sort of like Serena, that babe with whom I once skipped school to drink in Boston Commons, and there I was again, like never before, with Serena, slurring the words a little bit when I told her she was the first person who ever took the time to have a real conversation with me. First white chick. Because, I told Serena, people looked at an Asian kid in school they assumed he was a math and science geek, oh he's definitely smarter than everyone else, that's what I told her, such a sweet memory. Well, it was sweet anyway up until she told me that she already had a boyfriend, some college dude, why hadn't she told me before, didn't I deserve to be told, didn't I have some feelings too? No, probably I was an inscrutable kid from the East. Right? She didn't tell me because I was Chinese.

And I was in a bad spot, in a drug dealer's shooting gallery, probably going to be in really deep shit because if I didn't write something for the cartel about the history of Albertine, I was probably a dead Chinese kid, but I didn't care, because I believed I was drunk in the Boston Commons, and I was reciting poetry, for a girl with green eyes who would actually go on to be an actress in commercials, *There's a certain slant of light/Winter afternoons/That oppresses like the heft/Of cathedral tunes.* I could recite every poem I had ever memorized. It was amazing. Serena's face frozen in a kind of convulsive laughter, You are some crazy bastard, Kevin Lee. It was all good, it was all blessed, the trip. But then she said that thing about her boyfriend again, some would-be filmmaker.

And I was back in the office with Tara, girl with the blue hair. "Jesus, Lee, what happened? You don't look so good. Why didn't you call me? When I gave you the assignment, I assumed you were a professional, right? Because there are a lot of other people who would have jumped at the chance to write this piece." Glimpse of myself in the reflection of her office window. The city smoldering out the window, the whole empty city, myself superimposed over it. I looked like I hadn't eaten in two weeks. The part of my face that actually grew a beard had one of those beards that looked like a Vietnamese guy in a rice paddy. My eyes were sunken and red. I had the bruises under my eyes. Whatever viscous gunk was still irrigating my dry mouth had hardened at the corners into a crust. I had nothing to say. Nothing to do but hand over the notes. Twenty-nine thousand words. Tara paged through the beginning with an exasperated sigh. "What the fuck do you think we're going to do with this, Kevin? We're a fucking porn magazine? Remember?" As in dreams, I could feel the inability to do anything. I just watched the events glide by. From this quicksand of the future. I could see Tara with the blue pencil to match her blue hair receding in the reflection in the window.

And then there were a dozen more futures, each as unpleasant. Breaking into the bedroom of Bertrand, the administrator of the armory, stealing his beaker full of Teen, which he kept in his luxury fridge—he was the only guy in the entire armory who got to have a refrigerator—being discovered in the process of stealing his drugs by a woman who'd just recently gone out of her way to ask me where my family was, why I was living here alone. Seeing her face in the light from the fridge, the only light in the room. She was wearing army fatigues, the uniform of the future, everyone in army fatigues, everyone on high alert. And then I jumped a few rich people up in Park Slope, an affluent neighborhood that wasn't obliterated in the blast, I was wearing a warm-up suit, I was jumping some guy carrying groceries, and suddenly I was awake, with my face in my hands.

The guys at the folding table were laughing.

I wiped my leaking nose on my wrists. Stood up, weak-kneed.

"Good time?" said the administerer of poisons. "You need the boost; everybody needs it afterward. Don't worry yourself. You need the boost. To smooth it out."

He handed me a pill.

One of the security experts said to another: "Just the usual shit, man, names of cheap-ass girls kiss his ass when he was just a little Chinese boy eating his mommy's moo goo gai pan. Some shit."

That was it? That was what I was to them? Bunch of sentimental memories? The predictable twenty-five-dollar memories that coursed through here every day? What were they looking for? Later, I knew. They were looking for evidence that I had dropped off files with government agencies, or that I had ripped off rival gangs. Or they were looking to see if I'd had contact with Addict Number One. They were looking to see what I had put together, what I knew, where my researches had taken me, how much of the web of Albertine was already living in me, and therefore how much of it was available to you.

"Okay chump," bike messenger said to me, "free to go."

The door opened, and down a corridor I went, wearing handcuffs, back the way I'd come, like I could unlearn what I had learned—that I had the taste for the drug, and that the past was woefully lost. I'd been addicted by the drug overlord of my city, and now I was standing on his assembly-line floor again, though now Cassandra, or whoever she was, was missing, and the voice of the Cortez television announcer rang out, observing the following on the terms of my new employment: "We want you to learn the origin of Albertine, we want you to write down this origin, and all the rest of the history of Albertine, from its earliest days to the present time, and we don't want you to use any fancy language or waste any time, we just want you to write it down. And because what you're going to do is valuable to us, we are prepared to make it worth your while. We're going to give you plenty of our product as a memory aid, and we will give you a generous per diem. You'll dress like a man, you'll consider yourself a representative of Eddie Cortez, you'll avoid disrespectful persons and institutions. Remember, it's important for you to write and not worry about anything else. You fashion the sentences, you make them sing, we'll look after the rest."

"Sounds cool," I said, "especially since I'm already doing that for someone else."

"No, you aren't doing it for somebody else; you are doing it for us. Nobody else exists. The skin magazine doesn't exist, your friends don't exist. Your family doesn't exist. We exist."

I could feel how weak my legs were. I could feel the sweat trickling down the small of my back, soaking through my T-shirt. I was just hanging on. Because that's what my family did, they hung on. My grandfather, he left behind his country, never gave it another thought. My father, you never saw the guy sweat. My mother, she was on a plane that had to make an emergency landing once, she didn't even give it a second thought, as far as I could tell. Representatives of the Cortez cartel were tracking me on a monitor somewhere, or on some sequence of handheld computers, watching me, and they were broadcasting their messages to staff people who could be trusted. Who knew how many other people in the Eddie Cortez operation were being treated the way I was being treated today? Bring this guy into the fold, conquer him, if not, neutralize him, leave him out in the rubble of some building somewhere. It was an operation staffed by guys who all had guns, stun guns and cattle prods, real guns with bullets that could make an Abstract Expressionist painting out of a guy like me, and I was trying to get the fuck out of there, before I was dead, and I could barely think of anything else. Now they were taking me down this long hall, and it wasn't the corridor I was in before, because the building had all these layers, and it was hard to know where you were, relative to where you had been before, or maybe this is just the way I felt because of what the voice on the loudspeaker said next.

"Be sure to be vigilant about forgetting."

Which reminds me to remind you of the *diachronous theory of Albertine abuse,* which of course recognizes the forgetting as a social phenomenon coincident, big-time, with a certain pattern of Albertine penetration into the population. The manifestation of forgetting is easy to explain, see, because it has to do with bolstering the infrastructure of memory elsewhere. Like anyone who's a drinker knows, you borrow courage when you're drinking, and you lose it someplace else. Addiction is about credit. That amazing thing you said at the bar last night, that thing you would never say in person to anyone, it's a onetime occurrence, because tomorrow, in the light of dawn, when you are separated from your wallet and your money, when your girlfriend hates you, then you'll be unable to say that courageous thing again, because you are wrung out and lying on a mattress without sheets. You borrowed that courage, and it's gone.

So the thing with Albertine was that at night, under its influence, you remembered. Tonight the past was glorious and indelible—Serena in the park with the rum and the bittersweet revelation of her boyfriend—tonight was the beauty of almost being in love, which was a great beauty, but tomorrow, your memory was full of holes. Not a blackout, more like a brownout. You could remember that you once knew things, but they were indistinct now, and the understanding of them just flew out the window. It was like the early part of jet lag, or thorazine. Why did I come into this room? I was going to get something. Suddenly you had no idea, you stood looking at the pile of clothes in front of the dresser, clothes that were fascinating colors, that old pair of jeans, very interesting. Look at that color. It's so blue. Maybe you needed to do something, but you didn't, and you realized that things were going on in your body, and they were inexplicable to you. You were really thirsty. Maybe you ought to have had some juice, but on the way to the bottle of water on the table, you forgot.

The history of Albertine became a history of forgetting. A geometrically increasing history of forgetfulness. Men in charge of its distribution, by reason of the fact that they started using it for organizational reasons, to increase market share, they were as forgetful as the hard-core users, who after a while couldn't remember their own addresses, except occasionally, and who were therefore on the street, asking strangers, *Do you know my name? Do you happen to know where I live?* The history of the drug, requested by Cortez, was therefore important. How else to plan for the future? If the research and development team at Cortez Enterprises didn't forget how to read, then, as long as they had a hard copy of the history, everything was cool. I would write the story; they'd lock it away somewhere.

Before I had a chance to agree or disagree, I was going down in the industrial elevator, alone, and it was like being shat out the ass of the smelting factory. It was dawn with the light coming up under the lip of that relentless cloud. Dawn, the only time these days there was any glimmer on the horizon, before the debris clouds massed again. But, listen, I have to come clean on something. I missed Cassandra. That's what I was feeling. She'd sold me out to Eddie Cortez, made me his vassal, like she was his vassal. Trust and fealty, these words were just memories. So was Cassandra, just a memory. A lost person. Who'd reassured me for a few minutes. Who'd have sold out anyone for more drugs and a few minutes on a postindustrial sexual machine. Was I right that there was something there? For an Albertine second, the slowest second on the clock. Seemed like she was the threshold to some partially forgotten narrative, some inchoate past, some incomplete sign, like light coming in through window blinds. Boy, I was stupid, getting sentimental about the Asian mistress of a drug kingpin.

Daylight seemed serious, practical. It was the first time I could remember being out in the daylight since I started compiling these notes. On the way back to the armory, I waited on the line up the block for the one pay phone that still worked. Usually there were fifty or sixty people out front. All of them simmering with rage, because the connection was sketchy, the phone disconnected, and everyone listened to the other callers, listened to the conversations. Imagine the sound of the virtual automaton's computerized warmth, We're sorry, the parties you are contacting are unable to accept the call. Who was sorry exactly? The robot? A guy holding the receiver shouted, "I need to know the name of that prescription! I'm not a well man!" Then the disconnection. A woman begged her husband to take her back. Disconnection. And a kid who has lost his parents, trying to locate his grandparents. Disconnection. The phone booth had that multitude of sad stories hidden spinning around it.

Soon it was my turn, and my father got on. Man of few words.

"We told you not to call here anymore," he said.

"What?"

"You heard me."

"I haven't called in . . ."

I tried to put it all together. How long? Measuring time had become almost impossible. There was nothing to do but make a stab at it.

". . . three weeks."

"We can't give you anything more. Our own savings are nearly exhausted. You need to start thinking about how you're going to get out of the jam you're in without calling us every time it gets worse. It's you who is making it worse. Understand? Think about what you're doing!"

I could see the people behind me in the pay phone line leaning in toward the bad news, excited to get a few tidbits. Their own bad scrapes were not nearly as bad.

"What are you talking about?"

"I've told you before," he said. "Don't raise your voice with me."

His own voice defeated, brittle.

"Put Mom on the line!"

"Absolutely not."

"Let me talk to Mom!"

Then some more nonsense about how I had caused my mother unending sorrow, that it was her nature only to sacrifice, but I had squandered this generosity, had stamped up and down on it with my callousness, my American callousness, as if my family had not overcome innumerable obstacles to get me where I was. I made the selflessness of my heritage seem like a deluded joke. I had dishonored him, etc. etc., by my shameful activities, etc. etc. It was as good as if I had died during the blast.

A bona fide patriarchal dressing-down, of a sort that I thought I had left behind long ago. I was watching the faces of the people in the line behind me, and their faces were reflecting my own face. Incredulity. Confusion.

"Dad, I have no idea what you're talking about. Listen to me."

"You can't call here every day with your preposterous lies. Your imagined webs of conspiracy. We won't have it. We are exhausted. Your mother cannot get out of bed, and I am up at all hours frantic with worry about you. How are we supposed to live? Get some help!"

I smiled a befuddled smile for my audience, I replaced the receiver. In midstream. Of course, I hadn't called my parents recently, hadn't called them the day before, or the week before, or the week before that. Hadn't called them often at all. My crime, in fact, was that because of shame about where I lived and what I was doing I didn't really call anyone anymore. So what explained the circumstance?

I looked at the next guy in line. A melancholy African-American man, with a fringe of gray hair and eyeglasses patched with some duct tape. It was beginning to rain, of course, and I saw an obsidian blob splatter the surface of his glasses.

"I guess I just called them," I said. "I mean, I guess I forgot that I called them."

He pushed past me.

To forget was threatening now. Nobody wanted to have anything to do with a forgetter. A forgetter meant just the one thing. A forgetter had abscesses in his arm, or a forgetter had sold off the last of his possessions and was trying to sell them a second time, because he had forgotten that the apartment was already empty. The highest respect, the most admiration was accorded those with perfect recall—that was part of the diachronous theory, or if it wasn't yet, I predicted it would soon be part of that theory. Geeks with perfect recall would get up in public settings, with a circle of folding chairs around them, and then, in front of an amazed audience, these geeks would remember the perfect textures of things, Ah yes, the running mates of the losers in the last eight presidential elections, let me see. And the names of their wives. And weather on election day. Massive fraud would be perpetrated in certain cases, where these perfect-recall geeks would, it turned out, have needle tracks, just like the rest of us. Ohmygod! They were doping, and they would be escorted out into the street, in shame, where again rain was beginning to fall.

Which is why when I got back to the armory, and found the package on my bed, I felt that pornographic thrill. I could manage an eyedropper as good as the next guy, right? I'd work up to the needles. What else was there to hang around for? No one was waiting for me. Maybe I could get back to the night before, when I was talking to Cassandra. I said this little preliminary prayer, May this roll of the dice be the one in which I remember love, or teen sex, or that time when I had a lot of money from a summer job and I was barbecuing out in the back of the subdivision, and everybody was drinking beer and having a good time.

But, no, I would become a junky in a supply closet, and I would use a lantern I'd looted from a camping equipment store after the blast. I held the eyedropper above me, and the droplet of intoxicant was lingering there, and I was the oyster that was going to envelop it and make it my secret. The drop in the dropper was like the black rain of NYC which was like the money shot in a porn film which was like the tears from the Balkan statuary of the Virgin in the naïf style. The lantern shone up from underneath my supply closet shelves, and there was that rush of perfumes that I've already described, which meant that it was all beginning again; I was lucky for the perfumes I've known, other guys just know paperwork, but I've known the smell of people right before being naked with them, what an honor. All junkies are lapsed idealists, falling away from things as they were. I was a murderer of time. I'd taken the hours of my life out back of the armory and shoved them in the wood chipper or buried them in a swamp or bricked them up in the basement. But this thought was overwhelmed by the personal scent of a fashion student who lived near us when I was in California. It was on me like a new atmosphere. Along with the sheets of fog rolling in over the Bay.

It was all a fine movie. At least until something really horrible occurred to me, a bummer of a thought. How could it be? Thinking about that Serena, again, see, in the Boston Commons, drinking rum, remembering that she actually had Cherry Coke, not the soft drink once known as the Real Thing, to which I said, "Cherry Coke, girl, that's not Coke, because no Coke product that occurs, historically, after the advent of the New Coke—held by some to have been a reaction to sugar prices in Latin American countries—no Coke that occurs after that time is a legitimate Coke. Get it? The only Coke product that is genuine with respect to the rum and Cokes you're proposing to drink here is Mexican Coke, which you can still get in bottles, and which still features some actual cane sugar." An impressive speech, a flirtatious speech, but somewhere in the middle of remembering it—and who knew how many hours had passed now, who knew how many days—this thought I'm speaking about occurred to me:

Serena's boyfriend, the guy she was seeing besides me, or instead of me, *was Addict Number One.*

Years before, I mean. Way before he was the actual Addict Number One. Because we were in high school then, and Addict Number One wasn't killed yet, or hadn't vanished. Not in this version of the story. He was a college guy, and he wanted to make movies, went to NYU, lived downtown, wore a lot of black, just like Addict Number One. And he could tell you a lot about certain recordings that hardcore bands from Minneapolis made in the eighties, and he had a lot of opinions about architecture and politics and sitcoms and maybe bagels, I don't know. I could feel that it was true. It was a hunch, but it was a really good hunch. There was an intersection in the story where there hadn't been one before, and the intersection involved me, or at least tangentially it involved me. Before I was an observer, but now I was coming to see that there was no observing Albertine. Because Albertine was looking back into you. The thought was so unsettling that I was actually shaking with terror about it, but I was too high to stop remembering.

Serena said, "You won't have any idea whether this is Coke or Cherry Coke after the first half a cup. I could put varnish in here, you wouldn't know." She smiled and now I felt myself drunk just with the particulars of her smile. It was a humble, lopsided smile, and she was wearing those patched blue jeans, and she pulled off her green Dartmouth sweatshirt, to reveal a T-shirt with the sleeves cut off, the T-shirt advertising a particular girl deejay, and I could see the lower part of her belly underneath the T-shirt. The slope of her breasts. I mean, her smile promised things that never came to be, you know? While I was taking it in, turning over the irrefutable fact of her smile and a tiny series of beautiful lines, like parentheses, at the corners of her fantastic mouth, Serena began to fade. "Don't go," I said, "there's some stuff we need to cover," but it was like those cries in a dream, the cries that just wake you up. They don't actually bring help. They just wake you. I could see her fading, and in her stead, I saw a bunch of bare trees from some November trip to the malls of Jersey. Autumn.

I seized the eyedropper, which, because it had just been sitting on my roach-infested mattress while I was busy remembering, now seemed to have black specks all over the tip of it, and maybe there were some kinds of bugs crawling around on there, I don't know. I held back my eyelids. I was aching in my eye sockets.

The plan was to summon her back, to call her name in the old psychoanalytic way, you know. Names count for something. Strong feelings count for something. And such a beautiful name anyhow, right? Serena, like some ocean of calm lapping against the fucked-up landscape. I would ask her. If I could map the weird voyages of my younger self, that Asian kid trying to declare himself to a Yankee girl through really abstract complicated poetry, *If all time is eternally present,/All time is unredeemable./What might have been is an abstraction.*

Because if it was really true that Cassandra had somehow willed me to see what she knew about Eddie Cortez, just because she wanted me to see it, even if telling me the truth about Eddie was somehow a danger to her position as his mistress, then it was true that love and affection were important orienting forces in the Albertine epidemic. Like Eddie, who chased Addict Number One through the dingy recesses of his brain simply in the breadth of his malice and greed. Maybe the rememberer, in the intoxication of remembering, was always ultimately tempted to reach out the hand, and maybe this rememberer could do so, if his passion was strong enough. How else to look at it? What else did I have to go on? Because a hundred thousand Albertine addicts couldn't be wrong. Because they were all chasing the promise of some lost, glittering, perfect moment of love. Because some of them must have reached that Elysian destination in their floods of memory and forgetfulness. Because I sure loved Serena, because she had a lopsided smile, because she had nails called *lycanthrope,* because love is good when you have nothing, and I had nothing, except bike messengers watching my every move.

Instead of access to Serena, though, I got stuck in this fucked-up loop where all I could remember is a bunch of really horrible songs from my childhood. In particular, "Shake Your Bon-Bon," a song that definitely had not aged very well. Sounds tinny, like the sampling rate is bad somehow, you know, those early sampling rates on digital music, really tinny. And here's that little synthesizer loop that's supposed to sound like the Beatles during their sitar phase, girl backup singers, the attempt to make the glamorous leading man sound as though he didn't prefer boys, fine, really, but why pretend, man, knock yourself out. Seven hours, at least, passed in which I went over the minutiae of "Shake Your Bon-Bon." The utterly computerized sound of it, the vestiges of humanness in its barren musical palette, as if the singer dude couldn't be bothered to repeat the opening hook himself, no way, it'd sound better if they just looped it on Pro-Tools, and then the old-fashioned organ, which was a simulated organ, etc., and the relationship between the congas and the guitars, okay, and what about that Latin middle section? Demographically perfect! So twentieth century! I didn't want to think about the trombone solo at the end of "Shake Your Bon-Bon," buried in the back, that sultry trombone solo, but I did think about it, about the singer's Caribbean origins oozing out at the edges of the composition, and his homosexuality. Went on this way for a while, including a complete recollection of a remix that I think I only heard one time in my entire life, which was in some ways the superior version, because the more artificial the better, like when they take out all the rests between the vocal lines, so that the song has effectively become impossible to sing. Nowhere to take a breath. Was anyone on earth thinking about the singer in question, these days after the blast? I bet no one at all was thinking of him, except for certain stalkers from Yonkers or Port Chester. Where was he exactly? Had he managed to find refuge in a completely pink hotel in South Beach before the blast? And were his memories of showbiz dominance so great that the big new export market for Albertine was seducing him now like everyone else? Was South Beach falling into the vortex of memory, like New York before it?

Just when it seemed like I would never cast my eyes on Serena again, just when it seemed like it was all Ricky Martin from now on, she was a vision before me, you know, a thing of ether, a residuum, like lavender, like coffee regular. The odd thing was I got used to remembering that one portion of our time together. I forgot what came later. I forgot that just because she had this boyfriend, this college dude with short eyes, this college man who chased after teens, didn't mean that I stopped talking to her altogether, because the attachments you have then, when you're a kid, at least back before the trouble in the world began, these friendships are the one sustaining thing. I could see myself in some institutional corridor, high school passageway, and there she was, golden in the light of grimy shatterproof windows, as if women and light were as close as lungs and air. I was slumped by a locker. Serena came across the corridor, across speckled linoleum tiles, and it was like I had never looked at those tiles before, because she was wearing a certain sweatshop-manufactured brand of sneakers, and so I saw the linoleum, because the linoleum was improved by her and her sneakers.

"You okay?"

No. I was hyperventilating. Like I did back then. Anything could set me off. College entrance examinations, these caused me to hyperventilate, any dip in my grades. And I didn't tell anyone about it. Only my mother knew. I was an Asian kid and I was supposed to be incredibly smart. I was supposed to have calculus right at my fingertips, and I was supposed to know C++ and Visual Basic and Java and every other fucking computer language, and this all made me hyperventilate.

I said, "Tell me the name of the guy you're seeing. I just want to know his name. It's only fair."

"You really want to talk about this again?"

"Tell me once."

Battalions of teens slithered past, wearing their headphones and their MP3 players all playing the same moronic dirge of niche-marketed neo-grunge shit.

"Paley," she said. "First name, Irving, which I guess is a really weird name. He doesn't seem like an Irving to me. Is that enough?"

God sure put the big curse on Chinese kids, because when the raven of fate flew across their hearts, they just couldn't show it. We were supposed to be shut up in our hearts, because to do otherwise was not part of the collective plan, or maybe that was just how I felt about it. I felt like my heart was an overfilled water balloon, and I was hyperventilating.

"Kevin," she said, "you have to do something about the panic thing. They have drugs for it. You know?"

Do you know how much I think about you? I wanted to say. Do you want to know how you are preserved for all of human history? Because I have written you down, I have gotten down the way you pull your sweater sleeves over your hands, I have gotten down the way your eyeliner smudges. I have preserved the roll-out on the heels of your expensive sneakers, which you don't replace often enough. I know about you and nectarines, I know you like them better than anything else, and I know that you aren't happy first thing in the morning, not without a lot of coffee, and that you think your shoulders are fat, but that's ridiculous. All this is written down. And the times you yelled at your younger sister on the bus, I wrote down the entire exchange, and I don't want anything for it at all. I don't want you to feel that there's any obligation attached, except that you made me want to use writing for preservation, which is so great, because then I started preserving other things, like all the conversations I heard out in front of the Museum of Fine Arts, and I started describing the Charles River, rowboats on the Charles, I have written all of this down too, I have written it all down because of you.

This was enough! This was enough to redeem my sorry ass, because suddenly all the moments were one, this moment and that, lined up like the ducks on some Coney Island shooting game, chiming together, and I said, "Serena, I only got a second here, so listen up, I don't know any other way to put it, so just listen carefully. Something really horrible is going to happen to your friend Paley, so you have to tell him to stay out of Tompkins Square Park, no matter what, tell him never to go to Tompkins Square Park, tell him it's a reliable bet, and that maybe he should do his graduate work at USC or something. I'm telling you this because I just know it, so do it for me. I know, I know, it's crazy, but do like I say."

At which point, I was shaken rudely awake. *Oh, come on.* It was a time-travel moment. It was a memory-inside-a-memory moment, except that it might have been actually happening. I just wasn't sure. One of the bike messengers from Cortez Enterprises smacked me in the face. In my supply closet. I'd have been happy to talk, you know, but I was too high, and as so many accounts have suggested in the Albertine literature, trying to talk when you are high is like having all the radio stations on your radio playing at the same time. I could just make out the nasty sound of his voice, in the midst of a recollected lecture from my dad on the best way to bet on blackjack. *Lee, you are not attending to your duties.* Not true, no way, I tried to say, I'm a devoted employee, just got back here an hour ago, and I'm doing some more researches, and I'm finding out some very interesting things.

"You haven't produced shit," said the bike messenger. "We need to see some work. You need to be e-mailing us some attachments, Mr. Lee, and so far we haven't seen anything."

"Totally incorrect," I said. "I've been taking some notes. Somewhere around here. There are all kinds of notes."

There was the digital recorder, for example. But the batteries were dead.

"This conversation isn't going very well," replied the bike

messenger. "We have also heard that you have been moving product given to you as part of our agreement."

"There's just no way!"

"Don't make us have to remind you about the specifics of your responsibilities."

"Give me a break," I said. "I'm smarter than that."

Now the bike messenger flung open the door that led out of my supply closet. Like I had forgotten there was a world out there. And standing out in the hall was Tara from the tits-and-lit magazine, except she looked really disheveled, like she didn't want to be seen by anyone else, and I said, "Tara, what are you doing here? I thought I had at least another couple weeks—"

"You said you had the dropper. I don't know anything about all this. I gave you the money, so can I please just have the drugs? Then I'll get the fuck out of here."

I made some desperate pleas to the Cortez employee, looking at him looking at Tara, while Tara stood and watched. I stalled, demanded to know if there was a way for me to be sure that these guys, the bike messenger, and Tara weren't just figments of some future event that I was now "remembering," according to that theory about Albertine.

"Did you or did you not assign me an article about Albertine?"

Tara said, "Just set me up and let me get out of here."

And then Bertrand, the guy who doled out the habitable spaces in the armory, he got into the act too. Standing in the doorway, covered in grime, like he'd just come from his job at a filling station, except that as far as I knew it was just that Bertrand was an addict and had given up on personal hygiene, he gazed at me with a make-believe compassion.

"Kevin, listen, we've given you chances. We've looked the other way. We've been understanding for months. We've made excuses for you. We pulled you out of the gutter when you were passed out there. But people living here at the armory are afraid to walk by your apartment now. They're just afraid of what's going to happen. So where does that leave us?"

And even Bob, my early source, was standing behind Bertrand, hands on his hips. Trying to push past the throng of accusers, to get to me.

This was a moment when thinking carefully was more important than hallucinating. But because of the extremely dangerous amount of Albertine that was already overwhelming both my liver and my cerebral activity, reality just wasn't a station that I could tune very well. What I mean is, I went down under again. Right in front of all those people.

Soon I was hanging out on some sun porch in a subdivision in Massachusetts. All the houses, in whichever direction I turned, looked exactly the same. I bet they had electrical fireplaces in every room. It was like CAD had come through with a backhoe, bulldozed the whole region into uniformity. I could remember each tiny difference, each sign that some person, some family, had lived here for more than ten minutes. Serena's folks had a jack-o'-lantern on the porch. And over there was a guy with one arm mowing the common areas. That intoxicating smell of freshly cut grass. The sound of yellow jackets trying to get in through the screen.

Serena was reiterating that I had said something *really scary* to her at school today, and she needed to know if I'd said what I had said because of the panic thing. Were my symptoms causing me to say these crazy things, and if so, wouldn't it be better if I told someone what was happening, instead of carrying it around by myself? She knew, she said, about really serious mental illnesses, she knew about these things and she wanted me to know that I would still be her friend, her special friend, even if I had one of those mental illnesses, so I was not to worry about it. And now would I please try to explain?

"Listen, I know what I said, and there's no reason you should believe me," I tried, "but the fact is that the only reason I can explain to you about the future is because I'm in the future. And in the future I know how much you mean to me. In the future, this four months that we're close, they keep coming back around, again and again, like that day we were in the Boston Commons. It keeps coming back around.

I could tell you all this stuff about the future, about New York City and how it gets bombed into rubble, about drugs, about the epidemic that's coming, I could tell you how strung out I'm going to get. But that's not the point. Somehow you're the point. Serena, you're the *trompe l'oeil* in the triptych of the future, and that's because you know that guy. Paley. So you have to believe me, even though I probably wouldn't believe me, if I were you. Still, the thing is, you have to tell him what I've told you. Maybe none of this will happen, this stuff, I sure hope not. Maybe it will all turn out different, just because I'm telling you. But we can't plan on that. What we have to plan on is your telling Paley that he's in danger."

"Actually, Kevin, what I think we need to do is talk to your mom."

The jack-o'-lantern on the porch, of course. It was *autumn,* which was bad news, which meant I was on the comedown, and badly in need of a boost, and the whole scene was swirling away into an electromagnetic dwindling of stories. Serena was gone, and suddenly instead of being back in my room at the armory, where, suspended in a lost present, I was about to be evicted from my supply closet, I was back doing my job, the job of journalist, and what a relief. I had no idea what day it was. I had no idea if I was remembering the past or the future, or if I happened to be in the present. Albertine had messed with all that. I was confused. So was the guy I was interviewing, who happened to be the epidemiologist with the theory about the Albertine crisis, the one I told you about earlier, except that he was no epidemiologist at all. That was just his cover story. Actually, he was the anthropologist, Ernst Wentworth, and we were in his office in Brooklyn College, which wasn't really an office anymore, because there were about thirty thousand homeless people living on the campus of the college. At night there were vigilante raids in which the Arabic people living on one quad would be driven off the campus, out onto the streets of the Hot Zone, where stray gunshots from Eddie Cortez's crew took out at least two or three a night. It was trench warfare. No one was getting educated at Brooklyn College, and Wentworth was crowded into a single room with a half dozen other desks and twice as many file cabinets pushed against the windows.

He was having trouble following the thread of the interview. Me too. I couldn't remember if I had already asked certain questions:

Q: Check. Check. Check. Uh, okay, do you know anything about the origin of Albertine?

A: No one knows the origin actually. The most compelling theory, which is getting quite a bit of attention these days, is that Albertine has no origin. The physicists at the college have suggested the possibility that Albertine owes her proliferation to a recent intense shower of interstellar dark matter. The effect of this dark matter is such that time, right now, has become completely porous, completely randomized. Certain subatomic constituent particles are colliding with certain others. This would suggest that Albertine is a side effect of a space-time difficulty, a quantum indeterminacy, rather than a cause herself, and since she is not a cause, she has no origin, no specific beginning that we know of. She just tends to appear, on a statistical basis.

Q: Given that this is a possibility, why are Albertine's effects only visible in New York City?

A: The more provocative question would be, according to quantum indeterminacy, does New York City actually exist? At least, if you take the hypothesis of theoretical physics to its logical conclusion. This would be a brain-in-the-vat hypothesis. NYC as an illusion purveyed by a malevolent scientist. Except that the malevolent scientist here is Albertine herself. She leads us to believe in a certain New York City, a New York City with postapocalyptic, posttraumatic dimensions and obsessions. And yet perhaps this collective hallucination is merely a way to rationalize what is taking place: that it is now almost impossible to exist in linear time at all.

Q: So maybe in Kansas City, they have similar hallucinations. Kansas City is the center of some galloping drug epidemic. And the same thing in Tampa or Reno or Harrisburg?

A: Could be. Something like that. (*Pause.*) Can I borrow some of your—?

Q: There's only a little left. But, sure, get a buzz on. (*Getting serious.*) Have you attempted a catalogue of types of Albertine experiences?

A: Well, sociopaths seem to have a really bad time with the drug. We know that. And it's a startling fact, really. Since much of the distribution network is controlled by sociopaths. But at most dosage thresholds, sociopaths have stunted Albertine experiences. They'll remember their Driver Ed exam for hours on end. By sociopaths, I'm referring especially to individuals with poor intrapsychic bonding, poor social skills. Individuals who lack for compassion. It would be hard to imagine them taking much pleasure in Albertine. On the other hand, at the top end of the spectrum are the ambiguous experiences of which you are no doubt aware. People who claim to remember future events, people who claim to remember other people's memories, people who claim to have interacted with their memories. And so forth. At first we believed that these experiences, which characterized many of the people here conducting our studies—myself included—were only occurring, if that's the right word, among the enlightened. That is, we believed that ahistorical remembering was an aspect of wish fulfillment among the healthiest and most engaged personalities. But then we learned that malice, hatred, and murderous rage could be just as effective at creating these episodes. In either case, we became convinced that the frequency of these reports merited our attention. If true, the fact of ahistorical remembering would have to suggest that the fabric of time is not woven together as consistently as we once thought. We tried at first to analyze whether these logically impossible experiences were "true" on a factual level, but now we are more interested in whether or not they are repeatable, visible to more than one person, etc.

Q: Does your catalogue of experiences shed any light on Albertine's origin?
A: One compelling theory that's making the rounds among guys in the sciences here at the college is that Albertine has infinite origins. That she appeared in the environment all at once, at different locations, synchronously, according to some kind of philosophical or metaphysical randomness generator. There's no other perfect way to describe the effect. According to this view, the disorder she causes is so intense that her origin is concealed in an effacement of the moment of her origin, because to have a single origin violates the parameters of non-linearity. Didn't we already do this part about the origin?

Q: Shit. I guess you're right. Okay, hang on. (*Regroups.*) Do you, do you think it's possible to manipulate the origin of Albertine, to actually control the drug, so as to alter a specific narrative? Like, say, the rise of the Albertine crime syndicate?
A: Sure, persons of my acquaintance have done plenty of that. At least on an experimental basis. We have had no choice. But I'm not at liberty to go into that today.

Q: Let's go back to the issue of what to do about the epidemic. Do you have a specific policy formulation?
A: I did have some good ideas about that. (*Ponders.*) Okay, wait just a second. I'm going to look through my papers on the subject here. (*Riffles mounds on desk.*) I'm forgetting so much these days. Okay, my observation is that Albertine finds her allure in the fact that the human memory is, by its nature, imperfect. Every day, in every way, we are experiencing regret over the fact that we can conjure up some minimal part of the past, but not as much as we'd like. This imperfection of memory is built into the human animal, and as long as it's an issue, the

Albertine syndicates will be able to exploit it. Strategies for containment have to come from another direction, therefore. Which is to say that the only thing that could conceivably help in the long run would be to make distribution of the drug extremely widespread. We should make sure everybody has it.

Q: How would that help?
A: Since Albertine has forgetfulness as a long-term side effect, it's possible that we could actually make everyone forget that Albertine exists. It would have to be concerted, you understand. But let me make an analogy. At a certain point in heroin addiction, you no longer feel the effects of the opiate; you only service the withdrawal. A similar effect could take place here. At a certain point, everyone would be trying to avoid the forgetting, because they can't work effectively, they can't even remember where work is, and yet soon this forgetting would begin to invade even the drug experience, so that what you remember grows dimmer, because you are beginning to accelerate plaque buildup, and other anatomical effects. With enough of this forgetting everyone would forget that they were addicts, forget that they needed the drug to remember, forget that memory was imperfect, and then we would be back to some kind of lowest common denominator of civic psychology. Damaged, but equal.

Q: How would you go about doing this?
(*Ernst Wentworth gives the interviewer the once-over in a way he had not done before.*)
A: We're going to put it in the water supply.

Q: Hasn't that been tried already?
A: What do you mean?

Q: I think someone told me that an attack on the water supply was recently thwarted.
A: Are you serious?

Q: Well, unless someone was using disinformation—
A: (*Wentworth shouts.*) Guys, you recording all of this?

The room was bugged, of course, and on this signal a bunch of academics rushed into Wentworth's office, blindfolded me, and carried me out. I didn't struggle. When I was freed, I was in the Brooklyn College Astronomy Lab. It was Ernst Wentworth who gently removed my blindfold.

"You understand we have no choice but to take every precaution. Just a couple of days ago, Claude Jannings, from the linguistics department, watched his wife disappear in front of him. She was there, in the kitchen, talking about the dearth of political writings pertaining to the Albertine epidemic, and then she was gone, just absolutely gone. As if someone were listening to the conversation the whole time. Apparently, her remarks about Albertine, and inchoate plans to write on the subject, were enough to make her a target."

My eyes became accustomed to the dim light of the astronomy lab. The interior was all concrete, functional, except for the platform where you could get up and take a gander at the heavens. Around me, there was a circle of guys in tweed jackets and cardigan sweaters. A couple of bow ties. Khaki slacks.

"Wow, it's Kevin Lee! Right here in our lab!" Some good-natured chortling.

Huh?

Wentworth ventured further explanations. "We've developed a hierarchy for marking events, so we don't forget later. Whenever one of us goes out in public, we bring along a poster or sign indicating the date and time. That way, if we travel backwards on Albertine in search of particular events, we aren't thrown off or beguiled by unimportant days. And we bring clothing of various colors, red for an alert, green for an all-clear. It's a conspiracy of order, you understand, and that's a particularly revolutionary conspiracy right now. What we've additionally found, by cataloguing memories—and we have guys who are medicated twenty-four hours a day thinking about all this—is that there are certain people who turn up over and over. We refer to people who are present at large numbers of essential Albertine nodal points as memory catalysts. Eduardo Cortez, for example, is a *memory catalyst*, and not in a good way. And there are some other very odd examples I could give you. A talk-show host from ten or fifteen years ago seems to turn up quite a bit, perhaps just because his name is so memorable, Regis Philbin. You'd be surprised how close to the inner workings of the Albertine epidemic is Regis Philbin. When we're around Philbin, we are always wearing red. We don't know what he means yet, but we're working on it. And then there's you."

"Me?"

One doctoral candidate, standing by the base of the telescope, nonchalant, spoke up. "If we had baseball cards of the players in the Albertine epidemic, you'd be collectible. You'd be the power hitting shortstop."

"We have a theory," Wentworth said. "And the theory is that you're important because you're a writer."

"Yeah, but I'm not even a very good writer. I'm barely published."

Wentworth waved his plump hands.

"Doesn't matter. We've been trying to find out for a while who originally came up with your assignment. It wasn't your editor there. That we know. She's just another addict. It was someone above her, and if we can find out who it is, we think we'll be close to finding a spot where the Frost Communications holding company connects to Cortez Enterprises. Somewhere up the chain, you were being groomed for this moment. Unless you are simply some kind of emblem for Albertine. That's possible, too, of course."

Wentworth smiled, so that his tobacco-stained teeth shone forth in the gloomy light. "Additionally, you're a hero from the thick, roiling juices of the New York City melting pot. And that is very satisfying to us. Do you want to see? We know so much about you that it's almost embarrassing. We even know what you like to eat, and what kind of toothpaste you use. Don't worry, we won't make a big stink about it."

Later, of course, the constituency of the Brooklyn Resistance was a matter of much speculation. There were women there too, with mournful expressions, like they had come along with the Resistance, though they had grave doubts about its masculine power structure. Women in modest skirts or slightly unflattering pantsuits, like Jesse Simons, the Deconstructionist, who argued that doping the water supply was embracing the nomadic sign system of Albertine, which of course represented not some empirical astrophysical event, but, rather, a symbolic reaction to the crisis of instability caused by American Imperialism. And there were a couple of African-Americanists, wearing hints of kinte cloth with their tweeds and corduroys. They argued for intervention in the economic imperatives that led to drug dealing among the inner city poor. And there was the great postcolonialist writer Jean-Pierre Al-Sadir. He argued that the route to victory over civic chaos was infiltration of the Albertine cartels. However, Al-Sadir, because of his Algerian passport, had been mentioned as part of the conspiracy that detonated the New York City blast. Still, here he was, fighting with the patriots, if that's what they were. It was a testament to the desperation of the moment that none of these academic stars would normally have agreed on anything, you know? I mean, these people *hated* each other. If you'd gone to a faculty meeting at Columbia three years ago, you would have seen Al-Sadir call Simons an arrogant narcissist in front of a college president. That kind of thing. But infighting was forgotten for now, as the Resistance began plotting its strategies. Even when I was hanging around with them, there would be the occasional argument about the semiotics of wearing red, or about whether time as a system was inherently phallogocentric, such that its present adumbrated shape was preferable, as a representation of labial or vaginal narrative space.

"So you guys probably have one of those dials, on a machine, where we can go directly to a particular year and day and hour and second, right?"

"Fat chance," Wentworth said. "In fact, we have a room next door with a lot of cots in it—"

"A shooting gallery?"

"Just so. And we employ a lot of teaching assistants, keep them comfortable and intoxicated for a long time and see what happens. Whatever you might think, what we have here is a lot of affection for one another, so a lot of stories go around like lightning, a lot of conjecture, a lot of despair, a lot of elation, a lot of plans. You know? We see ourselves as junkies for history. Of which yours is one integral piece. Let's go have a look, shall we?"

It would be great if I could report that the shooting gallery of the Resistance was significantly better than the Cortez shooting gallery, but, really, the only difference was that these guys sterilized the needles after each use and swabbed their track marks. No abscesses in this crowd. Otherwise, it was only marginally more inviting. Some of the most important academics of my time were lying on cots, drooling, fighting their way through the cultural noise of fifty years—television programming, billboards, pornography, newspaper advertisements—in order to get back to the origin of Albertine, bitch goddess, in order to untangle the mess she'd made. The other important difference here was that these guys were synthesizing their own batches of the stuff, instead of buying it on the street, and when a bunch of chemists and biologists get into mixing up a drug, that drug *chimes* let me tell you. They explained the chemical derivation to me, too. Which looks kinda like this:

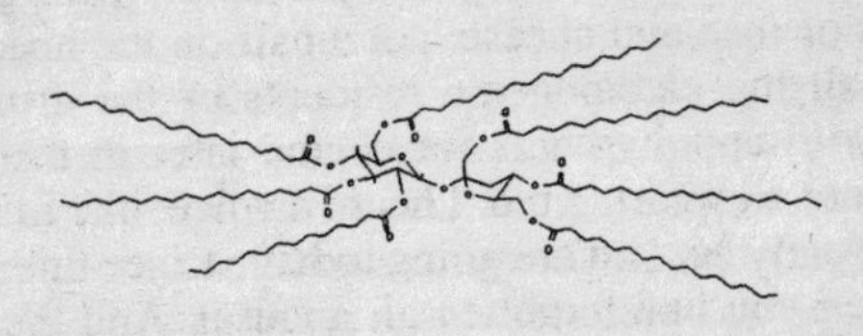

Apparently, the effect had to do with increasing oxygenated blood flow to neurotransmitters, thereby increasing electrical impulses. It wasn't that hard to do at all. Miraculous that no one had done it before now. The only physiognomic problem with Albertine was her tendency to burn out the cells, like in diseases of senescence. Albertine was sort of the neurochemical equivalent of steroid abuse.

I was lucky. Jesse Simons volunteered to be the prefect for my trip, and she and Wentworth stood awkwardly in the center of the room, as a grad student from the Renaissance Studies department pulled the rubber tie around my arm. It was the sweetest thing, tying off again. I didn't care anymore about writing, I only cared about the part where I stunned myself with Albertine. I was dreaming of being ravished by her, overwhelmed by her instruction, where perception was a maelstrom of time past, present, and future. The eons were neon, they were like the old Times Square, first time you ever saw it, first time you felt the rush of its hundreds of thousands of images, and I don't mean the Disney version, I mean the version with hookers and street violence and raving crack fiends. Albertine was like a soup of NYC neon. She was a catalogue of demonic euphonies. I felt the rubber cord unsnap, heard a sigh beside me, felt Jesse's arms around me, and the soft middle of sedentary Ernst Wentworth. Then we were rolling and tumbling in the thick of Albertine's forest. I was back in the armory, and there were a bunch of bike messengers leading me out, and I was screaming to Tara, and to Bertrand, and to Bob, *Save my notes, save my notes,* and the bike messengers were beating on me and I could feel the panic, in my chest, I could feel it, and I said, Where are you taking me? I passed a little circle of residents of the armory, carrying home their government rations of mac and cheese, not a hair on the head of any of them, all the carcinogenic residents of the armory, all of them with appointments for chemo later in the week, and they were all wearing red. I heard a voice, like in voice-over, We're sorry that you are going to have to see this. It was better when you had forgotten all about it. And the bike messengers took me on a tour of Brooklyn in their jeeps, up and down the empty streets of my borough, kicking my ass the whole way, until my lips were split and bleeding, until my blackened eyes were swollen shut. We came to a halt down on the waterfront, on the piers. They dumped me out of the jeep while it was still moving, and my last pair of jeans was shredded from all the broken glass and rubble. My knees and hips were gashed. But the syndicate wasn't through with me yet; some more of Cortez's flunkies took me inside a factory, a creepy institutional place, *where they manufactured the drug.*

Here it was. The Albertine sweatshop. There weren't many buildings left in downtown Brooklyn, you know, because it was within the event horizon of the dirty bomb, a lot of the stuff on the waterfront was rubble. But this building was still here somehow, which implied that Eddie Cortez was subjecting his production staff to radioactive hazards. That was the least of it, of course, because most of the staff was probably high. Maybe that was the one job benefit.

"What are we doing here?" I said to the goons leading me in past the surveillance gate, and in through a front hall that looked remarkably like the reception area of the tits-and-lit magazine that assigned my Albertine story in the first place. There was even one of those remote-control reception robots, just like at the magazine offices.

"Your questions will be answered in due course."

"Really? Because I have a big backlog—"

"Don't get smart, we *will* make it hurt, dig?"

More corridors, linkages of impossible interiors, then into an office. We were waved through without hesitation. The women and men in the typing pool with expressions of abject terror on their faces. Guys in red sweaters in every room, red neckties, matching socks. We passed a troika of potted ferns, and I was congratulating Eddie, silently, for using his ill-gotten profits for quality-of-life office accessories like potted palms, when I noticed an administrative assistant I recognized.

Deanna. Remember her? If you don't, you should lay off the sauce, gentle reader, because she was the character who told me about the plot to poison the water supply. The character who later became a hooker down by the Gowanus Canal. Have to say, considering the state of most of the people in the boroughs, Deanna was looking really great. I mean, she must have had some reconstructive dentistry, because back when I interviewed her, she had fewer teeth than fingers. Now she had on a slinky silk blouse, and what looked from this angle like a miniskirt. She still had long sleeves, of course. We recognized one another at the same moment, with a kind of disgust. I saw her eyes widen; I saw her glance quickly around herself. To make sure no one noticed. Was she working for Eddie now? Was she another employee drafted into the harem?

Then in the kind of frozen moment that can only happen in an era of completely subjective time, I began to understand that there was a commotion beginning around me, a commotion that had to do, I think, with Jesse Simons and Ernst Wentworth, who had remained so silent during the prior hour of torture and kidnapping that I had forgotten they were orbiting around me at all. They knew, I'd learned, what I knew; they saw what I saw. And I heard Jesse say to Ernst, *No, I have to do it, she's a woman, I don't want to hear about any guys shooting any women.* And Jesse Simons strode out of my memory, giving me a mournful glance on the way. Jesse, turns out, was carrying an enormous pistol, with a silencer on the end, and as soon as she was on the scene, I could see the Cortez guys also moving into position, with their submachine guns, there was a lot of yelling, someone was yelling Get him out of here, get him out of here, as if by removing me from the room, it would take Deanna of the picture, out of the story. I hung onto a desk. They beat on me with the butt ends of submachine guns, and I looked up just in time to see Deanna, whatever her surname was, if she even had a surname, disappear, at the muffled hiss and report of the silencer. The spot where Deanna had been sitting was emptied, and a plastic tape dispenser that she'd been holding in her hand was suspended briefly in midair. It fell to the wall-to-wall with a muffled thud. The men and women in the typing pool sent up a scream, many hands fluttered to gaping mouths. And that was when Cortez's people opened fire on the room. Cleaning out as many witnesses as they could get. As with Jesse and Ernst, who didn't want to leave Deanna alive to inform on their plan, Cortez didn't want any mnemonic jockeys recalling the scene. As if the solution to the disorder of time was the elimination of all possible perceivers of time. I want to allow a dignified space into the story where the Cortez typing pool was massacred, so if I move on with the facts, don't think that I don't know that all those people had families. Because I know.

Someone got hold of my feet, because I tried to make a quick escape myself, and they were swearing at me, dragging me down the corridor toward some blank, faceless office cubicle, where I too would be killed. Meanwhile, Ernst Wentworth, like the angelic presence that he was, again had the job of explanation: "Deanna knew about the trip to the water supply, for which we're embarking now, with many thanks to you for helping us to close the loophole. You were the only person who knew the identity of this informer. Jesse is sticking with you for the last few minutes, because there's one more thing you have to learn before you're done, and then, Kevin, you're a free man, with a load of forgetting in your future. I hope you write comic books or start a rock-and-roll band in your garage. And I hope you do it all somewhere far away from here."

Then the office door opened in.

I guess you already knew that Cassandra was sitting there. Wearing really high-end corporate gear from Italian designers who had managed to stay out of the international backlash against the American export market. Cortez Enterprises was about to have its limited public offering, I learned later, using a brokerage subsidiary that they owned themselves. So they had tarted up the office to impress some analysts. Cassandra was beautiful in a way I probably can't describe, because beauty, ultimately, is outside of language. Though it may have something to do with memory. She was wearing a red bow. One of Cortez's goons, unless it was Eddie himself, said, "Kevin, I guess you don't really remember your own mother?"

"My mother? What the hell are you talking about?"

Cassandra had cleaned up a lot since I saw her. Which I was starting to recognize might have been four months ago. It was hard to tell. Still, she was my age, more or less, maybe a few years younger, so how was she supposed to be my mother?

One thing I'll say for Cassandra, she had the kind of a compassionate expression a mother should have had. She asked if I was all right.

But the goons interfered with this tender moment.

"Okay, shoot 'em up."

"Wait," I said, "I'm already high, I'm already in somebody's memory, I don't even know if it's my own memory anymore, so you're getting me high inside a memory, that's a memory inside a memory, right? When do we come back out to the present, to the part where I'm just a kid trying to make his way?"

"Shut that motherfucker up."

Cassandra volunteered her arm, so I volunteered mine, covered with scars now, so much that they couldn't find a vein.

"Do him in the neck."

So they did. Without asking nicely.

I swirled into the rapture of the deep, far from all the shit that had accumulated since I first found out about Albertine. You know, my very first memory is of my grandfather, the Chinese immigrant patriarch, after his open-heart surgery. I was maybe three and a half years old. I never believed those memories. I never used to believe in the coherence of memory before an age when a kid could understand time. What comes before it? The rapture of the deep is what comes before. Before the scaffolding of time. Memories cartwheeling around in the empty heavens. Anyway, there he was on the stretcher in the living room, where he lived with us, doped on morphine. Doped for a good month anyway. I can remember the implacable smile on his face, I'm suffering now, but I came here for you, so you wouldn't have to suffer. So now go and do something. Make my sacrifices into your day at the beach. It lingered in my consciousness for a moment. From there the howling winds of recollection touched down on my abortive swimming lessons, then a summer on the Cape, walking on the beaches of the seashore, up through childhood, from one associative leap to the next, all memories with beaches in them, then all memories with singing in them, memories featuring varieties of pie, like this was the very last mainline I was going to have, like they were going to make a biopic about my short life from this footage scrolling through my brain. Everything was roses. I was the smartest kid in my elementary school class, I was the class president. I was a shortstop player. Everything was roses. *Until Serena showed up.* Serena, who was exactly contemporary with that nameless dread creeping into my daily life. I was the only Asian kid my parents had ever known who panicked, Asians just didn't panic, or they didn't fucking talk about it, man, that was for sure, like that afternoon when I was supposed to take some government-ordered placement exam and I was sitting in the bathroom puking, my father standing outside the door, telling me, in the severest language, that I was a disgrace. What was I going to do, drop out of society? Go work in a dry cleaner's? Recite poetry to the customers while I was doing alterations? Did I think my grandfather had come from Shanghai, etc. etc., on a boat that almost sank, etc. etc., so that I could . . . etc. etc., and then the sound of my mother's voice telling him to lay off, my mother the microbiologist, or epidemiologist, why couldn't I remember my mother's job, she was never home, actually, she was always working. *Come on.* I called out to the Cortez flunkies, Hey, you guys, give me another shot, because nothing is chiming, I am telling you there is not a chime left in the belfry, you guys, I was still pressing the wet rag against the wound in my neck when the guy slapped me in the back of the head and told me to shut the fuck up, and then I was again on the Ferris wheel of it all, but I could see my father's tassled loafers, and that's when Jesse Simons was talking to me again, suddenly I was recognizing her voice.

"Kevin, this is the end of the story, where you're going now, because your mother is about to lay her hand on yours, across the desk, Kevin, and that will be the signal that I have to let go. Here's what happens. This next ten minutes of your life enables us to dose the reservoir before Eddie Cortez finds out. We have just eliminated the person who informs on the plot to dose the reservoir, and so we are free to go back in time, by virtue of our collective affection for the city, to augment the water supply. And you know what that means, Kevin, it means that Eddie won't have time to drop the bomb, Kevin. *The bomb.* Because we believe Eddie

Cortez drops the bomb, to try to keep us from dosing the reservoir, and he drops it on lower Manhattan, because that's where *you* live in the fall of 2008. We believe that Eddie Cortez, not a highly trained sleeper cell of foreign nationals, detonates the uranium bomb, to ensure dominance of Cortez Enterprises and to wipe out a number of key Resistance players living in the East Village at that historical juncture. So take your time in the next few minutes because this gives us the element of surprise we need. Jean-Pierre Al-Sadir is driving a minivan up what's left of the interstate. And I believe he's playing Duke Ellington on the CD player, because he wants to hear something really great before his memory is wiped clean. You're the hero of the story, Kevin. And we're all really sorry we couldn't tell you earlier, and we're sorry you had to learn this way. But we want you to know this. We want you to know that all the traumatic events of the last few months, these were things we knew you could withstand. Like few others. You're the kid who made the story for us. We're proud. We wish you were our son. And in a way you are now. If that's any help at all. When you get to Manhattan, after talking to your mother, if it's still gone, that'll be the sign. Manhattan in ruins. Your ferry driver will be wearing green. That'll mean that Eddie doesn't need to go back in time to try to find you. That'll mean that Eddie has given up trying to control the past, in order to control the present. Well, unless, by poisoning the reservoir, we eliminate the future in which Eddie comes up with the idea of detonating the blast, in which case Manhattan will still be standing and this entire present, with the drug epidemic and the Brooklyn Resistance, will be non-actualizing. And it's also possible that the forgetting will have set in somewhere along the line, we aren't sure where yet, and that you may have forgotten certain important parts of the story. You may have forgotten that Manhattan was ever a city by the time you get home tonight. You might have forgotten all of this, all this rotten stuff, this loneliness, even this speech I'm giving you now. In fact, we have tried to pinpoint forgetting, Kevin, we have targeted it, in such a way as to wipe clean your own memories of the blast. Because you actually had a pretty rotten time that day. You saw some awful things. So if you have forgotten, we believe you are the first locally targeted forgetter. However, if in the future, during this next forgetting, you want to remember this or other events from your life we have a suggestion for the future, Kevin, *just play back your audio recordings*."

This is where my mom stole into memory of the past. My mom was so beautiful. Every time I saw her. Even when she was Cassandra, on the swing in Brooklyn. So beautiful that I couldn't even see the lines of time carved into her. Here in memory she's young again, she's perfect, young and brilliant, lit in the color of a fading silver halide print. My mom looks Kodak to me, always will, and she leads me out of the bathroom, away from my dad, and she explains that Serena telephoned her, and her syllables are carefully measured like on a metronome. It's not nearly as bad as it seems. If I could redo the color balance in this past, I would make it more ultramarine, because everything's too yellow: my mother taking me into the living room, where my grandfather once slept off his open-heart surgery. She sits me down. And she makes her diagnosis. She says, *I have been doing a lot of research into your chemical problem. And I have talked to a lot of professional friends on the subject. When you have a spare hour or so, later in the week, then we're going in to talk to some of them. But in the meantime, I want you to try something for me.*

So here it was. In a stoppered beaker.

"Just give this a try for me. I think it'll be more interesting than that stuff you and your friends have been smoking."

"Mom," I said. "Do you think I should?"

"I'm your mom."

"What is it?"

"Lithium, some SSRIs, and a memory enhancer we're trying out, in solution. It's supposed to sharpen cognition. Might help with those tests. In an Aspartame sauce."

Just like in the laboratory sequences, you know, from those black-and-white movies of yore. I drank up. And the fact is, I aced that exam. That's what I had forgotten. And I gave some to Serena, and she gave it to her boyfriend, Paley.

We called it Albertine, because it sounded like Aspartame. Or so I was remembering. I gave it to the others. We all did well on our tests. Just three kids from the subdivisions fucking up the entire future of the human race, in pursuit of kicks and decent board scores.

I didn't want to open my eyes. I didn't want to know. Didn't want to look across the desk at Cassandra, who may or may not have been my mother, may or may not have been the chief chemist for the Cortez syndicate, may or may not have been an informer for the Resistance, may or may not have been a young woman, may or may not have been home in Newton, refusing to come to the phone, may or may not have been an older Chinese woman with those sad eyes. I didn't want to hear her voice, from across the room, rationalizing, "Let time show why I've done what I've done." I didn't want to know. I didn't want to know the plans the Cortez operatives had for me, Addict Zero, didn't want to know why I was being put through this exercise—so that they could break me on the rack of information, or because they still wanted me to write down whatever it was that they wanted me to write down. I didn't want to know, finally, which memory was inside of which memory, didn't want to know if there was a truth on top of these other truths. In a few minutes' time, the water supply would be boiling with the stuff, eight weeks back. The cops at the reservoirs would be facedown in pools of blood, and the taps in Brooklyn, Queens, Staten Island, and the Bronx would be running bluer than usual, and there would be dancing in the streets, as though all this stuff I'm telling you hadn't happened at all. I mean, assuming the sweet forgetting didn't come like the instantaneous wave of radiation after the blast. Assuming I didn't forget all of this, how I got where I got, what I'd once known, the order in which I knew it, the cast of characters, my own name, the denouement.

What's memory? Memory's the groove. It's the all-stars laying down their groove, and it's you dancing, chasing the desperations of the heart, chasing something that's so gone, so ephemeral you know it only by its traces, how a certain plucked guitar string summons the thundering centuries, how a taste of fresh cherries calls up the indolent romancers on antebellum porches, all these stories rolling. Memory is the groove, the lie, the story you never get right, the better place. Memory is the bitch, the shame factory, the curse and the consolation. And that's where my journalistic exposé breaks down.

But I can offer a few last tidbits. If you're wondering what the future looks like, if you're one of the citizens from the past, wondering, let me tell you what it's like. First thing I'll tell you, gentle reader, is that the Brooklyn Bridge is gone, probably the most beautiful structure ever built according to the madness of New Yorkers. Brooklyn Bridge is gone, or at least the half of it on the New York side. The section on the Brooklyn side goes out as far as the first set of pillars, and after that it just crumbles away. Like the arms of Venus de Milo. It's a suggestion of an idealized relationship between parts of a city, a suggestion, not an actual relationship. And maybe that's why intrepid lovers go there now, lovers with thyroid cancer go up there at night, because it's finally a time in New York City history where you can see the night sky. That is, if the wind's blowing toward Jersey. They go up there, the lovers, they jump the police barriers, they walk out on that boardwalk, the part that's still remaining, they look across the East River, they make their protestations of loyalty, *I don't really have much time, so there's a few things I want to say to you.* I'll go even further. Because this instant is endless for me, and that's why I'm dictating these notes. What I do is, I find the ferryman on the Brooklyn side, out in Bay Ridge, old Irish guy, I pay my fresh coin to the Irish ferryman with the green windbreaker, pet his rottweiler. I say, I got some business over there, and the guy says, No can do, pal, and I point at it and I say, Business, and he says, No one has business there, but I do, I tell him, and I will make it worth your while, and he says, There's nothing over there, but in the end he accepts the offer, and then we are out upon the water, where the currents are stiff, and the waves treacherous, as if nature wants to wash this experiment of a city out into the sea, as if nature wants to clean the wound, flush the leftover uranium, the rubble, the human particulate, we're on the water, and right there is where that statue used to be, we'll get the new one from France before too long, and that's where New York Plaza used to be on the tip there, I tell the ferryman to take me farther up the coast, I want to know every rock and piling, every remaining I-beam, I want to know it all, so we go past the footprint of South Street seaport, and here are the things that we lost that I might have seen from here, the Municipal Building with its spires, City Hall, the World Financial Center, the New York Stock Exchange, where did all those bond traders go, what are they doing now, are they in Montclair or Greenwich, and then it's Chinatown, bombed almost to China, bombed down to the bedrock, edged by Canal Street, which is again a canal as it was way back when, and Little Italy is gone, those mobster hangouts are all gone, they're all working on the Jersey side now, trying to corner the Albertine market there, and Soho is gone, New York University is gone, Zeckendorf Towers gone, Union Square Park is gone, the building where Andy Warhol's Factory once was, what used to be Max's Kansas City, CBGB, and the Empire State Building is gone, which, when it fell sideways, crushed a huge chunk of lower Fifth Avenue, all the way to the Flatiron District, the area formerly known as the Ladies' Mile, the flower district is gone, the Fashion Institute of Technology, in fact, about the only thing they say is still somewhat intact, like the Acropolis of Athens, is the Public Library, but I can't see it from here. The bridges are blown out, the tram at 59th Street, gone, and as we pull alongside a section of the island where I'm guessing Stuyvesant Village used to be, I say, *Ferryman, put me down here,* pull your rowboat with its two-horsepower lawnmower engine alongside, because I'm going in, I'm going to Tompkins Square, man, I'm going backward, through that neighborhood of immigrants, so now I step on the easternmost part of the island, same place the Italians stepped, same place the Irish stepped, same place the Puerto Ricans stepped, and I'm going in there now, because as long as it's rubble I don't care how hot it is, I'm going in, it's like a desert of glass, sand and landfill burnt into glass, and I can hear the voices, even though it's been a while now, all those voices layered over one another, in their hundred and fifty languages, can't hear anything distinct about what they are saying, except that they're saying, *Hey, time for us to be heard.*

Story Copyrights